BARCHESTER TOWERS

BARCHESTER TOWERS

by

ANTHONY TROLLOPE

Abridged Edition

PRINTED IN — GREAT BRITAIN
DEAN & SON Ltd.
41/43 Ludgate Hill — LONDON E.C.4

TRADE MARK

MADE AND PRINTED IN GREAT BRITAIN BY PURNELL AND SONS, LTD.
PAULTON (SOMERSET) AND LONDON
603 03047 5

CONTENTS

Chapter		Page

CHAPTER I

WHO WILL BE THE NEW BISHOP?

In the latter days of July in the year 185—, a most important question was for ten days hourly asked in the cathedral city of Barchester, and answered every hour in various ways—Who was to be the new Bishop?

The death of old Dr. Grantly, who had for many years filled that chair with meek authority, took place exactly as the ministry of Lord —— was going to give place to that of Lord ——. The illness of the good old man was long and lingering, and it became at last a matter of intense interest to those concerned whether the new appointment should be made by a conservative or liberal government.

It was pretty well understood that the outgoing premier had made his selection, and that if the question rested with him, the mitre would descend on the head of Archdeacon Grantly, the old bishop's son. The archdeacon had long managed the affairs of the diocese; and for some months previous to the demise of his father, rumour had confidently assigned to him the reversion of his father's honours.

Bishop Grantly died as he had lived, peaceably, slowly, without pain and without excitement. The breath ebbed from him almost imperceptibly, and for a month before his death, it was a question whether he were alive or dead.

A trying time was this for the archdeacon, for whom was designed the reversion of his father's see by those who then had the giving away of episcopal thrones. I would not be understood to say that the prime minister had in so many words promised the bishopric to Dr. Grantly. He was too discreet a man for that. There is a proverb with reference to the killing of cats, and those who know anything either of high or low government places, will be well aware that a promise may be made without positive words, and that an expectant may be put into the highest state of encouragement, though the great man on whose breath he hangs may have done no more than whisper that "Mr. So-and-so is certainly a rising man."

Such a whisper had been made, and was known by those who heard it to signify that the cures of the diocese of Barchester should not be taken out of the hands of the archdeacon. The then prime minister was all in all at Oxford, and had lately passed a night at the house of the master of Lazarus. Now the master of Lazarus—which is, by the bye, in many respects the most comfortable, as well as the richest college at Oxford,—was the archdeacon's most intimate friend and most trusted counsellor. On the occasion of the prime minister's visit, Dr. Grantly was of course present, and the meeting was very gracious. On the following morning Dr. Gwynne, the master, told the archdeacon that in his opinion the thing was settled.

At this time the bishop was quite on his last legs; but the ministry also were tottering. Dr. Grantly returned from Oxford happy and elated, to resume his place in the palace, and to continue to perform for the father the last duties of a son; which, to give him his due, he performed with more tender care than was to be expected from his usual somewhat worldly manners.

A month since the physicians had named four weeks as the outside period during which breath could be supported within the body of the dying man. At the end of the month the physicians wondered, and named another fortnight. The old man lived on wine alone, but at the end of the fortnight he still lived; and the tidings of the fall of the ministry became more frequent. Sir Lamda Mewnew and Sir Omicron Pie, the two great London doctors, now came down for the fifth time, and declared, shaking their learned heads, that another week of life was impossible; and as they sat down to lunch in the episcopal dining-room, whispered to the archdeacon their own private knowledge that the ministry must fall within five days. The son returned to his father's room, and after administering with his own hands the sustaining modicum of madeira, sat down by the bedside to calculate his chances.

The ministry were to be out within five days: his father was to be dead within—No, he rejected that view of the subject. The ministry were to be out, and the diocese might probably be vacant at the same period. There was much doubt as to the names of the men who were to succeed to power, and a week must elapse before a Cabinet was formed. Would not vacancies be filled by the out-going men during this week? Dr. Grantly had a kind of idea that such would be the case, but did not know; and then he wondered at his own ignorance on such a question.

He tried to keep his mind away from the subject, but he could not. The race was so very close, and the stakes were so very high. He then looked at the dying man's impassive, placid face. There was no sign there of death or disease; it was something thinner than of yore, somewhat greyer, and the deep lines of age more marked; but, as far as he could judge, life might yet hang there for weeks to come. Sir Lamda Mewnew and Sir Omicron Pie had thrice been wrong, and might yet be wrong thrice again. The old bishop slept during twenty of the twenty-four hours, but during the short periods of his waking moments, he knew both his son and his dear old friend, Mr. Harding, the archdeacon's father-in-law, and would thank them tenderly for their care and love. Now he lay sleeping like a baby, resting easily on his back, his mouth just open, and his few grey hairs straggling from beneath his cap; his breath was perfectly noiseless, and his thin, wan hand, which lay above the coverlid, never moved. Nothing could be easier than the old man's passage from this world to the next.

But by no means easy were the emotions of him who sat there watching. He knew it must be now or never. He was already over fifty, and there was little chance that his friends who were now leaving office would soon return to it. No probable British prime minister but he who was now in, he who was so soon to be out, would think of making a bishop of Dr. Grantly. Thus he thought long and sadly, in deep silence, and then gazed at that still living face, and then at last dared to ask himself whether he really longed for his father's death.

The effort was a salutary one, and the question was answered in a moment. The proud, wishful, worldly man sank on his knees by the bedside, and taking the bishop's hand within his own, prayed eagerly that his sins might be forgiven him.

His face was still buried in the clothes when the door of the bedroom opened noiselessly, and Mr. Harding entered with a velvet step. Mr. Harding's attendance at that bedside had been nearly as constant as that of the archdeacon, and his ingress and egress was as much a matter of course as that of his son-in-law. He was standing close beside the archdeacon before he was perceived, and would also have knelt in prayer had he not feared that his doing so might have caused some sudden start, and have disturbed the dying man. Dr. Grantly, however, instantly perceived him, and rose from his knees. As he did so Mr. Harding took both his hands, and pressed them warmly. There was more fellowship between them at that moment than there had ever been before, and it so happened that after circumstances greatly preserved the feeling. As they stood there pressing each other's hands, the tears rolled freely down their cheeks.

"God bless you, my dears,"—said the bishop with feeble voice as he woke—"God bless you—may God bless you both, my dear children:" and so he died.

There was no loud rattle in the throat, no dreadful struggle, no palpable sign of death; but the lower jaw fell a little from its place, and the eyes, which had been so constantly closed in sleep, now remained fixed and open. Neither Mr. Harding nor Dr. Grantly knew that life was gone, though both suspected it.

"I believe it's all over," said Mr. Harding, still pressing the other's hands. "I think—nay, I hope it is."

"I will ring the bell," said the other, speaking all but in a whisper. "Mrs. Phillips should be here."

Mrs. Phillips, the nurse, was soon in the room, and immediately, with practised hand, closed those staring eyes.

"It's all over, Mrs. Phillips?" asked Mr. Harding.

"My lord's no more," said Mrs. Phillips, turning round and curseying low with solemn face; "his lordship's gone more like a sleeping babby than any that I ever saw."

"It's a great relief, archdeacon," said Mr. Harding, "a great relief—dear, good, excellent old man. Oh that our last moments may be as innocent and as peaceful as his!"

"Surely," said Mrs. Phillips. "The Lord be praised for all his mercies; but, for a meek, mild, gentle-spoken Christian, his lord-ship was——" and Mrs. Phillips, with unaffected but easy grief, put up her white apron to her flowing eyes.

"You cannot but rejoice that it is over," said Mr. Harding, still consoling his friend.

"No; I suppose not," said he, at last, in answer to Mr. Harding. "We have all expected it so long."

Mr. Harding took him by the arm and led him from the room. "We will see him again to-morrow morning," said he; "we had better leave the room now to the women." And so they went down stairs.

It was already evening and nearly dark. It was most important that the prime minister should know that night that the diocese was vacant. Everything might depend on it; and so, in answer to Mr. Harding's further consolation, the archdeacon suggested that a telegram message should immediately be sent off to London.

"Yes," said Dr. Grantly, collecting himself and shaking off his weakness, "we must send a message at once; we don't know what might be the consequence of delay. Will you do it?"

"I! oh yes; certainly: I'll do anything, only I don't know exactly what it is you want."

Dr. Grantly sat down before a writing table, and taking pen and ink, wrote on a slip of paper as follows:—

"By Electric Telegraph.
"For the Earl of ——, Downing Street, or elsewhere.
"'The Bishop of Barchester is dead.'
"Message sent by the Rev. Septimus Harding."

"There," said he, "just take that to the telegraph office at the railway station, and give it in as it is; they'll probably make you copy it on to one of their own slips; that's all you have to do: then you'll have to pay them half-a-crown;" and the archdeacon put his hand in his pocket and pulled out the necessary sum.

Mr. Harding felt very much like an errand-boy, and also felt that he was called on to perform his duties as such at rather an unseemly time; but he said nothing, and took the slip of paper and the proffered coin.

"But you've put my name into it, archdeacon."

"Yes," said the other, "there should be the name of some clergyman you know, and what name so proper as that of so old a friend as yourself? The Earl won't look at the name, you may be sure of that; but my dear Mr. Harding, pray don't lose any time."

Mr. Harding got as far as the library door on his way to the station, when he suddenly remembered the news with which he was fraught when he entered the poor bishop's bedroom. He had found the moment so inopportune for any mundane tidings, that he had repressed the words which were on his tongue, and immediately afterwards all recollection of the circumstance was for the time banished by the scene which had occurred.

"But, archdeacon," said he, turning back, "I forgot to tell you—the ministry are out."

"Out!" ejaculated the archdeacon, in a tone which too plainly showed his anxiety and dismay, although under the circumstances of the moment he endeavoured to control himself: "Out! who told you so?"

Mr. Harding explained that news to this effect had come down by electric telegraph, and that the tidings had been left at the palace door by Mr. Chadwick.

The archdeacon sat silent for awhile meditating, and Mr. Harding stood looking at him. "Never mind," said the archdeacon at last; "send the message all the same. The news must be sent to someone, and there is at present no one else in a position to receive it. Do it at once, my dear friend; you know I would not trouble you, were I in a state to do it myself. A few minutes' time is of the greatest importance."

Mr. Harding went out and sent the message, and it may be as well that we should follow it to its destination. Within thirty minutes of its leaving Barchester it reached the Earl of —— in his inner library. What elaborate letters, what eloquent appeals, what indignant remonstrances, he might there have to frame, at such a moment, may be conceived, but not described! How he was preparing his thunder for successful rivals, standing like a British peer with his back to the sea-coal fire, and his hands in his breeches pockets,—how his fine eye was lit up with anger, and his forehead gleamed with patriotism,—how he stamped his foot as he thought of his heavy associates,—how he all but swore as he remembered how much too clever one of them had been,—my creative readers may imagine. But was he so engaged? No: history and truth compel me to deny it. He was sitting easily in a lounging chair, conning over a Newmarket list, and by his elbow on the table was lying open an uncut French novel on which he was engaged.

He opened the cover in which the message was enclosed, and having read it, he took his pen and wrote on the back of it—

> "For the Earl of ——,
> "With the Earl of ——'s compliments."

and sent it off again on its journey.

Thus terminated our unfortunate friend's chance of possessing the glories of a bishopric.

The names of many divines were given in the papers as that of the bishop elect. "The British Grandmother" declared that Dr. Gwynne was to be the man, in compliment to the late ministry. This was a heavy blow to Dr. Grantly, but he was not doomed to see himself superseded by his friend. "The Anglican Devotee" put forward confidently the claims of a great London preacher of austere doctrines; and "The Eastern Hemisphere," an evening paper supposed to possess much official knowledge, declared in favour of an eminent naturalist, a gentleman most completely versed in the knowledge of rocks and minerals, but supposed by many to hold on religious subjects no special doctrines whatever. "The Jupiter," that daily paper, which, as we all know, is the only true source of infallibly correct information on all subjects, for a while was silent, but at last spoke out. The merits of all these candidates were discussed and somewhat irreverently disposed of, and then "The Jupiter" declared that Dr. Proudie was to be the man.

Dr. Proudie was the man. Just a month after the demise of the late bishop, Dr. Proudie kissed the Queen's hand as his successor elect.

We must beg to be allowed to draw a curtain over the sorrows of the archdeacon as he sat, sombre and sad at heart, in the study of his parsonage at Plumstead Episcopi. On the day subsequent to the despatch of the message he heard that the Earl of —— had consented to undertake the formation of a ministry, and from that moment he knew that his chance was over.

CHAPTER II

HIRAM'S HOSPITAL, ACCORDING TO ACT OF PARLIAMENT

It is hardly necessary that I should here give to the public any lengthened biography of Mr. Harding, up to the period of the commencement of this tale. The public cannot have forgotten how ill that sensitive gentleman bore the attack that was made on him in the columns of "The Jupiter", with reference to the income which he received as warden of Hiram's Hospital, in the city of Barchester. Nor can it yet be forgotten that a law-suit was instituted against him on the matter of that charity by Mr. John Bold, who afterwards married his, Mr. Harding's, younger and then only unmarried daughter. Under pressure of these attacks, Mr. Harding had resigned his wardenship, though strongly recommended to abstain from doing so, both by his friends and by his lawyers. He did, however, resign it, and betook himself manfully to the duties of the small parish of St. Cuthbert's, in the city, of which he was the vicar, continuing also to perform those of precentor of the cathedral, a situation of small emolument which had hitherto been supposed to be joined, as a matter of course, to the wardenship of the Hospital above spoken of.

Poor Eleanor Bold! I cannot say that with me John Bold was ever a favourite. I never thought him worthy of the wife he had won. But in her estimation he was most worthy. Hers was one of those feminine hearts which cling to a husband, not with idolatry, for worship can admit of no defect in its idol, but with the perfect tenacity of ivy. As the parasite plant will follow even the defects of the trunk which it embraces, so did Eleanor cling to and love the very faults of her husband. She had once declared that whatever her father did should in her eyes be right. She then transferred her allegiance, and became ever ready to defend the worst failings of her lord and master.

And John Bold was a man to be loved by a woman; he was himself affectionate, he was confiding and manly; and that arrogance of thought, unsustained by first-rate abilities, that attempt at being better than his neighbours which jarred so painfully on the feelings of his acquaintance, did not injure him in the estimation of his wife. Could she even have admitted that he had a fault, his early death would have blotted out the memory of it. She wept as for the loss of the most perfect treasure with which mortal woman had ever been endowed; for weeks after he was gone the idea of future happiness in this world was hateful to her; consolation, as it is called, was insupportable, and tears and sleep were her only relief.

But God tempers the wind to the shorn lamb. She knew that she had within her the living source of other cares. She knew that there was to be created for her another subject of weal or woe, of unutterable joy or despairing sorrow, as God in his mercy might vouchsafe to her. At first this did but augment her grief! To be the mother of a poor infant, orphaned before it was born, brought forth to the sorrows of an ever desolate hearth, nurtured admidst tears and wailing, and then turned adrift into the world without the aid of a father's care! There was at first no joy in this.

By degrees, however, her heart became anxious for another object, and, before its birth, the stranger was expected with all the eagerness of a longing mother. Just eight months after the father's death a second John Bold was born, and if the worship of one creature can be innocent in another, let us hope that the adoration offered over the cradle of the fatherless infant may not be imputed as a sin.

As regards the concerns of the world, John Bold had left his widow in prosperous circumstances. He had bequeathed to her all that he possessed, and that comprised an income much exceeding what she or her friends thought necessary for her. It amounted to nearly a thousand a year; and when she reflected on its extent, her dearest hope was to hand it over, not only unimpaired but increased, to her husband's son, to her own darling, to the little man who now lay sleeping on her knee, happily ignorant of the cares which were to be accumulated in his behalf.

When John Bold died she earnestly implored her father to come and live with her, but this Mr. Harding declined, though for some weeks he remained with her as a visitor. He could not be prevailed upon to forgo the possession of some small home of his own, and so remained in the lodgings he had first selected over a chemist's shop in the High Street of Barchester.

CHAPTER III

DR. AND MRS. PROUDIE

THIS narrative is supposed to commence immediately after the installation of Dr. Proudie. I will not describe the ceremony, as I do not precisely understand its nature. I am ignorant whether a bishop be chaired like a member of parliament, or carried in a gilt coach like a lord mayor, or sworn in like a justice of peace, or introduced like a peer to the upper house, or led between two brethren like a knight of the garter; but I do know that everything was properly done, and that nothing fit or becoming to a young bishop was omitted on the occasion.

In person Dr. Proudie is a good-looking man; spruce and dapper, and very tidy. He is somewhat below middle height, being about five feet four; but he makes up for the inches which he wants by the dignity with which he carries those which he has. It is no fault of his own if he has not a commanding eye, for he studies hard to assume it. His features are well formed, though perhaps the sharpness of his nose may give to his face in the eyes of some people an air of insignificance. If so, it is greatly redeemed by his mouth and chin, of which he is justly proud.

Dr. Proudie may well be said to have been a fortunate man, for he was not born to wealth, and he is now bishop of Barchester; but nevertheless he has his cares. He has a large family, of whom the three eldest are daughters, now all grown up and fit for fashionable life; and he has a wife. It is not my intention to breathe a word against the character of Mrs. Proudie, but I still cannot think that with all her virtues she adds much to her husband's happiness. The truth is that in matters domestic she rules supreme over her titular lord, and rules with a rod of iron. Nor is this all. Things domestic

Dr. Proudie might have abandoned to her, if not voluntarily, yet willingly. But Mrs. Proudie is not satisfied with such home dominion, and stretches her power over all his movements, and will not even abstain from things spiritual. In fact, the bishop is henpecked.

One other marked peculiarity in the character of the bishop's wife must be mentioned. Though not averse to the society and manners of the world, she is in her own way a religious woman; and the form in which this tendency shows itself in her is by a strict observance of Sabbatarian rule. Dissipation and low dresses during the week are, under her control, atoned for by three services, an evening sermon read by herself, and a perfect abstinence from any cheering employment on the Sunday. Unfortunately for those under her roof to whom the dissipation and low dresses are not extended, her servants namely and her husband, the compensating strictness of the Sabbath includes all. Woe betide the recreant housemaid who is found to have been listening to the honey of a sweetheart in the Regent's park, instead of the soul-stirring evening discourse of Mr. Slope. Not only is she sent adrift, but she is so sent with a character which leaves her little hope of a decent place. Woe betide the six-foot hero who escorts Mrs. Proudie to her pew in red plush breeches, if he slips away to the neighbouring beershop, instead of falling into the back seat appropriated to his use. Mrs. Proudie has the eyes of Argus for such offenders. Occasional drunkenness in the week may be overlooked, for six feet on low wages are hardly to be procured if the morals are always kept at a high pitch; but not even for grandeur or economy will Mrs. Proudie forgive a desecration of the Sabbath.

In such matters Mrs. Proudie allows herself to be often guided by that eloquent preacher, the Rev. Mr. Slope, and as Dr. Proudie is guided by his wife, it necessarily follows that the eminent man we have named has obtained a good deal of control over Dr. Proudie in matters concerning religion. Mr. Slope's only preferment has hitherto been that of reader and preacher in a London district church: and on the consecration of his friend the new bishop, he readily gave this up to undertake the onerous but congenial duties of domestic chaplain to his lordship.

Mr. Slope, however, on his first introduction must not be brought before the public at the tail of a chapter.

CHAPTER IV

THE BISHOP'S CHAPLAIN

OF the Rev. Mr. Slope's parentage I am not able to say much. I have heard it asserted that he is lineally descended from that eminent physician who assisted at the birth of Mr. T. Shandy, and that in early years he added an 'e' to his name, for the sake of euphony, as other great men have done before him. If this be so, I presume he was christened Obadiah, for that is his name, in commemoration of the conflict in which his ancestor so distinguished himself. All my researches on the subject have, however, failed in enabling me to fix the date on which the family changed its religion.

He had been a sizar at Cambridge, and had there conducted himself at any rate successfully, for in due process of time he was an M.A., having university pupils under his care. From thence he was transferred to London, and became preacher at a new district church built on the confines of Baker Street. He was in this position when congenial ideas on religious subjects recommended him to Mrs. Proudie, and the intercourse had become close and confidential.

Having been thus familiarly thrown among the Misses Proudie, it was no more than natural that some softer feeling than friendship should be engendered. There have been some passages of love between him and the eldest hope, Olivia; but they have hitherto resulted in no favourable arrangement. In truth, Mr. Slope having made a declaration of affection, afterwards withdrew it on finding that the doctor had no immediate worldly funds with which to endow his child; and it may easily be conceived that Miss Proudie, after such an announcement on his part, was not readily disposed to receive any further show of affection. On the appointment of Dr. Proudie to the bishopric of Barchester, Mr. Slope's views were in truth somewhat altered. Bishops, even though they be poor, can provide for clerical children, and Mr. Slope began to regret that he had not been more disinterested. He no sooner heard the tidings of the doctor's elevation, than he recommenced his siege, not violently, indeed, but respectfully, and at a distance. Olivia Proudie, however, was a girl of spirit: she had the blood of two peers in her veins, and, better still, she had another lover on her books; so Mr. Slope sighed in vain; and the pair soon found it convenient to establish a mutual bond of inveterate hatred.

Mr. Slope is tall, and not ill made. His feet and hands are large, as has ever been the case with all his family, but he has a broad chest and wide shoulders to carry off these excrescences, and on the whole his figure is good. His countenance, however, is not specially prepossessing. His hair is lank, and of a dull pale reddish hue. It is always formed into three straight lumpy masses, each brushed with admirable precision, and cemented with much grease; two of them adhere closely to the sides of his face, and the other lies at right angles above them. He wears no whiskers, and is always puncti- liously shaven. His face is nearly of the same colour as his hair, though perhaps a little redder: it is not unlike beef,—beef, however, one would say, of a bad quality. His forehead is capacious and high, but square and heavy, and unpleasantly shining. His mouth is large, though his lips are thin and bloodless; and his big, prominent, pale brown eyes inspire anything but confidence. His nose, however, is his redeeming feature: it is pronounced straight and well-formed; though I myself should have liked it better did it not possess a some- what spongy, porous appearance, as though it had been cleverly formed out of a red coloured cork.

I never could endure to shake hands with Mr. Slope. A cold, clammy perspiration always exudes from him, the small drops are ever to be seen standing on his brow, and his friendly grasp is unpleasant.

Such is Mr. Slope—such is the man who has suddenly fallen into the midst of Barchester Close, and is destined there to assume the station which has heretofore been filled by the son of the late bishop. Think, oh, my meditative reader, what an associate we have here for those comfortable prebendaries, those gentlemanlike clerical doctors, those happy well-used well-fed minor canons, who have grown into existence at Barchester under the kindly wings of Bishop Grantly!

But not as a mere associate for these does Mr. Slope travel down to Barchester with the bishop and his wife. He intends to be, if not their master, at least the chief among them. He intends to lead, and to have followers; he intends to hold the purse strings of the diocese, and draw round him an obedient herd of his poor and hungry brethren.

CHAPTER V

A MORNING VISIT

It was known that Dr. Proudie would immediately have to re- appoint to the wardenship of the hospital under the act of Parlia- ment to which allusion has been made; but no one imagined that any choice was left to him—no one for a moment thought that he could appoint any other than Mr. Harding. Mr. Harding himself, when he heard how the matter had been settled, without troubling himself much on the subject, considered it as certain that he would go back to his pleasant house and garden.

In such a frame of mind he proceeded to pay his respects at the palace the second day after the arrival of the bishop and his chaplain. But he did not go alone. Dr. Grantly proposed to accompany him, and Mr. Harding was not sorry to have a companion, who would remove from his shoulders the burden of the conversation in such an interview. In the affair of the consecration Dr. Grantly had been introduced to the bishop, and Mr. Harding had also been there. He had, however, kept himself in the background, and he was now to be presented to the great man for the first time.

His lordship was at home, and the two visitors were shown through the accustomed hall into the well-known room, where the good old bishop used to sit. The furniture had been bought at a valuation, and every chair and table, every bookshelf against the wall, and every square in the carpet, was as well known to each of them as their own bedrooms.

Our friends found Dr. Proudie sitting on the old bishop's chair, looking very nice in his new apron; they found, too, Mr. Slope standing on the hearthrug, persuasive and eager, just as the archdeacon used to stand; but on the sofa they also found Mrs. Proudie, an innovation for which a precedent might in vain be sought in all the annals of the Barchester bishopric!

There were four persons there, each of whom considered himself the most important personage in the diocese; himself, indeed, or herself, as Mrs. Proudie was one of them; and with such a difference of opinion it was not probable that they would get on pleasantly together. The bishop himself actually wore the visible apron, and trusted mainly to that—to that and his title, both being facts which could not be overlooked. The archdeacon knew his subject, and really understood the business of bishoping, which the others did not; and this was his strong ground. Mrs. Proudie had her sex to back her, and her habit of command, and was nothing daunted by the high tone of Dr. Grantly's face and figure. Mr. Slope had only himself and his own courage and tact to depend on, but he nevertheless was perfectly self-assured, and did not doubt but that he should soon get the better of weak men who trusted so much to externals, as both bishop and archdeacon appeared to do.

"Do you reside in Barchester, Dr. Grantly?" asked the lady with her sweetest smile.

Dr. Grantly explained that he lived in his own parish of Plumstead Episcopi, a few miles out of the city. Whereupon the lady hoped that the distance was not too great for country visiting, as she would be so glad to make the acquaintance of Mrs. Grantly. She would take the earliest opportunity, after the arrival of her horses at Barchester; their horses were at present in London; their horses were not immediately coming down, as the bishop would be obliged, in a few days, to return to town. Dr. Grantly was no doubt aware that the bishop was at present much called upon by the "University

Improvement Committee:" indeed, the Committee could not well proceed without him, as their final report had now to be drawn up. The bishop had also to prepare a scheme for the "Manufacturing Towns Morning and Evening Sunday School Society," of which he was a patron, or president, or director, and therefore the horses would not come down to Barchester at present; but whenever the horses did come down, she would take the earliest opportunity of calling at Plumstead Episcopi, providing the distance was not too great for country visiting.

The archdeacon made his fifth bow: he had made one at each mention of the horses; and promised that Mrs. Grantly would do herself the honour of calling at the palace on an early day. Mrs. Proudie declared that she would be delighted: she hadn't liked to ask, not being quite sure whether Mrs. Grantly had horses; besides, the distance might have been, &c. &c.

Dr. Grantly again bowed, but said nothing. He could have bought every individual possession of the whole family of the Proudies, and have restored them as a gift, without much feeling the loss; and had kept a separate pair of horses for the exclusive use of his wife since the day of his marriage; whereas Mrs. Proudie had been hitherto jobbed about the streets of London at so much a month during the season; and at other times had managed to walk, or hire a smart fly from the livery stables.

"Are the arrangements with reference to the Sabbath-day schools generally pretty good in your archdeaconry?" asked Mr. Slope.

"Sabbath-day schools!" repeated the archdeacon with an affectation of surprise. "Upon my word, I can't tell; it depends mainly on the parson's wife and daughters. There is none at Plumstead."

Mr. Slope merely opened his eyes wider, and slightly shrugged his shoulders. He was not, however, prepared to give up his darling project.

"I fear there is a great deal of Sabbath travelling here," said he. "On looking at the 'Bradshaw,' I see that there are three trains in and three out every Sabbath. Could nothing be done to induce the company to withdraw them? Don't you think, Dr. Grantly, that a little energy might diminish the evil?"

"Not being a director, I really can't say. But if you can withdraw the passengers, the company, I dare say, will withdraw the trains," said the doctor. "It's merely a question of dividends."

"But surely, Dr. Grantly," said the lady, "surely we should look at it differently. You and I, for instance, in our position: surely we should do all that we can to control so grievous a sin. Don't you think so, Mr. Harding?" and she turned to the precentor, who was sitting mute and unhappy.

Mr. Harding thought that all porters and stokers, guards, breaks-men and pointsmen ought to have an opportunity of going to church, and he hoped that they all had.

"But surely, surely," continued Mrs. Proudie, "surely that is not enough. Surely that will not secure such an observance of the Sabbath as we are taught to conceive is not only expedient but indispensable; surely——"

Come what come might, Dr. Grantly was not to be forced into a dissertation on a point of doctrine with Mrs. Proudie, nor yet with Mr. Slope; so without much ceremony he turned his back upon the sofa, and began to hope that Dr. Proudie had found that the palace repairs had been such as to meet his wishes.

Mrs. Proudie, though she had contrived to lend her assistance in recapitulating the palatial dilapidations, had not on that account given up her hold of Mr. Harding, nor ceased from her cross-examinations as to the iniquity of Sabbatical amusements. Over and over again she had thrown out her "Surely, surely," at Mr. Harding's devoted head, and ill had that gentleman been able to parry the attack.

He had never before found himself subject to such a nuisance. Ladies hitherto, when they had consulted him on religious subjects, had listened to what he might choose to say with some deference, and had differed, if they differed, in silence. But Mrs. Proudie interrogated him, and then lectured. "Neither thou, nor thy son, nor thy daughter, nor thy man servant, nor thy maid servant," said she, impressively, and more than once, as though Mr. Harding had forgotten the words. She shook her finger at him as she quoted the favourite law, as though menacing him with punishment; and then called upon him categorically to state whether he did not think that travelling on the Sabbath was an abomination and a desecration.

Mr. Harding had never been so hard pressed in his life. He felt that he ought to rebuke the lady for presuming so to talk to a gentleman and a clergyman many years her senior; but he recoiled from the idea of scolding the bishop's wife, in the bishop's presence, on his first visit to the palace; moreover, to tell the truth, he was somewhat afraid of her. She, seeing him sit silent and absorbed, by no means refrained from the attack.

"I hope, Mr. Harding," said she, shaking her head slowly and solemnly, "I hope you will not leave me to think that you approve of Sabbath travelling," and she looked a look of unutterable meaning into his eyes.

There was no standing this, for Mr. Slope was now looking at him, and so was the bishop, and so was the archdeacon, who had completed his adieux on that side of the room. Mr. Harding therefore got up also, and putting out his hand to Mrs. Proudie said: "If you will come to St. Cuthbert's some Sunday, I will preach you a sermon on that subject."

And so the archdeacon and the precentor took their departure, bowing low to the lady, shaking hands with the lord, and escaping from Mr. Slope in the best manner each could. Mr. Harding was again maltreated; but Dr. Grantly swore deeply at the bottom of his heart, that no earthly consideration should ever again induce him to touch the paw of that impure and filthy animal.

And now, had I the pen of a mighty poet, would I sing in epic verse the noble wrath of the archdeacon. The palace steps descend to a broad gravel sweep, from whence a small gate opens out into the street, very near the covered gateway leading into the close. The road from the palace door turns to the left, through the spacious gardens, and terminates on the London-road, half a mile from the cathedral.

Till they had both passed this small gate and entered the close, neither of them spoke a word; but the precentor clearly saw from his companion's face that a tornado was to be expected, nor was he himself inclined to stop it. Though by nature far less irritable than the archdeacon, even he was angry: he even—that mild and courteous man—was inclined to express himself in anything but courteous terms.

CHAPTER VI

WAR

Soon after his arrival the bishop had intimated to the dean that, with the permission of the canon then in residence, his chaplain would preach in the cathedral on the next Sunday. The canon in residence happened to be the Hon. and Rev. Dr. Vesey Stanhope, who at this time was very busy on the shores of the Lake of Como, adding to that unique collection of butterflies for which he is so famous. Or, rather, he would have been in residence but for the butterflies and other such summer-day considerations; and the vicar-choral, who was to take his place in the pulpit, by no means objected to having his work done for him by Mr. Slope.

Mr. Slope accordingly preached, and if a preacher can have satisfaction in being listened to, Mr. Slope ought to have been gratified. I have reason to think that he was gratified, and that he left the pulpit with the conviction that he had done what he intended to do when he entered it.

On this occasion the new bishop took his seat for the first time in the throne allotted to him. New scarlet cushions and drapery had been prepared, with new gilt binding and new fringe.

All Barchester went to hear Mr. Slope; either for that or to gaze at the new bishop.

Crowded audiences usually make good performers, and though Mr. Harding was not aware of any extraordinary exertion on his part, yet probably he rather exceeded his usual mark. Others were doing their best, and it was natural that he should emulate his brethren. So the service went on, and at last Mr. Slope got into the pulpit.

He chose for his text a verse from the precepts addressed by St. Paul to Timothy, as to the conduct necessary in a spiritual pastor and guide, and it was immediately evident that the good clergy of Barchester were to have a lesson.

"Study to show thyself approved unto God, a workman that needeth not to be ashamed, rightly dividing the word of truth." These were the words of his text, and with such a subject in such a place, it may be supposed that such a preacher would be listened to by such an audience. He was listened to with breathless attention, and not without considerable surprise. Whatever opinion of Mr. Slope might have been held in Barchester before he commenced his discourse, none of his hearers, when it was over, could mistake him either for a fool or a coward.

Mr. Slope, in commencing his sermon, showed no slight tact in his ambiguous manner of hinting that, humble as he was himself, he stood there as the mouthpiece of the illustrious divine who sat opposite to him; and having premised so much, he gave forth a very accurate definition of the conduct which that prelate would rejoice to see in the clergymen now brought under his jurisdiction. It is only necessary to say, that the peculiar points insisted upon were exactly those which were most distasteful to the clergy of the diocese, and most averse to their practice and opinions; and that all those peculiar habits and privileges which have always been dear to high-church priests, to that party which is now scandalously called the high-and-dry church, were ridiculed, abused, and anathematised. Now, the clergymen of the diocese of Barchester are all of the high-and-dry church.

Having thus, according to his own opinion, explained how a clergyman should show himself approved unto God, as a workman that needeth not to be ashamed, he went on to explain how the word of truth should be divided; and here he took a rather narrow view of the question, and fetched his arguments from afar. His object was to express his abomination of all ceremonious modes of utterance, to cry down any religious feeling which might be excited, not by the sense, but by the sound of words, and in fact to insult cathedral practices. Had St. Paul spoken of rightly pronouncing instead of rightly dividing the word of truth, this part of his sermon would have been more to the purpose; but the preacher's immediate object was to preach Mr. Slope's doctrine, and not St. Paul's, and he contrived to give the necessary twist to the text with some skill.

He could not exactly say, preaching from a cathedral pulpit, that chanting should be abandoned in cathedral services. By such an assertion, he would have overshot his mark and rendered himself absurd, to the delight of his hearers. He could, however, and did, allude with heavy denunciations to the practice of intoning in parish churches, although the practice was all but unknown in the diocese; and from thence he came round to the undue preponderance, which he asserted, music had over meaning in the beautiful service which they had just heard. He was aware, he said, that the practices of our ancestors could not be abandoned at a moment's notice; the feelings of the aged would be outraged, and the minds of respectable men would be shocked. There were many, he was aware, of not sufficient calibre of thought to perceive, of not sufficient education to know, that a mode of service, which was effective when outward ceremonies were of more moment than inward feelings, had become all but barbarous at a time when inward conviction was everything, when each word of the minister's lips should fall intelligibly into the listener's heart. Formerly the religion of the multitude had been an affair of the imagination: now, in these latter days, it had become necessary that a Christian should have a reason for his faith—should not only believe, but digest—not only hear, but understand. The words of our morning service, how beautiful, how apposite, how intelligible they were, when read with simple and distinct decorum! but how much of the meaning of the words was lost when they were produced with all the meretricious charms of melody! &c. &c.

Here was a sermon to be preached before Mr. Archdeacon Grantly, Mr. Precentor Harding, and the rest of them! before a whole dean and chapter assembled in their own cathedral! before men who had grown old in the exercise of their peculiar services, with a full conviction of their excellence for all intended purposes! This too from such a man, a clerical *parvenu*, a man without a cure, a mere chaplain, an intruder among them; a fellow raked up, so said Dr. Grantly, from the gutters of Marylebone! They had to sit through it! None of them, not even Dr. Grantly, could close his ears, nor leave the house of God during the hours of service. They were under an obligation of listening, and that too, without any immediate power of reply.

There was, at any rate, no tedium felt in listening to Mr. Slope on the occasion in question. His subject came too home to his audience to be dull; and, to tell the truth, Mr. Slope had the gift of using words forcibly. He was heard through his thirty minutes of eloquence with mute attention and open ears; but with angry eyes, which glared round from one enraged parson to another, with wide-spread nostrils from which already burst forth fumes of indignation, and with many shufflings of the feet and uneasy motions of the body, which betokened minds disturbed, and hearts not at peace with all the world.

At last the bishop, who, of all the congregation, had been most surprised, and whose hair almost stood on end with terror, gave the blessing in a manner not at all equal to that in which he had long

been practising it in his own study, and the congregation was free
to go their way.

All Barchester was in a tumult. Dr. Grantly could hardly get
himself out of the cathedral porch before he exploded in his wrath.
The old dean betook himself silently to his deanery, afraid to speak;
and there sat, half stupefied, pondering many things in vain. Mr.
Harding crept forth solitary and unhappy; and, slowly passing
beneath the elms of the close, could scarcely bring himself to believe
that the words which he had heard had proceeded from the pulpit
of Barchester cathedral. Was he again to be disturbed? was his
whole life to be shown up as a useless sham a second time? would he
have to abdicate his precentorship, as he had his wardenship, and
to give up chanting, as he had given up his twelve old bedesmen?
And what if he did! Some other Jupiter, some other Mr. Slope,
would come and turn him out of St. Cuthbert's. Surely he could
not have been wrong all his life in chanting the litany as he had
done! He began, however, to have his doubts. Doubting himself
was Mr. Harding's weakness. It is not, however, the usual fault of
his order.

Yes! All Barchester was in a tumult. It was not only the clergy
who were affected. The laity also had listened to Mr. Slope's new
doctrine, all with surprise, some with indignation, and some with a
mixed feeling, in which dislike of the preacher was not so strongly
blended. The old bishop and his chaplains, the dean and his
canons and minor canons, the old choir, and especially Mr. Harding who was at the head of it, had all been popular in Barchester.
They had spent their money and done good; the poor had not been
ground down; the clergy in society had neither been overbearing
nor austere; and the whole repute of the city was due to its ecclesiastical importance.

Dr. and Mrs. Proudie at once returned to London. They thought
it expedient not to have to encounter any personal application
from the dean and chapter respecting the sermon, till the violence of
the storm had expended itself; but they left Mr. Slope behind them
nothing daunted, and he went about his work zealously, flattering
such as would listen to his flattery, whispering religious twaddle
into the ears of foolish women, ingratiating himself with the few
clergy who would receive him, visiting the houses of the poor,
inquiring into all people, prying into everything, and searching
with his minutest eye into all palatial dilapidations. He did not,
however, make any immediate attempt to preach again in the
cathedral.

And so all Barchester was by the ears.

Among the ladies in Barchester who have hitherto acknowledged
Mr. Slope as their spiritual director, must not be reckoned either
the widow Bold, or her sister-in-law. On the first outbreak of the
wrath of the denizens of the close, none had been more animated

against the intruder than these two ladies. And this was natural. Who could be so proud of the musical distinction of their own cathedral as the favourite daughter of the precentor? Who would be so likely to resent an insult offered to the old choir? And in such matters Miss Bold and her sister-in-law had but one opinion.

This wrath, however, has in some degree been mitigated, and I regret to say that these ladies allowed Mr. Slope to be his own apologist. About a fortnight after the sermon had been preached, they were both of them not a little surprised by hearing Mr. Slope announced, as the page in buttons opened Mrs. Bold's drawing-room door. Indeed, what living man could, by a mere morning visit, have surprised them more? Here was the great enemy of all that was good in Barchester coming into their own drawing-room, and they had no strong arm, no ready tongue, near at hand for their protection. The widow snatched her baby out of its cradle into her lap, and Mary Bold stood up ready to die manfully in that baby's behalf, should, under any circumstances, such a sacrifice become necessary.

In this manner was Mr. Slope received. But when he left, he was allowed by each lady, to take her hand, and to make his adieux as gentlemen do who have been graciously entertained!

He commenced his acquaintance with Eleanor by praising her father. He had, he said, become aware that he had unfortunately offended the feelings of a man of whom he could not speak too highly; he would not now allude to a subject which was probably too serious for drawing-room conversation, but he would say, that it had been very far from him to utter a word in disparagement of a man, of whom all the world, at least the clerical world, spoke so highly as it did of Mr. Harding. And so he went on, unsaying a great deal of his sermon, expressing his highest admiration for the precentor's musical talents, eulogising the father and the daughter and the sister-in-law, speaking in that low silky whisper which he always had specially prepared for feminine ears, and, ultimately, gaining his object. When he left, he expressed a hope that he might again be allowed to call; and though Eleanor gave no verbal assent to this, she did not express dissent: and so Mr. Slope's right to visit at the widow's house was established.

The day after this visit Eleanor told her father of it, and expressed an opinion that Mr. Slope was not quite so black as he had been painted. Mr. Harding opened his eyes rather wider than usual when he heard what had occurred, but he said little; he could not agree in any praise of Mr. Slope, and it was not his practice to say much evil of any one. He did not, however, like the visit, and simple-minded as he was, he felt sure that Mr. Slope had some deeper motive than the mere pleasure of making soft speeches to two ladies.

CHAPTER VII

THE STANHOPE FAMILY

It is now three months since Dr. Proudie began his reign, and
changes have already been effected in the diocese which show at
least the energy of an active mind. Among other things absentee
clergymen have been favoured with hints much too strong to be
overlooked. Poor dear old Bishop Grantly had on this matter been
too lenient, and the archdeacon had been never inclined to be severe
with those who were absent on reputable pretences, and who provided
for their duties in a liberal way.

Among the greatest of the diocesan sinners in this respect was Dr.
Vesey Stanhope. Years had now passed since he had done a day's
duty; and yet there was no reason against his doing duty except a
want of inclination on his own part. He held a prebendal stall in
the diocese; one of the best residences in the close; and the two large
rectories of Crabtree Canonicorum and Stogpingum. Indeed, he
had the cure of three parishes, for that of Eiderdown was joined to
Stogpingum. He had resided in Italy for twelve years. His first
going there had been attributed to a sore throat; and that sore
throat, though never repeated in any violent manner, had stood
him in such stead, that it had enabled him to live in easy idleness
ever since.

He had now been summoned home—not, indeed, with rough
violence, or by any peremptory command, but by a mandate which
he found himself unable to disregard. Mr. Slope had written to
him by the bishop's desire. In the first place, the bishop much
wanted the valuable co-operation of Dr. Vesey Stanhope in the
diocese; in the next, the bishop thought it his imperative duty to
become personally acquainted with the most conspicuous of his
diocesan clergy; then the bishop thought it essentially necessary for
Dr. Stanhope's own interests, that Dr. Stanhope should, at any
rate for a time, return to Barchester; and lastly, it was said that
so strong a feeling was at the present moment evinced by the hierarchs
of the church with reference to the absence of its clerical members,
that it behoved Dr. Vesey Stanhope not to allow his name to stand
among those which would probably in a few months be submitted
to the councils of the nation.

There was something so ambiguously frightful in this last threat
that Dr. Stanhope determined to spend two or three summer
months at his residence in Barchester. His rectories were inhabited
by his curates, and he felt himself from disuse to be unfit for parochial duty; but his prebendal home was kept empty for him, and he

thought it probable that he might be able now and again to preach a prebendal sermon. He arrived, therefore, with all his family at Barchester, and he and they must be introduced to my readers.

The great family characteristic of the Stanhopes might probably be said to be heartlessness; but this want of feeling was, in most of them, accompanied by so great an amount of good nature as to make itself but little noticeable to the world. They were so prone to oblige their neighbours that their neighbours failed to perceive how indifferent to them was the happiness and well-being of those around them. The Stanhopes would visit you in your sickness (provided it were not contagious), would bring you oranges, French novels, and the last new bit of scandal, and then hear of your death or your recovery with an equally indifferent composure. Their conduct to each other was the same as to the world; they bore and forebore: and there was sometimes, as will be seen, much necessity for forebearing: but their love among themselves rarely reached above this. It is astonishing how much each of the family was able to do, and how much each did, to prevent the well-being of the other four.

For there were five in all; the doctor, namely, and Mrs. Stanhope, two daughters, and one son. The doctor, perhaps, was the least singular and most estimable of them all, and yet such good qualities as he possessed were all negative. He was a good looking rather plethoric gentleman of about sixty years of age. His hair was snow white, very plentiful, and somewhat like wool of the finest description. His whiskers were very large and very white, and gave to his face the appearance of a benevolent sleepy old lion. His dress was always unexceptionable.

Such was Dr. Stanhope. The features of Mrs. Stanhope's character were even less plainly marked than those of her lord. The *far niente* of her Italian life had entered into her very soul, and brought her to regard a state of inactivity as the only earthly good. In manner and appearance she was exceedingly prepossessing. She had been a beauty, and even now, at fifty-five, she was a handsome woman. Her dress was always perfect: she never dressed but once in the day, and never appeared till between three and four; but when she did appear, she appeared at her best. Whether the toil rested partly with her, or wholly with her handmaid, it is not for such a one as the author even to imagine. The structure of her attire was always elaborate, and yet never over laboured. In early life she had undergone great trials with reference to the doctor's dinners; but for the last ten or twelve years her eldest daughter Charlotte had taken that labour off her hands, and she had had little to trouble her;—little, that is, till the edict for this terrible English journey had gone forth: since, then, indeed, her life had been laborious enough. For such a one, the toil of being carried from the shores of Como to the city of Barchester is more than labour enough, let the care of the carriers be ever so vigilant. Mrs. Stanhope had been obliged to have every one of her dresses taken in from the effects of the journey.

Charlotte Stanhope was at this time about thirty-five years old; and, whatever may have been her faults, she had none of those which belong particularly to old young ladies. She neither dressed young, nor talked young, nor indeed looked young. She appeared to be perfectly content with her time of life, and in no way affected the graces of youth. She was a fine young woman; and had she been a man, would have been a very fine young man. All that was done in the house, and that was not done by servants, was done by her. She gave the orders, paid the bills, hired and dismissed the domestics, made the tea, carved the meat, and managed everything in the Stanhope household. She, and she alone, could ever induce her father to look into the state of his worldly concerns. She, and she alone, could in any degree control the absurdities of her sister. She, and she alone, prevented the whole family from falling into utter disrepute and beggary. It was by her advice that they now found themselves very unpleasantly situated in Barchester.

But the two most prominent members of the family still remain to be described. The second child had been christened Madeline, and had been a great beauty. We need not say had been, for she was never more beautiful than at the time of which we write, though her person for many years had been disfigured by an accident. It is unnecessary that we should give in detail the early history of Madeline Stanhope. She had gone to Italy when about seventeen years of age, and had been allowed to make the most of her surpassing beauty in the saloons of Milan, and among the crowded villas along the shores of the Lake of Como. She had become famous for adventures in which her character was just not lost, and had destroyed the hearts of a dozen cavaliers without once being touched in her own. Blood had flowed in quarrels about her charms, and she heard of these encounters with pleasurable excitement. It had been told of her that on one occasion she had stood by in the disguise of a page, and had seen her lover fall.

As is so often the case, she had married the very worst of those who sought her hand. Why she had chosen Paulo Neroni, a man of no birth and no property, a mere captain in the pope's guard, one who had come up to Milan either simply as an adventurer or else as a spy, a man of harsh temper and oily manners, mean in figure, swarthy in face, and so false in words as to be hourly detected, need not now be told. When the moment for doing so came, she had probably no alternative. He, at any rate, had become her husband; and after a prolonged honeymoon among the lakes, they had gone together to Rome, the papal captain having vainly endeavoured to induce his wife to remain behind him.

Six months afterwards she arrived at her father's house a cripple, and a mother. She had arrived without even notice, with hardly clothes to cover her, and without one of those many ornaments which had graced her bridal *trousseau*. Her baby was in the arms of a poor girl from Milan, whom she had taken in exchange for the Roman maid who had accompanied her thus far, and who had then, as her mistress said, become homesick and had returned. It was clear that the lady had determined that there should be no witness to tell stories of her life in Rome.

She had fallen, she said, in ascending a ruin, and had fatally injured the sinews of her knee; so fatally, that when she stood she lost eight inches of her accustomed height; so fatally, that when she essayed to move, she could only drag herself painfully along, with protruded hip and extended foot in a manner less graceful than that of a hunchback. She had consequently made up her mind, once and for ever, that she would never stand, and never attempt to move herself.

Stories were not slow to follow her, averring that she had been cruelly ill used by Neroni, and that to his violence had she owed her accident. Be that as it may, little had been said about her husband, but that little had made it clearly intelligible to the family that Signor Neroni was to be seen and heard of no more. There was no question as to re-admitting the poor ill used beauty to her old family rights, no question as to adopting her infant daughter beneath the Stanhope roof tree. Though heartless, the Stanhopes were not selfish. The two were taken in, petted, made much of, for a time all but adored, and then felt by the two parents to be great nuisances in the house. But in the house the lady was, and there she remained, having her own way, though that way was not very conformable with the customary usages of an English clergyman.

Madame Neroni, though forced to give up all motion in the world, had no intention whatever of giving up the world itself. The beauty of her face was uninjured, and that beauty was of a peculiar kind. Her copious rich brown hair was worn in Grecian *bandeaux* round her head, displaying as much as possible of her forehead and cheeks. Her forehead, though rather low, was very beautiful from its perfect contour and pearly whiteness. Her eyes were long and large, and marvellously bright; might I venture to say, bright as Lucifer's, I should perhaps best express the depth of their brilliancy. They were dreadful eyes to look at, such as would absolutely deter any man of quiet mind and easy spirit from attempting a passage of arms with such foes. There was talent in them, and the fire of passion and the play of wit, but there was no love. Cruelty was there instead, and courage, a desire of masterhood, cunning, and a wish for mischief. And yet, as eyes, they were very beautiful. The eyelashes were long and perfect, and the long steady unabashed gaze, with which she would look into the face of her admirer, fascinated while it frightened him. She was a basilisk from whom an ardent lover of beauty could make no escape. Her nose and mouth and

B

teeth and chin and neck and bust were perfect, much more so at twenty-eight than they had been at eighteen. What wonder that with such charms still glowing in her face, and with such deformity destroying her figure, she should resolve to be seen, but only to be seen reclining on a sofa.

Ethelbert Stanhope was in some respects like his younger sister, but he was less inestimable as a man than she as a woman. His great fault was an entire absence of that principle which should have induced him, as the son of a man without fortune, to earn his own bread. Many attempts had been made to get him to do so, but these had all been frustrated, not so much by idleness on his part, as by a disinclination to exert himself in any way not to his taste. He had been educated at Eton, and had been intended for the Church, but had left Cambridge in disgust after a single term, and notified to his father his intention to study for the bar. Preparatory to that, he thought it well that he should attend a German university, and consequently went to Leipsic. There he remained two years, and brought away a knowledge of German and a taste for the fine arts. He still, however, intended himself for the bar, took chambers, engaged himself to sit at the feet of a learned pundit, and spent a season in London. He there found that all his aptitudes inclined him to the life of an artist, and he determined to live by painting. With this object he returned to Milan, and had himself rigged out for Rome. As a painter he might have earned his bread, for he wanted only diligence to excel; but when at Rome his mind was carried away by other things: he soon wrote home for money, saying that he had been converted to the Mother Church, that he was already an acolyte of the Jesuits, and that he was about to start with others to Palestine on a mission for converting Jews.

Ethelbert did not long remain a Jew. He soon reappeared at the villa without prejudices on the subject of his religion, and with a firm resolve to achieve fame and fortune as a sculptor. He brought with him some models which he had originated at Rome, and which really gave such fair promise that his father was induced to go to further expense in furthering these views. Ethelbert opened an establishment, or rather took lodgings and a workshop, at Carrara, and there spoilt much marble, and made some few pretty images. Since that period, now four years ago, he had alternated between Carrara and the villa, but his sojourns at the workshop became shorter and shorter, and those at the villa longer and longer. 'Twas no wonder; for Carrara is not a spot in which an Englishman would like to dwell.

When the family started for England he had resolved not to be left behind, and with the assistance of his elder sister had carried his point against his father's wishes. It was necessary, he said, that he should come to England for orders. How otherwise was he to bring his profession to account?

In personal appearance Ethelbert Stanhope was the most singular of beings. He was certainly very handsome. He had his sister Madeline's eyes without their stare, and without their hard cunning cruel firmness. They were also very much lighter, and of so light and clear a blue as to make his face remarkable, if nothing else did so. On entering a room with him, Ethelbert's blue eyes would be the first thing you would see, and on leaving it almost the last you would forget. His light hair was very long and silky, coming down over his coat. His beard had been prepared in holy land, and was patriarchal. He never shaved, and rarely trimmed it. It was glossy, soft, clean, and altogether not unprepossessing. It was such, that ladies might desire to reel it off and work it into their patterns in lieu of floss silk. His complexion was fair and almost pink, he was small in height, and slender in limb, but well-made, and his voice was of peculiar sweetness.

In manner and dress he was equally remarkable. He had none of the *mauvaise honte* of an Englishman. He required no introduction to make himself agreeable to any person. He habitually addressed strangers, ladies as well as men, without any such formality, and in doing so never seemed to meet with rebuke. His costume cannot be described, because it was so various; but it was always totally opposed in every principle of colour and construction to the dress of those with whom he for the time consorted.

The Stanhopes were all known by name in Barchester, and Barchester was prepared to receive them with open arms. The doctor was one of her prebendaries, one of her rectors, one of her pillars of strength; and was, moreover, counted on, as a sure ally, both by Proudies and Grantlys.

He himself was the brother of one peer, and his wife was the sister of another—and both these peers were lords of whiggish tendency, with whom the new bishop had some sort of alliance. This was sufficient to give to Mr. Slope high hope that he might enlist Dr. Stanhope on his side, before his enemies could out-manoeuvre him. On the other hand, the old dean had many many years ago, in the days of the doctor's clerical energies, been instrumental in assisting him in his views as to preferment; and many many years ago also, the two doctors, Stanhope and Grantly, had, as young parsons, been joyous together in the common rooms of Oxford. Dr. Grantly, consequently, did not doubt but that the new comer would range himself under his banners.

Little did any of them dream of what ingredients the Stanhope family was now composed.

CHAPTER VIII

MRS. PROUDIE'S RECEPTION—COMMENCED

THE bishop and his wife had only spent three or four days in Barchester on the occasion of their first visit. His lordship had, as we have seen, taken his seat on his throne; but his demeanour there, into which it had been his intention to infuse much hierarchal dignity, had been a good deal disarranged by the audacity of his chaplain's sermon. He had hardly dared to look his clergy in the face, and to declare by the severity of his countenance that in truth he meant all that his factotum was saying on his behalf; nor yet did he dare to throw Mr. Slope over, and show to those around him that he was no party to the sermon, and would resent it.

He had accordingly blessed his people in a shambling manner, not at all to his own satisfaction, and had walked back to his palace with his mind very doubtful as to what he would say to his chaplain on the subject. He did not remain long in doubt. He had hardly doffed his lawn when the partner of all his toils entered his study, and exclaimed even before she had seated herself—

"Bishop, did you ever hear a more sublime, more spirit-moving, more appropriate discourse than that?"

"Well, my love; ha—hum—he!" The bishop did not know what to say.

"I hope, my lord, you don't mean to say you disapprove?"

There was a look about the lady's eye which did not admit of my lord's disapproving at that moment. He felt that if he intended to disapprove, it must be now or never; but he also felt that it could not be now. It was not in him to say to the wife of his bosom that Mr. Slope's sermon was ill-timed, impertinent and vexatious.

"No, no," replied the bishop. "No, I can't say I disapprove—a very clever sermon and very well intended, and I dare say will do a great deal of good." This last praise was added, seeing that what he had already said by no means satisfied Mrs. Proudie.

"I hope it will," said she. "I am sure it was well deserved. Did you ever in your life, bishop, hear anything so like play-acting as the way in which Mr. Harding sings the litany? I shall beg Mr. Slope to continue a course of sermons on the subject till all that is altered. We will have at any rate, in our cathedral, a decent, godly, modest morning service. There must be no more play-acting here now"; and so the lady rang for lunch.

The bishop knew more about cathedrals and deans, and precentors and church services than his wife did, and also more of a bishop's powers. But he thought it better at present to let the sub-ject drop.

"My dear," said he, "I think we must go back to London on Tuesday. I find my staying here will be very inconvenient to the Government."

The bishop knew that to this proposal his wife would not object; and he also felt that by thus retreating from the ground of battle, the heat of the fight might be got over in his absence.

"Mr. Slope will remain here, of course?" said the lady.

"Oh, of course," said the bishop.

Thus, after less than a week's sojourn in his palace, did the bishop fly from Barchester; nor did he return to it for two months, the London season being then over. During that time Mr. Slope was not idle, but he did not again essay to preach in the cathedral. In answer to Mrs. Proudie's letters, advising a course of sermons, he had pleaded that he would at any rate wish to put off such an undertaking till she was there to hear them.

He had employed his time in consolidating a Proudie and Slope party—or rather a Slope and Proudie party, and he had not employed his time in vain. He did not meddle with the dean and chapter, except by giving them little teasing intimations of the bishop's wishes about this and the bishop's feelings about that, in a manner which was to them sufficiently annoying, but which they could not resent. He preached once or twice in a distant church in the suburbs of the city, but made no allusion to the cathedral service. He commenced the establishment of two "Bishop's Bar-chester Sabbath-day Schools," gave notice of a proposed "Bishop's Barchester Young Men's Sabbath Evening Lecture Room,"—and wrote three or four letters to the manager of the Barchester branch railway, informing him how anxious the bishop was that the Sunday trains should be discontinued.

At the end of two months, however, the bishop and the lady reappeared; and as a happy harbinger of their return, heralded their advent by the promise of an evening party on the largest scale. The tickets of invitation were sent out from London—they were dated from Bruton Street, and were despatched by the odious Sabbath breaking railway, in a huge brown paper parcel to Mr. Slope. Everybody calling himself a gentleman, or herself a lady, within the city of Barchester, and a circle of two miles round it, was included. Tickets were sent to all the diocesan clergy, and also to many other persons of priestly note, of whose absence the bishop, or at least the bishop's wife, felt tolerably confident. It was in-tended, however, to be a thronged and noticeable affair, and pre-parations were made for receiving some hundreds.

People were to arrive at ten, supper was to last from twelve till one, and at half-past one everybody was to be gone. Carriages were to come in at the gate in the town and depart at the gate outside.

They were desired to take up at a quarter before one. It was managed excellently, and Mr. Slope was invaluable.

At half-past nine the bishop and his wife and their three daughters entered the great reception-room, and very grand and very solemn they were. Mr. Slope was down-stairs giving the last orders about the wine. He well understood that curates and country vicars with their belongings did not require so generous an article as the dignitaries of the close. There is a useful gradation in such things, and Marsala at 20s. a dozen did very well for the exterior supplementary tables in the corner.

"Bishop," said the lady, as his lordship sat himself down, "don't sit on that sofa, if you please ; it is to be kept separate for a lady."

The bishop jumped up and seated himself on a cane-bottomed chair. "*A* lady?" he inquired meekly ; "do you mean one particular lady, my dear?"

"Yes, Bishop, one particular lady," said his wife, disdaining to explain.

"She has got no legs, papa," said the youngest daughter, tittering.

"No legs!" said the bishop, opening his eyes.

"Nonsense, Netta, what stuff you talk," said Olivia. "She has got legs, but she can't use them. She has always to be kept lying down, and three or four men carry her about everywhere."

"Laws, how odd!" said Augusta. "Always carried about by four men! I'm sure I shouldn't like it. Am I right behind, mamma? I feel as if I was open ;" and she turned her back to her anxious parent.

"Open! to be sure you are," said she, "and a yard of petticoat strings hanging out. I don't know why I pay such high wages to Mrs. Richards, if she can't take the trouble to see whether or no you are fit to be looked at," and Mrs. Proudie poked the strings here, and twitched the dress there, and gave her daughter a shove and a shake, and then pronounced it all right.

"But," rejoined the bishop, who was dying with curiosity about the mysterious lady and her legs, "who is it that is to have the sofa? What's her name, Netta?"

A thundering rap at the front door interrupted the conversation. Mrs. Proudie stood up and shook herself gently, and touched her cap on each side as she looked in the mirror. Each of the girls stood on tiptoe, and re-arranged the bows on their bosoms ; and Mr. Slope rushed up stairs three steps at a time.

"But who is it, Netta?" whispered the bishop to his youngest daughter.

"La Signora Madeline Vesey Neroni," whispered back the daughter ; "and mind you don't let any one sit upon the sofa."

"La Signora Madeline Vicinironi!" muttered, to himself, the bewildered prelate. Had he been told that the Begum of Oude was to be there, or Queen Pomara of the Western Isles, he could not have been more astonished. La Signora Madeline Vicinironi, who, having no legs to stand on, had bespoken a sofa in his drawing-room!—who could she be? He however could now make no further inquiry, as Dr. and Mrs. Stanhope were announced. They had been sent on out of the way a little before the time, in order that the signora might have plenty of time to get herself conveniently packed into the carriage.

The bishop was all smiles for the prebendary's wife, and the bishop's wife was all smiles for the prebendary. Mr. Slope was presented, and was delighted to make the acquaintance of one of whom he had heard so much. The doctor bowed very low, and then looked as though he could not return the compliment as regarded Mr. Slope, of whom, indeed, he had heard nothing. The doctor, in spite of his long absence, knew an English gentleman when he saw him.

And then the guests came in shoals: Mr. and Mrs. Quiverful and their three grown daughters. Mr. and Mrs. Chadwick and their three daughters. The burly chancellor and his wife and clerical son from Oxford. The meagre little doctor without incumbrance. Mr. Harding with Eleanor and Miss Bold. The dean leaning on a gaunt spinster, his only child now living with him, a lady very learned in stones, ferns, plants and vermin, and who had written a book about petals. A wonderful woman in her way was Miss Trefoil. Mr. Finnie, the attorney, with his wife, was to be seen, much to the dismay of many who had never met him in a drawing-room before. The five Barchester doctors were all there, and old Scalpen, the retired apothecary and toothdrawer, who was first taught to consider himself as belonging to the higher orders by the receipt of the bishop's card. Then came the archdeacon and his wife, with their elder daughter Griselda, a slim pale retiring girl of seventeen, who kept close to her mother, and looked out on the world with quiet watchful eyes, one who gave promise of much beauty when time should have ripened it.

And so the rooms became full, and knots were formed, and every new comer paid his respects to my lord and passed on, not presuming to occupy too much of the great man's attention. The archdeacon shook hands very heartily with Doctor Stanhope, and Mrs. Grantly seated herself by the doctor's wife. And Mrs. Proudie moved about with well regulated grace, measuring out the quantity of her favours to the quality of her guests, just as Mr. Slope had been doing with the wine. But the sofa was still empty, and five-and-twenty ladies and five gentlemen had been courteously warned off it by the mindful chaplain.

"Why doesn't she come?" said the bishop to himself. His mind was so preoccupied with the signora, that he hardly remembered how to behave himself *en bishop*.

At last a carriage dashed up to the hall steps with a very different manner of approach from that of any other vehicle that had been there that evening. A perfect commotion took place. The doctor, who heard it as he was standing in the drawing-room, knew that his daughter was coming, and retired into the furthest corner, where he might not see her entrance. Mrs. Proudie perked herself up, feeling that some important piece of business was in hand. The bishop was instinctively aware that La Signora Vicinironi was come at last, and Mr. Slope hurried into the hall to give his assistance.

He was, however, nearly knocked down and trampled on by the cortège that he encountered on the hall steps. He got himself picked up as well as he could, and followed the cortège up stairs. The signora was carried head foremost, her head being the care of her brother and an Italian man-servant who was accustomed to the work; her feet were in the care of the lady's maid and the lady's Italian page; and Charlotte Stanhope followed to see that all was done with due grace and decorum. In this manner they climbed easily into the drawing-room, and a broad way through the crowd having been opened, the signora rested safely on her couch. She had sent a servant beforehand to learn whether it was a right or a left hand sofa, for it required that she should dress accordingly, particularly as regarded her bracelets.

And very becoming her dress was. It was white velvet, without any other garniture than rich white lace worked with pearls across her bosom, and the same round the armlets of her dress. Across her brow she wore a band of red velvet, on the centre of which shone a magnificent Cupid in mosaic, the tints of whose wings were of the most lovely azure, and the colour of his chubby cheeks the clearest pink. On the one arm which her position required her to expose she wore three magnificent bracelets, each of different stones. Beneath her on the sofa, and over the cushion and head of it, was spread a crimson silk mantle or shawl, which went under her whole body and concealed her feet. Dressed as she was and looking as she did, so beautiful and yet so motionless, with the pure brilliancy of her white dress brought out and strengthened by the colour beneath it, with that lovely head, and those large bold bright staring eyes, it was impossible that either man or woman should do other than look at her.

Neither man nor woman for some minutes did do other.

Her bearers too were worthy of note. The three servants were Italian, and though perhaps not peculiar in their own country, were very much so in the palace at Barchester. The man especially attracted notice, and created a doubt in the mind of some whether he were a friend or a domestic. The same doubt was felt as to Ethelbert. The man was attired in a loose-fitting common black cloth morning coat. He had a jaunty fat well-pleased clean face, on which no atom of beard appeared, and he wore round his neck a loose black silk neckhandkerchief. The bishop essayed to make him a bow, but the man, who was well-trained, took no notice of him, and walked out of the room quite at his ease, followed by the woman and the boy.

Ethelbert Stanhope was dressed in light blue from head to foot He had on the loosest possible blue coat, cut square like a shooting coat, and very short. It was lined with silk of azure blue. He had on a blue satin waistcoat, a blue neckhandkerchief which was fastened beneath his throat with a coral ring, and very loose blue trousers which almost concealed his feet. His soft glossy beard was softer and more glossy than ever.

The bishop, who had made one mistake, thought that he also was a servant, and therefore tried to make way for him to pass. But Ethelbert soon corrected the error.

CHAPTER IX

MRS. PROUDIE'S RECEPTION—CONCLUDED

"Bishop of Barchester, I presume?" said Bertie Stanhope, putting out his hand, frankly; "I am delighted to make your acquaintance. We are in rather close quarters here, a'nt we?"

In truth they were. They had been crowded up behind the head of the sofa : the bishop in waiting to receive his guest, and the other in carrying her; and they now had hardly room to move themselves.

The bishop gave his hand quickly, and made his little studied bow, and was delighted to make——. He couldn't go on, for he did not know whether his friend was a signor, or a count, or a prince.

"My sister really puts you all to great trouble," said Bertie.

"Not at all!" The bishop was delighted to have the opportunity of welcoming the Signora Vicinironi—so at least he said—and attempted to force his way round to the front of the sofa. He had, at any rate, learnt that his strange guests were brother and sister. The man, he presumed, must be Signor Vicinironi—or count, or prince, as it might be. It was wonderful what good English he spoke. There was just a twang of foreign accent, and no more.

"Do you like Barchester on the whole?" asked Bertie.

The bishop, looking dignified, said that he did like Barchester.

"You've not been here very long, I believe," said Bertie.

"No—not long," said the bishop, and tried again to make his way between the back of the sofa and a heavy rector, who was staring over it at the grimaces of the signora.

"You weren't a bishop before, were you?"

Dr. Proudie explained that this was the first diocese he had held.

"Ah—I thought so," said Bertie; "but you are changed about sometimes, a'nt you?"

"Translations are occasionally made," said Dr. Proudie; "but not so frequently as in former days."

"They've cut them all down to pretty nearly the same figure, haven't they?" said Bertie.

To this the bishop could not bring himself to make any answer, but again attempted to move the rector.

"But the work, I suppose, is different?" continued Bertie. "Is there much to do here, at Barchester?" This was said exactly in the tone that a young Admiralty clerk might use in asking the same question of a brother acolyte at the Treasury.

"The work of a bishop of the Church of England," said Dr. Proudie, with considerable dignity, "is not easy. The responsibility which he has to bear is very great indeed."

"Is it?" said Bertie, opening wide his wonderful blue eyes. "Well, I never was afraid of responsibility. I once had thoughts of being a bishop, myself."

"Had thoughts of being a bishop!" said Dr. Proudie, much amazed.

"That is, a parson—a parson first, you know, and a bishop afterwards. If I had once begun, I'd have stuck to it. But, on the whole, I like the Church of Rome the best."

The bishop could not discuss the point, so he remained silent.

"Now, there's my father," continued Bertie; "he hasn't stuck to it. I fancy he didn't like saying the same thing over so often. By the bye, Bishop, have you seen my father?"

The bishop was more amazed than ever. Had he seen his father? "No," he replied; "he had not yet had the pleasure: he hoped he might;" and, as he said so, he resolved to bear heavy on that fat, immovable rector, if ever he had the power of doing so.

"He's in the room somewhere," said Bertie, "and he'll turn up soon. By the bye, do you know much about the Jews?"

At last the bishop saw a way out. "I beg your pardon," said he; "but I'm forced to go round the room."

"Well—I believe I'll follow in your wake," said Bertie. "Terribly hot—isn't it?" This he addressed to the fat rector with whom he had brought himself into the closest contact. "They've got this sofa into the worst possible part of the room; suppose we move it. Take care, Madeline."

The sofa had certainly been so placed that those who were behind it found great difficulty in getting out;—there was but a narrow gangway, which one person could stop. This was a bad arrangement, and one which Bertie thought it might be well to improve.

"Take care, Madeline," said he; and turning to the fat rector, added, "Just help me with a slight push."

The rector's weight was resting on the sofa, and unwittingly lent all its impetus to accelerate and increase the motion which Bertie intentionally originated. The sofa rushed from its moorings, and ran half-way into the middle of the room. Mrs. Proudie was standing with Mr. Slope in front of the signora, and had been trying to be condescending and sociable; but she was not in the very best of tempers; for she found that, whenever she spoke to the lady, the lady replied by speaking to Mr. Slope. Mr. Slope was a favourite, no doubt; but Mrs. Proudie had no idea of being less thought of than the chaplain. She was beginning to be stately, stiff, and offended, when unfortunately the castor of the sofa caught itself in her lace train, and carried away there is no saying how much of her garniture. Gathers were heard to go, stitches to crack, plaits to fly open, flounces were seen to fall, and breadths to expose themselves;— a long ruin of rent lace disfigured the carpet, and still clung to the vile wheel on which the sofa moved.

So, when a granite battery is raised, excellent to the eyes of warfaring men, is its strength and symmetry admired. It is the work of years. Its neat embrasures, its finished parapets, its casemated stories, show all the skill of modern science. But, anon, a small spark is applied to the treacherous fusee—a cloud of dust arises to the heavens—and then nothing is to be seen but dirt and dust and ugly fragments.

We know what was the wrath of Juno when her beauty was despised. We know too what storms of passion even celestial minds can yield. As Juno may have looked at Paris on Mount Ida, so did Mrs. Proudie look on Ethelbert Stanhope when he pushed the leg of the sofa into her lace train.

"Oh, you idiot, Bertie!" said the signora, seeing what had been done, and what were to be the consequences.

"Idiot!" re-echoed Mrs. Proudie, as though the word were not half strong enough to express the required meaning; "I'll let him know——;" and then looking round to learn, at a glance, the worst, she saw that at present it behoved her to collect the scattered *débris* of her dress.

Bertie, when he saw what he had done, rushed over the sofa, and threw himself on one knee before the offended lady. His object, doubtless, was to liberate the torn lace from the castor; but he looked as though he were imploring pardon from a goddess.

"Unhand it, sir!" said Mrs. Proudie. From what scrap of dramatic poetry she had extracted the word cannot be said; but it must have rested on her memory, and now seemed opportunely dignified for the occasion.

"I'll fly to the looms of the fairies to repair the damage, if you'll only forgive me," said Ethelbert, still on his knees.

"Unhand it, sir!" said Mrs. Proudie, with redoubled emphasis, and all but furious wrath. This allusion to the fairies was a direct mockery, and intended to turn her into ridicule. So at least it seemed to her. "Unhand it, sir!" she almost screamed.

"It's not me; it's the cursed sofa," said Bertie, looking imploringly in her face, and holding up both his hands to show that he was not touching her belongings, but still remaining on his knees.

Hereupon the signora laughed; not loud, indeed, but yet audibly. And as the tigeress bereft of her young will turn with equal anger on any within reach, so did Mrs. Proudie turn upon her female guest.

"Madam!" she said—and it is beyond the power of prose to tell of the fire which flashed from her eyes.

The signora stared her full in the face for a moment, and then turning to her brother said, playfully, "Bertie, you idiot, get up."

By this time the bishop, and Mr. Slope, and her three daughters were around her, and had collected together the wide ruins of her magnificence. The girls fell into circular rank behind their mother, and thus following her and carrying out the fragments, they left the reception-rooms in a manner not altogether devoid of dignity. Mrs. Proudie had to retire and re-array herself.

As soon as the constellation had swept by, Ethelbert rose from his knees, and turning with mock anger to the fat rector, said: "After all it was your doing, sir—not mine. But perhaps you are waiting for preferment, and so I bore it."

Whereupon there was a laugh against the fat rector, in which both the bishop and the chaplain joined; and thus things got themselves again into order.

"Oh! my lord, I am so sorry for this accident," said the signora, putting out her hand so as to force the bishop to take it. "My brother is so thoughtless. Pray sit down, and let me have the pleasure of making your acquaintance. Though I am so poor a creature as to want a sofa, I am not so selfish as to require it all." Madeline could always dispose herself so as to make room for a gentleman, though, as she declared, the crinoline of her lady friends was much too bulky to be so accommodated.

"It was solely for the pleasure of meeting you that I have had myself dragged here," she continued. "Of course, with your occupation, one cannot even hope that you should have time to come to us, that is, in the way of calling. And at your English dinner-parties all is so dull and so stately. Do you know, my lord, that in coming to England my only consolation has been the thought that I should know you;" and she looked at him with the look of a she-devil.

The bishop, however, thought that she looked very like an angel, and accepting the proffered seat, sat down beside her. He uttered some platitude as to his deep obligation for the trouble she had taken, and wondered more and more who she was.

"Of course you know my sad story?" she continued.

The bishop didn't know a word of it. He knew, however, or thought he knew, that she couldn't walk into a room like other people, and so made the most of that. He put on a look of ineffable distress, and said that he was aware how God had afflicted her.

The signora just touched the corner of her eyes with the most lovely of pocket-handkerchiefs. Yes, she said—she had been sorely tried—tried, she thought, beyond the common endurance of humanity; but while her child was left to her, everything was left. "Oh! my lord," she exclaimed, "you must see that infant—the last bud of a wondrous tree: you must let a mother hope that you will lay your holy hands on her innocent head, and consecrate her for female virtues. May I hope it?" said she, looking into the bishop's eye, and touching the bishop's arm with her hand.

The bishop said he would, but where should he call.

"At papa's house," said the signora, with an air of some little surprise at the question.

The bishop actually wanted the courage to ask her who was her papa; so he was forced at last to leave her without fathoming the mystery. Mrs. Proudie, in her second best, had now returned to the rooms, and her husband thought it as well that he should not remain in too close conversation with the lady whom his wife appeared to hold in such slight esteem. Presently he came across his youngest daughter.

"Netta," said he, "do you know who is the father of that Signora Vicinironi?"

"It isn't Vicinironi, papa," said Netta; "but Vesey Neroni, and she's Doctor Stanhope's daughter. But I must go and do the civil to Griselda Grantly; I declare nobody has spoken a word to the poor girl this evening."

Dr. Stanhope! Dr. Vesey Stanhope! Dr. Vesey Stanhope's daughter, of whose marriage with a dissolute Italian scamp he now remembered to have heard something! And that impertinent blue cub who had examined him as to his episcopal bearings was old Stanhope's son, and the lady who had entreated him to come and visit her child was old Stanhope's daughter! the daughter of one of his own prebendaries! As these things flashed across his mind, he was nearly as angry as his wife had been. Nevertheless, he could not but own that she was an agreeable woman.

Dr. Proudie tripped out into the adjoining room, in which were congregated a crowd of Grantlyite clergymen, among whom the archdeacon was standing pre-eminent, while the old dean was sitting nearly buried in a huge arm-chair by the fire-place. The bishop was very anxious to be gracious, and, if possible, to diminish the bitterness which his chaplin had occasioned.

Mr. Slope in the mean time had taken the seat which the bishop had vacated on the signora's sofa, and remained with that lady till it was time to marshal the folk to supper. Not with contented eyes had Mrs. Proudie seen this. Had not this woman laughed at her distress, and had not Mr. Slope heard it? Was she not an intriguing Italian woman, half wife and half not, full of affectation, airs, and impudence? Was she not horribly bedizened with velvet and pearls, with velvet and pearls, too, which had not been torn off her back? Above all, did she not pretend to be more beautiful than her neighbours? To say that Mrs. Proudie was jealous would give a wrong idea of her feelings. She had not the slightest desire that Mr. Slope should be in love with herself. But she desired the incense of Mr. Slope's spiritual and temporal services, and did not choose that they should be turned out of their course to such an object as Signora Neroni. She considered also that Mr. Slope ought in duty to hate the signora; and it appeared from his manner that he was very far from hating her.

"Come, Mr. Slope," she said, sweeping by, and looking all that she felt; "can't you make yourself useful? Do pray take Mrs. Grantly down to supper."

Mrs. Grantly heard and escaped. The words were hardly out of Mrs. Proudie's mouth, before the intended victim had stuck her hand through the arm of one of her husband's curates, and saved herself. What would the archdeacon have said had he seen her walking down stairs with Mr. Slope?

Mr. Slope heard also, but was by no means so obedient as was expected. Indeed, the period of Mr. Slope's obedience to Mrs. Proudie was drawing to a close. He did not wish yet to break with her, nor to break with her at all, if it could be avoided. But he intended to be master in that palace, and as she had made the same resolution it was not improbable that they might come to blows.

Before leaving the signora he arranged a little table before her, and begged to know what he should bring her. She was quite indifferent, she said—nothing—anything. It was now she felt the misery of her position, now that she must be left alone. Well, a little chicken, some ham, and a glass of champagne.

Mr. Slope had to explain, not without blushing for his patron, that there was no champagne.

Sherry would do just as well. And then Mr. Slope descended with the learned Miss Trefoil on his arm. Could she tell him, he asked, whether the ferns of Barsetshire were equal to those of Cumberland? His strongest worldly passion was for ferns—and before she could answer him he left her wedged between the door and the sideboard. It was fifty minutes before she escaped, and even then unfed.

"You are not leaving us, Mr. Slope," said the watchful lady of the house, seeing her slave escaping towards the door, with stores of provisions held high above the heads of the guests.

Mr. Slope explained that the Signora Neroni was in want of her supper.

"Pray, Mr. Slope, let her brother take it to her," said Mrs. Proudie, quite out loud. "It is out of the question that you should be so employed. Pray, Mr. Slope, oblige me; I am sure Mr. Stanhope will wait upon his sister."

Ethelbert was most agreeably occupied in the furthest corner of the room, making himself both useful and agreeable to Mrs. Proudie's youngest daughter.

"I couldn't get out, madam, if Madeline were starving for her supper," said he; "I'm physically fixed, unless I could fly."

The lady's anger was increased by seeing that her daughter also had gone over to the enemy; and when she saw, that in spite of her remonstrances, in the teeth of her positive orders, Mr. Slope went off to the drawing-room, the cup of her indignation ran over, and she could not restrain herself. "Such manners I never saw," she said, muttering. "I cannot, and will not permit it;" and then, after fussing and fuming for a few minutes, she pushed her way through the crowd, and followed Mr. Slope.

When she reached the room above, she found it absolutely deserted, except by the guilty pair. The signora was sitting very comfortably up to her supper, and Mr. Slope was leaning over her and administering to her wants. They had been discussing the merits of Sabbath-day schools, and the lady had suggested that as she could not possibly go to the children, she might be indulged in the wish of her heart by having the children brought to her.

"And when shall it be, Mr. Slope?" said she.

Mr. Slope was saved the necessity of committing himself to a promise by the entry of Mrs. Proudie. She swept close up to the sofa so as to confront the guilty pair, stared full at them for a moment, and then said as she passed on to the next room, "Mr. Slope, his lordship is especially desirous of your attendance below; you will greatly oblige me if you will join him." And so she stalked on.

Mr. Slope muttered something in reply, and prepared to go downstairs. As for the bishop's wanting him, he knew his lady patroness well enough to take that assertion at what it was worth; but he did not wish to make himself the hero of a scene, or to become conspicuous for more gallantry than the occasion required.

"Is he always like this?" said the signora.

"Yes—always—madam," said Mrs. Proudie, returning; "always the same—always equally adverse to impropriety of conduct of every description;" and she stalked back through the room again, following Mr. Slope out of the door.

The signora couldn't follow her, or she certainly would have done so. But she laughed loud, and sent the sound of it ringing through the lobby and down the stairs after Mrs. Proudie's feet. Had she been as active as Grimaldi, she could probably have taken no better revenge.

"Mr. Slope," said Mrs. Proudie, catching the delinquent at the door, "I am surprised that you should leave my company to attend on such a painted Jezebel as that."

"But she's lame, Mrs. Proudie, and cannot move. Somebody must have waited upon her."

"Lame," said Mrs. Proudie; "I'd lame her if she belonged to me. What business had she here at all?—such impertinence—such affectation."

In the hall and adjacent rooms all manner of cloaking and shawling was going on, and the Barchester folk were getting themselves gone. Mrs. Proudie did her best to smirk at each and every one, as they made their adieux, but she was hardly successful. Her temper had been tried fearfully. By slow degrees, the guests went.

"Send back the carriage quick," said Ethelbert, as Dr. and Mrs. Stanhope took their departure.

The younger Stanhopes were left to the very last, and an uncomfortable party they made with the bishop's family. They all went into the dining-room, and then the bishop observing that "the lady" was alone in the drawing-room, they followed him up. Mrs. Proudie kept Mr. Slope and her daughters in close conversation, resolving that he should not be indulged, nor they polluted. The bishop, in mortal dread of Bertie and the Jews, tried to converse with Charlotte Stanhope about the climate of Italy. Bertie and the signora had no resource but in each other.

"Did you get your supper, at last, Madeline?" said the impudent or else mischievous young man.

"Oh, yes," said Madeline; "Mr. Slope was so very kind as to bring it me. I fear, however, he put himself to more inconvenience than I wished."

Mrs. Proudie looked at her, but said nothing. The meaning of her look might have been thus translated: "If ever you find yourself within these walls again, I'll give you leave to be as impudent and affected, and as mischievous as you please."

At last the carriage returned with the three Italian servants, and La Signora Madeline Vesey Neroni was carried out, as she had been carried in.

The lady of the palace retired to her chamber by no means contented with the result of her first grand party at Barchester.

CHAPTER X

SLOPE VERSUS HARDING

Two or three days after the party, Mr. Harding received a note, begging him to call on Mr. Slope, at the palace, at an early hour the following morning. There was nothing uncivil in the communication, and yet the tone of it was thoroughly displeasing. It was as follows:

"My dear Mr. Harding,—Will you favour me by calling on me at the palace to-morrow morning at 9.30 a.m. The bishop wishes me to speak to you touching the hospital. I hope you will excuse my naming so early an hour. I do so as my time is greatly occupied. If, however, it is positively inconvenient to you, I will change it to 10. You will, perhaps, be kind enough to let me have a note in reply.

> "Believe me to be,
> "My dear Mr. Harding,
> "Your assured friend,
> "OBH. SLOPE.

"The Palace, Monday morning,
  "20th August, 185—."

And on the following morning, punctually at half-past nine, he knocked at the palace door, and asked for Mr. Slope.

The bishop had one small room allotted to him on the ground-floor, and Mr. Slope had another. Into this latter Mr. Harding was shown, and asked to sit down. Mr. Slope was not yet there. The ex-warden stood up at the window looking into the garden, and could not help thinking how very short a time had passed since the whole of that house had been open to him, as though he had been a child of the family, born and bred in it.

It was nearly ten when Mr. Slope hurried into the room, and, muttering something about the bishop and diocesan duties, shook Mr. Harding's hand ruthlessly, and begged him to be seated.

Now the air of superiority which this man assumed, did go against the grain of Mr. Harding; and yet he did not know how to resent it. The whole tendency of his mind and disposition was opposed to any contra-assumption of grandeur on his own part, and he hadn't the worldly spirit or quickness necessary to put down insolent pretensions by downright and open rebuke, as the archdeacon would have done. There was nothing for Mr. Harding but to submit, and he accordingly did so.

"About the hospital, Mr. Harding?" began Mr. Slope, speaking of it as the head of a college at Cambridge might speak of some sizarship which had to be disposed of.

Mr. Harding crossed one leg over another, and then one hand over the other on the top of them, and looked Mr. Slope in the face; but he said nothing.

"It's to be filled up again," said Mr. Slope. Mr. Harding said that he had understood so.

"Of course, you know, the income will be very much reduced," continued Mr. Slope. "The bishop wished to be liberal, and he therefore told the government that he thought it ought to be put at not less than £450. I think on the whole the bishop was right; for though the services required will not be of a very onerous nature, they will be more so than they were before. And it is, perhaps, well that the clergy immediately attached to the cathedral town should be made as comfortable as the extent of the ecclesiastical means at our disposal will allow. Those are the bishop's ideas, and I must say mine also."

Mr. Harding sat rubbing one hand on the other, but said not a word.

"So much for the income, Mr. Harding. The house will, of course, remain to the warden, as before. It should, however, I think, be stipulated that he should paint inside every seven years, and outside every three years, and be subject to dilapidations, in the event of vacating, either by death or otherwise. But this is a matter on which the bishop must yet be consulted."

Mr. Harding still rubbed his hands, and still sat silent, gazing up into Mr. Slope's unprepossessing face.

"Then, as to the duties," continued he, "I believe, if I am rightly informed, there can hardly be said to have been any duties hitherto," and he gave a sort of half laugh, as though to pass off the accusation in the guise of a pleasantry.

Mr. Harding thought of the happy, easy years he had passed in his old home; of the worn-out, aged men whom he had succoured; of his good intentions; and of his work, which had certainly been of the lightest. He thought of these things, doubting for a moment whether he did or did not deserve the sarcasm. He gave his enemy the benefit of the doubt, and did not rebuke him. He merely observed, very tranquilly, and perhaps with too much humility, that the duties of the situation, such as they were, had, he believed, been done to the satisfaction of the late bishop.

Mr. Slope again smiled, and this time the smile was intended to operate against the memory of the late bishop, rather than against the energy of the ex-warden; and so it was understood by Mr. Harding. The colour rose to his cheeks, and he began to feel very angry.

"You must be aware, Mr. Harding, that things are a good deal changed in Barchester," said Mr. Slope.

Mr. Harding said that he was aware of it. "And not only in Barchester, Mr. Harding, but in the world at large. It is not only in Barchester that a new man is carrying out new measures and casting away the useless rubbish of past centuries. The same thing is going on throughout the country. Work is now required from every man who receives wages; and they who have to superintend the doing of work, and the paying of wages, are bound to see that this rule is carried out. New men, Mr. Harding, are now needed, and are now forthcoming in the church, as well as in other professions."

All this was wormwood to our old friend. He had never rated very high his own abilities or activity; but all the feelings of his heart were with the old clergy, and any antipathies of which his heart was susceptible, were directed against those new, busy, uncharitable, self-lauding men, of whom Mr. Slope was so good an example.

"Perhaps," said he, "the bishop will prefer a new man at the hospital?"

"By no means," said Mr. Slope. "The bishop is very anxious that you should accept the appointment; but he wishes you should understand beforehand what will be the required duties. In the first place, a Sabbath-day school will be attached to the hospital."

"What! for the old men?" asked Mr. Harding.

"No, Mr. Harding, not for the old men, but for the benefit of the children of such of the poor of Barchester as it may suit. The bishop will expect that you shall attend this school, and the teachers shall be under your inspection and care."

Mr. Harding slipped his topmost hand off the other, and began to rub the calf of the leg which was supported.

"As to the old men," continued Mr. Slope, "and the old women who are to form a part of the hospital, the bishop is desirous that you shall have morning and evening service on the premises every Sabbath, and one week-day service; that you shall preach to them once at least on Sundays; and that the whole hospital be always collected for morning and evening prayer. The bishop thinks that this will render it unnecessary that any separate seats in the cathedral should be reserved for the hospital inmates."

Mr. Slope paused, but Mr. Harding still said nothing.

"Indeed, it would be difficult to find seats for the women; and, on the whole, Mr. Harding, I may as well say at once, that for people of that class the cathedral service does not appear to me the most useful,—even if it be so for any class of people."

"We will not discuss that, if you please," said Mr. Harding.

"I am not desirous of doing so; at least, not at the present moment. I hope, however, you fully understand the bishop's wishes about the new establishment of the hospital; and if, as I do not doubt, I shall receive from you an assurance that you accord with his lordship's views, it will give me very great pleasure to be the bearer from his lordship to you of the presentation to the appointment."

"But if I disagree with his lordship's views?" asked Mr. Harding.

"But I hope you do not," said Mr. Slope.

"But if I do?" again asked the other.

"If such unfortunately should be the case, which I can hardly conceive, I presume your own feelings will dictate to you the propriety of declining the appointment."

"But if I accept the appointment, and yet disagree with the bishop, what then?"

This question rather bothered Mr. Slope. It was true that he had talked the matter over with the bishop, and had received a sort of authority for suggesting to Mr. Harding the propriety of a Sunday school, and certain hospital services; but he had no authority for saying that these propositions were to be made peremptory conditions attached to the appointment. The bishop's idea had been that Mr. Harding would of course consent, and that the school would become, like the rest of those new establishments in the city, under the control of his wife and his chaplain. Mr. Slope's idea had been more correct. He intended that Mr. Harding should refuse the situation, and that an ally of his own should get it: but he had not conceived the possibility of Mr. Harding openly accepting the appointment, and as openly rejecting the conditions.

"It is not, I presume, probable," said he, "that you will accept from the hands of the bishop a piece of preferment, with a fixed predetermination to disacknowledge the duties attached to it."

"If I become warden," said Mr. Harding, "and neglect my duty, the bishop has means by which he can remedy the grievance."

"I hardly expected such an argument from you, or I may say the suggestion of such a line of conduct," said Mr. Slope, with a great look of injured virtue.

"Nor did I expect such a proposition."

"I shall be glad at any rate to know what answer I am to make to his lordship," said Mr. Slope.

"I will take an early opportunity of seeing his lordship myself," said Mr. Harding.

"Such an arrangement," said Mr. Slope, "will hardly give his lordship satisfaction. Indeed, it is impossible that the bishop should himself see every clergyman in the diocese on every subject of patronage that may arise. The bishop, I believe, did see you on the matter, and I really cannot see why he should be troubled to do so again."

"Do you know, Mr. Slope, how long I have been officiating as a clergyman in this city?" Mr. Slope's wish was now nearly fulfilled. Mr. Harding had become angry, and it was probable that he might commit himself.

"I really do not see what that has to do with the question. You cannot think the bishop would be justified in allowing you to regard as a sinecure a situation that requires an active man, merely because you have been employed for many years in the cathedral."

"But it might induce the bishop to see me, if I asked him to do so. I shall consult my friends in this matter, Mr. Slope; but I mean to be guilty of no subterfuge,—you may tell the bishop that as I alto-gether disagree with his views about the hospital, I shall decline the situation if I find that any such conditions are attached to it as those you have suggested;" and so saying, Mr. Harding took his hat and went his way.

Mr. Slope was contented. He considered himself at liberty to accept Mr. Harding's last speech as an absolute refusal of the appointment. At least, he so represented it to the bishop and to Mrs. Proudie.

"That is very surprising," said the bishop.

"Not at all," said Mrs. Proudie; "you little know how determined the whole set of them are to withstand your authority."

"But Mr. Harding was so anxious for it," said the bishop.

"Yes," said Mr. Slope, "if he can hold it without the slightest acknowledgement of your lordship's jurisdiction."

"That is out of the question," said the bishop.

"I should imagine it to be quite so," said the chaplain.

"Indeed, I should think so," said the lady.

"I really am sorry for it," said the bishop.

"I don't know that there is much cause for sorrow," said the lady. "Mr. Quiverful is a much more deserving man, more in need of it, and one who will make himself much more useful in the close neighbourhood of the palace."

"I suppose I had better see Quiverful?" said the chaplain.

"I suppose you had," said the bishop.

CHAPTER XI

THE RUBBISH CART

MR. HARDING after leaving the palace, walked slowly for an hour or so beneath the shady elms of the close, and then betook himself to his daughter's house. He had at any rate made up his mind that he would go out to Plumstead to consult Dr. Grantly, and that he would in the first instance tell Eleanor what had occurred.

And now he was doomed to undergo another misery. Mr. Slope had forestalled him at the widow's house. He had called there on the preceding afternoon. He could not, he had said, deny himself the pleasure of telling Mrs. Bold that her father was about to return to the pretty house at Hiram's hospital. He had been instructed by the bishop to inform Mr. Harding that the appointment would now be made at once. The bishop was of course only too happy to be able to be the means of restoring to Mr. Harding the preferment which he had so long adorned. And then by degrees Mr. Slope had introduced the subject of the pretty school which he hoped before long to see attached to the hospital. He had quite fascinated Mrs. Bold by his description of this picturesque, useful, and charitable appendage, and she had gone so far as to say that she had no doubt her father would approve, and that she herself would gladly undertake a class.

Any one who had heard the entirely different tone, and seen the entirely different manner in which Mr. Slope had spoken of this projected institution to the daughter and to the father, could not have failed to own that Mr. Slope was a man of genius. He said nothing to Mrs. Bold about the hospital sermons and services, nothing about the exclusion of the old men from the cathedral, nothing about dilapidation and painting, nothing about carting away the rubbish. Eleanor had said to herself that certainly she did not like Mr. Slope personally, but that he was a very active, zealous clergyman, and would no doubt be useful in Barchester. All this paved the way for much additional misery to Mr. Harding.

Eleanor put on her happiest face as she heard her father on the stairs, for she thought she had only to congratulate him; but directly she saw his face, she knew that there was but little matter for congratulation. She had seen him with the same weary look of sorrow on one or two occasions before, and remembered it well. She had seen him when he first read that attack upon himself in the Jupiter which had ultimately caused him to resign the hospital; and she had seen him also when the archdeacon had persuaded him to remain there against his own sense of propriety and honour. She knew at a glance that his spirit was in deep trouble.

"Oh, papa, what is it?" said she, putting down her boy to crawl upon the floor.

"I came to tell you, my dear," said he, "that I am going out to Plumstead: you won't come with me, I suppose?"

"To Plumstead, papa? Shall you stay there?"

"I suppose I shall, to-night: I must consult the archdeacon about this weary hospital. Ah me! I wish I had never thought of it again."

"Why, papa, what is the matter?"

"I've been with Mr. Slope, my dear, and he isn't the pleasantest companion in the world, at least not to me." Eleanor gave a sort of half blush; but she was wrong if she imagined that her father in any way alluded to her acquaintance with Mr. Slope.

"Well, papa."

"He wants to turn the hospital into a Sunday school and a preaching house; and I suppose he will have his way. I do not feel myself adapted for such an establishment, and therefore, I suppose, I must refuse the appointment."

"What would be the harm of the school, papa?"

"The want of a proper schoolmaster, my dear."

"But that would of course be supplied."

"Mr. Slope wishes to supply it by making me his schoolmaster. But as I am hardly fit for such work, I intend to decline."

"Oh, papa! Mr. Slope doesn't intend that. He was here yesterday, and what he intends——"

"He was here yesterday, was he?" asked Mr. Harding.

"Yes, papa."

"And talking about the hospital?"

"He was saying how glad he would be, and the bishop too, to see you back there again. And then he spoke about the Sunday school; and to tell the truth I agreed with him; and I thought you would have done so too. Mr. Slope spoke of a school, not inside the hospital, but just connected with it, of which you would be the patron and visitor; and I thought you would have liked such a school as that; and I promised to look after it and to take a class —and it all seemed so very——. But, oh, papa! I shall be so miserable if I find I have done wrong."

"Nothing wrong at all, my dear," said he, gently, very gently rejecting his daughter's caress. "There can be nothing wrong in your wishing to make yourself useful; indeed, you ought to do so by all means. Everyone must now exert himself who would not choose to go to the wall." Poor Mr. Harding thus attempted in his misery to preach the new doctrine to his child. "Himself or herself, it's all the same," he continued; "you will be quite right, my dear, to do something of this sort; but——"

"Well, papa."

"I am not quite sure that if I were you I would select Mr. Slope for my guide."

"But I never have done so, and never shall."

"It would be very wicked of me to speak evil of him, for to tell the truth I know no evil of him; but I am not quite sure that he is honest. That he is not gentleman-like in his manners, of that I am quite sure."

"I never thought of taking him for my guide, papa."

"As for myself, my dear," continued he, "we know the old proverb—'It's bad teaching an old dog tricks.' I must decline the Sunday school, and shall therefore probably decline the hospital also. But I will first see your brother-in-law." So he took up his hat, kissed the baby, and withdrew, leaving Eleanor in as low spirits as himself.

He walked away to the inn to order a fly, went home to put up his carpet bag, and then started for Plumstead. There was, at any rate, no danger that the archdeacon would fraternise with Mr. Slope; but then he would recommend internecine war, public appeals, loud reproaches, and all the paraphernalia of open battle. Now that alternative was hardly more to Mr. Harding's taste than the other.

When Mr. Harding reached the parsonage he found that the archdeacon was out, and would not be home till dinner-time, so he began his complaint to his elder daughter.

Mrs. Grantly soon learnt that her sister Eleanor had promised to assist Mr. Slope in the affairs of the hospital; and it was on this point that her attention soon fixed itself.

"How can Eleanor endure him?" said she.

"He is a very crafty man," said her father, "and his craft has been successful in making Eleanor think that he is a meek, charitable, good clergyman. God forgive me, if I wrong him, but such is not his true character in my opinion."

"His true character, indeed!" said she, with something approaching to scorn for her father's moderation. "I only hope he won't have craft enough to make Eleanor forget herself and her position."

"Do you mean marry him?" said he, startled out of his usual demeanour by the abruptness and horror of so dreadful a proposition.

"What is there so improbable in it? Of course that would be his own object if he thought he had any chance of success. Eleanor has a thousand a year entirely at her own disposal, and what better fortune could fall to Mr. Slope's lot than the transferring of the disposal of such a fortune to himself?"

To give Eleanor her due, any suspicion as to the slightest inclination on her part towards Mr. Slope was a wrong to her. She had no more idea of marrying Mr. Slope than she had of marrying the bishop; and the idea that Mr. Slope would present himself as a suitor had never occurred to her.

And as to him, it must also be affirmed that he was hitherto equally innocent of the crime imputed to him. How it had come to pass that a man whose eyes were generally so widely open to everything around him had not perceived that this young widow was rich as well as beautiful, cannot probably now be explained. But such was the fact. Mr. Slope had ingratiated himself with Mrs. Bold, merely as he had done with other ladies, in order to strengthen his party in the city. He subsequently amended his error; but it was not till after the interview between him and Mr. Harding.

CHAPTER XII

THE NEW CHAMPION

THE archdeacon did not return to the parsonage till close upon the hour of dinner, and there was therefore no time to discuss matters before that important ceremony. He seemed to be in an especial good humour, and welcomed his father-in-law with a sort of jovial earnestness that was usual with him when things on which he was intent were going on as he would have them.

"It's all settled, my dear," said he to his wife as he washed his hands in his dressing-room, while she, according to her wont, sat listening in the bedroom; "Arabin has agreed to accept the living. He'll be here next week." And the archdeacon scrubbed his hands and rubbed his face with a violent alacrity, which showed that Arabin's coming was a great point gained.

"Will he come here to Plumstead?" said the wife.

"He has promised to stay a month with us," said the archdeacon, "so that he may see what his parish is like. You'll like Arabin very much. He's a gentleman in every respect, and full of humour."

"He's very queer, isn't he?" asked the lady.

"Well—he is a little odd in some of his fancies; but there's nothing about him you won't like. He is as staunch a churchman as there is at Oxford. I really don't know what we should do without Arabin. It's a great thing for me to have him so near me; and if anything can put Slope down, Arabin will do it."

The Reverend Francis Arabin was a fellow of Lazarus, the favoured disciple of the great Dr. Gwynne, a high churchman at all points; so high, indeed, that at one period of his career he had all but toppled over into the cesspool of Rome; a poet and also a polemical writer, a great pet in the common rooms at Oxford, an eloquent clergyman, a droll, odd, humorous, energetic, conscientious man, and, as the archdeacon had boasted of him, a thorough gentleman. As he will hereafter be brought more closely to our notice, it is now only necessary to add, that he had just been presented to the vicarage of St. Ewold by Dr. Grantly, in whose gift as archdeacon the living lay. St. Ewold is a parish lying just without the city of Barchester. The suburbs of the new town, indeed, are partly within its precincts, and the pretty church and parsonage are not much above a mile distant from the city gate.

St. Ewold is not a rich piece of preferment—it is worth some three or four hundred a year at most, and has generally been held by a clergyman attached to the cathedral choir. The archdeacon, however, felt, when the living on this occasion became vacant, that it imperatively behoved him to aid the force of his party with some tower of strength, if any such tower could be got to occupy St. Ewold's. He had discussed the matter with his brethren in Barchester; not in any weak spirit as the holder of patronage to be used for his own or his family's benefit, but as one to whom was committed a trust, on the due administration of which much of the church's welfare might depend. He had submitted to them the name of Mr. Arabin, as though the choice had rested with them all in conclave, and they had unanimously admitted that, if Mr. Arabin would accept St. Ewold's no better choice could possibly be made.

If Mr. Arabin would accept St. Ewold's! There lay the difficulty. Mr. Arabin was a man standing somewhat prominently before the world, that is, before the Church of England world. He was not a rich man, it is true, for he held no preferment but his fellowship; but he was a man not over anxious for riches, not married of course, and one whose time was greatly taken up in discussing, both in print and on platforms, the privileges and practices of the church to which he belonged. As the archdeacon had done battle for its temporalities, so did Mr. Arabin do battle for its spiritualities; and both had done so conscientiously; that is, not so much each for his own benefit as for that of others.

Holding such a position as Mr. Arabin did, there was much reason to doubt whether he would consent to become the parson of

St. Ewold's, and Dr. Grantly had taken the trouble to go himself to Oxford on the matter. Dr. Gwynne and Dr. Grantly together had succeeded in persuading this eminent divine that duty required him to go to Barchester. There were wheels within wheels in this affair. For some time past Mr. Arabin had been engaged in a tremendous controversy with no less a person than Mr. Slope, respecting the apostolic succession. These two gentlemen had never seen each other, but they had been extremely bitter in print. Mr. Slope had endeavoured to strengthen his cause by calling Mr. Arabin an owl, and Mr. Arabin had retaliated by hinting that Mr. Slope was an infidel. This battle had been commenced in the columns of the daily Jupiter, a powerful newspaper, the manager of which was very friendly to Mr. Slope's view of the case. The matter, however, had become too tedious for the readers of the Jupiter, and a little note had therefore been appended to one of Mr. Slope's most telling rejoinders, in which it had been stated that no further letters from the reverend gentleman could be inserted except as advertisements.

Whether or no the near neighbourhood of the foe may have acted in any way as an inducement to Mr. Arabin to accept the living of St. Ewold, we will not pretend to say; but it had at any rate been settled in Dr. Gwynne's library, at Lazarus, that he would accept it, and that he would lend his assistance towards driving the enemy out of Barchester, or, at any rate, silencing him while he remained there.

All through dinner the archdeacon's good humour shone brightly in his face. He ate of the good things heartily, he drank wine with his wife and daughter, he talked pleasantly of his doings at Oxford, told his father-in-law that he ought to visit Dr. Gwynne at Lazarus, and launched out again in praise of Mr. Arabin.

"Is Mr. Arabin married, papa?" asked Griselda.

"No, my dear; the fellow of a college is never married."

"Is he a young man, papa?"

"About forty, I believe," said the archdeacon.

"Oh!" said Griselda. Had her father said eighty. Mr. Arabin would not have appeared to her to be very much older.

When the two gentlemen were left alone over their wine, Mr. Harding told his tale of woe. But even this, sad as it was, did not much diminish the archdeacon's good humour, though it greatly added to his pugnacity.

"He can't do it," said Dr. Grantly over and over again, as his father-in-law explained to him the terms on which the new warden of the hospital was to be appointed; "he can't do it. What he says is not worth the trouble of listening to. He can't alter the duties of the place."

"Who can't?" asked the ex-warden.

"Neither the bishop nor the chaplain, nor yet the bishop's wife, who, I take it, has really more to say to such matters than either of the other two. The whole body corporate of the palace together have no power to turn the warden of the hospital in to a Sunday schoolmaster."

"But the bishop has the power to appoint whom he pleases, and——"

"I don't know that; I rather think he'll find he has no such power. Let him try it, and see what the press will say. For once we shall have the popular cry on our side. But Proudie, ass as he is, knows the world too well to get such a hornet's nest about his ears."

Mr. Harding winced at the idea of the press. He had had enough of that sort of publicity, and was unwilling to be shown up a second time either as a monster or as a martyr. He gently remarked that he hoped the newspapers would not get hold of his name again, and then suggested that perhaps it would be better that he should abandon his object. "I am getting old," said he; "and after all I doubt whether I am fit to undertake new duties."

"New duties!" said the archdeacon: "don't I tell you there shall be no new duties?"

"Or, perhaps, old duties either," said Mr. Harding; "I think I will remain content as I am." The picture of Mr. Slope carting away the rubbish was still present to his mind.

The archdeacon drank off his glass of claret, and prepared himself to be energetic. "I do hope," said he, "that you are not going to be so weak as to allow such a man as Mr. Slope to deter you from doing what you know it is your duty to do. You know it is your duty to resume your place at the hospital now that parliament has so settled the stipend as to remove those difficulties which induced you to resign it. You cannot deny this; and should your timidity now prevent you from doing so, your conscience will hereafter never forgive you;" and as he finished this clause of his speech, he pushed over the bottle to his companion.

"Your conscience will never forgive you," he continued. "You resigned the place from conscientious scruples, scruples which I greatly respected, though I did not share them. All your friends respected them, and you left your old house as rich in reputation as you were ruined in fortune. It is now expected that you will return. Dr. Gwynne was saying only the other day——"

"Dr. Gwynne does not reflect how much older a man I am now than when he last saw me."

"Old—nonsense!" said the archdeacon; "you never thought yourself old till you listened to the impudent trash of that coxcomb at the palace."

"I shall be sixty-five if I live till November," said Mr. Harding.

"And seventy-five, if you live till November ten years," said the archdeacon. "And you bid fair to be as efficient then as you were ten years ago. But for heaven's sake let us have no pretence in this matter. Your plea of old age is only a pretence. But you're not drinking your wine. It is only a pretence. The fact is, you are half afraid of this Slope, and would rather subject yourself to comparative poverty and discomfort, than come to blows with a man who will trample on you, if you let him."

"I certainly don't like coming to blows, if I can help it."

"Nor I neither—but sometimes we can't help it. This man's object is to induce you to refuse the hospital, that he may put some creature of his own into it; that he may show his power, and insult us all by insulting you, whose cause and character are so intimately bound up with that of the chapter. You owe it to us all to resist him in this, even if you have no solicitude for yourself. But surely, for your own sake, you will not be so lily-livered as to fall into this trap which he has baited for you, and let him take the very bread out of your mouth without a struggle."

Mr. Harding did not like being called lily-livered, and was rather inclined to resent it. "I doubt there is any true courage," said he, "in squabbling for money."

"If honest men did not squabble for money, in this wicked world of ours, the dishonest men would get it all; and I do not see that the cause of virtue would be much improved. No,—we must use the means which we have. If we were to carry your argument home, we might give away every shilling of revenue which the church has; and I presume you are not prepared to say that the church would be strengthened by such a sacrifice." The archdeacon filled his glass and then emptied it, drinking with much reverence a silent toast to the well-being and permanent security of those temporalities which were so dear to his soul.

"I think all quarrels between a clergyman and his bishop should be avoided," said Mr. Harding.

"I think so too; but it is quite as much the duty of the bishop to look to that as of his inferior. I tell you what, my friend; I'll see the bishop in this matter, that is, if you will allow me; and you may be sure I will not compromise you. My opinion is, that all this trash about the Sunday-schools and the sermons has originated wholly with Slope and Mrs. Proudie, and that the bishop knows nothing about it. The bishop can't very well refuse to see me, and I'll come upon him when he has neither his wife nor his chaplain by him. I think you'll find that it will end in his sending you the appointment without any condition whatever. And as to the seats in the cathedral, we may safely leave that to Mr. Dean. I believe the fool positively thinks that the bishop could walk away with the cathedral if he pleased."

And so the matter was arranged between them. Mr. Harding had come expressly for advice, and therefore felt himself bound to take the advice given him. He had known, moreover, beforehand, that the archdeacon would not hear of his giving the matter up, and accordingly though he had in perfect good faith put forward his own views, he was prepared to yield.

They therefore went into the drawing-room in good humour with each other, and the evening passed pleasantly in prophetic discussions on the future wars of Arabin and Slope. The frogs and the mice would be nothing to them, nor the angers of Agamemnon and Achilles. How the archdeacon rubbed his hands, and plumed himself on the success of his last move. He could not himself descend into the arena with Slope, but Arabin would have no such scruples. Arabin was exactly the man for such work, and the only man whom he knew that was fit for it.

The archdeacon's good humour and high buoyancy continued till, when reclining on his pillow, Mrs. Grantly commenced to give him her view of the state of affairs at Barchester. And then certainly he was startled. The last words he said that night were as follows:—

"If she does, by heaven I'll never speak to her again. She dragged me into the mire once, but I'll not pollute myself with such filth as that——" And the archdeacon gave a shudder which shook the whole room, so violently was he convulsed with the thought which then agitated his mind.

Now in this matter, the widow Bold was scandalously ill-treated by her relatives. She had spoken to the man three or four times, and had expressed her willingness to teach in a Sunday-school. Such was the full extent of her sins in the matter of Mr. Slope. Poor Eleanor! But time will show.

The next morning Mr. Harding returned to Barchester, no further word having been spoken in his hearing respecting Mr. Slope's acquaintance with his younger daughter. But he observed that the archdeacon at breakfast was less cordial than he had been on the preceding evening.

CHAPTER XIII

THE WIDOW'S SUITORS

MR. SLOPE lost no time in availing himself of the bishop's permission to see Mr. Quiverful, and it was in his interview with this worthy pastor that he first learned that Mrs. Bold was worth the wooing. He rode out to Puddingdale to communicate to the embryo warden the good will of the bishop in his favour, and during the discussion on the matter it was not unnatural that the pecuniary resources of Mr. Harding and his family should become the subject of remark.

Mr. Quiverful, with his fourteen children and his four hundred a year, was a very poor man, and the prospect of this new preferment, which was to be held together with his living, was very grateful to him. To what clergyman so circumstanced would not such a prospect be very grateful? But Mr. Quiverful had long been acquainted with Mr. Harding, and had received kindness at his hands, so that his heart misgave him as he thought of supplanting a friend at the hospital. Nevertheless, he was extremely civil, cringingly civil, to Mr. Slope; treated him quite as the great man; entreated this great man to do him the honour to drink a glass of sherry, at which, as it was very poor Marsala, the now pampered Slope turned up his nose; and ended by declaring his extreme obligation to the bishop and Mr. Slope, and his great desire to accept the hospital, if—if it were certainly the case that Mr. Harding had refused it.

What man, as needy as Mr. Quiverful, would have been more disinterested?

"Mr. Harding did positively refuse it," said Mr. Slope, with a certain air of offended dignity, "when he heard of the conditions to which the appointment is now subjected. Of course, you understand, Mr. Quiverful, that the same conditions will be imposed on yourself."

Mr. Quiverful cared nothing for the conditions. He would have undertaken to preach any number of sermons Mr. Slope might have chosen to dictate, and to pass every remaining hour of his Sundays within the walls of a Sunday-school. What sacrifices, or, at any rate, what promises, would have been too much to make for such an addition to his income, and for such a house! But his mind still recurred to Mr. Harding.

"To be sure," said he; "Mr. Harding's daughter is very rich, and why should he trouble himself with the hospital?"

"You mean Mrs. Grantly," said Slope.

"I meant his widowed daughter," said the other. "Mrs. Bold has twelve hundred a year of her own, and I suppose Mr. Harding means to live with her."

"Twelve hundred a year of her own!" said Slope, and very shortly afterwards took his leave, avoiding, as far as it was possible for him to do, any further allusion to the hospital. Twelve hundred a year, said he to himself, as he rode slowly home. If it were the fact that Mrs. Bold had twelve hundred a year of her own, what a fool would he be to oppose her father's return to his old place. The train of Mr. Slope's ideas will probably be plain to all my readers. Why should he not make the twelve hundred a year his own? and if he did so, would it not be well for him to have a father-in-law comfortably provided with the good things of this world? would it not, moreover, be much more easy for him to gain the daughter, if he did all in his power to forward the father's views?

It was with such resolve as this that he reached Barchester. He would at once ascertain what the truth might be as to the lady's wealth, and having done this, he would be ruled by circumstances in his conduct respecting the hospital. If he found that he could turn round and secure the place for Mr. Harding without much self-sacrifice, he would do so; but if not, he would woo the daughter in opposition to the father. But in no case would he succumb to the archdeacon.

He saw his horse taken round to the stable, and immediately went forth to commence his inquiries. To give Mr. Slope his due, he was not a man who ever let much grass grow under his feet.

Poor Eleanor! She was doomed to be the intended victim of more schemes than one.

About the time that Mr. Slope was visiting the vicar of Pudding-dale, a discussion took place respecting her charms and wealth at Dr. Stanhope's house in the close. There had been morning callers there, and people had told some truth and also some falsehood respecting the property which John Bold had left behind him. By degrees the visitors went, and as the doctor went with them, and as the doctor's wife had not made her appearance, Charlotte Stanhope and her brother were left together. He was sitting idly at the table, scrawling caricatures of Barchester notables, then yawning, then turning over a book or two, and evidently at a loss how to kill his time without much labour.

"You haven't done much, Bertie, about getting any orders," said his sister.

"Orders!" said he; "who on earth is there at Barchester to give one orders? Who among the people here could possibly think it worth his while to have his head done into marble?"

"Then you mean to give up your profession," said she.

"No, I don't," said he, going on with some absurd portrait of the bishop. "Look at that, Lotte; isn't it the little man all over, apron and all? I'd go on with my profession at once, as you call it, if the governor would set me up with a studio in London; but as to sculpture at Barchester—I suppose half the people here don't know what a torso means."

"The governor will not give you a shilling to start you in London," said Lotte. "Indeed, he can't give you what would be sufficient, for he has not got it. But you might start yourself very well, if you pleased."

"How the deuce am I to do it?" said he.

"To tell you the truth, Bertie, you'll never make a penny by any profession."

"That's what I often think myself," said he, not in the least offended. "Some men have a great gift of making money, but they can't spend it. Others can't put two shillings together, but they have a great talent for all sorts of outlay. I begin to think that my genius is wholly in the latter line."

"How do you mean to live then?" asked the sister.

"I suppose I must regard myself as a young raven, and look for heavenly manna; besides, we have all got something when the governor goes."

"Yes—you'll have enough to supply yourself with gloves and boots; that is, if the Jews have not got the possession of it all. I believe they have the most of it already. I wonder, Bertie, at your indifference; that you, with your talents and personal advantages, should never try to settle yourself in life. I look forward with dread to the time when the governor must go. Mother, and Madeline, and I,—we shall be poor enough, but you will have absolutely nothing."

"Sufficient for the day is the evil thereof," said Bertie.

"Will you take my advice?" said his sister.

"*Cela dépend*," said the brother.

"Will you marry a wife with money?"

"At any rate," said he, "I won't marry one without: wives with money a'nt so easy to get now-a-days; the parsons pick them all up."

"And a parson will pick up the wife I mean for you, if you do not look quickly about it; the wife I mean is Mrs. Bold."

"Whew-w-w-w!" whistled Bertie, "a widow!"

"She is very beautiful," said Charlotte.

"With a son and heir all ready to my hand," said Bertie.

"A baby that will very likely die," said Charlotte.

"I don't see that," said Bertie. "But however, he may live for me—I don't wish to kill him; only, it must be owned that a ready-made family is a drawback."

"There is only one after all," pleaded Charlotte.

"And that a very little one, as the maid-servant said," rejoined Bertie.

"Beggars mustn't be choosers, Bertie; you can't have everything."

"God knows I am not unreasonable," said he, "nor yet opinionated; and if you'll arrange it all for me, Lotte, I'll marry the lady. Only mark this; the money must be sure, and the income at my own disposal, at any rate for the lady's life."

Charlotte was explaining to her brother that he must make love for himself if he meant to carry on the matter, and was encouraging him to do so, by warm eulogiums on Eleanor's beauty, when the signora was brought into the drawing-room. When at home, and subject to the gaze of none but her own family, she allowed herself to be dragged about by two persons, and her two bearers now deposited her on her sofa. She was not quite so grand in her apparel as she had been at the bishop's party, but yet she was dressed with much care, and though there was a look of care and pain about her eyes, she was, even by daylight, extremely beautiful.

"Well, Madeline; so I'm going to be married," Bertie began, as soon as the servants had withdrawn.

"There's no other foolish thing left, that you haven't done," said Madeline, "and therefore you are quite right to try that."

"Oh, you think it's a foolish thing, do you?" said he. "There's

Lotte advising me to marry by all means. But on such a subject your opinion ought to be the best; you have experience to guide you."

"Yes, I have," said Madeline, with a sort of harsh sadness in her tone, which seemed to say—What is it to you if I am sad? I have never asked your sympathy.

Bertie was sorry when he saw that she was hurt by what he said, and he came and squatted on the floor close before her face to make his peace with her.

"Come, Mad, I was only joking; you know that. But in sober earnest, Lotte is advising me to marry. She wants me to marry this Mrs. Bold. She's a widow with lots of tin, a fine baby, a beautiful complexion, and the *George and Dragon* hotel up in the High Street. By Jove, Lotte, if I marry her, I'll keep the public house myself— it's just the life to suit me."

"What?" said Madeline, "that vapid swarthy creature!" The signora never allowed any woman to be beautiful.

"Instead of being vapid," said Lotte. "I call her a very lovely woman. She was by far the loveliest woman in the rooms the other night; that is, excepting you, Madeline."

"If it be true that she has got twelve hundred a year quite at her own disposal, and she be not utterly vulgar in her manners, I would advise you to marry her. I dare say she is to be had for the asking: and as you are not going to marry her for love, it doesn't much matter whether she is good-looking or not. As to your really marry-ing a woman for love, I don't believe *you* are fool enough for that."

But let the gentle-hearted reader be under no apprehension what-soever. It is not destined that Eleanor shall marry Mr. Slope or Bertie Stanhope.

I would not for the value of this chapter have it believed by a single reader that my Eleanor could bring herself to marry Mr. Slope, or that she should be sacrificed to a Bertie Stanhope. But among the good folk of Barchester many believed both the one and the other.

CHAPTER XIV

BABY WORSHIP

"DIDDLE, diddle, diddle, diddle, dum, dum, dum," said or sung Eleanor Bold.

"Diddle, diddle, diddle, diddle, dum, dum, sum," continued Mary Bold, taking up the second part of this concerted piece.

The only audience at the concert was the baby, who however gave such vociferous applause, that the performers presuming it to amount to an encore, commenced again.

c

"Diddle, diddle, diddle, diddle, dum, dum, dum: hasn't he got lovely legs?" said the rapturous mother.

"H'm 'm 'm 'm 'm," simmered Mary, burying her lips in the little fellow's fat neck, by way of kissing him.

At this moment the door opened, and Mr. Slope was announced. Up jumped Eleanor, and with a sudden quick motion of her hands pushed back her hair over her shoulders. It would have been perhaps better for her that she had not, for she thus showed more of her confusion than she would have done had she remained as she was. Mr. Slope, however, immediately recognised her loveliness, and thought to himself, that irrespective of her fortune, she would be an inmate that a man might well desire for his house, a partner for his bosom's care very well qualified to make care lie easy.

"I have to apologise for calling at so very early an hour," began Mr. Slope, "but I was really so anxious to speak to you that I hope you and Miss Bold will excuse me."

Eleanor muttered something in which the words "certainly," and "of course," and "not early at all," were just audible, and then apologised for her own appearance, declaring with a smile, that her baby was becoming such a big boy that he was quite unmanageable.

"He's a great big naughty boy," said she to the child; "and we must send him away to a great big rough romping school, where they have great big rods, and do terrible things to naughty boys who don't do what their own mammas tell them;" and she then commenced another course of kissing, being actuated thereto by the terrible idea of sending her child away which her own imagination had depicted.

"And where the masters don't have such beautiful long hair to be dishevelled," said Mr. Slope, taking up the joke and paying a compliment at the same time.

Eleanor thought he might as well have left the compliment alone; but she said nothing and looked nothing, being occupied as she was with the baby.

"Let me take him," said Mary. "His clothes are nearly off his back with his romping," and so saying she left the room with the child. Miss Bold had heard Mr. Slope say he had something pressing to say to Eleanor, and thinking that she might be *de trop*, took this opportunity of getting herself out of the room.

"Don't be long, Mary," said Eleanor, as Miss Bold shut the door.

"I am glad, Mrs. Bold, to have the opportunity of having ten minutes' conversation with you alone," began Mr. Slope. "Will you let me openly ask you a plain question?"

"Certainly," said she.

"And I am sure you will give me a plain and open answer."

"Either that or none at all," said she, laughing.

"My question is this, Mrs. Bold; is your father really anxious to go back to the hospital?"

"Why do you ask me?" said she. "Why don't you ask himself?"

"My dear Mrs. Bold, I'll tell you why. There are wheels within wheels, all of which I would explain to you, only I fear that there is not time. It is essentially necessary that I should have an answer to this question, otherwise I cannot know how to advance your father's wishes; and it is quite impossible that I should ask himself. No one can esteem your father more than I do, but I doubt if this feeling is reciprocal." It certainly was not. "I must be candid with you as the only means of avoiding ultimate consequences, which may be most injurious to Mr. Harding. I fear there is a feeling, I will not even call it a prejudice, with regard to myself in Barchester, which is not in my favour. You remember that sermon——"

"Oh! Mr. Slope, we need not go back to that," said Eleanor.

"For one moment, Mrs. Bold. It is not that I may talk of myself, but because it is so essential that you should understand how matters stand. That sermon may have been ill-judged,—it was certainly misunderstood; but I will say nothing about that now; only this, that it did give rise to a feeling against myself which your father shares with others. It may be that he has proper cause, but the result is that he is not inclined to meet me on friendly terms. I put it to yourself whether you do not know this to be the case."

Eleanor made no answer, and Mr. Slope, in the eagerness of his address, edged his chair a little nearer to the widow's seat, unperceived by her.

"Such being so," continued Mr. Slope, "I cannot ask him this question as I can ask it of you. In spite of my delinquencies since I came to Barchester you have allowed me to regard you as a friend." Eleanor made a little motion with her head which was hardly confirmatory, but Mr. Slope if he noticed it, did not appear to do so. "To you I can speak openly, and explain the feelings of my heart. This your father would not allow. Unfortunately the bishop has thought it right that this matter of the hospital should pass through my hands. There have been some details to get up with which he would not trouble himself, and thus it has come to pass that I was forced to have an interview with your father on the matter."

"I am aware of that," said Eleanor.

"Of course," said he. "In that interview Mr. Harding left the impression on my mind that he did not wish to return to the hospital."

"How could that be?" said Eleanor, at last stirred up to forget the cold propriety of demeanour which she had determined to maintain.

"My dear Mrs. Bold, I give my word that such was the case," said he, again getting a little nearer to her. "And what is more than that, before my interview with Mr. Harding, certain persons at the palace, I do not mean the bishop, had told me that such was the fact. I own, I hardly believed it; I own, I thought that your father would wish on every account, for conscience' sake, for the sake of those old men, for old association, and the memory of dear days long gone by, on every account I thought that he would wish to resume his duties. But I was told that such was not his wish; and he certainly left me with the impression that I had been told the truth."

"Well!" said Eleanor, now sufficiently roused on the matter.

"I hear Miss Bold's step," said Mr. Slope; "would it be asking too great a favour to beg you to—— I know you can manage anything with Miss Bold."

Eleanor did not like the word manage, but still she went out, and asked Mary to leave them alone for another quarter of an hour.

"Thank you, Mrs. Bold,—I am so very grateful for this confidence. Well, I left your father with this impression. Indeed, I may say that he made me understand that he declined the appointment."

"Not the appointment," said Eleanor. "I am sure he did not decline the appointment. But he said that he would not agree,—that is, that he did not like the scheme about the schools and the services, and all that. I am quite sure he never said that he wished to refuse the place."

"Oh, Mrs. Bold!" said Mr. Slope, in a manner almost impassioned. "I would not, for the world, say to so good a daughter a word against so good a father. But you must, for his sake, let me show you exactly how the matter stands at present. Mr. Harding was a little flurried when I told him of the bishop's wishes about the school. I did so, perhaps, with the less caution because you yourself had so perfectly agreed with me on the same subject. He was a little put out and spoke warmly. 'Tell the bishop,' said he, 'that I quite disagree with him,—and shall not return to the hospital as such conditions are attached to it.' What he said was to that effect; indeed, his words were, if anything, stronger than those. I had no alternative but to repeat them to his lordship, who said that he could look on them in no other light than a refusal. He also had heard the report that your father did not wish for the appointment, and putting all these things together, he thought he had no choice, but to look for some one else. He has consequently offered the place to Mr. Quiverful."

"Offered the place to Mr. Quiverful!" repeated Eleanor, her eyes suffused with tears. "Then, Mr. Slope, there is an end of it."

"No, my friend—not so," said he. "It is to prevent such being the end of it that I am now here. I may at any rate presume that I have got an answer to my question, and that Mr. Harding is desirous of returning."

"Desirous of returning—of course he is," said Eleanor; "of course he wishes to have back his house and his income, and his place in the world; to have back what he gave up with such self-denying honesty, if he can have them without restraints on his conduct to which at his age it would be impossible that he should submit. How can the bishop ask a man of his age to turn schoolmaster to a pack of children?"

"Out of the question," said Mr. Slope, laughing slightly; "of course no such demand shall be made on your father. I can at any rate promise you that I will not be the medium of any so absurd a requisition. We wished your father to preach in the hospital, as the inmates may naturally be too old to leave it; but even that shall not be insisted on. We wished also to attach a Sabbath-day school to the hospital, thinking that such an establishment could not but be useful under the surveillance of so good a clergyman as Mr. Harding, and also under your own. But, dear Mrs. Bold; we won't talk of these things now. One thing is clear; we must do what we can to annul this rash offer the bishop has made to Mr. Quiverful. Your father wouldn't see Quiverful, would he? Quiverful is an honourable man, and would not, for a moment, stand in your father's way."

"What?" said Eleanor; "ask a man with fourteen children to give up his preferment! I am quite sure he will do no such thing."

"I suppose not," said Slope; and he again drew near to Mrs. Bold, so that now they were very close to each other. Eleanor did not think much about it, but instinctively moved away a little. How greatly would she have increased the distance could she have guessed what had been said about her at Plumstead! "I suppose not. But it is out of the question that Quiverful should supersede your father,—quite out of the question. The bishop has been too rash. But pray let me assure you that your father's interests shall not be sacrificed if it be possible for me to protect them. I will tell the bishop openly what are the facts. I will explain to him that he has hardly the right to appoint any other than your father, and will show him that if he does so he will be guilty of great injustice,—and you, Mrs. Bold, you will have the charity at any rate to believe this of me, that I am truly anxious for your father's welfare,—for his and for your own."

And so he took his leave, pressing the widow's hand rather more closely than usual. Circumstances, however, seemed just then to make this intelligible, and the lady did not feel called on to resent it.

"I cannot understand him," said Eleanor to Mary Bold, a few minutes afterwards. "I do not know whether he is a good man or a bad man—whether he is true or false."

"Then give him the benefit of the doubt," said Mary, "and believe the best."

"On the whole, I think I do," said Eleanor. "I think I do believe that he means well—and if so, it is a shame that we should revile him, and make him miserable while he is among us. But, oh, Mary, I fear papa will be disappointed in the hospital."

CHAPTER XV

WHO SHALL BE COCK OF THE WALK?

ALL this time things were going on somewhat uneasily at the palace. The hint or two which Mr. Slope had given was by no means thrown away upon the bishop. He had a feeling that if he ever meant to oppose the now almost unendurable despotism of his wife, he must lose no further time in doing so; that if he ever meant to be himself master in his own diocese, let alone his own house, he should begin at once.

To-morrow he would have to declare to the archdeacon either that Mr. Harding should have the appointment, or that he should not have it. The bishop felt that he could not honestly throw over the Quiverfuls without informing Mrs. Proudie, and he resolved at last to brave the lioness in her den and tell her that circumstances were such that it behoved him to reappoint Mr. Harding. He did not feel that he should at all derogate from his new courage by promising Mrs. Proudie that the very first piece of available preferment at his disposal should be given to Quiverful to atone for the injury done to him. If he could mollify the lioness with such a sop, how happy would he think his first efforts to have been!

Not without many misgivings did he find himself in Mrs. Proudie's boudoir.

"Ahem—my dear," began the bishop, "if you are disengaged, I wished to speak to you." Mrs. Proudie put her pencil down carefully at the point to which she had dotted her figures, marked down in her memory the sum she had arrived at, and then looked up, sourly enough, into her helpmate's face. "If you are busy, another time will do as well," continued the bishop, whose courage like Bob Acres' had oozed out, now that he found himself on the ground of battle.

"What is it about, Bishop?" asked the lady.

"Well—it was about those Quiverfuls—but I see you are engaged. Another time will do just as well for me."

"What about the Quiverfuls? It is quite understood I believe, that they are to come to the hospital. There is to be no doubt about that, is there?" and as she spoke she kept her pencil sternly and vigorously fixed on the column of figures before her.

"Why, my dear, there is a difficulty," said the bishop.

"A difficulty!" said Mrs. Proudie, "what difficulty? The place has been promised to Mr. Quiverful, and of course he must have it. He has made all his arrangements. He has written for a curate for Puddingdale, he has spoken to the auctioneer about selling his farm, horses, and cows, and in all respects considers the place as his own. Of course he must have it."

"Well, my dear, I merely wanted to suggest to you that Mr. Slope seems to think that if Mr. Harding be not appointed, public feeling in the matter would be against us, and that the press might perhaps take it up."

"Mr. Slope seems to think!" said Mrs. Proudie, in a tone of voice which plainly showed the bishop that he was right in looking for a breach in that quarter. "And what has Mr. Slope to do with it? I hope, my lord, you are not going to allow yourself to be governed by a chaplain." And now in her eagerness the lady lost her place in her account.

"Certainly not, my dear. Nothing I can assure you is less probable. But still Mr. Slope may be useful in finding how the wind blows, and I really thought that if we could give something else as good to the Quiverfuls——"

"Nonsense," said Mrs. Proudie; "it would be years before you could give them anything else that could suit them half as well, and as for the press and the public, and all that, remember there are two ways of telling a story. If Mr. Harding is fool enough to tell his tale, we can also tell ours. The place was offered to him, and he refused it. It has now been given to some one else, and there's an end of it. At least, I should think so."

"Well, my dear, I rather believe you are right;" said the bishop, and sneaking out of the room, he went down stairs, troubled in his mind as to how he should receive the archdeacon on the morrow. He felt himself not very well just at present; and began to consider that he might, not improbably, be detained in his room the next morning by an attack of bile. He was, unfortunately, very subject to bilious annoyances.

CHAPTER XVI

THE WIDOW'S PERSECUTION

EARLY on the following morning Mr. Slope was summoned to the bishop's dressing-room. His lordship complained of being rather unwell, had a slight headache, and was not quite the thing in his stomach; but there was nothing the matter with his temper.

"Oh, Slope," said he, taking the chaplain's proffered hand, "Archdeacon Grantly is to call on me this morning, and I really am not fit to see him. I fear I must trouble you, to see him for me;"

and then Dr. Proudie proceeded to explain what it was that must be said to Dr. Grantly. He was to be told in fact in the civilest words in which the tidings could be conveyed, that Mr. Harding having refused the wardenship, the appointment had been offered to Mr. Quiverful and accepted by him.

Mr. Slope felt pretty sure that Dr. Grantly would decline the honour of seeing him, and such turned out to be the case. The archdeacon, when the palace door was opened to him, was greeted by a note. Mr. Slope presented his compliments, &c. &c. The bishop was ill in his room, and very greatly regretted, &c. &c. Mr. Slope had been charged with the bishop's views, and if agreeable to the archdeacon, would do himself the honour, &c. &c. The archdeacon, however, was not agreeable, and having read his note in the hall, crumpled it up in his hand, and muttering something about sorrow for his lordship's illness, took his leave, without sending as much as a verbal message in answer to Mr. Slope's note.

"Ill!" said the archdeacon to himself as he flung himself into his brougham. "The man is absolutely a coward. He is afraid to see me. Ill, indeed!" The archdeacon was never ill himself, and did not therefore understand that any one else could in truth be prevented by illness from keeping an appointment. He regarded all such excuses as subterfuges, and in the present instance he was not far wrong.

Dr. Grantly desired to be driven to his father-in-law's lodgings in the High Street, and hearing from the servant that Mr. Harding was at his daughter's, followed him to Mrs. Bold's house, and there found him. The archdeacon was fuming with rage when he got into the drawing-room, and had by this time nearly forgotten the pusillanimity of the bishop in the villany of the chaplain.

"Look at that," said he, throwing Mr. Slope's crumpled note to Mr. Harding. "I am to be told that if I choose I may have the honour of seeing Mr. Slope, and that too, after a positive engagement with the bishop."

"But he says the bishop is ill," said Mr. Harding.

"Pshaw! You don't mean to say that you are deceived by such an excuse as that. He was well enough yesterday. Now I tell you what, I will see the bishop; and I will tell him also very plainly what I think of his conduct. I will see him, or else Barchester will soon be too hot to hold him."

Eleanor was sitting in the room, but Dr. Grantly had hardly noticed her in his anger. Eleanor now said to him, with the greatest innocence, "I wish you had seen Mr. Slope, Dr. Grantly, because I think perhaps it might have done good."

The archdeacon turned on her with almost brutal wrath. Had she at once owned that she had accepted Mr. Slope for her second husband, he could hardly have felt more convinced of her belonging body and soul to the Slope and Proudie party than he now did on hearing her express such a wish as this. Poor Eleanor!

"See him!" said the archdeacon glaring at her; "and why am I to be called on to lower myself in the world's esteem and my own by coming in contact with such a man as that? I have hitherto lived among gentlemen, and do not mean to be dragged into other company by anybody."

Poor Mr. Harding well knew what the archdeacon meant, but Eleanor was as innocent as her own baby. She could not understand how the archdeacon could consider himself to be dragged into bad company by condescending to speak to Mr. Slope for a few minutes when the interests of her father might be served by his doing so.

"I was talking for a full hour yesterday to Mr. Slope," said she, with some little assumption of dignity, "and I did not find myself lowered by it."

"Perhaps not," said he. "But if you'll be good enough to allow me, I shall judge for myself in such matters. And I tell you what, Eleanor; it will be much better for you if you will allow yourself to be guided also by the advice of those who are your friends. If you do not you will be apt to find that you have no friends left who can advise you."

"I believe you greatly wrong Mr. Slope," continued Eleanor; "but I have explained this to papa already; and as you do not seem to approve of what I say, Dr. Grantly, I will with your permission leave you and papa together," and so saying she walked slowly out of the room.

All this made Mr. Harding very unhappy. It was quite clear that the archdeacon and his wife had made up their minds that Eleanor was going to marry Mr. Slope. Mr. Harding could not really bring himself to think that she would do so, but yet he could not deny that circumstances made it appear that the man's company was not disagreeable to her. She was now constantly seeing him, and yet she received visits from no other unmarried gentleman. She always took his part when his conduct was canvassed, although she was aware how personally objectionable he was to her friends.

"She'll marry that man as sure as two and two make four," said the practical archdeacon.

The two now turned into the cathedral library, which was used by the clergymen of the close as a sort of ecclesiastical club-room, for writing sermons and sometimes letters; also for reading theological works, and sometimes magazines and newspapers. The theological works were not disturbed, perhaps, quite as often as from the appearance of the building the outside public might have been led to expect. Here the two allies settled on their course of action. The archdeacon wrote a letter to the bishop, strongly worded, but still respectful, in which he put forward his father-in-law's claim to the appointment, and expressed his own regret that he had not been able to see his lordship when he called. Of Mr. Slope he made no mention whatsoever. It was then settled that Mr. Harding should go out to Plumstead on the following day; and after considerable discussion on the matter, the archdeacon proposed to ask Eleanor there also, so as to withdraw her, if possible, from Mr. Slope's attentions. "A week or two," said he, "may teach her what he is, and while she is there she will be out of harm's way. Mr. Slope won't come there after her."

Eleanor was not a little surprised when her brother-in-law came back and very civilly pressed her to go out to Plumstead with her father. She instantly perceived that her father had been fighting her battles for her behind her back. She felt thankful to him, and for his sake she would not show her resentment to the archdeacon by refusing his invitation. But she could not, she said, go on the morrow; she had an invitation to drink tea at the Stanhopes which she had promised to accept. She would, she added, go with her father on the next day, if he would wait; or she would follow him.

"The Stanhopes!" said Dr. Grantly; "I did not know you were so intimate with them."

"I did not know it myself," said she, "till Miss Stanhope called yesterday. However, I like her very much, and I have promised to go and play chess with some of them."

"Have they a party there?" said the archdeacon, still fearful of Mr. Slope.

"Oh, no," said Eleanor; "Miss Stanhope said there was to be nobody at all. But she had heard that Mary had left me for a few weeks, and she had learnt from some one that I play chess, and so she came over on purpose to ask me to go in."

"Well, that's very friendly," said the ex-warden. "They certainly do look more like foreigners than English people, but I dare say they are none the worse for that."

The archdeacon was inclined to look upon the Stanhopes with favourable eyes, and had nothing to object on the matter. It was therefore arranged that Mr. Harding should postpone his visit to Plumstead for one day, and then take with him Eleanor, the baby, and the nurse.

Mr. Slope is certainly becoming of some importance in Barchester.

CHAPTER XVII

BARCHESTER BY MOONLIGHT

THERE was much cause for grief and occasional perturbation of spirits in the Stanhope family, but yet they rarely seemed to be grieved or to be disturbed. It was the peculiar gift of each of them that each was able to bear his or her own burden without complaint, and perhaps without sympathy. They habitually looked on the sunny side of the wall, if there was a gleam on either side for them to look at; and, if there was none, they endured the shade with an indifference which, if not stoical, answered the end at which the Stoics aimed. Old Stanhope could not but feel that he had ill-performed his duties as a father and a clergyman; and could hardly look forward to his own death without grief at the position in which he would leave his family. His income for many years had been as high as 3000*l*. a year, and yet they had among them no other provision than their mother's fortune of 10,000*l*. He had not only spent his income, but was in debt. Yet with all this, he seldom showed much outward sign of trouble.

They all met together in the drawing-room at nine o'clock, in perfect good humour with each other; and about that hour Mrs. Bold was announced. She had never been in the house before, though she had of course called; and now she felt it strange to find herself there in her usual evening dress, entering the drawing-room of these strangers in this friendly unceremonious way, as though she had known them all her life. But in three minutes they made her at home. Charlotte tripped down stairs and took her bonnet from her, and Bertie came to relieve her from her shawl, and the signora smiled on her as she could smile when she chose to be gracious, and the old doctor shook hands with her in a kind benedictory manner that went to her heart at once, and made her feel that he must be a good man.

She had not been seated for above five minutes when the door again opened, and Mr. Slope was announced. She felt rather surprised, because she was told that nobody was to be there, and it was very evident from the manner of some of them, that Mr. Slope was unexpected. But still there was not much in it. In such invitations a bachelor or two more or less are always spoken of as nobodies, and there was no reason why Mr. Slope should not drink tea at Dr. Stanhope's as well as Eleanor herself. He, however, was very much surprised and not very much gratified at finding that his own embryo spouse made one of the party. He had come there to gratify himself by gazing on Madame Neroni's beauty, and listening to and returning her flattery: and though he had not owned as much to himself, he still felt that if he spent the evening as he had intended to do, he might probably not thereby advance his suit with Mrs. Bold.

The signora, who had no idea of a rival, received Mr. Slope with her usual marks of distinction. As he took her hand, she made some confidential communication to him in a low voice, declaring that she had a plan to communicate to him after tea, and was evidently prepared to go on with her work of reducing the chaplain to a state of captivity. Poor Mr. Slope was rather beside himself. He thought that Eleanor could not but have learnt from his demeanour that he was an admirer of her own, and he had also flattered himself that the idea was not unacceptable to her. What would she think of him if he now devoted himself to a married woman!

But Eleanor was not inclined to be severe in her criticisms on him in this respect, and felt no annoyance of any kind, when she found herself seated between Bertie and Charlotte Stanhope. She had no suspicion of Mr. Slope's intentions; she had no suspicion even of the suspicion of other people; but still she felt well pleased not to have Mr. Slope too near to her.

When tea was over Charlotte went to the open window and declared loudly that the full harvest moon was much too beautiful to be disregarded, and called them all to look at it. To tell the truth, there was but one there who cared much about the moon's beauty, and that one was not Charlotte; but she knew how valuable an aid to her purpose the chaste goddess might become, and could easily create a little enthusiasm for the purpose of the moment. Eleanor and Bertie were soon with her. The doctor was now quiet in his armchair, and Mrs. Stanhope in hers, both prepared for slumber.

"Are you a Whewellite or a Brewsterite, or a t'othermanite, Mrs. Bold?" said Charlotte, who knew a little about everything, and had read about a third of each of the books to which she alluded.

"Oh!" said Eleanor; "I have not read any of the books, but I feel sure that there is one man in the moon at least, if not more."

"You don't believe in the pulpy gelatinous matter?" said Bertie.

"I heard about that," said Eleanor; "and I really think it's almost wicked to talk in such a manner. How can we argue about God's power in the other stars from the laws which he has given for our rule in this one?"

"How indeed!" said Bertie. "Why shouldn't there be a race of salamanders in Venus? and even if there be nothing but fish in Jupiter, why shouldn't the fish there be as wide awake as the men and women here?"

"That would be saying very little for them," said Charlotte. "I am for Dr. Whewell myself; for I do not think that men and women are worth being repeated in such countless worlds. There may be souls in other stars, but I doubt their having any bodies attached to them. But come, Mrs. Bold, let us put our bonnets on and walk round the close. If we are to discuss sidereal questions, we shall do so much better under the towers of the cathedral, than stuck in this narrow window."

Mrs. Bold made no objection, and a party was made to walk out. Charlotte Stanhope well knew the rule as to three being no company, and she had therefore to induce her sister to allow Mr. Slope to accompany them.

"Come, Mr. Slope," she said; "I'm sure you'll join us. We shall be in again in a quarter of an hour, Madeline."

Madeline read in her eye all that she had to say, knew her object, and as she had to depend on her sister for so many of her amusements, she felt that she must yield. It was hard to be left alone while others of her own age walked out to feel the soft influence of the bright night, but it would be harder still to be without the sort of sanction which Charlotte gave to all her flirtations and intrigues. Charlotte's eye told her that she must give up just at present for the good of the family, and so Madeline obeyed.

But Charlotte's eyes said nothing of the sort to Mr. Slope. He had no objection at all to the *tête-à-tête* with the signora, which the departure of the other three would allow him, and gently whispered to her, "I shall not leave you alone."

"Oh, yes," she said; "go—pray go, pray go, for my sake. Do not think that I am so selfish. It is understood that nobody is kept within for me. You will understand this too when you know me better. Pray join them, Mr. Slope, but when you come in speak to me for five minutes before you leave us."

Mr. Slope understood that he was to go, and he therefore joined the party in the hall. He would have had no objection at all to this arrangement, if he could have secured Mrs. Bold's arm; but this of course was out of the question. Indeed, his fate was very soon settled, for no sooner had he reached the hall-door than Miss Stanhope put her hand within his arm, and Bertie walked off with Eleanor just as naturally as though she were already his own property.

And so they sauntered forth; first they walked round the close, according to their avowed intent; then they went under the old arched gateway below St. Cuthbert's little church, and then they turned behind the grounds of the bishop's palace, and so on till they came to the bridge just at the edge of the town, from which passers-by can look down into the gardens of Hiram's Hospital; and here Charlotte and Mr. Slope, who were in advance, stopped till the other two came up to them. Mr. Slope knew that the gable-ends, and old brick chimneys which stood up so prettily in the moonlight, were those of Mr. Harding's late abode, and would not have stopped on such a spot, in such company, if he could have avoided it; but Miss Stanhope would not take the hint which he tried to give.

"This is a very pretty place, Mrs. Bold," said Charlotte; "by far the prettiest place near Barchester. I wonder your father gave it up."

It was a very pretty place, and now by the deceitful light of the moon looked twice larger, twice prettier, twice more antiquely picturesque than it would have done in truth-telling daylight. Who does not know the air of complex multiplicity and the mysterious interesting grace which the moon always lends to old gabled buildings half surrounded, as was the hospital, by fine trees! As seen from the bridge on the night of which we are speaking, Mr. Harding's late abode did look very lovely; and though Eleanor did not grieve at her father's having left it, she felt at the moment an intense wish that he might be allowed to return.

"He is going to return to it almost immediately, is he not?" asked Bertie.

Eleanor made no immediate reply. Many such a question passes unanswered, without the notice of the questioner; but such was not now the case. They all remained silent as though expecting her to reply, and after a moment or two, Charlotte said, "I believe it is settled that Mr. Harding returns to the hospital, is it not?"

"I don't think anything about it is settled yet," said Eleanor.

When they had parted company with Mr. Slope Eleanor explained how he had at first endeavoured to tyrannise over her father, but how he had latterly come round, and done all he could to talk the bishop over in Mr. Harding's favour. "But my father," said she, "is hardly inclined to trust him; they all say he is so arrogant to the old clergymen of the city."

"Take my word for it," said Bertie, "your father is right. If I am not very much mistaken, that man is both arrogant and false."

They strolled up to the top of the hill, and then returned through the fields by a footpath which leads by a small wooden bridge, or rather a plank with a rustic rail to it, over the river to the other side of the cathedral from that at which they had started. They had thus walked round the bishop's grounds, through which the river runs, and round the cathedral and adjacent fields, and it was past eleven before they reached the doctor's door.

"It is very late," said Eleanor, "it will be a shame to disturb your mother again at such an hour."

"Oh," said Charlotte, laughing, "you won't disturb mamma; I dare say she is in bed by this time, and Madeline would be furious if you did not come in and see her. Come, Bertie, take Mrs. Bold's bonnet from her."

They went up stairs, and found the signora alone, reading. She looked somewhat sad and melancholy, but not more so perhaps than was sufficient to excite additional interest in the bosom of Mr. Slope; and she was soon deep in whispered intercourse with that happy gentleman, who was allowed to find a resting-place on her sofa. The signora had a way of whispering that was peculiarly her own, and was exactly the reverse of that which prevails among great tragedians. The great tragedian hisses out a positive whisper, made with bated breath, and produced by inarticulated tongue-formed sounds, but yet he is audible through the whole house. The signora however used no hisses, and produced all her words in a clear silver tone, but they could only be heard by the ear into which they were poured.

Charlotte hurried and skurried about the room hither and thither, doing, or pretending to do many things; and then saying something about seeing her mother, ran up stairs. Eleanor was thus left alone with Bertie, and she hardly felt an hour fly by her. To give Bertie his due credit, he could not have played his cards better. He did not make love to her, nor sigh, nor look languishing; but he was amusing and familiar, yet respectful; and when he left Eleanor at her own door at one o'clock, which he did by the bye with the assistance of the now jealous Slope, she thought that he was one of the most agreeable men, and the Stanhopes decidedly the most agreeable family, that she had ever met.

CHAPTER XVIII

ST. EWOLD'S PARSONAGE

THE Rev. Francis Arabin, fellow of Lazarus, late professor of poetry at Oxford, and present vicar of St. Ewold, in the diocese of Barchester, must now be introduced personally to the reader.

Of his doings in the world, and of the sort of fame which he has achieved, enough has been already said. It has also been said that he is forty years of age, and still unmarried.

Exteriorly, he was not a remarkable person. He was above the middle height, well made, and very active. His hair which had been jet black, was now tinged with grey, but his face bore no sign of years. It would perhaps be wrong to say that he was handsome, but his face was, nevertheless, pleasant to look upon. The cheek bones were rather too high for beauty, and the formation of the forehead too massive and heavy: but the eyes, nose, and mouth were perfect. There was a continual play of lambent fire about his eyes, which gave promise of either pathos or humour whenever he essayed to speak, and that promise was rarely broken. There was a gentle play about his mouth which declared that his wit never descended to sarcasm, and that there was no ill-nature in his repartee.

Such was Mr. Arabin, the new vicar of St. Ewold, who is going to stay with the Grantlys, at Plumstead Episcopi.

Mr. Arabin reached Plumstead the day before Mr. Harding and Eleanor, and the Grantly family were thus enabled to make his acquaintance and discuss his qualifications before the arrival of the other guests.

In the archdeacon's drawing-room, Mr. Arabin had sparkled with his usual unaffected brilliancy, but when he retired to his bedroom, he sat there sad, at his open window, repining within himself that he also had no wife, no bairns, no soft sward of lawn duly mown for him to lie on, no herd of attendant curates, no bowings from the banker's clerks, no rich rectory. That apostleship that he had thought of had evaded his grasp, and he was now only vicar of St. Ewold's, with a taste for a mitre. Truly he had fallen between two stools.

When Mr. Harding and Mrs. Bold reached the rectory on the following morning, the archdeacon and his friend were at St. Ewold's. They had gone over that the new vicar might inspect his church, and be introduced to the squire, and were not expected back before dinner. Mr. Harding rambled out by himself, and strolled, as was his wont at Plumstead, about the lawn and round the church; and as he did so, the two sisters naturally fell into conversation about Barchester.

There was not much sisterly confidence between them. Mrs. Grantly was ten years older than Eleanor, and had been married while Eleanor was yet a child. They had never, therefore, poured into each other's ears their hopes and loves; and now that one was a wife and the other a widow, it was not probable that they would begin to do so. They lived too much asunder to be able to fall into that kind of intercourse which makes confidence between sisters almost a necessity; and, moreover, that which is so easy at eighteen is often very difficult at twenty-eight. Mrs. Grantly knew this, and did not, therefore, expect confidence from her sister; and yet she longed to ask her whether in real truth Mr. Slope was agreeable to her.

It was by no means difficult to turn the conversation to Mr. Slope. That gentleman had become so famous at Barchester, had so much to do with all clergymen connected with the city, and was so specially concerned in the affairs of Mr. Harding, that it would have been odd if Mr. Harding's daughters had not talked about him. Mrs. Grantly was soon abusing him, which she did with her whole heart; and Mrs. Bold was nearly as eager to defend him. She positively disliked the man, would have been delighted to learn that he had taken himself off so that she should never see him again, had indeed almost a fear of him, and yet she constantly found herself taking his part. The abuse of other people, and abuse of a nature that she felt to be unjust, imposed this necessity on her, and at last made Mr. Slope's defence an habitual course of argument with her.

From Mr. Slope the conversation turned to the Stanhopes, and Mrs. Grantly was listening with some interest to Eleanor's account of the family, when it dropped out that Mr. Slope made one of the party. "What!" said the lady of the rectory, "was Mr. Slope there too?"

Eleanor merely replied that such had been the case.

"Why, Eleanor, he must be very fond of you, I think; he seems to follow you everywhere."

Even this did not open Eleanor's eyes. She merely laughed, and said that she imagined Mr. Slope found other attraction at Dr. Stanhope's. And so they parted. Mrs. Grantly felt quite convinced that the odious match would take place; and Mrs. Bold as convinced that that unfortunate chaplain, disagreeable as he must be allowed to be, was more sinned against than sinning.

The archdeacon of course heard before dinner that Eleanor had remained the day before in Barchester with the view of meeting Mr. Slope, and that she had so met him. He remembered how she had positively stated that there were to be no guests at the Stanhopes, and he did not hesitate to accuse her of deceit. Moreover, the fact, or rather presumed fact, of her being deceitful on such a matter, spoke but too plainly in evidence against her as to her imputed crime of receiving Mr. Slope as a lover.

"I am afraid that anything we can do will be too late," said the archdeacon. "I own I am fairly surprised. I never liked your sister's taste with regard to men; but still I did not give her credit for—ugh!"

"And so soon, too," said Mrs. Grantly, who thought more, perhaps, of her sister's indecorum in having a lover before she had put off her weeds, than her bad taste in having such a lover as Mr. Slope.

"Well, my dear, I shall be sorry to be harsh, or to do anything that can hurt your father; but, positively, neither that man nor his wife shall come within my doors."

Mrs. Grantly sighed, and then attempted to console herself and her lord by remarking that, after all, the thing was not accomplished yet. Now that Eleanor was at Plumstead, much might be done to wean her from her fatal passion. Poor Eleanor!

The evening passed off without anything to make it remarkable. Before they all retired it was settled that the whole party should drive over on the following day to inspect the parsonage at St. Ewold. The three clergymen were to discuss dilapidations, and the two ladies were to lend their assistance in suggesting such changes as might be necessary for a bachelor's abode. Accordingly, soon after breakfast, the carriage was at the door. There was only room for four inside, and the archdeacon got upon the box. Eleanor found herself opposite to Mr. Arabin, and was, therefore, in a manner forced into conversation with him. They were soon on comfortable terms together; and had she thought about it, she would have thought that, in spite of his black cloth, Mr. Arabin would not have been a bad addition to the Stanhope family party.

Now that the archdeacon was away, they could all trifle. Mr. Harding began by telling them in the most innocent manner imaginable an old legend about Mr. Arabin's new parish. There was, he said, in days of yore, an illustrious priestess of St. Ewold, famed through the whole country for curing all manner of diseases. She had a well, as all priestesses have ever had, which well was extant to this day, and shared in the minds of many of the people the sanctity which belonged to the consecrated ground of the parish church. Mr. Arabin declared that he should look on such tenets on the part of his parishioners as anything but orthodox. And Mrs. Grantly replied that she so entirely disagreed with him as to think that no parish was in a proper state that had not its priestess as well as its priest. "The duties are never well done," said she, "unless they are so divided."

"I suppose, papa," said Eleanor, "that in the olden times the priestess bore all the sway herself. Mr. Arabin, perhaps, thinks that such might be too much the case now if a sacred lady were admitted within the parish."

"I think, at any rate," said he, "that it is safer to run no such risk. No priestly pride has ever exceeded that of sacerdotal females. A very lowly curate I might, perhaps, essay to rule; but a curatess would be sure to get the better of me."

"There are certainly examples of such accidents happening," said Mrs. Grantly. "They do say that there is a priestess at Barchester who is very imperious in all things touching the altar. Perhaps the fear of such a fate as that is before your eyes."

When they were joined by the archdeacon on the gravel before the vicarage, they descended again to grave dullness. Not that Archdeacon Grantly was a dull man; but his frolic humours were of a cumbrous kind; and his wit, when he was witty, did not generally extend itself to his auditory. On the present occasion he was soon making speeches about wounded roofs and walls, which he declared to be in want of some surgeon's art. There was not a partition that he did not tap, nor a block of chimneys that he did not narrowly examine; all water-pipes, flues, cisterns, and sewers underwent an investigation; and he even descended in the care of his friend, so far as to bore sundry boards in the floors with a bradawl.

Mr. Arabin accompanied him through the rooms, trying to look wise in such domestic matters, and the other three also followed. Mrs. Grantly showed that she had not herself been priestess of a parish twenty years for nothing, and examined the bells and window panes in a very knowing way.

"You will, at any rate, have a beautiful prospect out of your own window, if this is to be your private sanctum," said Eleanor. She was standing at the lattice of a little room up stairs, from which the view certainly was very lovely. It was from the back of the vicarage, and there was nothing to interrupt the eye between the house and the glorious grey pile of the cathedral. The intermediate ground, however, was beautifully studded with timber. In the immediate foreground ran the little river which afterwards skirted the city; and, just to the right of the cathedral, the pointed gables and chimneys of Hiram's Hospital, peeped out of the elms which encompass it.

"Yes," said he, joining her. "I shall have a beautifully complete view of my adversaries. I shall sit down before the hostile town, and fire away at them at a very pleasant distance. I shall just be able to lodge a shot in the hospital, should the enemy ever get possession of it; and as for the palace, I have it within full range."

"I never saw anything like you clergymen," said Eleanor; "you are always thinking of fighting each other."

"Either that," said he, "or else supporting each other. The pity is that we cannot do the one without the other. But are we not here to fight? Is not ours a church militant? What is all our work but fighting, and hard fighting, if it be well done?"

"But not with each other."

Here they were interrupted by the archdeacon, whose voice was heard from the cellar shouting to the vicar.

"Arabin, Arabin,"—and then turning to his wife, who was apparently at his elbow—"where has he gone to? This cellar is perfectly abominable. It would be murder to put a bottle of wine into it till it has been roofed, walled, and floored. How on earth old Goodenough ever got on with it, I cannot guess. But then Goodenough never had a glass of wine that any man could drink."

"What is it, archdeacon?" said the vicar, running down stairs, and leaving Eleanor above to her meditations.

"This cellar must be roofed, walled, and floored," repeated the archdeacon. "Now mind what I say, and don't let the architect persuade you that it will do; half of these fellows know nothing about wine. This place as it is now would be damp and cold in winter, and hot and muggy in summer. I wouldn't give a straw for the best wine that ever was vinted, after it had lain here a couple of years."

Mr. Arabin assented, and promised that the cellar should be reconstructed according to the archdeacon's receipt.

"And, Arabin, look here; was such an attempt at a kitchen grate ever seen?"

"The grate is really very bad," said Mrs. Grantly; "I am sure the priestess won't approve of it, when she is brought home to the scene of her future duties. Really, Mr. Arabin, no priestess accustomed to such an excellent well as that above could put up with such a grate as this."

"If there must be a priestess at St. Ewold's at all, Mrs. Grantly, I think we will leave her to her well, and not call down her divine wrath on any of the imperfections rising from our human poverty. However, I own I am amenable to the attractions of a well-cooked dinner, and the grate shall certainly be changed."

By this time the archdeacon had again ascended, and was now in the dining-room. "Arabin," said he, speaking in his usual loud clear voice, and with that tone of dictation which was so common to him; "you must positively alter this dining-room, that is, remodel it altogether; look here, it is just sixteen feet by fifteen; did anybody ever hear of a dining-room of such proportions!" and the archdeacon stepped the room long-ways and cross-ways with ponderous steps, as though a certain amount of ecclesiastical dignity could be imparted even to such an occupation as that by the manner of doing it. "Barely sixteen; you may call it a square."

Mr. Arabin, however, did not appear well inclined to enter into speculative expenses, and therefore, any material alterations in the house, the cost of which could not fairly be made to lie at the door either of the ecclesiastical commissioners or of the estate of the late incumbent, were tabooed. With this essential exception, the archdeacon ordered, suggested, and carried all points before him in a manner very much to his own satisfaction. A close observer, had

there been one there, might have seen that his wife had been quite
as useful in the matter as himself. No one knew better than Mrs.
Grantly the appurtenances necessary to a comfortable house. She
did not, however, think it necessary to lay claim to any of the glory
which her lord and master was so ready to appropriate as his own.

Having gone through their work effectually and systematically,
the party returned to Plumstead well satisfied with their expedition.

CHAPTER XIX

THE THORNES OF ULLATHORNE

ON the following Sunday Mr. Arabin was to read himself in at
his new church. It was agreed at the rectory that the archdeacon should go over with him and assist at the reading-desk,
and that Mr. Harding should take the archdeacon's duty at Plumstead Church. Mrs. Grantly had her school and her buns to attend
to, and professed that she could not be spared; but Mrs. Bold was to
accompany them. It was further agreed also, that they would lunch
at the squire's house, and return home after the afternoon
service.

Wilfred Thorne, Esq., of Ullathorne, was the squire of St. Ewold's;
or rather the squire of Ullathorne; for the domain of the modern
landlord was of wider notoriety than the fame of the ancient saint.
He was a fair specimen of what that race has come to in our days,
which a century ago was, as we are told, fairly represented by
Squire Western. If that representation be a true one, few classes of
men can have made faster strides in improvement. Mr. Thorne,
however, was a man possessed of quite a sufficient number of foibles
to lay him open to much ridicule. He was still a bachelor, being
about fifty, and was not a little proud of his person.

Mr. Thorne did not live in solitude at Ullathorne. He had a
sister, who was ten years older than himself, and who participated
in his prejudices and feelings so strongly, that she was a living
caricature of all his foibles. She would not open a modern quarterly,
did not choose to see a magazine in her drawing-room, and would
not have polluted her fingers with a shred of the "Times" for any
consideration.

In her person and her dress she was perfect, and well she knew her
own perfection. She was a small elegantly made old woman, with a
face from which the glow of her youth had not departed without
leaving some streaks of a roseate hue. She was proud of her colour,
proud of her grey hair which she wore in short crisp curls peering out
all around her face from the dainty white lace cap. To think of all
the money that she spent in lace used to break the heart of poor

Mrs. Quiverful with her seven daughters. She was proud of her teeth, which were still white and numerous, proud of her bright cheery eye, proud of her short jaunty step, and very proud of the neat, precise, small feet with which those steps were taken. She was proud also, ay, very proud, of the rich brocaded silk in which it was her custom to ruffle through her drawing-room.

For all this rich attire Miss Thorne was not indebted to the generosity of her brother. She had a very comfortable independence of her own, which she divided among juvenile relatives, the milliners, and the poor, giving much the largest share to the latter. It may be imagined, therefore, that with all her little follies she was not unpopular. All her follies have, we believe, been told. Her virtues were too numerous to describe, and not sufficiently interesting to deserve description.

Mr. Thorne's house was called Ullathorne Court, and was properly so called; for the house itself formed two sides of a quadrangle, which was completed on the other two sides by a wall about twenty feet high.

CHAPTER XX

MR. ARABIN READS HIMSELF IN AT ST. EWOLD'S

On the Sunday morning the archdeacon with his sister-in-law and Mr. Arabin drove over to Ullathorne, as had been arranged. On their way thither the new vicar declared himself to be considerably disturbed in his mind at the idea of thus facing his parishioners for the first time. He had, he said, been always subject to *mauvaise honte* and an annoying degree of bashfulness, which often unfitted him for any work of a novel description; and now he felt this so strongly that he feared he should acquit himself badly in St. Ewold's reading-desk. He knew, he said, that those sharp little eyes of Miss Thorne would be on him, and that they would not approve. All this the archdeacon greatly ridiculed. He himself knew not, and had never known, what it was to be shy.

Mr. and Miss Thorne were standing ready dressed for church in the hall, and greeted their clerical visitors with cordiality. The archdeacon was an old favourite. He was a clergyman of the old school, and this recommended him to the lady. The little bell was tinkling, and the rural population of the parish were standing about the lane, leaning on the church stile, and against the walls of the old court, anxious to get a look at their new minister as he passed from the house to the rectory. The archdeacon's servant had already preceded them thither with the vestments.

They all went forth together; and when the ladies passed into the church the three gentlemen tarried a moment in the lane, that Mr.

Thorne might name to the vicar with some kind of one-sided introduction the most leading among his parishioners.

Mr. Arabin read the lessons and preached. It was enough to put a man a little out, let him have been ever so used to pulpit reading, to see the knowing way in which the farmers cocked their ears, and set about a mental criticism as to whether their new minister did or did not fall short of the excellence of him who had lately departed from them. A mental and silent criticism it was for the existing moment, but soon to be made public among the elders of St. Ewold's over the green graves of their children and forefathers. The excellence, however, of poor old Mr. Goodenough had not been wonderful, and there were few there who did not deem that Mr. Arabin did his work sufficiently well, in spite of the slightly nervous affection which at first impeded him, and which nearly drove the archdeacon beside himself.

There is a rule in our church which forbids the younger order of our clergymen to perform a certain portion of the service. The absolution must be read by a minister in priest's orders. If there be no such minister present, the congregation can have the benefit of no absolution but that which each may succeed in administering to himself. The rule may be a good one, though the necessity for it hardly comes home to the general understanding. But this forbearance on the part of youth would be much more appreciated if it were extended likewise to sermons. The only danger would be that congregations would be too anxious to prevent their young clergymen from advancing themselves in the ranks of the ministry. Clergymen who could not preach would be such blessings that they would be bribed to adhere to their incompetence.

Mr. Arabin, however, had not the modesty of youth to impede him, and he succeeded with his sermon even better than with the lessons.

Then came the lunch at Ullathorne. As soon as they were in the hall Miss Thorne took Mr. Arabin's hand, and assured him that she received him into her house, into the temple, she said, in which she worshipped, and bade him God speed with all her heart. Mr. Arabin was touched, and squeezed the spinster's hand without uttering a word in reply. Then Mr. Thorne expressed a hope that Mr. Arabin found the church easy to fill, and Mr. Arabin having replied that he had no doubt he should do so as soon as he had learnt to pitch his voice to the building, they all sat down to the good things before them.

The archdeacon made a very good lunch, and talked to his host about turnip-drillers and new machines for reaping: while the host, thinking it only polite to attend to a stranger, and fearing that perhaps he might not care about turnip crops on a Sunday, mooted all manner of ecclesiastical subjects.

At three o'clock they again went into church; and now Mr.

Arabin read the service and the archdeacon preached. Nearly the same congregation was present, with some adventurous pedestrians from the city, who had not thought the heat of the mid-day August sun too great to deter them. The archdeacon took his text from the Epistle of Philemon. "I beseech thee for my son Onesimus, whom I have begotten in my bonds." From such a text it may be imagined the kind of sermon which Dr. Grantly preached, and on the whole it was neither dull, nor bad, nor out of place.

He told them that it had become his duty to look about for a pastor for them, to supply the place of one who had been long among them; and that in this manner he regarded as a son him whom he had selected, as St. Paul had regarded the young disciple whom he sent forth. Then he took a little merit to himself for having studiously provided the best man he could without reference to patronage or favour; but he did not say that the best man according to his views was he who was best able to subdue Mr. Slope, and make that gentleman's situation in Barchester too hot to be comfortable. As to the bonds, they had consisted in the exceeding struggle which he had made to get a good clergyman for them. He deprecated any comparison between himself and St. Paul, but said that he was entitled to beseech them for their good will towards Mr. Arabin, in the same manner that the apostle had besought Philemon and his household with regard to Onesimus.

The archdeacon's sermon, text, blessing and all, was concluded within the half hour. Then they shook hands with their Ullathorne friends, and returned to Plumstead. 'Twas thus that Mr. Arabin read himself in at St. Ewold's.

CHAPTER XXI

MR. SLOPE MANAGES MATTERS VERY CLEVERLY AT PUDDINGDALE

THE next two weeks passed pleasantly enough at Plumstead. The whole party there assembled seemed to get on well together. Eleanor made the house agreeable, and the archdeacon and Mrs. Grantly seemed to have forgotten her iniquity as regarded Mr. Slope. Mr. Harding had his violoncello, and played to them while his daughters accompanied him. Johnny Bold, by the help either of Mr. Rerechild or else by that of his coral and carrot-juice, got through his teething troubles. There had been gaieties too of all sorts. They had dined at Ullathorne, and the Thornes had dined at the Rectory. Eleanor had been duly put to stand on her box, and in that position had found herself quite unable to express her opinion on the merits of flounces, such having been the subject given to try her elocution. Mr. Arabin had of course been much in his own parish, looking to the doings at his vicarage, calling on his parishioners, and taking on himself the duties of his new calling. But still he had been every evening at Plumstead, and Mrs. Grantly was partly willing to agree with her husband that he was a pleasant inmate in a house.

They had also been at a dinner party at Dr. Stanhope's, of which Mr. Arabin had made one. He also, moth-like, burnt his wings in the flames of the signora's candle. Mrs. Bold, too, had been there, and had felt somewhat displeased with the taste, want of taste she called it, shown by Mr. Arabin in paying so much attention to Madame Neroni. It was as infallible that Madeline should displease and irritate the women, as that she should charm and captivate the men. The one result followed naturally on the other. It was quite true that Mr. Arabin had been charmed. He thought her a very clever and a very handsome woman; he thought also that her peculiar affliction entitled her to the sympathy of all. He had never, he said, met so much suffering joined to such perfect beauty and so clear a mind.

So things went on at Plumstead, and on the whole not unpleasantly, till a huge storm darkened the horizon, and came down upon the inhabitants of the rectory with all the fury of a water-spout. It was astonishing how in a few minutes the whole face of the heavens was changed. The party broke up from breakfast in perfect harmony; but fierce passions had arisen before the evening, which did not admit of their sitting at the same board for dinner. To explain this, it will be necessary to go back a little.

It will be remembered that the bishop expressed to Mr. Slope in his dressing-room, his determination that Mr. Quiverful should be confirmed in his appointment to the hospital, and that his lordship requested Mr. Slope to communicate this decision to the archdeacon. It will also be remembered that the archdeacon had indignantly declined seeing Mr. Slope, and had, instead, written a strong letter to the bishop, in which he all but demanded the situation of warden for Mr. Harding. To this letter the archdeacon received an immediate formal reply from Mr. Slope, in which it was stated that the bishop had received and would give his best consideration to the archdeacon's letter.

The archdeacon felt himself somewhat checkmated by this reply. What could he do with a man who would neither see him, nor argue with him by letter, and who had undoubtedly the power of appointing any clergyman he pleased? He had consulted with Mr. Arabin, who had suggested the propriety of calling in the aid of the master of Lazarus. "If," said he, "you and Dr. Gwynne formally declare your intention of waiting upon the bishop, the bishop will not dare to refuse to see you; and if two such men as you are see him together, you will probably not leave him without carrying your point."

The archdeacon did not quite like admitting the necessity of his being backed by the master of Lazarus before he could obtain admission into the episcopal palace of Barchester; but still he felt that the advice was good, and he resolved to take it. He wrote again to the bishop, expressing a hope that nothing further would be done in the matter of the hospital, till the consideration promised by his lordship had been given, and then sent off a warm appeal to his friend the master, imploring him to come to Plumstead and assist in driving the bishop into compliance. The master had rejoined, raising some difficulty, but not declining; and the archdeacon had again pressed his point, insisting on the necessity for immediate action. Dr. Gwynne unfortunately had the gout, and could therefore name no immediate day, but still agreed to come, if it should be finally found necessary. So the matter stood, as regarded the party at Plumstead.

But Mr. Harding had another friend fighting his battle for him, quite as powerful as the master of Lazarus, and this was Mr. Slope.

The bishop had declared that Mr. Quiverful should be the new warden. As Mr. Slope went down stairs prepared to see the archdeacon if necessary, but fully satisfied that no such necessity would arise, he declared to himself that Mr. Harding should be warden. With the object of carrying this point, he rode over to Puddingdale, and had a further interview with the worthy expectant of clerical good things.

Mrs. Quiverful, as soon as she saw his horse coming up the avenue from the vicarage gate, hastily packed up her huge basket of needlework, and hurried herself and her daughter out of the room in which she was sitting with her husband. "It's Mr. Slope," she said. "He's come to settle with you about the hospital. I do hope we shall now be able to move at once." And she hastened to bid the maid of all work go to the door, so that the welcome great man might not be kept waiting.

Mr. Slope thus found Mr. Quiverful alone. Mrs. Quiverful went off to her kitchen and back settlements with anxious beating heart, almost dreading that there might be some slip between the cup of her happiness and the lip of her fruition, but yet comforting herself with the reflection that after what had taken place, any such slip could hardly be possible.

Mr. Slope was all smiles as he shook his brother clergyman's hand, and said that he had ridden over because he thought it right at once to put Mr. Quiverful in possession of the facts of the matter regarding the wardenship of the hospital. As he spoke, the poor expectant husband and father saw at a glance that his brilliant hopes were to be dashed to the ground, and that his visitor was now there for the purpose of unsaying what on his former visit he had said. There was something in the tone of the voice, something in the glance of the eye, which told the tale. Mr. Quiverful knew it all at once.

CHAPTER XXII

A LOVE SCENE

MR. SLOPE returned from the Puddingdale with a feeling of considerable triumph. Not that he thought that his difficulties were all over; he did not so deceive himself; but he felt that he had played his first move well, as well as the pieces on the board would allow; and that he had nothing with which to reproach himself. He first of all posted the letter to the archbishop, and having made that sure he proceeded to push the advantage which he had gained. Had Mrs. Bold been at home, he would have called on her; but he knew that she was at Plumstead, so he wrote the following note. It was the beginning of what, he trusted, might be a long and tender series of epistles.

"My dear Mrs. Bold,—You will understand perfectly that I cannot at present correspond with your father. I heartily wish that I could, and hope the day may be not long distant when mists shall have cleared away, and we may know each other. But I cannot preclude myself from the pleasure of sending you these few lines to say that Mr. Q. has to-day, in my presence, resigned any title that he ever had to the wardenship of the hospital, and that the bishop has assured me that it is his intention to offer it to your esteemed father.

"Will you, with my respectful compliments, ask him, who I believe is now a fellow-visitor with you, to call on the bishop either on Wednesday or Thursday, between ten and one. *This is by the bishop's desire.* If you will so far oblige me as to let me have a line naming either day, and the hour which will suit Mr. Harding, I will take care that the servants shall have orders to show him in without delay. Perhaps I should say no more, —but still I wish you could make your father understand that no subject will be mooted between his lordship and him, which will refer at all to the method in which he may choose to perform his duty. I for one, am persuaded that no clergyman could perform it more satisfactorily than he did, or than he will do again.

"On a former occasion I was indiscreet and much too impatient, considering your father's age and my own. I hope he will not now refuse my apology. I still hope also that with your aid and sweet pious labours, we may live to attach such a Sabbath school to the old endowment, as may, by God's grace and furtherance, be a blessing to the poor of this city.

"You will see at once that this letter is confidential. The

subject, of course, makes it so. But, equally of course, it is for your parent's eye as well as for your own, should you think proper to show it to him.

"I hope my darling little friend Johnny is as strong as ever, —dear little fellow. Does he still continue his rude assaults on those beautiful long silken tresses?

"I can assure you your friends miss you from Barchester sorely; but it would be cruel to begrudge you your sojourn among flowers and fields during this truly sultry weather.

"Pray believe me, my dear Mrs. Bold,

"Yours most sincerely,

"OBADIAH SLOPE.

"Barchester, Friday."

Now this letter, taken as a whole, and with the consideration that Mr. Slope wished to assume a great degree of intimacy with Eleanor, would not have been bad, but for the allusion to the tresses. Gentlemen do not write to ladies about their tresses, unless they are on very intimate terms indeed. But Mr. Slope could not be expected to be aware of this. He longed to put a little affection into his epistle, and yet he thought it injudicious, as the letter would, he knew, be shown to Mr. Harding. He would have insisted that the letter should be strictly private and seen by no eyes but Eleanor's own, had he not felt that such an injunction would have been disobeyed. He therefore restrained his passion, did not sign himself "yours affectionately," and contented himself instead with the compliment to the tresses.

Having finished his letter, he took it to Mrs. Bold's house, and learning there, from the servant, that things were to be sent out to Plumstead that afternoon, left it, with many injunctions, in her hands.

We will now follow Mr. Slope so as to complete the day with him, and then return to his letter and its momentous fate in the next chapter.

There is an old song which gives us some very good advice about courting:—

It's gude to be off with the auld luve
Before ye be on wi' the new.

Of the wisdom of this maxim Mr. Slope was ignorant, and accordingly, having written his letter to Mrs. Bold, he proceeded to call upon the Signora Neroni. Indeed it was hard to say which was the old love and which the new. Mr. Slope having been smitten with both so nearly at the same time. Perhaps he thought it not amiss to have two strings to his bow. But two strings to Cupid's bow are always dangerous to him on whose behalf they are to be used. A man should remember that between two stools he may fall to the ground.

Mr. Slope having added to his person all such adornments as are possible to a clergyman making a morning visit, such as a clean neck tie, clean handkerchief, new gloves, and a *soupçon* of not unnecessary scent called about three o'clock at the doctor's door. At about this hour the signora was almost always alone in the back drawing-room. The mother had not come down. The doctor was out or in his own room. Bertie was out, and Charlotte at any rate left the room if any one called whose object was specially with her sister. Such was her idea of being charitable and sisterly.

Mr. Slope, as was his custom, asked for Mr. Stanhope, and was told, as was the servant's custom, that the signora was in the drawing-room. Upstairs he accordingly went. He found her, as he always did, lying on her sofa with a French volume before her, and a beautiful little inlaid writing case open on her table. At the moment of his entrance she was in the act of writing.

"Ah my friend," said she, putting out her left hand to him across her desk, "I did not expect you to-day and was this very instant writing to you——"

Mr. Slope, taking the soft fair delicate hand in his, and very soft and fair and delicate it was, bowed over it his huge red head and kissed it. It was a sight to see, a deed to record if the author could fitly do it, a picture to put on canvass. Mr. Slope was big, awkward, cumbrous, and having his heart in his pursuit was ill at ease. The lady was fair, as we have said, and delicate; every thing about her was fine and refined; her hand in his looked like a rose lying among carrots, and when he kissed it he looked as a cow might do on finding such a flower among her food. She was graceful as a couchant goddess, and, moreover, as self-possessed as Venus must have been when courting Adonis.

Oh, that such grace and such beauty should have condescended to waste itself on such a pursuit!

"I was in the act of writing to you," said she, "but now my scrawl may go into the basket;" and she raised the sheet of gilded note paper from off her desk as though to tear it.

"Indeed it shall not," said he, laying the embargo of half a stone weight of human flesh and blood upon the devoted paper. "Nothing that you write for my eyes, signora, shall be so desecrated," and he took up the letter, put that also among the carrots and fed on it, and then proceeded to read it.

"Gracious me! Mr. Slope," said she, "I hope you don't mean to say that you keep all the trash I write to you. Half my time I don't know what I write, and when I do, I know it is only fit for the back of the fire. I hope you have not that ugly trick of keeping letters."

"At any rate, I don't throw them into a waste-paper basket. If destruction is their doomed lot, they perish worthily, and are burnt on a pyre, as Dido was of old."

"With a steel pen stuck through them, of course," said she, "to make the simile more complete. Of all the ladies of my acquaintance I think Lady Dido was the most absurd. Why did she not do as Cleopatra did? Why did she not take out her ships and insist on going with him? She could not bear to lose the land she had got by a swindle; and then she could not bear the loss of her lover. So she fell between two stools. Mr. Slope, whatever you do, never mingle love and business."

"Your love should be sufficient to satisfy the dream of a monarch," said Mr. Slope, not quite clear as to the meaning of his words.

"Say an archbishop, Mr. Slope," said she. Poor fellow! she was very cruel to him. He went round again upon his cork on this allusion to his profession. He tried, however, to smile, and gently accused her of joking on a matter, which was, he said, to him of such vital moment.

"Why—what gulls do you men make of us," she replied. "How you fool us to the top of our bent; and of all men you clergymen are the most fluent of your honeyed caressing words. Now look me in the face, Mr. Slope, boldly and openly."

Mr. Slope did look at her with a languishing loving eye, and as he did so, he again put forth his hand to get hold of hers.

"I told you to look at me boldly, Mr. Slope; but confine your boldness to your eyes."

"Oh, Madeline!" he sighed.

"Well, my name is Madeline," said she; "but none except my own family usually call me so. Now look me in the face, Mr. Slope. Am I to understand that you say you love me?"

Mr. Slope never had said so. If he had come there with any formed plan at all, his intention was to make love to the lady without uttering any such declaration. It was, however, quite impossible that he should now deny his love. He had, therefore, nothing for it, but to go down on his knees distractedly against the sofa, and swear that he did love her with a love passing the love of man.

The signora received the assurance with very little palpitation or appearance of surprise. "And now answer me another question," said she; "when are you to be married to my dear friend Eleanor Bold?"

Poor Mr. Slope went round and round in mortal agony. In such a condition as his it was really very hard for him to know what answer to give. And yet no answer would be his surest condemnation. He might as well at once plead guilty to the charge brought against him.

"And why do you accuse me of such dissimulation?" said he.

"Dissimulation! I said nothing of dissimulation. I made no charge against you, and make none. Pray don't defend yourself to me. You swear that you are devoted to my beauty, and yet you are on the eve of matrimony with another. I feel this to be rather a compliment. It is to Mrs. Bold that you must defend yourself. That you may find difficult; unless, indeed, you can keep her in the dark. You clergymen are cleverer than other men."

"Signora, I have told you that I loved you, and now you rail at me?"

"Rail at you. God bless the man; what would he have? Come, answer me this at your leisure,—not without thinking now, but leisurely and with consideration,—Are you not going to be married to Mrs. Bold?"

"I am not," said he. And as he said it, he almost hated, with an exquisite hatred, the woman whom he could not help loving with an exquisite love.

"But surely you are a worshipper of hers?"

"I am not," said Mr. Slope, to whom the word worshipper was peculiarly distasteful. The signora had conceived that it would be so.

"I wonder at that," said she. "Do you not admire her? To my eye she is the perfection of English beauty. And then she is rich too. I should have thought she was just the person to attract you. Come, Mr. Slope, let me give you advice on this matter. Marry the charming widow! she will be a good mother to your children, and an excellent mistress of a clergyman's household."

"Oh, signora, how can you be so cruel?"

"Cruel," said she, changing the voice of banter which she had been using for one which was expressively earnest in its tone; "is that cruelty?"

"How can I love another, while my heart is entirely your own?"

"If that were cruelty, Mr. Slope, what might you say of me if I were to declare that I returned your passion? What would you think if I bound you even by a lover's oath to do daily penance at this couch of mine? What can I give in return for a man's love? Ah, dear friend, you have not realised the conditions of my fate."

"Were you free to marry, I would take you to my house to-morrow and wish no higher privilege."

"I am free;" said she, almost starting up in her energy. For though there was no truth in her pretended regard for her clerical admirer, there was a mixture of real feeling in the scorn and satire with which she spoke of love and marriage generally. "I am free; free as the winds. Come; will you take me as I am? Have your wish: sacrifice the world, and prove yourself a true man."

Mr. Slope should have taken her at her word. She would have drawn back, and he would have had the full advantage of the offer. But he did not. Instead of doing so, he stood wrapt in astonishment, passing his fingers through his lank red hair, and thinking as he stared upon her animated countenance that her wondrous beauty grew more and more wonderful as he gazed on it. "Ha! ha! ha!" she laughed out loud. "Come Mr. Slope; don't talk of sacrificing the world again. People beyond one-and-twenty should never dream of such a thing. You and I, if we have the dregs of any love left in us, if we have the remnants of a passion remaining in our hearts, should husband our resources better. We are not in our *première jeunesse*. The world is a very nice place. Your world, at any rate, is so. You have all manner of fat rectories to get, and possible bishoprics to enjoy. Come, confess; on second thoughts you would not sacrifice such things for the smiles of a lame lady?"

It was impossible for him to answer this. In order to be in any way dignified, he felt that he must be silent.

"Come," said she—"don't boody with me: don't be angry because I speak out some home truths. Alas, the world, as I have found it, has taught me bitter truth. Come, tell me that I am forgiven. Are we not to be friends?" and she again put out her hand to him.

He sat himself down in the chair beside her, and took her proffered hand and leant over her.

"There," said she, with her sweetest softest smile—a smile to withstand which a man should be cased in triple steel, "there; seal your forgiveness on it," and she raised it towards his face. He kissed it again and again, and stretched over her as though desirous of extending the charity of his pardon beyond the hand that was offered to him. She managed, however, to check his ardour. For one so easily allured as this poor chaplain, her hand was surely enough.

"Oh, Madeline!" said he, "tell me that you love me—do you— do you love me?"

"Hush," said she. "There is my mother's step. Our *tête-à-tête* has been of monstrous length. Now you had better go. But we shall see you soon again, shall we not?"

Mr. Slope promised that he would call again on the following day.

"And, Mr. Slope," she continued, "pray answer my note. You have it in your hand, though I declare during these two hours you have not been gracious enough to read it. It is about the Sabbath school and the children. You know how anxious I am to have them here. I have been learning the catechism myself, on purpose. You must manage it for me next week. I will teach them, at any rate, to submit themselves to their spiritual pastors and masters."

Mr. Slope said but little on the subject of Sabbath schools, but he made his adieu, and betook himself home with a sad heart, troubled mind, and uneasy conscience.

CHAPTER XXIII

MRS. BOLD IS ENTERTAINED BY DR. AND MRS. GRANTLY AT PLUMSTEAD

IT will be remembered that Mr. Slope, when leaving his *billet doux* at the house of Mrs. Bold, had been informed that it would be sent out to her at Plumstead that afternoon. The archdeacon and Mr. Harding had in fact come into town together in the brougham, and it had been arranged that they should call for Eleanor's parcels as they left on their way home. Accordingly they did so call, and the maid, as she handed to the coachman a small basket and large bundle carefully and neatly packed, gave in at the carriage window Mr. Slope's epistle. The archdeacon, who was sitting next to the window, took it, and immediately recognised the hand-writing of his enemy.

"Who left this?" said he.

"Mr. Slope called with it himself, your reverence," said the girl; "and was very anxious that missus should have it to-day."

So the brougham drove off, and the letter was left in the arch-deacon's hand. He looked at it as though he held a basket of adders. He could not have thought worse of the document had he read it and discovered it to be licentious and atheistical. He did, moreover, what so many wise people are accustomed to do in similar circumstances; he immediately condemned the person to whom the letter was written, as though she were necessarily a *particeps criminis*.

Poor Mr. Harding, though by no means inclined to forward Mr. Slope's intimacy with his daughter, would have given any-thing to have kept the letter from his son-in-law. But that was now impossible. There it was in his hand; and he looked as thoroughly disgusted as though he were quite sure that it contained all the rhapsodies of a favoured lover.

"It's very hard on me," said he, after awhile, "that this should go on under my roof."

"I think you are very hard upon Eleanor," replied Mr. Harding. "I will not allow that she has disgraced herself, nor do I think it likely that she will do so. She has a right to correspond with whom she pleases, and I shall not take upon myself to blame her because she gets a letter from Slope."

"I suppose," said Dr. Grantly, "you don't wish her to marry the man. I suppose you'll admit that she would disgrace herself if she did do so."

"I do not wish her to marry him," said the perplexed father; "I do not like him, and do not think he would make a good husband. But if Eleanor chooses to do so, I shall certainly not think that she disgraces herself."

"Good heavens!" exclaimed Dr. Grantly, and threw himself back into the corner of his brougham. Mr. Harding said nothing more, but commenced playing a dirge, with an imaginary fiddle bow upon an imaginary violoncello, for which there did not appear to be quite room enough in the carriage; and he con-tinued the tune, with sundry variations, till he arrived at the rectory door.

The archdeacon had been meditating sad things in his mind. Hitherto he had always looked on his father-in-law as a true partisan, though he knew him to be a man devoid of all the combative qualifications for that character. He had felt no fear that Mr. Harding would go over to the enemy, though he had never counted much on the ex-warden's prowess in breaking the hostile ranks. Now, however, it seemed that Eleanor, with her wiles, had completely trepanned and bewildered her father, cheated him out of his judgment, robbed him of the predilections and tastes of his life, and caused him to be tolerant of a man whose arrogance and vulgarity would, a few years since, have been unendurable to him. That the whole thing was as good as arranged between Eleanor and Mr. Slope there was no longer any room to doubt. That Mr. Harding knew that such was the case, even this could hardly be doubted. It was too manifest that he at any rate suspected it, and was prepared to sanction it.

And thus these two men, each miserable enough in his own way, returned to Plumstead.

It was getting late when they arrived there, and the ladies had already gone up to dress. Nothing more was said as the two parted in the hall. As Mr. Harding passed to his own room he knocked at Eleanor's door and handed in the letter. The archdeacon hurried to his own territory, there to unburden his heart to his faithful partner.

What colloquy took place between the marital chamber and the adjoining dressing-room shall not be detailed. The reader, now intimate with the persons concerned, can well imagine it. The whole tenor of it also might be read in Mrs. Grantly's brow as she came down to dinner.

Eleanor, when she received the letter from her father's hand, had no idea from whom it came. She had never seen Mr. Slope's hand-writing, or if so had forgotten it; and did not think of him as she twisted the letter as people do twist letters when they do not immediately recognise their correspondents either by the writing or the seal. She was sitting at her glass brushing her hair, and rising every other minute to play with her boy who was sprawling on the bed, and who engaged pretty nearly the whole attention of the maid as well as of his mother.

At last, sitting before her toilet table, she broke the seal, and turning over the leaf saw Mr. Slope's name. She first felt surprised, and then annoyed, and then anxious. As she read it she became interested. She was so delighted to find that all obstacles to her father's return to the hospital were apparently removed that she did not observe the fulsome language in which the tidings were conveyed. She merely perceived that she was commissioned to tell her father that such was the case, and she did not realise the fact that such a communication should not have been made, in the first instance, to her by an unmarried young clergyman. She felt, on the whole, grateful to Mr. Slope, and anxious to get on her dress.

D

that she might run with the news to her father. Then she came to
the allusion to her own pious labours, and she said in her heart
that Mr. Slope was an affected ass. Then she went on again and
was offended by her boy being called Mr. Slope's darling—he
was nobody's darling but her own; or at any rate not the darling
of a disagreeable stranger like Mr. Slope. Lastly she arrived at
the tresses and felt a qualm of disgust. She looked up in the glass,
and there they were before her, long and silken, certainly, and very
beautiful. I will not say but that she knew them to be so, but
she felt angry with them and brushed them roughly and carelessly.
She crumpled the letter up with angry violence, and resolved,
almost without thinking of it, that she would not show it to her
father. She would merely tell him the contents of it. She then
comforted herself again with her boy, had her dress fastened, and
went down to dinner.

As she tripped down the stairs she began to ascertain that there
was some difficulty in her situation. She could not keep from her
father the news about the hospital, nor could she comfortably
confess the letter from Mr. Slope before the Grantlys. Her father
had already gone down. She had heard his step upon the lobby.
She resolved therefore to take him aside, and tell him her little
bit of news. Poor girl! she had no idea how severely the unfortunate
letter had already been discussed.

When she entered the drawing-room the whole party were there,
including Mr. Arabin, and the whole party looked glum and sour.
The two girls sat silent and apart as though they were aware that
something was wrong. Even Mr. Arabin was solemn and silent.
Eleanor had not seen him since breakfast. He had been the whole
day at St. Ewold's, and such having been the case it was natural
that he should tell how matters were going on there. He did nothing
of the kind, however, but remained solemn and silent. They were
all solemn and silent. Eleanor knew in her heart that they had been
talking about her, and her heart misgave her as she thought of
Mr. Slope and his letter. At any rate she felt it to be quite impossible
to speak to her father alone while matters were in this state.

Dinner was soon announced, and Dr. Grantly, as was his wont,
gave Eleanor his arm. But he did so as though the doing it were
an outrage on his feelings rendered necessary by sternest necessity.
With quick sympathy Eleanor felt this, and hardly put her fingers
on his coat sleeve. It may be guessed in what way the dinner-hour
was passed. Dr. Grantly said a few words to Mr. Arabin, Mr.
Arabin said a few words to Mrs. Grantly, she said a few words to
her father, and he tried to say a few words to Eleanor. She felt
that she had been tried and found guilty of something, though she
knew not what. She longed to say out to them all, "Well, what is
it that I have done; out with it, and let me know my crime; for
heaven's sake let me hear the worst of it;" but she could not. She

could say nothing, but sat there silent, half feeling that she was guilty, and trying in vain to pretend even to eat her dinner.

At last the cloth was drawn, and the ladies were not long following it. When they were gone the gentlemen were somewhat more sociable but not much so. They could not of course talk over Eleanor's sins. The archdeacon had indeed so far betrayed his sister-in-law as to whisper into Mr. Arabin's ear in the study, as they met there before dinner, a hint of what he feared. He did so with the gravest and saddest of fears, and Mr. Arabin became grave and apparently sad enough as he heard it. He opened his eyes and his mouth and said in a sort of whisper "Mr. Slope!" in the same way as he might have said "The Cholera!" had his friend told him that that horrid disease was in his nursery. "I fear so, I fear so," said the archdeacon, and then together they left the room.

Thus the three men sat over their wine, all thinking of the same subject, but unable to speak of it to each other. So we will leave them, and follow the ladies into the drawing-room.

Mrs. Grantly had received a commission from her husband, and had undertaken it with some unwillingness. He had desired her to speak gravely to Eleanor, and to tell her that, if she persisted in her adherence to Mr. Slope, she could no longer look for the countenance of her present friends. Mrs. Grantly probably knew her sister better than the doctor did, and assured him that it would be in vain to talk to her. The only course likely to be of any service in her opinion was to keep Eleanor away from Barchester. Perhaps she might have added, for she had a very keen eye in such things, that there might also be ground for hope in keeping Eleanor near Mr. Arabin. Of this, however, she said nothing. But the arch-deacon would not be talked over, he spoke much of his conscience, and declared that if Mrs. Grantly would not do it he would. So instigated, the lady undertook the task, stating, however, her full conviction that her interference would be worse than useless. And so it proved.

As soon as they were in the drawing-room Mrs. Grantly found some excuse for sending her girls away, and then began her task. She knew well that she could exercise but very slight authority over her sister. Their various modes of life, and the distance between their residences, had prevented any very close confidence. They had hardly lived together since Eleanor was a child. Eleanor had moreover, especially in latter years, resented in a quiet sort of way the dictatorial authority which the archdeacon seemed to exercise over her father, and on this account had been unwilling to allow the archdeacon's wife to exercise authority over herself.

"You got a note just before dinner, I believe," began the eldest sister.

Eleanor acknowledged that she had done so, and felt that she turned red as she acknowledged it. She would have given anything to have kept her colour, but the more she tried to do so the more signally she failed.

"Was it not from Mr. Slope?"

Eleanor said that the letter was from Mr. Slope.

"Is he a regular correspondent of yours, Eleanor?"

"Not exactly," said she, already beginning to feel angry at the cross-examination. She determined, and why it would be difficult to say, that nothing should induce her to tell her sister Susan what was the subject of the letter. Mrs. Grantly, she knew, was instigated by the archdeacon, and she would not plead to any arraignment made against her by him.

"But, Eleanor dear, why do you get letters from Mr. Slope at all, knowing, as you do, he is a person so distasteful to papa, and to the archdeacon, and indeed to all your friends?"

"In the first place, Susan, I don't get letters from him; and in the next place, as Mr. Slope wrote the one letter which I have got, and as I only received it, which I could not very well help doing, as papa handed it to me, I think you had better ask Mr. Slope instead of me."

"What was his letter about, Eleanor?"

"I cannot tell you," said she, "because it was confidential. It was on business respecting a third person."

"It was in no way personal to yourself, then?"

"I won't exactly say that, Susan," said she, getting more and more angry at her sister's questions.

"Well, I must say it's rather singular," said Mrs. Grantly, affecting to laugh, "that a young lady in your position should receive a letter from an unmarried gentleman of which she will not tell the contents, and which she is ashamed to show to her sister."

"I am not ashamed," said Eleanor blazing up; "I am not ashamed of anything in the matter, only I do not choose to be cross-examined as to my letters by any one."

"Well, dear," said the other, "I cannot but tell you that I do not think Mr. Slope a proper correspondent for you."

"If he be ever so improper, how can I help his having written to me? But you are all prejudiced against him to such an extent, that that which would be kind and generous in another man is odious and impudent in him. I hate a religion that teaches one to be so onesided in one's charity."

"I am sorry, Eleanor, that you hate the religion you find here; but surely you should remember in such matters the archdeacon must know more of the world than you do. I don't ask you to respect or comply with me, although I am, unfortunately, so many years your senior; but surely, in such a matter as this, you might consent to be guided by the archdeacon. He is most anxious to be your friend if you will let him."

"In such a matter as what?" said Eleanor very testily. "Upon my word I don't know what this is all about."

"We all want you to drop Mr. Slope."

"You all want me to be as illiberal as yourselves. That I shall never be. I see no harm in Mr. Slope's acquaintance, and I shall not insult the man by telling him that I do. He has thought it necessary to write to me, and I do not want the archdeacon's advice about the letter. If I did I would ask it."

"Then, Eleanor, it is my duty to tell you," and now she spoke with a tremendous gravity, "that the archdeacon thinks that such a correspondence is disgraceful, and that he cannot allow it to go on in his house."

Eleanor's eyes flashed fire as she answered her sister, jumping up from her seat as she did so. "You may tell the archdeacon that wherever I am I shall receive what letters I please and from whom I please. And as for the word disgraceful, if Dr. Grantly has used it of me he has been unmanly and inhospitable," and she walked off to the door. "When papa comes from the dining-room I will thank you to ask him to step up to my bed-room. I will show him Mr. Slope's letter, but I will show it to no one else." And so saying she retreated to her baby.

She had not been long in her room before her father joined her. As he left the drawing-room Mrs. Grantly took her husband into the recess of the window, and told him how signally she had failed.

"I will speak to her myself before I go to bed," said the archdeacon.

"Pray do no such thing," said she; "you can do no good and will only make an unseemly quarrel in the house. You have no idea how headstrong she can be."

Mr. Harding looked worn and woebegone as he entered his daughter's room. These sorrows worried him sadly. He felt that if they were continued he must go to the wall in the manner so kindly prophesied to him by the chaplain. He knocked gently at his daughter's door, waited till he was distinctly bade to enter, and then appeared as though he and not she were the suspected criminal.

Eleanor's arm was soon within his, and she had soon kissed his forehead and caressed him, not with joyous but with eager love. "Oh, papa," she said, "I do so want to speak to you. They have been talking about me down stairs to-night; don't you know they have, papa?"

Mr. Harding confessed with a sort of murmur that the archdeacon had been speaking of her.

"I shall hate Dr. Grantly soon——"

"Oh my dear!"

"Well; I shall. I cannot help it. He is so uncharitable, so unkind, so suspicious of every one that does not worship himself: and then he is so monstrously arrogant to other people who have a right to their opinions as well as he has to his own."

"He is an earnest, eager man, my dear: but he never means to be unkind."

"He is unkind, papa, most unkind. There, I got that letter from Mr. Slope before dinner. It was you yourself who gave it to me. There; pray read it. It is all for you. It should have been addressed to you. You know how they have been talking about it down stairs. You know how they behaved to me at dinner. And since dinner Susan has been preaching to me, till I could not remain in the room with her. Read it, papa; and then say whether that is a letter that need make Dr. Grantly so outrageous."

Mr. Harding took his arm from his daughter's waist, and slowly read the letter. She expected to see his countenance lit with joy as he learnt that his path back to the hospital was made so smooth; but she was doomed to disappointment, as had once been the case before on a somewhat similar occasion. His first feeling was one of unmitigated disgust that Mr. Slope should have chosen to interfere in his behalf. He had been anxious to get back to the hospital, but he would have infinitely sooner resigned all pretensions to the place, than have owed it in any manner to Mr. Slope's influence in his favour. Then he thoroughly disliked the tone of Mr. Slope's letter; it was unctuous, false, and unwholesome, like the man. He saw, which Eleanor had failed to see, that much more had been intended than was expressed. The appeal to Eleanor's pious labours as separate from his own grated sadly against his feelings as a father. And then when he came to the "darling boy" and the "silken tresses," he slowly closed and folded the letter in despair. It was impossible that Mr. Slope should so write unless he had been encouraged. It was impossible Eleanor should have received such a letter, and have received it without annoyance, unless she were willing to encourage him. So at least Mr. Harding argued to himself.

And he, foolish weak loving man, would not say one word, though one word would have cleared up everything. There would have been a deluge of tears, and in ten minutes every one in the house would have understood how matters really were. The father would have been delighted. The sister would have kissed her sister and begged a thousand pardons. The archdeacon would have apologised and wondered, and raised his eyebrows, and gone to bed a happy man. And Mr. Arabin—Mr. Arabin would have dreamt of Eleanor, have awoke in the morning with ideas of love, and retired to rest the next evening with schemes of marriage. But, alas! all this was not to be.

Mr. Harding slowly folded the letter, handed it back to her, kissed her forehead and bade God bless her. He then crept slowly away to his own room.

As soon as he had left the passage another knock was given at Eleanor's door, and Mrs. Grantly's very demure own maid, entering on tiptoe, wanted to know would Mrs. Bold be so kind as to speak to the archdeacon for two minutes, in the archdeacon's study, if not disagreeable. The archdeacon's compliments, and he wouldn't detain her two minutes.

Eleanor thought it was very disagreeable; she was tired and fagged and sick at heart; her present feelings towards Dr. Grantly were anything but those of affection. She was, however, no coward, and therefore promised to be in the study in five minutes. So she arranged her hair, tied on her cap, and went down with a palpitating heart.

CHAPTER XXIV

A SERIOUS INTERVIEW

THERE are people who delight in serious interviews, especially when to them appertains the part of offering advice or administering rebuke, and perhaps the archdeacon was one of these. Yet on this occasion he did not prepare himself for the coming conversation with much anticipation of pleasure. Whatever might be his faults he was not an inhospitable man, and he almost felt that he was sinning against hospitality in upbraiding Eleanor in his own house. Then, also he was not quite sure that he would get the best of it. His wife had told him that he decidedly would not, and he usually gave credit to what his wife said. He was, however, so convinced of what he considered to be the impropriety of Eleanor's conduct, and so assured also of his own duty in trying to check it, that his conscience would not allow him to take his wife's advice and go to bed quietly.

Eleanor's face as she entered the room was not such as to reassure him. As a rule she was always mild in manner and gentle in conduct; but there was that in her eye which made it not an easy task to scold her. In truth she had been little used to scolding. No one since her childhood had tried it but the archdeacon, and he had generally failed when he did try it. He had never done so since her marriage; and now, when he saw her quiet easy step, as she entered his room, he almost wished that he had taken his wife's advice.

He began by apologising for the trouble he was giving her. She begged him not to mention it, assured him that walking down stairs was no trouble to her at all, and then took a seat and waited patiently for him to begin his attack.

"My dear Eleanor," he said, "I hope you believe me when I assure you that you have no sincerer friend than I am." To this Eleanor answered nothing, and therefore he proceeded. "If you had a brother of your own I should not probably trouble you with what I am going to say. But as it is I cannot but think that it must be a comfort to you to know that you have near you one who is as anxious for your welfare as any brother of your own could be."

"I never had a brother," said she.

"I know you never had, and it is therefore that I speak to you."

"I never had a brother," she repeated; "but I have hardly felt the want. Papa has been to me both father and brother."

"Your father is the fondest and most affectionate of men. But—"

"He is—the fondest and most affectionate of men, and the best of counsellors. While he lives I can never want advice."

This rather put the archdeacon out. He could not exactly contradict what his sister-in-law said about her father; and yet he did not at all agree with her. He wanted her to understand that he tendered his assistance because her father was a soft good-natured gentleman, not sufficiently knowing in the ways of the world; but he could not say this to her. So he had to rush into the subject-matter of his proffered counsel without any acknowledgment on her part that she could need it, or would be grateful for it.

"Susan tells me that you received a letter this evening from Mr. Slope."

"Yes; papa brought it in the brougham. Did he not tell you?"

"And Susan says that you objected to let her know what it was about."

"I don't think she asked me. But had she done so I should not have told her. I don't think it nice to be asked about one's letters. If one wishes to show them one does so without being asked."

"True. Quite so. What you say is quite true. But is not the fact of your receiving letters from Mr. Slope, which you do not wish to show to your friends, a circumstance which must excite some—some surprise—some suspicion—"

"Suspicion!" said she, not speaking above her usual voice, speaking still in a soft womanly tone, but yet with indignation; "suspicion! and who suspects me, and of what?" And then there was a pause, for the archdeacon was not quite ready to explain the ground of his suspicion. "No, Dr. Grantly, I did not choose to show Mr. Slope's letter to Susan. I could not show it to any one till papa had seen it. If you have any wish to read it now, you can do so," and she handed the letter to him over the table.

This was an amount of compliance which he had not at all expected, and which rather upset him in his tactics. However, he took the letter, perused it carefully, and then refolding it, kept it on the table under his hand. To him it appeared to be in almost every respect the letter of a declared lover; it seemed to corroborate his worst suspicions; and the fact of Eleanor's showing it to him was all but tantamount to a declaration on her part, that it was her pleasure to receive love-letters from Mr. Slope. He almost entirely overlooked the real subject-matter of the epistle; so intent was he on the forthcoming courtship and marriage.

"I'll thank you to give it me back, if you please, Dr. Grantly."

He took it in his hand and held it up, but made no immediate overture to return it. "And Mr. Harding has seen this?" said he.

"Of course he has," said she; "it was written that he might see it. It refers solely to his business—of course I showed it to him."

"And, Eleanor, do you think that is a proper letter for you—for a person in your condition—to receive from Mr. Slope?"

"Quite a proper letter," said she, speaking, perhaps, a little out of obstinacy; probably forgetting at the moment the objectionable mention of her silken curls.

"Then, Eleanor, it is my duty to tell you that I wholly differ from you."

"So I suppose," said she, instigated now by sheer opposition and determination not to succumb. "You think Mr. Slope is a messenger direct from Satan. I think he is an industrious, well meaning clergyman. It's a pity that we differ as we do. But, as we do differ, we had probably better not talk about it."

"Eleanor, you are forgetting yourself," said he, looking very sternly at her. "Otherwise you would never tell me that I conceive any man to be a messenger from Satan."

"But you do," said she. "Nothing is too bad for him. Give me that letter, if you please;" and she stretched out her hand and took it from him. "He has been doing his best to serve papa, doing more than any of papa's friends could do; and yet, because he is the chaplain of a bishop whom you don't like, you speak of him as though he had no right to the usage of a gentleman."

"He has done nothing for your father."

"I believe that he has done a great deal; and, as far as I am concerned, I am grateful to him. Nothing that you can say can prevent my being so. I judge people by their acts, and his, as far as I can see them, are good." She then paused for a moment. "If you have nothing further to say, I shall be obliged by being permitted to say good night—I am very tired."

Dr. Grantly had, as he thought, done his best to be gracious to his sister-in-law. He had endeavoured not to be harsh to her, and had striven to pluck the sting from his rebuke. But he did not intend that she should leave him without hearing him.

"I have something to say, Eleanor; and I fear I must trouble you to hear it. You profess that it is quite proper that you should receive from Mr. Slope such letters as that you have in your hand. Susan and I think very differently. You are, of course, your own mistress, and much as we both must grieve should anything separate you from us, we have no power to prevent you from taking steps which may lead to such a separation. If you are so wilful as to reject the counsel of your friends, you must be allowed to cater for yourself. But Eleanor, I may at any rate ask you this. Is it worth your while to break away from all those you have loved—from all who love you—for the sake of Mr. Slope?"

"I don't know what you mean, Dr. Grantly; I don't know what you're talking about. I don't want to break away from anybody."

"But you will do so if you connect yourself with Mr. Slope. Eleanor, I must speak out to you. You must choose between your sister and myself and our friends, and Mr. Slope and his friends. I say nothing of your father, as you may probably understand his feelings better than I do."

"What do you mean, Dr. Grantly? What am I to understand? I never heard such wicked prejudice in my life."

"It is no prejudice, Eleanor. I have known the world longer than you have done. Mr. Slope is altogether beneath you. You ought to know and feel that he is so. Pray—pray think of this before it is too late."

"Too late!"

"Or if you will not believe me, ask Susan; you cannot think she is prejudiced against you. Or even consult your father, he is not prejudiced against you. Ask Mr. Arabin——"

"You haven't spoken to Mr. Arabin about this!" said she, jumping up and standing before him.

"Eleanor, all the world in and about Barchester will be speaking of it soon."

"But have you spoken to Mr. Arabin about me and Mr. Slope?"

"Certainly I have, and he quite agrees with me."

"Agrees with what?" said she. "I think you are trying to drive me mad."

"He agrees with me and Susan that it is quite impossible you should be received at Plumstead as Mrs. Slope."

Not being favourites with the tragic muse we do not dare to attempt any description of Eleanor's face when she first heard the name of Mrs. Slope pronounced as that which would or should or might at some time appertain to herself. The look, such as it was, Dr. Grantly did not soon forget. For a moment or two she could find no words to express her deep anger and deep disgust; and, indeed, at this conjuncture, words did not come to her very freely.

"How dare you be so impertinent?" at last she said; and then hurried out of the room, without giving the archdeacon the opportunity of uttering another word. It was with difficulty she contained herself till she reached her own room; and then locking the door, she threw herself on her bed and sobbed as though her heart would break.

But even yet she had no conception of the truth. She had no idea that her father and her sister had for days past conceived in sober earnest the idea that she was going to marry this man. She did not even then believe that the archdeacon thought that she would do so. By some manœuvre of her brain, she attributed the origin of the accusation to Mr. Arabin, and as she did so her anger against him was excessive, and the vexation of her spirit almost unendurable. She could not bring herself to think that the charge was made seriously. It appeared to her most probable that the archdeacon and Mr. Arabin had talked over her objectionable acquaintance with Mr. Slope; that Mr. Arabin, in his jeering, sarcastic way, had suggested the odious match as being the severest way of treating with contumely her acquaintance with his enemy; and that the archdeacon, taking the idea from him, thought proper to punish her by the allusion. The whole night she lay awake thinking of what had been said, and this appeared to be the most probable solution.

But the reflection that Mr. Arabin should have in any way mentioned her name in connection with that of Mr. Slope was overpowering; and the spiteful ill-nature of the archdeacon, in repeating the charge to her, made her wish to leave his house almost before the day had broken. One thing was certain: nothing should make her stay there beyond the following morning, and nothing should make her sit down to breakfast in company with Dr. Grantly. When she thought of the man whose name had been linked with her own, she cried from sheer disgust. It was only because she would be thus disgusted, thus pained and shocked and cut to the quick, that the archdeacon had spoken the horrid word. He wanted to make her quarrel with Mr. Slope, and therefore he had outraged her by his abominable vulgarity. She determined that at any rate he should know that she appreciated it.

Nor was the archdeacon a bit better satisfied with the result of his serious interview than was Eleanor. He gathered from it, as indeed he could hardly fail to do, that she was very angry with him; but he thought that she was thus angry, not because she was suspected of an intention to marry Mr. Slope, but because such an intention was imputed to her as a crime. Dr. Grantly regarded this supposed union with disgust; but it never occurred to him that Eleanor was outraged, because she looked at it exactly in the same light.

On the following morning Eleanor's maid was commissioned to send word into the dining-room that her mistress was not well enough to attend prayers, and that she would breakfast in her own room. Here she was visited by her father and declared to him her intention of returning immediately to Barchester. He was hardly surprised by the announcement. All the household seemed to be aware that something had gone wrong. Every one walked about with subdued feet, and people's shoes seemed to creak more than usual. There was a look of conscious intelligence on the faces of the women: and the men attempted, but in vain, to converse as though nothing were the matter. All this had weighed heavily on the heart of Mr. Harding; and when Eleanor told him that her immediate return to Barchester was a necessity, he merely sighed piteously, and said that he would be ready to accompany her.

But here she objected strenuously. She had a great wish, she said, to go alone; a great desire that it might be seen that her father was not implicated in her quarrel with Dr. Grantly. To this at last he gave way; but not a word passed between them about Mr. Slope—not a word was said, not a question asked as to the serious interview on the preceding evening. There was, indeed, very little confidence between them, though neither of them knew why it should be so. Eleanor once asked him whether he would not call upon the bishop; but he answered rather tartly that he did not know—he did not think he should, but he could not say just at present. And so they parted. Each was miserably anxious for some show of affection, for some return of confidence, for some sign of the feeling that usually bound them together. But none was given. The father could not bring himself to question his daughter about her supposed lover; and the daughter would not sully her mouth by repeating the odious word with which Dr. Grantly had roused her wrath. And so they parted.

There was some trouble in arranging the method of Eleanor's return. She begged her father to send for a postchaise; but when Mrs. Grantly heard of this, she objected strongly. If Eleanor would go away in dudgeon with the archdeacon, why should she let all the servants and all the neighbourhood know that she had done so? So at last Eleanor consented to make use of the Plumstead carriage; and as the archdeacon had gone out immediately after breakfast and was not to return till dinner-time, she also consented to postpone her journey till after lunch, and to join the family at that time. As to the subject of the quarrel not a word was said by any one. The affair of the carriage was arranged by Mr. Harding, who acted as Mercury between the two ladies; they, when they met, kissed each other very lovingly, and then sat down each to her crochet work as though nothing was amiss in all the world.

CHAPTER XXV

ANOTHER LOVE SCENE

BUT there was another visitor at the rectory whose feelings in this unfortunate matter must be somewhat strictly analysed. Mr. Arabin had heard from his friend of the probability of Eleanor's marriage with Mr. Slope with amazement, but not with incredulity. It has been said that he was not in love with Eleanor, and up to this period this certainly had been true. But as soon as he heard that she loved some one else, he began to be very fond of her himself. He did not make up his mind that he wished to have her for his wife; he had never thought of her, and did not now think of her, in connection with himself; but he experienced an inward indefinable feeling of deep regret, a gnawing sorrow, an unconquerable depression of spirits, and also a species of self-abasement that he—he Mr. Arabin—had not done something to prevent that other he, that vile he, whom he so thoroughly depised, from carrying off this sweet prize.

Eleanor had not passed a pleasant morning. She was irritated with every one, and not least with herself. She felt that she had been hardly used, but she felt also that she had not played her own cards well. She should have held herself so far above suspicion as to have received her sister's innuendoes and the archdeacon's lecture with indifference. She had not done this, but had shown herself angry and sore, and was now ashamed of her own petulance, and yet unable to discontinue it.

The greater part of the morning she had spent alone; but after a while her father joined her. He had fully made up his mind that, come what come might, nothing should separate him from his younger daughter.

He was sitting with her in the drawing-room, with his arm round her waist, saying every now and then some little soft words of affection, and working hard with his imaginary fiddle-bow, when Mr. Arabin entered the room. He immediately got up, and the two made some trite remarks to each other, neither thinking of what he was saying, while Eleanor kept her seat on the sofa mute and moody. Mr. Arabin was included in the list of those against whom her anger was excited. He, too, had dared to talk about her acquaintance with Mr. Slope; he, too, had dared to blame her for not making an enemy of his enemy. She had not intended to see him before her departure, and was now but little inclined to be gracious.

There was a feeling through the whole house that something was wrong. Mr. Arabin, when he saw Eleanor, could not succeed in looking or in speaking as though he knew nothing of all this.

"I am sorry to hear that you are to leave us so soon," said he, striving in vain to use his ordinary voice. In answer to this she muttered something about the necessity of her being in Barchester, and betook herself most industriously to her crochet work.

Then there was a little more trite conversation between Mr. Arabin and Mr. Harding; trite, and hard, and vapid, and senseless. Neither of them had anything to say to the other, and yet neither at such a moment liked to remain silent. At last Mr. Harding, taking advantage of a pause, escaped out of the room, and Eleanor and Mr. Arabin were left together.

"We have had a very pleasant month here," said he; "at least I have, and I am sorry it should be so soon over."

"I have already been from home longer than I intended," said she; "and it is time that I should return."

"Well, pleasant hours and pleasant days must come to an end. It is a pity that so few of them are pleasant; or perhaps, rather——"

"It is a pity, certainly, that men and women do so much to destroy the pleasantness of their days," said she, interrupting him. "It is a pity that there should be so little charity abroad."

"Charity should begin at home," said he; and he was proceeding to explain that he as a clergyman could not be what she would call charitable at the expense of those principles which he considered it his duty to teach, when he remembered that it would be worse than vain to argue on such a matter with the future wife of Mr. Slope. "But you are just leaving us," he continued, "and I will not weary your last hour with another lecture. As it is, I fear I have given you too many."

She paused for a while, and then looking full in his face, she said, "You are not bold enough, Mr. Arabin, to speak out to me openly and plainly, and yet you expect me, a woman, to speak openly to you. Why did you speak calumny of me to Dr. Grantly behind my back?"

"Calumny!" said he, and his whole face became suffused with blood; "what calumny? If I have spoken calumny of you, I will beg your pardon, and his to whom I spoke it, and God's pardon also. But what calumny have I spoken of you to Dr. Grantly?"

She also blushed deeply. She could not bring herself to ask him whether he had not spoken of her as another man's wife. "You know that best yourself," said she; "but I ask you as a man of honour, if you have not spoken of me as you would not have spoken of your own sister; or rather I will not ask you," she continued, finding that he did not immediately answer her. "I will not put you to the necessity of answering such a question. Dr. Grantly has told me what you said."

"Dr. Grantly certainly asked me for my advice, and I gave it. He asked me——"

"I know he did, Mr. Arabin. He asked you whether he would be doing right to receive me at Plumstead, if I continued my acquaintance with a gentleman who happens to be personally disagreeable to yourself and to him?"

"You are mistaken, Mrs. Bold. I have no personal knowledge of Mr. Slope; I never met him in my life."

"You are not the less individually hostile to him. It is not for me to question the propriety of your enmity; but I had a right to expect that my name should not have been mixed up in your hostilities. This has been done, and been done by you in a manner the most injurious and the most distressing to me as a woman. I must confess, Mr. Arabin, that from you I expected a different sort of usage."

As she spoke she with difficulty restrained her tears; but she did restrain them. Had she given way and sobbed aloud, as in such cases a woman should do, he would have melted at once, implored her pardon, perhaps knelt at her feet and declared his love. Everything would have been explained, and Eleanor would have gone back to Barchester with a contented mind. How easily would she have forgiven and forgotten the archdeacon's suspicions had she but heard the whole truth from Mr. Arabin. But then where would have been my novel? She did not cry, and Mr. Arabin did not melt.

"You do me an injustice," said he. "My advice was asked by Dr. Grantly, and I was obliged to give it."

"Dr. Grantly has been most officious, most impertinent. I have as complete a right to form my acquaintance as he has to form his. What would you have said, and I consulted you as to the propriety of my banishing Dr. Grantly from my house because he knows Lord Tattenham Corner? I am sure Lord Tattenham is quite as objectionable an acquaintance for a clergyman as Mr. Slope is for a clergyman's daughter."

"I do not know Lord Tattenham Corner."

"No; but Dr. Grantly does. It is nothing to me if he knows all the young lords on every racecourse in England. I shall not interfere with him; nor shall he with me."

"I am sorry to differ with you, Mrs. Bold; but as you have spoken to me on this matter, and especially as you blame me for what little I said on the subject, I must tell you that I do differ from you. Dr. Grantly's position as a man in the world gives him a right to choose his own acquaintances, subject to certain influences. If he chooses them badly, those influences will be used. If he consorts with persons unsuitable to him, his bishop will interfere. What the bishop is to Dr. Grantly, Dr. Grantly is to you."

"I deny it. I utterly deny it," said Eleanor, jumping from her seat, and literally flashing before Mr. Arabin, as she stood on the drawing-room floor. He had never seen her so excited, he had never seen her look half so beautiful.

"I utterly deny it," said she. "Dr. Grantly has no sort of jurisdiction over me whatsoever. Do you and he forget that I am not altogether alone in the world? Do you forget that I have a father? Dr. Grantly, I believe, always has forgotten it.

"From you, Mr. Arabin," she continued, "I would have listened to advice because I should have expected it to have been given as one friend may advise another; not as a schoolmaster gives an order to a pupil. I might have differed from you; on this matter I should have done so; but had you spoken to me in your usual manner and with your usual freedom I should not have been angry. But now——was it manly of you, Mr. Arabin, to speak of me in this way——, so disrespectful—so——? I cannot bring myself to repeat what you said. You must understand what I feel. Was it just of you to speak of me in such a way, and to advise my sister's husband to turn me out of my sister's house, because I chose to know a man of whose doctrine you disapprove?"

"I have no alternative left to me, Mrs. Bold," said he, standing with his back to the fire-place, looking down intently at the carpet pattern, and speaking with a slow measured voice, "but to tell you plainly what did take place between me and Dr. Grantly."

"Well," said she, finding that he paused for a moment.

"I am afraid that what I may say may pain you."

"It cannot well do so more than what you have already done," said she.

"Dr. Grantly asked me whether I thought it would be prudent for him to receive you in his house as the wife of Mr. Slope, and I told him that I thought it would be imprudent. Believing it to be utterly impossible that Mr. Slope and——"

"Thank you, Mr. Arabin, that is sufficient. I do not want to know your reasons," said she, speaking with a terribly calm voice. "I have shown to this gentleman the common-place civility of a neighbour; and because I have done so, because I have not indulged against him in all the rancour and hatred which you and Dr. Grantly consider due to all clergymen who do not agree with yourselves, you conclude that I am to marry him;—or rather you do not conclude so—no rational man could really come to such an outrageous conclusion without better ground;—you have not thought so—but, as I am in a position in which such an accusation must be peculiarly painful, it is made in order that I may be terrified into hostility against this enemy of yours."

As she finished speaking, she walked to the drawing-room window and stepped out into the garden. Mr. Arabin was left in the room, still occupied in counting the pattern on the carpet. He had, however, distinctly heard and accurately marked every word that she had spoken. Was it not clear from what she had said, that the archdeacon had been wrong in imputing to her any attachment to Mr. Slope? Was it not clear that Eleanor was still free to make another choice? It may seem strange that he should for a moment have had a doubt; and yet he did doubt. She had not absolutely denied the charge; she had not expressly said that it was untrue. Mr. Arabin understood little of the nature of a woman's feelings, or he would have known how improbable it was that she should make any clearer declaration than she had done. Few men do understand the nature of a woman's heart, till years have robbed such understanding of its value. And it is well that it should be so, or men would triumph too easily.

Mr. Arabin stood counting the carpet, unhappy, wretchedly unhappy, at the hard words that had been spoken to him; and yet happy, exquisitely happy, as he thought that after all the woman whom he so regarded was not to become the wife of the man whom he so much disliked. As he stood there be began to be aware that he was himself in love. Forty years had passed over his head, and as yet woman's beauty had never given him an uneasy hour. His present hour was very uneasy.

Not that he remained there for half or a quarter of that time. In spite of what Eleanor had said, Mr. Arabin was, in truth, a manly man. Having ascertained that he loved this woman, and having now reason to believe that she was free to receive his love, at least if she pleased to do so, he followed her into the garden to make such wooing as he could.

He was not long in finding her. She was walking to and fro beneath the avenue of elms that stood in the archdeacon's grounds, skirting the churchyard. What had passed between her and Mr. Arabin, had not, alas, tended to lessen the acerbity of her spirit. She was very angry; more angry with him than with any one. How could he have so misunderstood her? She had been so intimate with him, had allowed him such latitude in what he had chosen to say to her, had complied with his ideas, cherished his views, fostered his precepts, cared for his comforts, made much of him in every way in which a pretty woman can make much of an unmarried man without committing herself or her feelings! She had been doing this, and while she had been doing it he had regarded her as the affianced wife of an another man.

As she passed along the avenue, every now and then an unbidden tear would force itself on her cheek, and as she raised her hand to brush it away she stamped with her little foot upon the sward with very spite to think that she had been so treated.

Mr. Arabin was very near to her when she first saw him, and she turned short round and retraced her steps down the avenue, trying to rid her cheeks of all trace of the tell-tale tears. It was a needless endeavour, for Mr. Arabin was in a state of mind that hardly allowed him to observe such trifles. He followed her down the walk, and overtook her just as she reached the end of it.

He had not considered how he would address her; he had not thought what he would say. He had only felt that it was wretchedness to him to quarrel with her, and that it would be happiness to be allowed to love her. And yet he could not lower himself by asking her pardon. He had done her no wrong. He had not calumniated her, not injured her, as she had accused him of doing. He could not confess sins of which he had not been guilty. He could only let the past be past, and ask her as to her and his hopes for the future.

"I hope we are not to part as enemies?" said he.

"There shall be no enmity on my part," said Eleanor; "I endeavour to avoid all enmities. It would be a hollow pretence were I to say that there can be true friendship between us after what has just passed. People cannot make their friends of those whom they despise."

"And am I despised?"

"*I* must have been so before you could have spoken of me as you did. And I was deceived, cruelly deceived. I believed that you thought well of me; I believed that you esteemed me."

"Thought well of you and esteemed you!" said he. "In justifying myself before you, I must use stronger words than those." He paused for a moment, and Eleanor's heart beat with painful violence within her bosom as she waited for him to go on. "I have esteemed, do esteem you, as I never yet esteemed any woman. Think well of you! I never thought to think so well, so much of any human creature. Speak calumny of you! Insult you! Wilfully injure you! I wish it were my privilege to shield you from calumny, insult, and injury. Calumny! ah, me. 'Twere almost better that it were so. Better than to worship with a sinful worship; sinful and vain also." And then he walked along beside her, with his hands clasped behind his back, looking down on the grass beneath his feet, and utterly at a loss how to express his meaning. And Eleanor walked beside him determined at least to give him no assistance.

"Ah me!" he uttered at last, speaking rather to himself than to her. "Ah me! these Plumstead walks were pleasant enough, if one could have but heart's ease; but without that the dull dead stones of Oxford were far preferable; and St. Ewold's too; Mrs. Bold, I am beginning to think that I mistook myself when I came hither. A Romish priest now would have escaped all this. Oh, father of heaven! how good for us would it be, if thou couldest vouchsafe to us a certain rule."

"And have we not a certain rule, Mr. Arabin?"

"Yes—yes, surely; 'Lead us not into temptation but deliver us from evil.' But what is temptation? what is evil? Is this evil,—is this temptation?"

Poor Mr. Arabin! It would not come out of him, that deep true love of his. He could not bring himself to utter it in plain language that would require and demand an answer. He knew not how to say to the woman by his side, "Since the fact is that you do not love that other man, that you are not to be his wife, can you love me, will you be my wife?" These were the words which were in his heart, but with all his sighs he could not draw them to his lips. He would have given anything, everything for power to ask this simple question; but glib as was his tongue in pulpits and on platforms, now he could not find a word wherewith to express the plain wish of his heart.

And yet Eleanor understood him as thoroughly as though he had declared his passion with all the elegant fluency of a practised Lothario. With a woman's instinct she followed every bend of his mind, as he spoke of the pleasantness of Plumstead and the stones of Oxford; as he alluded to the safety of the Romish priest and the hidden perils of temptation. She knew that it all meant love. She knew that this man at her side, this accomplished scholar, this practised orator, this great polemical combatant, was striving and striving in vain to tell her that his heart was no longer his own.

She knew this, and felt a sort of joy in knowing it; and yet she would not come to his aid. He had offended her deeply, had treated her unworthily, the more unworthily seeing that he had learnt to love her, and Eleanor could not bring herself to abandon her revenge. She did not ask herself whether or no she would ultimately accept his love. She did not even acknowledge to herself that she now perceived it with pleasure. At the present moment it did not touch her heart; it merely appeased her pride and flattered her vanity. Mr. Arabin had dared to associate her name with that of Mr. Slope, and now her spirit was soothed by finding that he would fain associate it with his own. And so she walked on beside him inhaling incense, but giving out no sweetness in return.

"Answer me this," said Mr. Arabin, stopping suddenly in his walk, and stepping forward so that he faced his companion. "Answer me this one question. You do not love Mr. Slope? you do not intend to be his wife?"

Mr. Arabin certainly did not go the right way to win such a woman as Eleanor Bold. Just as her wrath was evaporating, as it was disappearing before the true warmth of his untold love, he rekindled it by a most useless repetition of his original sin. Had he known what he was about he should never have mentioned Mr. Slope's name before Eleanor Bold, till he had made her all his own. Then, and not till then, he might have talked of Mr. Slope with as much triumph as he chose.

"I shall answer no such question," said she; "and what is more, I must tell you that nothing can justify your asking it. Good morning!"

And so saying she stepped proudly across the lawn, and passing through the drawing-room window joined her father and sister at lunch in the dining-room. Half an hour afterwards she was in the carriage, and so she left Plumstead without again seeing Mr. Arabin.

CHAPTER XXVI

THE BISHOP'S LIBRARY

AND thus the pleasant party at Plumstead was broken up. It had been a very pleasant party as long as they had all remained in good humour with one another. Mrs. Grantly had felt her house to be gayer and brighter than it had been for many a long day, and the archdeacon had been aware that the month had passed pleasantly without attributing the pleasure to any other special merits than those of his own hospitality. Within three or four days of Eleanor's departure Mr. Harding had also returned, and Mr. Arabin had gone to Oxford to spend one week there previous to his settling at the vicarage of St. Ewold's. He had gone laden with many messages to Dr. Gwynne touching the iniquity of the doings in Barchester palace, and the peril in which it was believed the hospital still stood in spite of the assurances contained in Mr. Slope's inauspicious letter.

During Eleanor's drive into Barchester she had not much opportunity of reflecting on Mr. Arabin. She had been constrained to divert her mind both from his sins and his love by the necessity of conversing with her sister, and maintaining the appearance of parting with her on good terms. When the carriage reached her own door, and while she was in the act of giving her last kiss to her sister and nieces, Mary Bold ran out and exclaimed,

"Oh! Eleanor,—have you heard?—oh! Mrs. Grantly, have you heard what has happened? The poor dean!"

"Good heavens!" said Mrs. Grantly; "what—what has happened?"

"This morning at nine he had a fit of apoplexy, and he has not spoken since. I very much fear that by this time he is no more."

Mrs. Grantly had been very intimate with the dean, and was therefore much shocked. Eleanor had not known him so well; nevertheless she was sufficiently acquainted with his person and manners to feel startled and grieved also at the tidings she now received. "I will go at once to the deanery," said Mrs. Grantly; "the archdeacon, I am sure, will be there. If there is any news to send you I will let Thomas call before he leaves town." And so the carriage drove off, leaving Eleanor and her baby with Mary Bold.

Mrs. Grantly had been quite right. The archdeacon was at the deanery. He had come into Barchester that morning by himself, not caring to intrude himself upon Eleanor, and he also immediately on his arrival had heard of the dean's fit. There was, as we have before said, a library or reading room connecting the cathedral with the dean's house. This was generally called the bishop's library, because a certain bishop of Barchester was supposed to have added it to the cathedral.

On the morning in question most of the resident clergymen who constituted the chapter, and some few others, were here assembled, and among them as usual the archdeacon towered with high authority. He had heard of the dean's fit before he was over the bridge which led into the town, and had at once come to the well known clerical trysting place. He had been there by eleven o'clock, and had remained ever since. From time to time the medical men who had been called in came through from the deanery into the library, uttered little bulletins, and then returned. There was it appears very little hope of the old man's rallying, indeed no hope of any thing like a final recovery. The only question was whether he must die at once speechless, unconscious, stricken to death by his first heavy fit; or whether by due aid of medical skill he might not be so far brought back to this world as to become conscious of his state, and enabled to address one prayer to his Maker before he was called to meet Him face to face at the judgment seat.

Sir Omicron Pie had been sent for from London. That great man had shown himself a wonderful adept at keeping life still moving within an old man's heart in the case of good old Bishop Grantly, and it might be reasonably expected that he would be equally successful with a dean. In the mean time Dr. Fillgrave and Mr. Rerechild were doing their best; and poor Miss Trefoil sat at the head of her father's bed, longing, as in such cases daughters do long, to be allowed to do something to show her love; if it were only to chafe his feet with her hands, or wait in menial offices on those autocratic doctors; anything so that now in the time of need she might be of use.

The archdeacon alone of the attendant clergy had been admitted for a moment into the sick man's chamber. He had crept in with creaking shoes, had said with smothered voice a word of consolation to the sorrowing daughter, had looked on the distorted face of his old friend with solemn but yet eager scrutinising eye, as though he said in his heart "and so some day it will probably be with me;" and then having whispered an unmeaning word or two to the doctors, had creaked his way back again into the library.

"He'll never speak again, I fear," said the archdeacon as he noiselessly closed the door, as though the unconscious dying man, from whom all sense had fled, would have heard in his distant chamber the spring of the lock which was now so carefully handled.

"Indeed! indeed! is he so bad?" said the meagre little prebendary, turning over in his own mind all the probable candidates for the deanery, and wondering whether the archdeacon would think it worth his while to accept it. "The fit must have been very violent."

"When a man over seventy has a stroke of apoplexy, it seldom comes very lightly," said the burly chancellor.

"He was an excellent, sweet-tempered man," said one of the vicars choral. "Heaven knows how we shall repair his loss."

"He was indeed," said a minor canon, "and a great blessing to all those privileged to take a share of the services of our cathedral. I suppose the government will appoint, Mr. Archdeacon. I trust we may have no stranger."

"We will not talk about his successor," said the archdeacon, "while there is yet hope."

"Oh no, of course not," said the minor canon. "It would be exceedingly indecorous, but——"

"I know of no man," said the meagre little prebendary, "who has better interest with the present government than Mr. Slope."

"Pooh!" said the burly chancellor. At this moment the door opened, and in came Dr. Fillgrave.

"How is he?" "Is he conscious?" "Can he speak?" "I hope not dead?" "No worse news, doctor, I trust?" "I hope, I trust, something better, doctor?" said half a dozen voices all at once, each in a tone of extremest anxiety. It was pleasant to see how popular the good old dean was among his clergy.

"No change, gentlemen; not the slightest change—but a telegraphic message has arrived—Sir Omicron Pie will be here by the 9.15 p.m. train. If any man can do anything Sir Omicron Pie will do it. But all that skill can do has been done."

"We are sure of that, Dr. Fillgrave," said the archdeacon; "we are quite sure of that. But yet you know——"

"Oh! quite right," said the doctor, "quite right—I should have done just the same—I advised it at once. I said to Rerechild at once that with such a life and such a man, Sir Omicron should be summoned—of course I knew the expense was nothing—so distinguished, you know, and so popular. Nevertheless, all that human skill can do has been done."

Just at this period Mrs. Grantly's carriage drove into the close, and the archdeacon went down to confirm the news which she had heard before.

By the 9.15 p.m. train Sir Omicron Pie did arrive. And in the course of the night a sort of consciousness returned to the poor old dean. Whether this was due to Sir Omicron Pie is a question on which it may be well not to offer an opinion. Dr. Fillgrave was very clear in his own mind, but Sir Omicron himself is thought to have differed from that learned doctor. At any rate Sir Omicron expressed an opinion that the dean had yet some days to live.

For the eight or ten next days, accordingly, the poor dean remained in the same state, half conscious and half comatose, and the attendant clergy began to think that no new appointment would be necessary for some few months to come.

CHAPTER XXVII

A NEW CANDIDATE FOR ECCLESIASTICAL HONOURS

THE dean's illness occasioned much mental turmoil in other places besides the deanery and adjoining library; and the idea which occurred to the meagre little prebendary about Mr. Slope did not occur to him alone.

The bishop was sitting listlessly in his study when the news reached him of the dean's illness. It was brought to him by Mr. Slope, who of course was not the last person in Barchester to hear it. It was also not slow in finding its way to Mrs. Proudie's ears. It may be presumed that there was not just then much friendly intercourse between these two rival claimants for his lordship's obedience. Indeed, though living in the same house, they had not met since the stormy interview between them in the bishop's study on the preceding day.

On that occasion Mrs. Proudie had been defeated. That the prestige of continual victory should have been torn from her standards was a subject of great sorrow to that militant lady; but though defeated, she was not overcome. She felt that she might yet recover her lost ground, that she might yet hurl Mr. Slope down to the dust from which she had picked him, and force her sinning lord to sue for pardon in sackcloth and ashes.

On that memorable day, memorable for his mutiny and rebellion against her high behests, he had carried his way with a high hand, and had really begun to think it possible that the days of his slavery were counted. He had begun to hope that he was now about to enter into a free land, a land delicious with milk which he himself might quaff, and honey which would not tantalise him by being only honey to the eye. When Mrs. Proudie banged the door, as she left his room, he felt himself every inch a bishop. To be sure his spirit had been a little cowed by his chaplain's subsequent lecture; but on the whole he was highly pleased with himself, and flattered himself that the worst was over. "Ce n'est que le premier pas qui coûte," he reflected; and now that the first step had been so magnanimously taken, all the rest would follow easily.

He met his wife as a matter of course at dinner, where little or nothing was said that could ruffle the bishop's happiness. His daughters and the servants were present and protected him.

He made one or two trifling remarks on the subject of his projected visit to the archbishop, in order to show to all concerned that he intended to have his own way; and the very servants perceiving the change transferred a little of their reverence from their mistress to their master. All which the master perceived; and so also did the mistress. But Mrs. Proudie bided her time.

After dinner he returned to his study where Mr. Slope soon found him, and there they had tea together and planned many things. For some few minutes the bishop was really happy; but as the clock on the chimney piece warned him that the stilly hours of night were drawing on, as he looked at his chamber candlestick and knew that he must use it, his heart sank within him again. He was as a ghost, all whose power of wandering free through these upper regions ceases at cock-crow; or rather he was the opposite of the ghost, for till cock-crow he must again be a serf. And would that be all? Could he trust himself to come down to breakfast a free man in the morning?

He was nearly an hour later than usual, when he betook himself to his rest. Rest! what rest! However, he took a couple of glasses of

sherry, and mounted the stairs. Far be it from us to follow him
thither. There are some things which no novelist, no historian,
should attempt; some few scenes in life's drama which even no poet
should dare to paint. Let that which passed between Dr. Proudie
and his wife on this night be understood to be among them.

He came down the following morning a sad and thoughtful man.
He was attenuated in appearance; one might almost say emaciated.
I doubt whether his now grizzled locks had not palpably become
more grey than on the preceding evening. At any rate he had aged
materially. Years do not make a man old gradually and at an even
pace. Look through the world and see if this is not so always, except
in those rare cases in which the human being lives and dies without
joys and without sorrows, like a vegetable. A man shall be possessed
of florid youthful blooming health till, it matters not what age.
Thirty—forty—fifty, then comes some nipping frost, some period
of agony, that robs the fibres of the body of their succulence, and the
hale and hearty man is counted among the old.

He came down and breakfasted alone; Mrs. Proudie being indisposed took her coffee in her bed-room, and her daughters waited
upon her there. He ate his breakfast alone, and then, hardly knowing what he did, he betook himself to his usual seat of his study. He
tried to solace himself with his coming visit to the archbishop. That
effort of his own free will at any rate remained to him as an enduring
triumph. But somehow, now that he had achieved it, he did not
seem to care so much about it. It was his ambition that had
prompted him to take his place at the archi-episcopal table, and his
ambition was now quite dead within him.

He was thus seated when Mr. Slope made his appearance, with
breathless impatience.

"My lord, the dean is dead."

"Good heavens!" exclaimed the bishop, startled out of his
apathy by an announcement so sad and so sudden.

"He is either dead or now dying. He has had an apoplectic fit,
and I am told that there is not the slightest hope; indeed, I do not
doubt that by this time he is no more."

Bells were rung, and servants were immediately sent to inquire.
In the course of the morning, the bishop, leaning on his chaplain's
arm, himself called at the deanery door. Mrs. Proudie sent to Miss
Trefoil all manner of offers of assistance. The Miss Proudies sent
also, and there was immense sympathy between the palace and the
deanery. The answer to all inquiries was unvaried. The dean was
just the same; and Sir Omicron Pie was expected down by the
9.15 p.m. train.

And then Mr. Slope began to meditate, as others also had done,
as to who might possibly be the new dean; and it occurred to him, as
it had also occurred to others, that it might be possible that he
should be the new dean himself. And then the question as to the

twelve hundred, or fifteen hundred, or two thousand, ran in his mind, as it had run through those of the other clergymen in the cathedral library.

Whether it might be two thousand, or fifteen or twelve hundred, it would in any case undoubtedly be a great thing for him, if he could get it. The gratification to his ambition would be greater even than that of his covetousness. How glorious to out-top the arch-deacon in his own cathedral city; to sit above prebendaries and canons, and have the cathedral pulpit and all the cathedral services altogether at his own disposal!

But it might be easier to wish for this than to obtain it. Mr. Slope, however, was not without some means of forwarding his views, and he at any rate did not let the grass grow under his feet. In the first place he thought—and not vainly—that he could count upon what assistance the bishop could give him. He immediately changed his views with regard to his patron; he made up his mind that if he became dean, he would hand his lordship back again to his wife's vassalage; and he thought it possible that his lordship might not be sorry to rid himself of one of his mentors. Mr. Slope had also taken some steps towards making his name known to other men in power. There was a certain chief-commissioner of national schools who at the present moment was presumed to stand especially high in the good graces of the government big wigs, and with him Mr. Slope had contrived to establish a sort of epistolary intimacy. He thought that he might safely apply to Sir Nicholas Fitzwhiggin; and he felt sure that if Sir Nicholas chose to exert himself, the promise of such a piece of preferment would be had for the asking for.

Then he also had the press at his bidding, or flattered himself that he had so. The daily Jupiter had taken his part in a very thorough manner in those polemical contests of his with Mr. Arabin; he had on more than one occasion absolutely had an interview with a gentleman on the staff of that paper, who, if not the editor, was as good as the editor; and had long been in the habit of writing telling letters on all manner of ecclesiastical abuses, which he signed with his initials, and sent to his editorial friend with private notes signed in his own name. Indeed, he and Mr. Towers—such was the name of the powerful gentleman of the press with whom he was connected—were generally very amiable with each other. Mr. Slope's little productions were always printed and occasionally commented upon; and thus, in a small sort of way, he had become a literary celebrity. This public life had great charms for him, though it certainly also had its drawbacks. On one occasion, when speaking in the presence of reporters, he had failed to uphold and praise and swear by that special line of conduct which had been upheld and praised and sworn by in the Jupiter, and then he had been much surprised and at the moment not a little irritated to find himself lacerated most un-mercifully by his old ally. He was quizzed and bespattered and made a fool of, just as though, or rather worse than if, he had been a constant enemy instead of a constant friend. He had hitherto not learnt that a man who aspires to be on the staff of the Jupiter must surrender all individuality. But ultimately this little castigation had broken no bones between him and his friend Mr. Towers. Mr. Slope was one of those who understood the world too well to show himself angry with such a potentate as the Jupiter. He had kissed the rod that scourged him, and now thought that he might fairly look for his reward. He determined that he would at once let Mr. Towers know that he was a candidate for the place which was about to become vacant. More than one piece of preferment had lately been given away much in accordance with advice tendered to the government in the columns of the Jupiter.

But it was incumbent on Mr. Slope first to secure the bishop. He specially felt that it behoved him to do this before the visit to the archbishop was made. It was really quite providential that the dean should have fallen ill just at the very nick of time. If Dr. Proudie could be instigated to take the matter up warmly, he might manage a good deal while staying at the archbishop's palace. Feeling this very strongly Mr. Slope determined to sound the bishop that very afternoon. He was to start on the following morning to London, and therefore not a moment could be lost with safety.

He went into the bishop's study about five o'clock, and found him still sitting alone. It might have been supposed that he had hardly moved since the little excitement occasioned by his walk to the dean's door. He still wore on his face that dull dead look of half unconscious suffering. He was doing nothing, reading nothing, thinking of nothing, but simply gazing on vacancy when Mr. Slope for the second time that day entered his room.

"Well, Slope," said he, somewhat impatiently; for, to tell the truth, he was not anxious just at present to have much conversation with Mr. Slope.

"Your lordship will be sorry to hear that as yet the poor dean has shown no sign of amendment."

"Oh—ah—hasn't he? Poor man! I'm sure I'm very sorry. I suppose Sir Omicron has not arrived yet?"

"No; not till the 9.15 p.m. train."

"I wonder they didn't have a special. They say Dr. Trefoil is very rich."

"Very rich, I believe," said Mr. Slope. "But the truth is, all the doctors in London can do no good; no other good than to show that every possible care has been taken. Poor Dr. Trefoil is not long for this world, my lord."

"I suppose not—I suppose not."

"Oh no; indeed, his best friends could not wish that he should outlive such a shock, for his intellects cannot possibly survive it."

"Poor man! poor man!" said the bishop.

"It will naturally be a matter of much moment to your lordship who is to succeed him," said Mr. Slope. "It would be a great thing if you could secure the appointment for some person of your own way of thinking on important points. The party hostile to us are very strong here in Barchester—much too strong."

"Yes, yes. If poor Dr. Trefoil is to go, it will be a great thing to get a good man in his place."

"It will be everything to your lordship to get a man on whose co-operation you can reckon. Only think what trouble we might have if Dr. Grantly, or Dr. Hyandry, or any of that way of thinking, were to get it."

"It is not very probable that Lord —— will give it to any of that school; why should he?"

"No. Not probable; certainly not; but it's possible. Great interest will probably be made. If I might venture to advise your lordship, I would suggest that you should discuss the matter with his grace next week. I have no doubt that your wishes, if made known and backed by his grace, would be paramount with Lord ——."

"Well, I don't know that; Lord —— has always been very kind to me, very kind. But I am unwilling to interfere in such matters unless asked. And indeed if asked, I don't know whom, at this moment, I should recommend."

Mr. Slope, even Mr. Slope, felt at the present rather abashed. He hardly knew how to frame his little request in language sufficiently modest. He had recognised and acknowledged to himself the necessity of shocking the bishop in the first instance by the temerity of his application, and his difficulty was how best to remedy that by his adroitness and eloquence. "I doubted myself," said he, "whether your lordship would have any one immediately in your eye, and it is on this account that I venture to submit to you an idea that I have been turning over in my own mind. If poor Dr. Trefoil must go, I really do not see why, with your lordship's assistance, I should not hold the preferment myself."

"You!" exclaimed the bishop, in a manner that Mr. Slope could hardly have considered complimentary.

The ice was now broken, and Mr. Slope became fluent enough. "I have been thinking of looking for it. If your lordship will press the matter on the archbishop, I do not doubt but I shall succeed. You see I shall be the first to move, which is a great matter. Then I can count upon assistance from the public press: my name is known, I may say, somewhat favourably known to that portion of the press which is now most influential with the government, and I have friends also in the government. But, nevertheless, it is to you, my lord, that I look for assistance. It is from your hands that I would most willingly receive the benefit. And, which should ever be the chief consideration in such matters, you must know better than any other person whatsoever what qualifications I possess."

The bishop sat for a while dumbfounded. Mr. Slope dean of Barchester! The idea of such a transformation of character would never have occurred to his own unaided intellect. At first he went on thinking why, for what reasons, on what account, Mr. Slope should be dean of Barchester. But by degrees the direction of his thoughts changed, and he began to think why, for what reasons, on what account, Mr. Slope should not be dean of Barchester. As far as he himself, the bishop, was concerned, he could well spare the services of his chaplain. That little idea of using Mr. Slope as a counterpoise to his wife had well nigh evaporated. He had all but acknowledged the futility of the scheme. If indeed he could have slept in his chaplain's bed-room instead of his wife's there might have been something in it. But —— ——. And thus as Mr. Slope was speaking, the bishop began to recognise the idea that that gentleman might become dean of Barchester without impropriety; not moved, indeed, by Mr. Slope's eloquence, for he did not follow the tenor of his speech; but led thereto by his own cogitations.

"I need not say," continued Mr. Slope, "that it would be my chief desire to act in all matters connected with the cathedral as far as possible in accordance with your views. I know your lordship so well (and I hope you know me well enough to have the same feelings) that I am satisfied that my being in that position would add materially to your own comfort, and enable you to extend the sphere of your useful influence. As I said before, it is most desirable that there should be but one opinion among the dignitaries of the same diocese. I doubt much whether I would accept such an appointment in any diocese in which I should be constrained to differ much from the bishop. In this case there would be a delightful uniformity of opinion."

Mr. Slope perfectly well perceived that the bishop did not follow a word that he said, but nevertheless he went on talking. He knew it was necessary that Dr. Proudie should recover from his surprise, and he knew also that he must give him the opportunity of appearing to have been persuaded by argument. So he went on, and produced a multitude of fitting reasons all tending to show that no one on earth could make so good a dean of Barchester as himself, that the government and the public would assuredly coincide in desiring that he, Mr. Slope, should be dean of Barchester; but that for high considerations of ecclesiastical polity it would be especially desirable that this piece of preferment should be so bestowed through the instrumentality of the bishop of the diocese.

"But I really don't know what I could do in the matter," said the bishop.

"If you would mention it to the archbishop; if you could tell his grace that you consider such an appointment very desirable, that you have it much at heart with a view to putting an end to schism in the diocese; if you did this with your usual energy, you would probably find no difficulty in inducing his grace to promise that he would mention it to Lord ——. Of course you would let the archbishop know that I am not looking for the preferment solely through his intervention; that you do not exactly require him to ask it as a favour; that you expect that I shall get it through other sources, as is indeed the case; but that you are very anxious that his grace should express his approval of such an arrangement to Lord ——"

It ended in the bishop promising to do as he was bid. Not that he so promised without a stipulation. "About that hospital," he said, in the middle of the conference. "I was never so troubled in my life;" which was about the truth. "You haven't spoken to Mr. Harding since I saw you?"

Mr. Slope assured his patron that he had not.

"Ah well, then—I think upon the whole it will be better to let Quiverful have it. It has been half promised to him, and he has a large family and is very poor. I think on the whole it will be better to make out the nomination for Mr. Quiverful."

"But, my lord," said Mr. Slope, still thinking that he was bound to make a fight for his own view on this matter, and remembering that it still behoved him to maintain his lately acquired supremacy over Mrs. Proudie, lest he should fail in his views regarding the deanery,—"but my lord, I am really much afraid——"

"Remember, Mr. Slope," said the bishop, "I can hold out no sort of hope to you in this matter of succeeding poor Dr. Trefoil. I will certainly speak to the archbishop, as you wish it, but I cannot think——"

"Well, my lord," said Mr. Slope, fully understanding the bishop, and in his turn interrupting him, "perhaps your lordship is right about Mr. Quiverful. I have no doubt I can easily arrange matters with Mr. Harding, and I will make out the nomination for your signature as you direct."

"Yes, Slope, I think that will be best; and you may be sure that any little that I can do to forward your views shall be done."

And so they parted.

Mr. Slope had now much business on his hands. He had to make his daily visit to the signora. This common prudence should have now induced him to omit, but he was infatuated; and could not bring himself to be commonly prudent. He determined therefore that he would drink tea at the Stanhopes'; and he determined also, or thought that he determined, that having done so he would go thither no more. He had also to arrange his matters with Mrs. Bold. He was of opinion that Eleanor would grace the deanery as perfectly as she would the chaplain's cottage; and he thought, moreover, that Eleanor's fortune would excellently repair any dilapidations and curtailments in the dean's stipend which might have been made by that ruthless ecclesiastical commission.

Touching Mrs. Bold his hopes now soared high. Mr. Slope was

one of that numerous multitude of swains who think that all is fair in love, and he had accordingly not refrained from using the services of Mrs. Bold's own maid. From her he had learnt much of what had taken place at Plumstead; not exactly with truth, for "the own maid" had not been able to divine the exact truth, but with some sort of similitude to it. He had been told that the archdeacon and Mrs. Grantly and Mr. Harding and Mr. Arabin had all quarrelled with "missus" for having received a letter from Mr. Slope; that "missus" had positively refused to give the letter up; that she had received from the archdeacon the option of giving up either Mr. Slope and his letter, or else the society of Plumstead rectory; and that "missus" had declared with much indignation, that "she didn't care a straw for the society of Plumstead rectory," and that she wouldn't give up Mr. Slope for any of them.

Considering the course from whence this came, it was not quite so untrue as might have been expected. It showed pretty plainly what had been the nature of the conversation in the servants' hall; and coupled as it was with the certainty of Eleanor's sudden return, it appeared to Mr. Slope to be so far worthy of credit as to justify him in thinking that the fair widow would in all human probability accept his offer.

All this work was therefore to be done. It was desirable he thought that he should make his offer before it was known that Mr. Quiverful was finally appointed to the hospital. In his letter to Eleanor he had plainly declared that Mr. Harding was to have the appointment. It would be very difficult to explain this away; and were he to write another letter to Eleanor, telling the truth and throwing the blame on the bishop, it would naturally injure him in her estimation. He determined therefore to let that matter disclose itself as it would, and to lose no time in throwing himself at her feet.

Then he had to solicit the assistance of Sir Nicholas Fitzwhiggin and Mr. Towers, and he went directly from the bishop's presence to compose his letters to those gentlemen. As Mr. Slope was esteemed an adept at letter writing, they shall be given in full.

"(Private.)   Palace, Barchester, Sept. 185—.

"My dear Sir Nicholas,—I hope that the intercourse which has been between us will preclude you from regarding my present application as an intrusion. You cannot I imagine have yet heard that poor dear old Dr. Trefoil has been seized with apoplexy. It is a subject of profound grief to every one in Barchester, for he has always been an excellent man—excellent as a man and as a clergyman. He is, however, full of years, and his life could not under any circumstances have been much longer spared. You may probably have known him.

"There is, it appears, no probable chance of his recovery. Sir Omicron Pie, is I believe, at present with him. At any rate the medical men here have declared that one or two days more must limit the tether of his mortal coil. I sincerely trust that his soul may wing its flight to that haven where it may for ever be at rest and for ever be happy.

"The bishop has been speaking to me about the preferment, and he is anxious that it should be conferred on me. I confess that I can hardly venture, at my age, to look for such advancement; but I am so far encouraged by his lordship, that I believe I shall be induced to do so. His lordship goes to —— to-morrow, and is intent on mentioning the subject to the archbishop.

"I know well how deservedly great is your weight with the present government. In any matter touching church preferment you would of course be listened to. Now that the matter has been put into my head, I am of course anxious to be successful. If you can assist me by your good word, you will confer on me one additional favour.

"I had better add, that Lord —— cannot as yet know of this piece of preferment having fallen in, or rather of its certainty of falling (for poor dear Dr. Trefoil is past hope). Should Lord —— first hear it from you, that might probably be thought to give you a fair claim to express your opinion.

"Of course our grand object is, that we should all be of one opinion in church matters. This is most desirable at Barchester; it is this that makes our good bishop so anxious about it. You may probably think it expedient to point this out to Lord —— if it shall be in your power to oblige me by mentioning the subject to his lordship.

"Believe me, my dear Sir Nicholas,
"Your most faithful servant,
"OBADIAH SLOPE."

His letter to Mr. Towers was written in quite a different strain. Mr. Slope conceived that he completely understood the difference in character and position of the two men whom he addressed. He knew that for such a man as Sir Nicholas Fitzwhiggin a little flummery was necessary, and that it might be of the easy everyday description. Accordingly his letter to Sir Nicholas was written *currente calamo*, with very little trouble. But to such a man as Mr. Towers it was not so easy to write a letter that should be effective and yet not offensive, that should carry its point without undue interference. It was not difficult to flatter Dr. Proudie or Sir Nicholas Fitzwhiggin, but very difficult to flatter Mr. Towers without letting the flattery declare itself. This, however, had to be done. Moreover, this letter must, in appearance at least, be written without effort, and be fluent, un-constrained, and demonstrative of no doubt or fear on the part of the writer. Therefore the epistle to Mr. Towers was studied, and re-copied, and elaborated at the cost of so many minutes, that Mr.

Slope had hardly time to dress himself and reach Dr. Stanhope's that evening.

When despatched it ran as follows:

" (Private.)   Barchester. Sept. 185—. "
(He purposely omitted any allusion to the "palace," thinking that Mr. Towers might not like it. A great man, he remembered, had been once much condemned for dating a letter from Windsor Castle.)

"My dear Sir,—We were all a good deal shocked here this morning by hearing that poor old Dean Trefoil had been stricken with apoplexy. The fit took him about 9 a.m. I am writing now to save the post, and he is still alive, but past all hope, or possibility I believe, of living. Sir Omicron Pie is here, or will be very shortly; but all that even Sir Omicron can do, is to ratify the sentence of his less distinguished brethren that nothing can be done. Poor Dr. Trefoil's race on this side the grave is run. I do not know whether you knew him. He was a good, quiet, charitable man, of the old school of course, as any clergyman over seventy years of age must necessarily be.

"But I do not write merely with the object of sending you such news as this: doubtless some one of your Mercuries will have seen and heard and reported so much; I write, as you usually do yourself, rather with a view to the future than to the past.

"Rumour is already rife here as to Dr. Trefoil's successor, and among those named as possible future deans your humble servant is, I believe, not the least frequently spoken of; in short I am looking for the preferment. You may probably know that since Bishop Proudie came to this diocese I have exerted myself here a good deal; and I may certainly say not without some success. He and I are nearly always of the same opinion on points of doctrine as well as church discipline, and therefore I have had, as his confidential chaplain, very much in my own hands; but I confess to you that I have a higher ambition than to remain the chaplain of any bishop.

"There are no positions in which more energy is now needed than those of our deans. The whole of our enormous cathedral establishments have been allowed to go to sleep,—nay, they are all but dead and ready for the sepulchre! And yet of what prodigious moment they might be made, if, as was intended, they were so managed as to lead the way and show an example for all our parochial clergy!

"The bishop here is most anxious for my success; indeed, he goes to-morrow to press the matter on the archbishop. I believe also I may count on the support of at least one most effective member of the government. But I confess that the support of the Jupiter, if I be thought worthy of it, would be more gratifying to me than any other; more gratifying if by it I should be successful: and more gratifying also, if, although so supported, I should be unsuccessful.

"The time has, in fact, come in which no government can venture to fill up the high places of the Church in defiance of the public press. The age of honourable bishops and noble deans has gone by; and any clergyman however humbly born can now hope for success, if his industry, talent, and character be sufficient to call forth the manifest opinion of the public in his favour.

"At the present moment we all feel that any counsel given in such matters by the Jupiter has the greatest weight—is, indeed, generally followed; and we feel also—I am speaking of clergymen of my own age and standing—that it should be so. There can be no patron less interested than the Jupiter, and none that more thoroughly understands the wants of the people.

"I am sure you will not suspect me of asking from you any support which the paper with which you are connected cannot conscientiously give me. My object in writing is to let you know that I am a candidate for the appointment. It is for you to judge whether or no you can assist my views. I should not, of course, have written to you on such a matter had I not believed (and I have had good reason so to believe) that the Jupiter approves of my views on ecclesiastical polity.

"The bishop expresses a fear that I may be considered too young for such a station, my age being thirty-six. I cannot think that at the present day any hesitation need be felt on such a point. The public has lost its love for antiquated servants. If a man will ever be fit to do good work he will be fit at thirty-six years of age.

"Believe me very faithfully yours,

"T. Towers, Esq   "OBADIAH SLOPE.
    "——Court,
  "Middle Temple."

Having thus exerted himself, Mr. Slope posted his letters, and passed the remainder of the evening at the feet of his mistress.

Mr. Slope will be accused of deceit in his mode of canvassing. It will be said that he lied in the application he made to each of his three patrons. I believe it must be owned that he did so. He could not hesitate on account of his youth, and yet be quite assured that he was not too young. He could not count chiefly on the bishop's support, and chiefly also on that of the newspaper. He did not think that the bishop was going to —— to press the matter on the arch-bishop. It must be owned that in his canvassing Mr. Slope was as false as he well could be.

Let it, however, be asked of those who are conversant with such matters, whether he was more false than men usually are on such occasions. We English gentlemen hate the name of a lie; but how often do we find public men who believe each other's words?

E

CHAPTER XXVIII

MRS. PROUDIE VICTRIX

THE next week passed over at Barchester with much apparent
tranquillity. The hearts, however, of some of the inhabitants
were not so tranquil as the streets of the city. The poor old dean still
continued to live, just as Sir Omicron Pie had prophesied that he
would do, much to the amazement, and some thought disgust, of Dr.
Fillgrave. The bishop still remained away. He had stayed a day
or two in town, and had also remained longer at the archbishop's
than he had intended. Mr. Slope had as yet received no line in
answer to either of his letters; but he had learnt the cause of this.
Sir Nicholas was stalking a deer, or attending the Queen, in the
Highlands; and even the indefatigable Mr. Towers had stolen an
autumn holiday, and had made one of the yearly tribe who now
ascend Mont Blanc. Mr. Slope learnt that he was not expected back
till the last day of September.

Mrs. Bold was thrown much with the Stanhopes, of whom she
became fonder and fonder. If asked, she would have said that
Charlotte Stanhope was her especial friend, and so she would have
thought. But, to tell the truth, she liked Bertie nearly as well; she
had no more idea of regarding him as a lover than she would have
had of looking at a big tame dog in such a light. Bertie had become
very intimate with her, and made little speeches to her, and said
little things of a sort very different from the speeches and sayings of
other men. But then this was almost always done before his sisters;
and he, with his long silken beard, his light blue eyes and strange
dress, was so unlike other men. She admitted him to a kind of
familiarity which she had never known with any one else, and of
which she by no means understood the danger. She blushed once at
finding that she had called him Bertie, and on the same day only
barely remembered her position in time to check herself from playing upon him some personal practical joke to which she was instigated
by Charlotte.

In all this Eleanor was perfectly innocent, and Bertie Stanhope
could hardly be called guilty. But every familiarity into which
Eleanor was entrapped was deliberately planned by his sister. She
knew well how to play her game, and played it without mercy; she
knew, none so well, what was her brother's character, and she would
have handed over to him the young widow, and the young widow's
money, and the money of the widow's child, without remorse. With
her pretended friendship and warm cordiality, she strove to connect
Eleanor so closely with her brother as to make it impossible that she
should go back even if she wished it. But Charlotte Stanhope knew

As soon as he had dressed himself she returned to his room. "I hope you enjoyed yourself at——" said she, seating herself on one side of the fire while he remained in his arm-chair on the other, stroking the calves of his legs. It was the first time he had had a fire in his room since the summer, and it pleased him; for the good bishop loved to be warm and cozy. Yes, he said, he had enjoyed himself very much. Nothing could be more polite than the archbishop; and Mrs. Archbishop had been equally charming.

Mrs. Proudie was delighted to hear it; nothing, she declared, pleased her so much as to think

Her bairn respectit like the lave.

She did not put it precisely in these words, but what she said came to the same thing; and then, having petted and fondled her little man sufficiently, she proceeded to business.

"The poor dean is still alive," said she.

"So I hear, so I hear," said the bishop. "I'll go to the deanery directly after breakfast to-morrow."

"We are going to this party at Ullathorne to-morrow morning, my dear; we must be there early, you know,—by twelve o'clock I suppose."

"Oh,—ah!" said the bishop; "then I'll certainly call the next day."

"Was much said about it at——?" asked Mrs. Proudie.

"About what?" said the bishop.

"Filling up the dean's place," said Mrs. Proudie. As she spoke a spark of the wonted fire returned to her eye, and the bishop felt himself to be a little less comfortable than before.

"Filling up the dean's place; that is, if the dean dies?—very little, my dear. It was mentioned, just mentioned."

"And what did you say about it, bishop?"

"Why, I said that I thought that if, that is, should—should the dean die, that is, I said I thought——" As he went on stammering and floundering, he saw that his wife's eyes was fixed sternly on him. Why should he encounter such evil for a man whom he loved so slightly as Mr. Slope? Why should he give up his enjoyments and his ease, and such dignity as might be allowed to him, to fight a losing battle for a chaplain? The chaplain after all, if successful, would be as great a tyrant as his wife. Why fight at all? why contend? why be uneasy? From that moment he determined to fling Mr. Slope to the winds, and take the goods the gods provided.

"I am told," said Mrs. Proudie, speaking very slowly, "that Mr. Slope is looking to be the new dean."

"Yes,—certainly, I believe he is," said the bishop.

"And what does the archbishop say about that?" asked Mrs. Proudie.

"Well, my dear, to tell the truth, I promised Mr. Slope to speak to the archbishop. Mr. Slope spoke to me about it. It is very arrogant of him, I must say,—but that is nothing to me."

"Arrogant!" said Mrs. Proudie; "it is the most impudent piece of pretention I ever heard of in my life. Mr. Slope dean of Barchester, indeed! And what did you do in the matter, bishop?"

"Why, my dear, I did speak to the archbishop."

"You don't mean to tell me," said Mrs. Proudie, "that you are going to make yourself ridiculous by lending your name to such a preposterous attempt as this? Mr. Slope dean of Barchester, indeed!" And she tossed her head, and put her arms a-kimbo, with an air of confident defiance that made her husband quite sure that Mr. Slope never would be Dean of Barchester. In truth, Mrs. Proudie was all but invincible; had she married Petruchio, it may be doubted whether that arch wife-tamer would have been able to keep her legs out of those garments which are presumed by men to be peculiarly unfitted for feminine use.

"It is preposterous, my dear."

"Then why have you endeavoured to assist him?"

"Why,—my dear, I haven't assisted him—much."

"But why have you done it at all? why have you mixed your name up in any thing so ridiculous? What was it you did say to the archbishop?"

"Why, I just did mention it; I just did say that—that in the event of the poor dean's death, Mr. Slope would—would——"

"Would what?"

"I forget how I put it,—would take it if he could get it; something of that sort. I didn't say much more than that."

"You shouldn't have said anything at all. And what did the archbishop say?"

"He didn't say anything; he just bowed and rubbed his hands. Somebody else came up at the moment, and as we were discussing the new parochial universal school committee, the matter of the new dean dropped; after that I didn't think it wise to renew it."

"Renew it! I am very sorry you ever mentioned it. What will the archbishop think of you?"

"You may be sure, my dear, the archbishop thought very little about it."

"But why did you think about it, bishop? how could you think of making such a creature as that Dean of Barchester?—Dean of Barchester! I suppose he'll be looking for a bishopric some of these days—a man that hardly knows who his own father was; a man that I found without bread to his mouth, or a coat to his back. Dean of Barchester, indeed! I'll dean him."

Mrs. Proudie considered herself to be in politics a pure Whig; all her family belonged to the Whig party. Now among all ranks of Englishmen and Englishwomen (Mrs. Proudie should, I think, be ranked among the former, on the score of her great strength of mind), no one is so hostile to lowly born pretenders to high station as the pure Whig.

The bishop thought it necessary to exculpate himself. "Why, my dear," said he, "it appeared to me that you and Mr. Slope did not get on quite so well as you used to do."

"Get on!" said Mrs. Proudie, moving her foot uneasily on the hearth-rug, and compressing her lips in a manner that betokened much danger to the subject of their discourse.

"I began to find that he was objectionable to you,"—Mrs. Proudie's foot worked on the hearth-rug with great rapidity,—"and that you would be more comfortable if he was out of the palace,"— Mrs. Proudie smiled, as a hyena may probably smile before he begins his laugh,—"and therefore I thought that if he got this place, and so ceased to be my chaplain, you might be pleased at such an arrangement."

And then the hyena laughed out. Pleased at such an arrangement! pleased at having her enemy converted into a dean with twelve hundred a year! Medea, when she decribes the customs of her native country (I am quoting from Robson's edition), assures her astonished auditor that in her land captives, when taken, are eaten. "You pardon them?" says Medea. "We do indeed," says the mild Grecian. "We eat them!" says she of Colchis, with terrific energy. Mrs. Proudie was the Medea of Barchester; she had no idea of not eating Mr. Slope. Pardon him! merely get rid of him! make a dean of him! It was not so they did with their captives in her country, among people of her sort! Mr. Slope had no such mercy to expect; she would pick him to the very last bone.

"Oh, yes, my dear, of course he'll cease to be your chaplain," said she. "After what has passed, that must be a matter of course. I couldn't for a moment think of living in the same house with such a man. Besides, he has shown himself quite unfit for such a situation; making broils and quarrels among the clergy, getting you, my dear, into scrapes, and taking upon himself as though he were as good as bishop himself. Of course he'll go. But because he leaves the palace, that is no reason why he should get into the deanery."

"Oh, of course not!" said the bishop; "but to save appearances you know, my dear——"

"I don't want to save appearances; I want Mr. Slope to appear just what he is—a false, designing, mean, intriguing man. I have my eye on him; he little knows what I see. He is misconducting himself in the most disgraceful way with that lame Italian woman. That family is a disgrace to Barchester, and Mr. Slope is a disgrace to Barchester! If he doesn't look well to it, he'll have his gown stripped off his back instead of having a dean's hat on his head. Dean, indeed! The man has gone mad with arrogance."

The bishop said nothing further to excuse either himself or his chaplain, and having shown himself passive and docile was again taken into favour. They soon went to dinner, and he spent the pleasantest evening he had had in his own house for a long time. His daughter played and sang to him as he sipped his coffee and read his newspaper, and Mrs. Proudie asked good-natured little questions about the archbishop; and then he went happily to bed, and slept as quietly as though Mrs. Proudie had been Griselda herself. While shaving himself in the morning and preparing for the festivities of Ullathorne, he fully resolved to run no more tilts against a warrior so fully armed at all points as was Mrs. Proudie.

CHAPTER XXIX

OXFORD—THE MASTER AND TUTOR OF LAZARUS

MR. ARABIN, as we have said, had but a sad walk of it under the trees of Plumstead churchyard. He did not appear to any of the family till dinner time, and then he seemed, as far as their judgment went, to be quite himself. He had, as was his wont, asked himself a great many questions, and given himself a great many answers; and the upshot of this was that he had set himself down for an ass. He had determined that he was much too old and much too rusty to commence the manoeuvres of love-making; that he had let the time slip through his hands which should have been used for such purposes; and that now he must lie on his bed as he had made it. Then he asked himself whether in truth he did love this woman; and he answered himself, not without a long struggle, but at last honestly, that he certainly did love her. He then asked himself whether he did not also love her money; and he again answered himself that he did so. But here he did not answer honestly. It was and ever had been his weakness to look for impure motives for his own conduct. No doubt, circumstanced as he was, with a small living and a fellowship, accustomed as he had been to collegiate luxuries and expensive comforts, he might have hesitated to marry a penniless woman had he felt ever so strong a predilection for the woman herself; no doubt Eleanor's fortune put all such difficulties out of the question; but it was equally without doubt that his love for her had crept upon him without the slightest idea on his part that he could ever benefit his own condition by sharing her wealth.

When he had stood on the hearth-rug, counting the pattern, and counting also the future chances of his own life, the remembrances of Mrs. Bold's comfortable income had not certainly damped his first assured feeling of love for her. And why should it have done so? Need it have done so with the purest of men? Be that as it may, Mr. Arabin decided against himself; he decided that it had done so in his case, and that he was not the purest of men.

He also decided, which was more to his purpose, that Eleanor did not care a straw for him, and that very probably she did care a straw for his rival. Then he made up his mind not to think of her any more, and went on thinking of her till he was almost in a state to drown himself in the little brook which ran at the bottom of the archdeacon's grounds.

And ever and again his mind would revert to the Signora Neroni, and he would make comparisons between her and Eleanor Bold, not always in favour of the latter. The signora had listened to him, and flattered him, and believed in him; at least she had told him so. Mrs. Bold had also listened to him, but had never flattered him; had not always believed in him; and now had broken from him in violent rage. The signora, too, was the more lovely woman of the two, and had also the additional attraction of her affliction; for to him it was an attraction.

But he never could have loved the Signora Neroni as he felt that he now loved Eleanor! and so he flung stones into the brook, instead of flinging in himself, and sat down on its margin as sad a gentleman as you shall meet in a summer's day.

He heard the dinner-bell ring from the churchyard, and he knew that it was time to recover his self-possession. He felt that he was disgracing himself in his own eyes, that he had been idling his time and neglecting the high duties which he had taken upon himself to perform. He should have spent this afternoon among the poor at St. Ewold's, instead of wandering about at Plumstead, an ancient love-lorn swain, dejected and sighing, full of imaginary sorrows and Wertherian grief. He was thoroughly ashamed of himself, and determined to lose no time in retrieving his character, so damaged in his own eyes. Thus when he appeared at dinner he was as animated as ever, and was the author of most of the conversation which graced the archdeacon's board on that evening. Mr. Harding was ill at ease and sick at heart, and did not care to appear more comfortable than he really was; what little he did say was said to his daughter. He thought that the archdeacon and Mr. Arabin had leagued together against Eleanor's comfort; and his wish now was to break away from the pair, and undergo in his Barchester lodgings whatever Fate had in store for him. He hated the name of the hospital; his attempt to regain his lost inheritance there had brought upon him so much suffering. As far as he was concerned, Mr. Quiverful was now welcome to the place.

And the archdeacon was not very lively. The poor dean's illness was of course discussed in the first place. Dr. Grantly did not mention Mr. Slope's name in connexion with the expected event of Dr. Trefoil's death; he did not wish to say anything about Mr. Slope just at present, nor did he wish to make known his sad surmises; but the idea that his enemy might possibly become Dean of Barchester made him very gloomy. Should such an event take place, such a dire catastrophe come about, there would be an end to his life as far as his life was connected with the city of Barchester. He must give up all his old haunts, all his old habits, and live quietly as a retired rector at Plumstead. It had been a severe trial for him to have Dr. Proudie in the palace; but with Mr. Slope also in the deanery, he felt that he should be unable to draw his breath in Barchester close.

Thus it came to pass that in spite of the sorrow at his heart, Mr. Arabin was apparently the gayest of the party. Both Mr. Harding and Mrs. Grantly were in a slight degree angry with him on account of his want of gloom. To the one it appeared as though he were triumphing at Eleanor's banishment, and to the other that he was not affected as he should have been by all the sad circumstances of the day, Eleanor's obstinacy, Mr. Slope's success, and the poor dean's apoplexy. And so they were all at cross purposes.

Mr. Harding left the room almost together with the ladies, and then the archdeacon opened his heart to Mr. Arabin. He still harped upon the hospital. "What did that fellow mean," said he, "by saying in his letter to Mrs. Bold, that if Mr. Harding would call on the bishop it would be all right? Of course I would not be guided by anything he might say; but still it may be well that Mr. Harding should see the bishop. It would be foolish to let the thing slip through our fingers because Mrs. Bold is determined to make a fool of herself."

Mr. Arabin hinted that he was not quite so sure that Mrs. Bold would make a fool of herself. He said that he was not convinced that she did regard Mr. Slope so warmly as she was supposed to do. The archdeacon questioned and cross-questioned him about this, but elicited nothing; and at last remained firm in his own conviction that he was destined, *malgré lui*, to be the brother-in-law of Mr. Slope. Mr. Arabin strongly advised that Mr. Harding should take no step regarding the hospital in connexion with, or in consequence of, Mr. Slope's letter. "If the bishop really means to confer the appointment on Mr. Harding," argued Mr. Arabin, "he will take care to let him have some other intimation than a message conveyed through a letter to a lady. Were Mr. Harding to present himself at the palace he might merely be playing Mr. Slope's game;" and thus it was settled that nothing should be done till the great Dr. Gwynne's arrival, or at any rate without that potentate's sanction.

It was droll to observe how these men talked of Mr. Harding as though he were a puppet, and planned their intrigues and small ecclesiastical manoeuvres in reference to Mr. Harding's future position, without dreaming of taking him into their confidence. There was a comfortable house and income in question, and it was very desirable, and certainly very just, that Mr. Harding should have them; but that, at present, was not the main point; it was expedient to beat the bishop, and if possible to smash Mr. Slope.

Mr. Slope had set up, or was supposed to have set up, a rival candidate. Of all things the most desirable would have been to have had Mr. Quiverful's appointment published to the public, and then annulled by the clamour of an indignant world, loud in the defence of Mr. Harding's rights. But of such an event the chance was small; a slight fraction only of the world would be indignant, and that fraction would be one not accustomed to loud speaking. And then the preferment had in a sort of way been offered to Mr. Harding, and had in a sort of way been refused by him.

Mr. Slope's wicked, cunning hand had been peculiarly conspicuous in the way in which this had been brought to pass, and it was the success of Mr. Slope's cunning which was so painfully grating to the feelings of the archdeacon. That which of all things he most dreaded was that he should be out-generalled by Mr. Slope; and just at present it appeared probable that Mr. Slope would turn his flank, steal a march on him, cut off his provisions, carry his strong town by a *coup de main*, and at last beat him thoroughly in a regular pitched battle. The archdeacon felt that his flank had been turned when desired to wait on Mr. Slope instead of the bishop, that a march had been stolen when Mr. Harding was induced to refuse the bishop's offer, that his provisions would be cut off when Mr. Quiverful got the hospital, that Eleanor was the strong town doomed to be taken, and that Mr. Slope, as Dean of Barchester, would be regarded by all the world as the conqueror in the final conflict.

Dr. Gwynne was the *Deus ex machinâ* who was to come down upon the Barchester stage, and bring about deliverance from these terrible evils. But how can melodramatic *dénouements* be properly brought about, how can vice and Mr. Slope be punished, and virtue and the archdeacon be rewarded, while the avenging god is laid up with the gout? In the mean time evil may be triumphant, and poor innocence, transfixed to the earth by an arrow from Dr. Proudie's quiver, may lie dead upon the ground, not to be resuscitated even by Dr. Gwynne.

Two or three days after Eleanor's departure, Mr. Arabin went to Oxford, and soon found himself closeted with the august head of his college. It was quite clear that Dr. Gwynne was not very sanguine as to the effects of his journey to Barchester, and not over anxious to interfere with the bishop. He had had the gout but was very nearly convalescent, and Mr. Arabin at once saw that had the mission been one of which the master thoroughly approved, he would before this have been at Plumstead.

As it was, Dr. Gwynne was resolved on visiting his friend, and willingly promised to return to Barchester with Mr. Arabin. He could not bring himself to believe that there was any probability that Mr. Slope would be made Dean of Barchester. Rumour, he said, had reached even his ears, not at all favourable to that gentleman's character, and he expressed himself strongly of opinion that any such appointment was quite out of the question. At this stage of the proceedings, the master's right-hand man, Tom Staple, was called in to assist at the conference. Tom Staple was the Tutor of Lazarus, and moreover a great man at Oxford. Though universally known by a species of nomenclature so very undignified, Tom Staple was one who maintained a high dignity in the University. He was, as it were, the leader of the Oxford tutors, a body of men who consider themselves collectively as being by very little, if at all, second in importance to the heads themselves. It is not always the case that the master, or warden, or provost, or principal can hit it off exactly with his tutor. A tutor is by no means indisposed to have a will of his own. But as Lazarus they were great friends and firm allies at the time of which we are writing.

Tom Staple was a hale strong man of about forty-five; short in stature, swarthy in face, with strong sturdy black hair, and crisp black beard, of which very little was allowed to show itself in shape of whiskers. He always wore a white neckcloth, clean indeed, but not tied with that scrupulous care which now distinguishes some of our younger clergy. He was, of course, always clothed in a seemly suit of solemn black. Mr. Staple was a decent cleanly liver, not over addicted to any sensuality; but nevertheless a somewhat warmish hue was beginning to adorn his nose, the peculiar effect, as his friends averred, of a certain pipe of port introduced into the cellars of Lazarus the very same year in which the tutor entered it as a freshman. There was also, perhaps, a little redolence of port wine, as it were the slightest possible twang, in Mr. Staple's voice.

In these latter days Tom Staple was not a happy man; University reform had long been his bugbear, and now was his bane. It was not with him as with most others, an affair of politics, respecting which, when the need existed, he could, for parties' sake or on behalf of principle, maintain a certain amount of necessary zeal; it was not with him a subject for dilettante warfare, and courteous commonplace opposition. To him it was life and death. The *statu quo* of the University was his only idea of life, and any reformation was as bad to him as death. He would willingly have been a martyr in the cause, had the cause admitted of martyrdom.

At the present day, unfortunately, public affairs will allow of no martyrs, and therefore it is that there is such a deficiency of zeal. Could gentlemen of 10,000*l.* a year have died on their own doorsteps in defence of protection, no doubt some half-dozen glorious old baronets would have so fallen, and the school of protection would at this day have been crowded with scholars. Who can fight strenuously in any combat in which there is no danger. Tom Staple would have willingly been impaled before a Committee of the House, could he by such self-sacrifice have infused his own spirit into the component members of the hebdomadal board.

Tom Staple was one of those who in his heart approved of the credit system which had of old been in vogue between the students and tradesmen of the University. He knew and acknowledged to himself that it was useless in these degenerate days publicly to contend with the Jupiter on such a subject. The Jupiter had undertaken to rule the University, and Tom Staple was well aware that the Jupiter was too powerful for him. But in secret, and among his safe companions, he would argue that the system of credit was an ordeal good for young men to undergo.

The bad men, said he, the weak and worthless, blunder into danger and burn their feet; but the good men, they who have any character, they who have that within them which can reflect credit on their Alma Mater, they come through scatheless. What merit will there be to a young man to get through safely, if he be guarded and protected and restrained like a school-boy? By so doing, the period of the ordeal is only postponed, and the manhood of the man will be deferred from the age of twenty to that of twenty-four. If you bind him with leading-strings at college, he will break lose while eating for the bar in London; bind him there, and he will break loose afterwards, when he is a married man. The wild oats must be sown somewhere. 'Twas thus that Tom Staple would argue of young men; not, indeed, with much consistency, but still with some practical knowledge of the subject gathered from long experience.

And now Tom Staple proffered such wisdom as he had for the assistance of Dr. Gwynne and Mr. Arabin.

"Quite out of the question," said he, arguing that Mr. Slope could not possibly be made the new Dean of Barchester.

"So I think," said the master. "He has no standing, and, if all I hear be true, very little character."

"As to character," said Tom Staple, "I don't think much of that. They rather like loose parsons for deans; a little fast living, or a dash of infidelity, is no bad recommendation to a cathedral close. But they couldn't make Mr. Slope; the last two deans have been Cambridge men; you'll not show me an instance of their making three men running from the same University. We don't get our share, and never shall, I suppose; but we must at least have one out of three."

"Those sort of rules are all gone by now," said Mr. Arabin.

"Everything has gone by, I believe," said Tom Staple. "The cigar has been smoked out, and we are the ashes."

"Speak for yourself, Staple," said the master.

"I speak for all," said the tutor, stoutly. "It is coming to that, that there will be no life left anywhere in the country. No one is any longer fit to rule himself, or those belonging to him. The Government is to find us all in everything, and the press is to find the Government. Nevertheless, Mr. Slope won't be Dean of Barchester."

"And who will be warden of the hospital?" said Mr. Arabin.

"I hear that Mr. Quiverful is already appointed," said Tom Staple.

"I think not," said the master. "And I think, moreover, that Dr. Proudie will not be so short-sighted as to run against such a rock: Mr. Slope should himself have sense enough to prevent it."

"But perhaps Mr. Slope may have no objection to see his patron on a rock," said the suspicious tutor.

"What could he get by that?" asked Mr. Arabin.

"It is impossible to see the doubles of such a man," said Mr. Staple. "It seems quite clear that Bishop Proudie is altogether in his hands, and it is equally clear that he has been moving heaven and earth to get this Mr. Quiverful into the hospital, although he must know that such an appointment would be most damaging to the bishop. It is impossible to understand such a man, and dreadful to think," added Tom Staple, sighing deeply, "that the welfare and fortunes of good men may depend on his intrigues."

Dr. Gwynne or Mr. Staple were not in the least aware, nor even was Mr. Arabin, that this Mr. Slope, of whom they were talking, had been using his utmost efforts to put their own candidate into the hospital; and that in lieu of being permanent in the palace, his own expulsion therefrom had been already decided on by the high powers of the diocese.

"I'll tell you what," said the tutor, "if this Quiverful is thrust into the hospital and Dr. Trefoil does die, I should not wonder if the Government were to make Mr. Harding Dean of Barchester. They would feel bound to do something for him after all that was said when he resigned."

Dr. Gwynne at the moment made no reply to this suggestion; but it did not the less impress itself on his mind. If Mr. Harding could not be warden of the hospital, why should he not be Dean of Barchester?

And so the conference ended without any very fixed resolution, and Dr. Gwynne and Mr. Arabin prepared for their journey to Plumstead on the morrow.

CHAPTER XXX

MISS THORNE'S FÊTE CHAMPÊTRE

THE day of the Ullathorne party arrived, and all the world were there; or at least so much of the world as had been included in Miss Thorne's invitation. As we have said, the bishop returned home on the previous evening, and on the same evening, and by the same train, came Dr. Gwynne and Mr. Arabin from Oxford. The arch-deacon with his brougham was in waiting for the Master of Lazarus, so that there was a goodly show of church dignitaries on the platform of the railway.

The Stanhope party was finally arranged in the odious manner already described, and Eleanor got into the doctor's carriage full of apprehension and presentiment of further misfortune, whereas Mr. Slope entered the vehicle elate with triumph.

He had received that morning a very civil note from Sir Nicholas Fitzwhiggin; not promising much indeed; but then Mr. Slope knew or fancied that he knew, that it was not etiquette for government officers to make promises. Though Sir Nicholas promised nothing he implied a good deal; declared his conviction that Mr. Slope would make an excellent dean, and wished him every kind of success. To be sure he added that, not being in the cabinet, he was never consulted on such matters, and that even if he spoke on the subject his voice would go for nothing. But all this Mr. Slope took for the prudent reserve of official life. To complete his anticipated triumphs, another letter was brought to him just as he was about to start to Ullathorne.

Mr. Slope also enjoyed the idea of handing Mrs. Bold out of Dr. Stanhope's carriage before the multitude at Ullathorne gate, as much as Eleanor dreaded the same ceremony. He had fully made up his mind to throw himself and his fortune at the widow's feet, and had almost determined to select the present propitious morning for doing so. The signora had of late been less than civil to him. She had indeed admitted his visits, and listened, at any rate without anger, to his love; but she had tortured him and reviled him, jeered at him and ridiculed him, while she allowed him to call her the most beautiful of living women, to kiss her hand, and to proclaim himself with reiterated oaths her adorer, her slave, and worshipper.

The Ullathorne household was early on the move. Cooks were cooking in the kitchen long before daylight, and men were dragging out tables and hammering red baize on to benches at the earliest dawn. With what dread eagerness did Miss Thorne look out at the weather as soon as the parting veil of night permitted her to look at all! In this respect at any rate there was nothing to grieve her. The glass had been rising for the last three days, and the morning broke with that dull chill steady grey haze which in autumn generally presages a clear and dry day. By seven she was dressed and down. Miss Thorne knew nothing of the modern luxury of *déshabilles*. She would as soon have thought of appearing before her brother without her stockings as without her stays; and Miss Thorne's stays were no trifle.

And yet there was nothing for her to do when down. She fidgeted out to the lawn, and then back into the kitchen. She put on her high-heeled clogs, and fidgeted out into the paddock. Then she went into the small home park where the quintain was erected. The pole and cross bar and the swivel, and the target and the bag of flour were all complete. She got up on a carpenter's bench and touched the target with her hand; it went round with beautiful ease; the swivel had been oiled to perfection. She almost wished to take old Plomacy at his word, to get on a side saddle and have a tilt at it herself.

At about nine the lower orders began to congregate in the paddock and park, under the surveillance of Mr. Plomacy and the head gardener and head groom, who were sworn in as his deputies, and were to assist him in keeping the peace and promoting the sports. Many of the younger inhabitants of the neighbourhood, thinking that they could not have too much of a good thing, had come at a very early hour, and the road between the house and the church had been thronged for some time before the gates were thrown open.

And then another difficulty of huge dimensions arose, a difficulty which Mr. Plomacy had indeed foreseen and for which he was in some sort provided. Some of those who wished to share Miss Thorne's hospitality were not so particular as they should have been as to the preliminary ceremony of an invitation. They doubtless conceived that they had been overlooked by accident; and instead of taking this in dudgeon, as their betters would have done, they good-naturedly put up with the slight, and showed that they did so by presenting themselves at the gate in their Sunday best.

Mr. Plomacy, however, well knew who were welcome and who were not. To some, even though uninvited, he allowed ingress. "Don't be too particular, Plomacy," his mistress had said; "especially with the children. If they live anywhere near, let them in."

Acting on this hint, Mr. Plomacy did let in many an eager urchin, and a few tidily dressed girls with their swains, who in no way belonged to the property. But to the denizens of the city he was inexorable. Many a Barchester apprentice made his appearance there that day, and urged with piteous supplication that he had been working all the week in making saddles and boots for the use of Ullathorne, in compounding doses for the horses, or cutting up carcases for the kitchen. No such claim was allowed. Mr. Plomacy knew nothing about the city apprentices; he was to admit the tenants and labourers on the estate; Miss Thorne wasn't going to take in the whole city of Barchester; and so on.

Nevertheless, before the day was half over, all this was found to be useless. Almost anybody who chose to come made his way into the park, and the care of the guardians was transferred to the tables on which the banquet was spread. Even here there was many an unauthorized claimant for a place, of whom it was impossible to get quit without more commotion than the place and food were worth.

CHAPTER XXXI

ULLATHORNE SPORTS—ACT I

THE trouble in civilised life of entertaining company, as it is called too generally without much regard to strict veracity, is so great that it cannot but be matter of wonder that people are so fond of attempting it. It is difficult to ascertain what is the *quid pro quo*. If they who give such laborious parties, and who endure such toil and turmoil in the vain hope of giving them successfully, really enjoyed the parties given by others, the matter could be understood. A sense of justice would induce men and women to undergo, in behalf of others, those miseries which others had undergone in their behalf. But they all profess that going out is as great a bore as receiving; and to look at them when they are out, one cannot but believe them.

Entertain! Who shall have sufficient self-assurance, who shall feel sufficient confidence in his own powers to dare to boast that he can entertain his company? A clown can sometimes do so, and sometimes a dancer in short petticoats and stuffed pink legs; occasionally, perhaps, a singer. But beyond these, success in this art of entertaining is not often achieved. Young men and girls linking themselves kind with kind, pairing like birds in spring because nature wills it, they, after a simple fashion, do entertain each other. Few others even try.

Ladies, when they open their houses, modestly confessing, it may be presumed, their own incapacity, mainly trust to wax candles and upholstery. Gentlemen seem to rely on their white waistcoats. To these are added, for the delight of the more sensual, champagne and such good things of the table as fashion allows to be still considered as comestible. Even in this respect the world is deteriorating. All the good soups are now tabooed; and at the houses of one's accustomed friends, small barristers, doctors, government clerks, and such like (for we cannot all of us always live as grandees, surrounded by an elysium of livery servants), one gets a cold potato handed to one as a sort of finale to one's slice of mutton. Alas! for those happy days when one could say to one's neighbourhood, "Jones, shall I give you some mashed turnip?—may I trouble you for a little cabbage?" And then the pleasure of drinking wine with Mrs. Jones and Miss Smith; with all the Joneses and all the Smiths! These latter-day habits are certainly more economical.

Miss Thorne, however, boldly attempted to leave the modern beaten track, and made a positive effort to entertain her guests. Alas! she did so with but moderate success. They had all their own way of going, and would not go her way. She piped to them, but they would not dance. She offered to them good honest household cake, made of currants and flour and eggs and sweetmeat; but they would feed themselves on trashy wafers from the shop of the Barchester pastry-cook, on chalk and gum and adulterated sugar. Poor Miss Thorne! yours is not the first honest soul that has vainly striven to recall the glories of happy days gone by! If fashion suggests to a Lady De Courcy that when invited to a *déjeûner* at twelve she ought to come at three, no eloquence of thine will teach her the advantage of a nearer approach to punctuality.

She had fondly thought that when she called on her friends to come at twelve, and specially begged them to believe that she meant it, she would be able to see them comfortably seated in their tents at two. Vain woman—or rather ignorant woman—ignorant of the advances of that civilisation which the world had witnessed while she was growing old. At twelve she found herself alone, dressed in all the glory of the newest of her many suits of raiment; with strong shoes however, and a serviceable bonnet on her head, and a warm rich shawl on her shoulders. Thus clad she peered out into the tent, went to the ha-ha, and satisfied herself that at any rate the youngsters were amusing themselves, spoke a word to Mrs. Greenacre over the ditch, and took one look at the quintain. Three or four young farmers were turning the machine round and round, and poking at the bag of flour in manner not at all intended by the inventor of the game; but no mounted sportsmen were there. Miss Thorne looked at her watch. It was only fifteen minutes past twelve, and it was understood that Harry Greenacre was not to begin till the half hour.

Miss Thorne returned to her drawing-room rather quicker than was her wont, fearing that the countess might come and find none to welcome her. She need not have hurried, for no one was there. At half-past twelve she peeped into the kitchen; at a quarter to one she was joined by her brother; and just then the first fashionable arrival took place. Mrs. Clantantram was announced.

No announcement was necessary, indeed; for the good lady's voice was heard as she walked across the court-yard to the house scolding the unfortunate postilion who had driven her from Barchester. At the moment, Miss Thorne could not but be thankful that the other guests were more fashionable, and were thus spared the fury of Mrs. Clantantram's indignation.

"Oh, Miss Thorne, look here!" said she, as soon as she found herself in the drawing-room; "do look at my roquelaure! It's clean spoilt, and for ever. I wouldn't but wear it because I knew you wished us all to be grand to-day; and yet I had my misgivings. Oh dear, oh dear! It was five-and-twenty shillings a yard."

The Barchester post horses had misbehaved in some unfortunate manner just as Mrs. Clantantrum was getting out of the chaise and had nearly thrown her under the wheel.

Mrs. Clantantram belonged to other days, and therefore, though she had but little else to recommend her, Miss Thorne was to a certain extent fond of her. She sent the roquelaure away to be cleaned, and lent her one of her best shawls out of her own wardrobe.

The next comer was Mr. Arabin, who was immediately informed of Mrs. Clantantram's misfortune, and of her determination to pay neither master nor post-boy; although, as she remarked, she intended to get her lift home before she made known her mind upon that matter. Then a good deal of rustling was heard in the sort of lobby that was used for the ladies' outside cloaks; and the door having been thrown wide open, the servant announced, not in the most confident of voices, Mrs. Lookaloft, and the Miss Lookalofts, and Mr. Augustus Lookaloft.

Poor man!—we mean the footman. He knew, none better, that Mrs. Lookaloft had no business there, that she was not wanted there, and would not be welcome. But he had not the courage to tell a stout lady with a low dress, short sleeves, and satin at eight shillings a yard, that she had come to the wrong tent; he had not dared to hint to young ladies with white dancing shoes and long gloves, that there was a place ready for them in the paddock. And, thus Mrs. Lookaloft carried her point, broke through the guards, and made her way into the citadel. That she would have to pass an uncomfortable time there, she had surmised before. But nothing now could rob her of the power of boasting that she had consorted on the lawn with the squire and Miss Thorne, with a countess, a bishop, and the country grandees, while Mrs. Greenacre and such like were walking about with the ploughboys in the park. It was a great point gained by Mrs. Lookaloft, and it might be fairly expected that from this time forward the tradesmen of Barchester would, with undoubting pens, address her husband as T. Lookaloft, Esquire.

Mrs. Lookaloft's pluck carried her through everything, and she walked triumphant into the Ullathorne drawing-room; but her children did feel a little abashed at the sort of reception they met with. It was not in Miss Thorne's heart to insult her own guests; but neither was it in her disposition to overlook such effrontery.

"Oh, Mrs. Lookaloft, is this you," said she; "and your daughters and son? Well, we're very glad to see you; but I'm sorry you've come in such low dresses, as we are all going out of doors. Could we lend you anything?"

"Oh dear no! thank ye, Miss Thorne," said the mother; "the girls and myself are quite used to low dresses, when we're out."

"Are you, indeed?" said Miss Thorne shuddering; but the shudder was lost on Mrs. Lookaloft.

"And where's Lookaloft?" said the master of the house, coming up to welcome his tenant's wife. Let the faults of the family be what they would, he could not but remember that their rent was well paid; he was therefore not willing to give them a cold shoulder.

"Such a headache, Mr. Thorne!" said Mrs. Lookaloft. "In fact he couldn't stir, or you may be certain on such a day he would not have absented hisself."

"Dear me," said Miss Thorne. "If he is so ill, I'm sure you'd wish to be with him."

"Not at all!" said Mrs. Lookaloft. "Not at all, Miss Thorne. It is only bilious you know, and when he's that way he can bear nobody nigh him."

The fact however was that Mr. Lookaloft, having either more sense or less courage than his wife, had not chosen to intrude on Miss Thorne's drawing-room; and as he could not very well have gone among the plebeians while his wife was with the patricians, he thought it most expedient to remain at Rosebank.

Mrs. Lookaloft soon found herself on a sofa, and the Miss Lookalofts on two chairs, while Mr. Augustus stood near the door; and here they remained till in due time they were seated all four together at the bottom of the dining-room table.

Then the Grantlys came; the archdeacon and Mrs. Grantly and the two girls, and Dr. Gwynne and Mr. Harding; and as ill luck would have it, they were closely followed by Dr. Stanhope's carriage. As Eleanor looked out of the carriage window, she saw her brother-in-law helping the ladies out, and threw herself back into her seat, dreading to be discovered. She had had an odious journey. Mr. Slope's civility had been more than ordinarily greasy; and now, though he had not in fact said anything which she could notice, she had for the first time entertained a suspicion that he was intending to make love to her. Was it after all true that she had been conducting herself in a way that justified the world in thinking that she liked the man? After all, could it be possible that the archdeacon and Mr. Arabin were right, and that she was wrong? Charlotte Stanhope had also been watching Mr. Slope, and had come to the conclusion that it behoved her brother to lose no further time, if he meant to gain the widow. She almost regretted that it had not been contrived that Bertie should be at Ullathorne before them.

Dr. Grantly did not see his sister-in-law in company with Mr. Slope, but Mr. Arabin did. Mr. Arabin came out with Mr. Thorne to the front door to welcome Mrs. Grantly, and he remained in the courtyard till all their party had passed on. Eleanor hung back in the carriage as long as she well could, but she was nearest to the door, and when Mr. Slope, having alighted, offered her his hand, she had no alternative but to take it. Mr. Arabin standing at the open door, while Mrs. Grantly was shaking hands with some one within, saw a clergyman alight from the carriage whom he at once knew to be Mr. Slope, and then he saw this clergyman hand out Mrs. Bold. Having seen so much, Mr. Arabin, rather sick at heart, followed Mrs. Grantly into the house.

Eleanor was, however, spared any further immediate degradation, for Dr. Stanhope gave her his arm across the courtyard, and Mr. Slope was fain to throw away his attention upon Charlotte.

They had hardly passed into the house, and from the house to the lawn, when, with a loud rattle and such noise as great men and great women are entitled to make in their passage through the world, the Proudies drove up. It was soon apparent that no every day comer was at the door. One servant whispered to another that it was the bishop, and the word soon ran through all the hangers-on and strange grooms and coachmen about the place. There was quite a little cortège to see the bishop and his "lady" walk across the courtyard, and the good man was pleased to see that the church was held in such respect in the parish of St. Ewold's.

And now the guests came fast and thick, and the lawn began to be crowded, and the room to be full. Voices buzzed, silk rustled against silk, and muslin crumpled against muslin. Miss Thorne became more happy than she had been, and again bethought her of her sports. There were targets and bows and arrows prepared at the further end of the lawn. Here the gardens of the place encroached with a somewhat wide sweep upon the paddock, and gave ample room for the doings of the toxophilites. Miss Thorne got together such daughters of Diana as could bend a bow, and marshalled them to the targets. There were the Grantly girls and the Proudie girls and the Chadwick girls, and the two daughters of the burly chancellor, and Miss Knowle; and with them went Frederick and Augustus Chadwick, and young Knowle of Knowle park, and Frank Foster of the Elms, and Mr. Velem Deeds the dashing attorney of the High Street, and the Rev. Mr. Green, and the Rev. Mr. Brown, and the Rev. Mr. White, all of whom, as in duty bound, attended the steps of the three Miss Proudies.

"Did you ever ride at the quintain, Mr. Foster?" said Miss Thorne, as she walked with her party, across the lawn.

"The quintain?" said young Foster, who considered himself a dab at horsemanship. "Is it a sort of gate, Miss Thorne?"

Miss Thorne had to explain the noble game she spoke of, and Frank Foster had to own that he never had ridden at the quintain.

"Would you like to come and see?" said Miss Thorne. "There'll be plenty here without you, if you like it."

"Well, I don't mind," said Frank; "I suppose the ladies can come too."

"Oh yes," said Miss Thorne; "those who like it; I have no doubt they'll go to see your prowess, if you'll ride, Mr. Foster."

Mr. Foster looked down at a most unexceptionable pair of pantaloons, which had arrived from London only the day before. They were the very things, at least he thought so, for a picnic or fête champêtre; but he was not prepared to ride in them. Nor was he more encouraged than had been Mr. Thorne, by the idea of being attacked from behind by the bag of flour which Miss Thorne had graphically described to him.

"Well, I don't know about riding, Miss Thorne," said he; "I fear I'm not quite prepared."

Miss Thorne sighed, but said nothing further. She left the toxophilites to their bows and arrows, and returned towards the house. But as she passed by the entrance to the small park, she thought that she might at any rate encourage the yeoman by her presence, as she could not induce her more fashionable guests to mix with them in their manly amusements. Accordingly she once more betook herself to the quintain post.

Here to her great delight she found Harry Greenacre ready mounted, with his pole in his hand, and a lot of comrades standing round him, encouraging him to the assault. She stood at a little distance and nodded to him in token of her good pleasure.

"Shall I begin, ma'am?" said Harry fingering his long staff in a rather awkward way, while his horse moved uneasily beneath him, not accustomed to a rider armed with such a weapon.

"Yes, yes," said Miss Thorne, standing triumphant as the queen of beauty, on an inverted tub which some chance had brought thither from the farm-yard.

"Here goes then," said Harry as he wheeled his horse round to get the necessary momentum of a sharp gallop. The quintain post stood right before him, and the square board at which he was to tilt was fairly in his way. If he hit that duly in the middle, and maintained his pace as he did so, it was calculated that he would be carried out of reach of the flour bag, which, suspended at the other end of the cross-bar on the post, would swing round when the board was struck. It was also calculated that if the rider did not maintain his pace, he would get a blow from the flour bag just at the back of his head, and bear about him the signs of his awkwardness to the great amusement of the lookers-on.

Harry Greenacre did not object to being powdered with flour in the service of his mistress, and therefore gallantly touched his steed with his spur, having laid his lance in rest to the best of his ability. But his ability in this respect was not great, and his appurtenances probably not very good; consequently, he struck his horse with his pole unintentionally on the side of the head as he started. The animal swerved and shied, and galloped off wide of the quintain. Harry well accustomed to manage a horse, but not to do so with a twelve-foot rod on his arm, lowered his right hand to the bridle and thus the end of the lance came to the ground, and got between the legs of the steed. Down came rider and steed and staff. Young Greenacre was thrown some six feet over the horse's head, and poor Miss Thorne almost fell off her tub in a swoon.

"Oh gracious, he's killed," shrieked a woman who was near him when he fell.

"The Lord be good to him! his poor mother, his poor mother!" said another.

"Well, drat them dangerous plays all the world over," said an old crone.

"He has broke his neck sure enough, if ever man did," said a fourth.

Poor Miss Thorne. She heard all this and yet did not quite swoon. She made her way through the crowd as best she could, sick herself almost to death. Oh, his mother—his poor mother! how could she ever forgive herself. The agony of that moment was terrific. She could hardly get to the place where the poor lad was lying, as three or four men in front were about the horse which had risen with some difficulty; but at last she found herself close to the young farmer.

"Has he marked himself? for heaven's sake tell me that; has he marked his knees?" said Harry, slowly rising and rubbing his left shoulder with his right hand, and thinking only of his horse's legs. Miss Thorne soon found that he had not broken his neck, nor any of his bones, nor been injured in any essential way. But from that time forth she never instigated any one to ride at a quintain.

Eleanor left Dr. Stanhope as soon as she could do so civilly, and went in quest of her father whom she found on the lawn in company with Mr. Arabin. She was not sorry to find them together. She was anxious to disabuse at any rate her father's mind as to this report which had got abroad respecting her, and would have been well pleased to have been able to do the same with regard to Mr. Arabin. She put her own through her father's arm, coming up behind his back, and then tendered her hand also to the vicar of St. Ewold's.

"And how did you come?" said Mr. Harding, when the first greeting was over.

"The Stanhopes brought me," said she; "their carriage was obliged to come twice, and has now gone back for the signora." As she spoke she caught Mr. Arabin's eye, and saw that he was looking pointedly at her with a severe expression. She understood at once the accusation contained in his glance. It said as plainly as an eye could speak, "Yes, you came with the Stanhopes, but you did so in order that you might be in company with Mr. Slope."

"Our party," said she, still addressing her father, "consisted of the doctor and Charlotte Stanhope, myself, and Mr. Slope." As she mentioned the last name she felt her father's arm quiver slightly beneath her touch. At the same moment Mr. Arabin turned away from them, and joining his hands behind his back strolled slowly away by one of the paths.

"Papa," said she, "it was impossible to help coming in the same carriage with Mr. Slope; it was quite impossible. I had promised to come with them before I dreamt of his coming, and afterwards I could not get out of it without explaining and giving rise to talk.

You weren't at home, you know, I couldn't possibly help it." She said all this so quickly that by the time her apology was spoken she was quite out of breath.

"I don't know why you should have wished to help it, my dear," said her father.

"Yes, papa, you do; you must know, you do know all the things they said at Plumstead. I am sure you do. You know all the arch-deacon said. How unjust he was; and Mr. Arabin too. He's a horrid man, a horrid odious man, but——"

"Who is an odious man, my dear? Mr. Arabin?"

"No; but Mr. Slope. You know I mean Mr. Slope. He's the most odious man I ever met in my life, and it was most unfortunate my having to come here in the same carriage with him. But how could I help it?"

A great weight began to move itself off Mr. Harding's mind. So, after all, the archdeacon with all his wisdom, and Mrs. Grantly with all her tact, and Mr. Arabin with all his talent, were in the wrong. His own child, his Eleanor, the daughter of whom he was so proud was not to become the wife of a Mr. Slope. He had been about to give his sanction to the marriage, so certified had he been of the fact; and now he learnt that this imputed lover of Eleanor's was at any rate as much disliked by her as by any one of the family. Mr. Harding, however, was by no means sufficiently a man of the world to conceal the blunder he had made. He could not pretend that he had entertained no suspicion; he could not make believe that he had never joined the archdeacon in his surmises. He was greatly surprised, and gratified beyond measure, and he could not help showing that such was the case.

"My darling girl," said he, "I am so delighted, so overjoyed. My own child; you have taken such a weight off my mind."

"But surely, papa, *you* didn't think——"

"I didn't know what to think, my dear. The archdeacon told me that——"

"The archdeacon!" said Eleanor, her face lighting up with passion. "A man like the archdeacon might, one would think, be better employed than in traducing his sister-in-law, and creating bitterness between a father and his daughter!"

"He didn't mean to do that, Eleanor."

"What did he mean then? Why did he interfere with me, and fill your mind with such falsehood?"

"Never mind it now, my child; never mind it now. We shall all know you better now."

"Oh, papa, that you should have thought it! that you should have suspected me!"

"I don't know what you mean by suspicion, Eleanor. There would be nothing disgraceful, you know; nothing wrong in such a marriage. Nothing that could have justified my interfering as your father." And Mr. Harding would have proceeded in his own defence to make out that Mr. Slope after all was a very good sort of man, and a very fitting second husband for a young widow, had he not been interrupted by Eleanor's greater energy.

"It would be disgraceful," said she; "it would be wrong; it would be abominable. Could I do such a horrid thing, I should expect no one to speak to me. Ugh——" and she shuddered as she thought of that matrimonial torch which her friends had been so ready to light on her behalf. "I don't wonder at Dr. Grantly; I don't wonder at Susan; but, oh, papa, I do wonder at you. How could you, how could you believe it?" Poor Eleanor, as she thought of her father's defalcation, could resist her tears no longer, and was forced to cover her face with her handkerchief.

The place was not very opportune for her grief. They were walking through the shrubberies, and there were many people near them. Poor Mr. Harding stammered out his excuse as best he could, and Eleanor with an effort controlled her tears, and returned her handkerchief to her pocket. She did not find it difficult to forgive her father, nor could she altogether refuse to join him in the returning gaiety of spirit to which her present avowal gave rise. It was such a load off his heart to think that he should not be called on to welcome Mr. Slope as his son-in-law. It was such a relief to him to find that his daughter's feelings and his own were now, as they ever had been, in unison. He had been so unhappy for the last six weeks about this wretched Mr. Slope! He was so indifferent as to the loss of the hospital, so thankful for the recovery of his daughter, that, strong as was the ground for Eleanor's anger, she could not find it in her heart to be long angry with him.

"Dear papa," she said, hanging closely to his arm, "never suspect me again: promise me that you never will. Whatever I do, you may be sure I shall tell you first; you may be sure I shall consult you."

And Mr. Harding did promise, and owned his sin, and promised again. And so, while he promised amendment and she uttered forgiveness, they returned together to the drawing-room windows.

And what had Eleanor meant when she declared that *whatever she did*, she would tell her father first? What was she thinking of doing?

So ended the first act of the melodrama which Eleanor was called on to perform this day at Ullathorne.

And now the eating and drinking began in earnest. Dr. Grantly, to his great horror, found himself leagued to Mrs. Clantantram. Mrs. Clantantram had a great regard for the archdeacon, which was not cordially returned; and when she, coming up to him, whispered in his ear, "Come, archdeacon, I'm sure you won't begrudge an old friend the favour of your arm," and then proceeded to tell him the whole history of her roquelaure, he resolved that he would shake her off before he was fifteen minutes older. But latterly the archdeacon had not been successful in his resolutions; and on the present occasion Mrs. Clantantram stuck to him till the banquet was over.

Dr. Gwynne got a baronet's wife, and Mrs. Grantly fell to the lot of a baronet. Charlotte Stanhope attached herself to Mr. Harding in order to make room for Bertie, who succeeded in sitting down in the dining-room next to Mrs. Bold. To speak sooth, now that he had love in earnest to make, his heart almost failed him.

Eleanor had been right glad to avail herself of his arm seeing that Mr. Slope was hovering nigh her. In striving to avoid that terrible Charybdis of a Slope she was in great danger of falling into an unseen Scylla on the otherhand, that Scylla being Bertie Stanhope. Nothing could be more gracious than she was to Bertie. She almost jumped at his proffered arm. Charlotte perceived this from a distance, and triumphed in her heart; Bertie felt it, and was encouraged; Mr. Slope saw it, and glowered with jealousy. Eleanor and Bertie sat down to table in the dining-room; and as she took her seat at his right hand, she found that Mr. Slope was already in possession of the chair at her own.

As these things were going on in the dining-room, Mr. Arabin was hanging enraptured and alone over the signora's sofa; and Eleanor from her seat could look through the open door and see that he was doing so.

CHAPTER XXXII

THE BISHOP SITS DOWN TO BREAKFAST, AND THE DEAN DIES

THE bishop of Barchester said grace over the wellspread board in the Ullathorne dining-room; and while he did so the last breath was flying from the dean of Barchester as he lay in his sick room in the deanery. When the bishop of Barchester raised his first glass of champagne to his lips, the deanship of Barchester was a good thing in the gift of the prime minister. Before the bishop of Barchester had left the table, the minister of the day was made aware of the fact at his country seat in Hampshire, and had already turned over in his mind the names of five very respectable aspirants for the preferment. It is at present only necessary to say that Mr. Slope's name was not among the five.

"'Twas merry in the hall when the beards wagged all;" and the clerical beards wagged merrily in the hall of Ullathorne that day. It was not till after the last cork had been drawn, the last speech made, the last nut cracked, that tidings reached and were whispered about that the poor dean was no more. It was well for the happiness of the clerical beards that this little delay took place, as otherwise decency would have forbidden them to wag at all.

But there was one sad man among them that day. Mr. Arabin's beard did not wag as it should have done. He had come there hoping the best, striving to think the best, about Eleanor; turning over in his mind all the words he remembered to have fallen from her about Mr. Slope, and trying to gather from them a conviction unfavourable to his rival. He had not exactly resolved to come that day to some decisive proof as to the widow's intention; but he had meant, if possible, to re-cultivate his friendship with Eleanor; and in his present frame of mind any such re-cultivation must have ended in a declaration of love.

He had passed the previous night alone at his new parsonage, and it was the first night that he had so passed. It had been dull and sombre enough. Mrs. Grantly had been right in saying that a priestess would be wanting at St. Ewold's. He had sat there alone with his glass before him, and then with his teapot, thinking about Eleanor Bold. As is usual in such meditations, he did little but blame her; blame her for liking Mr. Slope, and blame her for not liking him; blame her for her cordiality to himself, and blame her for her want of cordiality; blame her for being stubborn, headstrong, and passionate; and yet the more he thought of her the higher she rose in his affection. If only it should turn out, if only it could be made to turn out, that she had defended Mr. Slope, not from love, but on principle, all would be right. Such principle in itself would be admirable, loveable, womanly; he felt that he could be pleased to allow Mr. Slope just so much favour as that. But if —— And then Mr. Arabin poked his fire most unnecessarily, spoke crossly to his new parlour-maid who came in for the tea-things and threw himself back in his chair determined to go to sleep. Why had she been so stiffnecked when asked a plain question? She could not but have known in what light he regarded her. Why had she not answered a plain question, and so put an end to his misery? Then, instead of going to sleep in his arm-chair, Mr. Arabin walked about the room as though he had been possessed.

On the following morning, when he attended Miss Thorne's behests, he was still in a somewhat confused state. His first duty had been to converse with Mrs. Clantantram, and that lady had found it impossible to elicit the slightest sympathy from him on the subject of her roquelaure. Miss Thorne had asked him whether Mrs. Bold was coming with the Grantlys; and the two names of Bold and Grantly together had nearly made him jump from his seat.

He was in this state of confused uncertainty, hope, and doubt, when he saw Mr. Slope, with his most polished smile, handing Eleanor out of her carriage. He thought of nothing more. He never considered whether the carriage belonged to her or to Mr.

Slope, or to any one else to whom they might both be mutually
obliged without any concert between themselves. This sight in
his present state of mind was quite enough to upset him and his
resolves. It was clear as noonday. Had he seen her handed into
a carriage by Mr. Slope at a church door with a white veil over her
head, the truth could not be more manifest. He went into the
house, and, as we have seen, soon found himself walking with Mr.
Harding. Shortly afterwards Eleanor came up; and then he had
to leave his companion, and either go about alone or find another.
While in this state he was encountered by the archdeacon.

"I wonder," said Dr. Grantly, "if it be true that Mr. Slope and
Mrs. Bold came here together. Susan says she is almost sure she
saw their faces in the same carriage as she got out of her own."

Mr. Arabin had nothing for it but to bear his testimony to the
correctness of Mrs. Grantly's eyesight.

"It is perfectly shameful," said the archdeacon; "or I should
rather say, shameless. She was asked here as my guest; and if she
be determined to disgrace herself, she should have feeling enough
not to do so before my immediate friends. I wonder how that man
got himself invited. I wonder whether she had the face to bring
him."

To this Mr. Arabin could answer nothing, nor did he wish to
answer anything. Though he abused Eleanor to himself, he did
not choose to abuse her to any one else, nor was he well pleased to
hear any one else speak ill of her. Dr. Grantly, however, was very
angry, and did not spare his sister-in-law. Mr. Arabin therefore
left him as soon as he could, and wandered back into the house.

He had not been there long, when the signora was brought in.
For some time he kept himself out of temptation, and merely
hovered round her at a distance; but as soon as Mr. Thorne had
left her, he yielded himself up to the basilisk, and allowed himself
to be made prey of.

It is impossible to say how the knowledge had been acquired,
but the signora had a sort of instinctive knowledge that Mr. Arabin
was an admirer of Mrs. Bold. Men hunt foxes by the aid of dogs,
and are aware that they do so by the strong organ of smell with
which the dog is endowed. They do not, however, in the least
comprehend how such a sense can work with such acuteness. The
organ by which women instinctively, as it were, know and feel
how other women are regarded by men, and how also men are
regarded by other women, is equally strong, and equally incom-
prehensible. A glance, a word, a motion, suffices: by some such
acute exercise of her feminine senses the signora was aware that
Mr. Arabin loved Eleanor Bold; and therefore, by a further exercise
of her peculiar feminine propensities, it was quite natural for her
to entrap Mr. Arabin into her net.

The work was half done before she came to Ullathorne, and when could she have a better opportunity of completing it? She had had almost enough of Mr. Slope, though she could not quite resist the fun of driving a very sanctimonious clergyman to madness by a desperate and ruinous passion. Mr. Thorne had fallen too easily to give much pleasure in the chase. His position as a man of wealth might make his alliance of value, but as a lover he was very second-rate. We may say that she regarded him somewhat as a sportsman does a pheasant. The bird is so easily shot, that he would not be worth the shooting were it not for the very respectable appearance that he makes in a larder. The signora would not waste much time in shooting Mr. Thorne, but still he was worth bagging for family uses.

But Mr. Arabin was game of another sort. The signora was herself possessed of quite sufficient intelligence to know that Mr. Arabin was a man more than usually intellectual. She knew also, that as a clergyman he was of a much higher stamp than Mr. Slope, and that as a gentleman he was better educated than Mr. Thorne. She would never have attempted to drive Mr. Arabin into ridiculous misery as she did Mr. Slope, nor would she think it possible to dispose of him in ten minutes as she had done with Mr. Thorne.

Such were her reflections about Mr. Arabin. As to Mr. Arabin, it cannot be said that he reflected at all about the signora. He knew that she was beautiful, and he felt that she was able to charm him. He required charming in his present misery, and therefore he went and stood at the head of her couch. She knew all about it. Such were her peculiar gifts. It was her nature to see that he required charming, and it was her province to charm him. As the Eastern idler swallows his dose of opium, as the London re-probate swallows his dose of gin, so with similar desires and for similar reasons did Mr. Arabin prepare to swallow the charms of the Signora Neroni.

"Why an't you shooting with bows and arrows, Mr. Arabin?" said she, when they were nearly alone together in the drawing-room; "or talking with young ladies in shady bowers, or turning your talents to account in some way? What was a bachelor like you asked here for? Don't you mean to earn your cold chicken and champagne? Were I you, I should be ashamed to be so idle."

Mr. Arabin murmured some sort of answer. Though he wished to be charmed, he was hardly yet in a mood to be playful in return.

"Why, what ails you, Mr. Arabin?" said she, "here you are in your own parish; Miss Thorne tells me that her party is given expressly in your honour; and yet you are the only dull man at it. Your friend Mr. Slope was with me a few minutes since, full of life and spirits; why don't you rival him?"

It was not difficult for so acute an observer as Madeline Neroni to see that she had hit the nail on the head and driven the bolt home. Mr. Arabin winced visibly before her attack, and she knew at once that he was jealous of Mr. Slope.

"But I look on you and Mr. Slope as the very antipodes of men," said she. "There is nothing in which you are not each the reverse of the other, except in belonging to the same profession; and even in that you are so unlike as perfectly to maintain the rule. He is gregarious, you are given to solitude. He is active, you are passive. He works, you think. He likes women, you despise them. He is fond of position and power, and so are you, but for directly different reasons. He loves to be praised, you very foolishly abhor it. He will gain his rewards, which will be an insipid useful wife, a comfortable income, and a reputation for sanctimony. You will also gain yours."

"Well, and what will they be?" said Mr. Arabin, who knew that he was being flattered, and yet suffered himself to put up with it. "What will be my rewards?"

"The heart of some woman whom you will be too austere to own that you love, and the respect of some few friends which you will be too proud to own that you value."

"Rich rewards," said he; "but of little worth if they are to be so treated."

"Oh, you are not to look for such success as awaits Mr. Slope. He is born to be a successful man. He suggests to himself an object, and then starts for it with eager intention. Nothing will deter him from his pursuit. He will have no scruples, no fears, no hesitation. His desire is to be a bishop with a rising family, the wife will come first, and in due time the apron. You will see all this, and then——"

"Well, and what then?"

"Then you will begin to wish that you had done the same."

Mr. Arabin looked placidly out at the lawn, and resting his shoulder on the head of the sofa, rubbed his chin with his hand. It was a trick he had when he was thinking deeply; and what the signora said made him think. Was it not all true? Would he not hereafter look back, if not at Mr. Slope, at some others, perhaps not equally gifted with himself, who had risen in the world while he had lagged behind, and then wish that he had done the same?

"Is not such the doom of all speculative men of talent?" said she. "Do they not all sit rapt as you now are, cutting imaginary silken cords with fine edges, while those not so highly tempered sever the every-day Gordian knots of the world's struggle, and win wealth and renown? Steel too highly polished, edges too sharp, do not do for this world's work, Mr. Arabin."

Who was this woman that thus read the secrets of his heart, and re-uttered to him the unwelcome bodings of his own soul? He looked full into her face when she had done speaking, and said, "Am I one of those foolish blades, too sharp and too fine to do a useful day's work?"

"Why do you let the Slopes of the world out-distance you?" said she. "Is not the blood in your veins as warm as his? does not your pulse beat as fast? Has not God made you a man, and intended you to do a man's work here, ay, and to take a man's wages also?"

Mr. Arabin sat ruminating and rubbing his face, and wondering why these things were said to him; but he replied nothing. The signora went on—

"The greatest mistake any man ever made is to suppose that the good things of the world are not worth the winning. And it is a mistake so opposed to the religion which you preach! Why does God permit his bishops one after another to have their five thousands and ten thousands a year if such wealth be bad and not worth having? Why are beautiful things given to us, and luxuries and pleasant enjoyments, if they be not intended to be used? They must be meant for some one, and what is good for a layman cannot surely be bad for a clerk. You try to despise these good things, but you only try; you don't succeed."

"Don't I?" said Mr. Arabin, still musing, and not knowing what he said.

"I ask you the question; do you succeed?"

Mr. Arabin looked at her piteously. It seemed to him as though he were being interrogated by some inner spirit of his own, to whom he could not refuse an answer, and to whom he did not dare to give a false reply.

"Come, Mr. Arabin, confess; do you succeed? Is money so contemptible? Is worldly power so worthless? Is feminine beauty a trifle to be so slightly regarded by a wise man?"

"Feminine beauty!" said he, gazing into her face, as though all the feminine beauty in the world were concentrated there. "Why do you say I do not regard it?"

"If you look at me like that, Mr. Arabin, I shall alter my opinion— or should do so, were I not of course aware that I have no beauty of my own worth regarding."

The gentleman blushed crimson, but the lady did not blush at all. A slightly increased colour animated her face, just so much so as to give her an air of special interest. She expected a compliment from her admirer, but she was rather grateful than otherwise by finding that he did not pay it to her. Messrs. Slope and Thorne, Messrs. Brown, Jones and Robinson, they all paid her compliments. She was rather in hopes that she would ultimately succeed in inducing Mr. Arabin to abuse her.

"But your gaze," said she, "is one of wonder, and not of admiration. You wonder at my audacity in asking you such questions about yourself."

"Well, I do rather," said he.

"Nevertheless I expect an answer, Mr. Arabin. Why were women made beautiful if men are not to regard them?"

F

"But men do regard them," he replied.

"And why not you?"

"You are begging the question, Madame Neroni."

"I am sure I shall beg nothing, Mr. Arabin, which you will not grant, and I do beg for an answer. Do you not as a rule think women below your notice as companions? Let us see. There is the widow Bold looking round at you from her chair this minute. What would you say to her as a companion for life?"

Mr. Arabin, rising from his position, leaned over the sofa and looked through the drawing room door to the place where Eleanor was seated between Bertie Stanhope and Mr. Slope. She at once caught his glance, and averted her own. She was not pleasantly placed in her present position. Mr. Slope was doing his best to attract her attention; and she was striving to prevent his doing so by talking to Mr. Stanhope, while her mind was intently fixed on Mr. Arabin and Madame Neroni. Bertie Stanhope endeavoured to take advantage of her favours, but he was thinking more of the manner in which he would by-and-by throw himself at her feet, than of amusing her at the present moment.

"There," said the signora. "She was stretching her beautiful neck to look at you, and now you have disturbed her. Well I declare, I believe I am wrong about you; I believe that you do think Mrs. Bold a charming woman. Your looks seem to say so; and by her looks I should say that she is jealous of me. Come, Mr. Arabin, confide in me, and if it is so, I'll do all in my power to make up the match."

It is needless to say that the signora was not very sincere in her offer. She was never sincere on such subjects. She never expected others to be so, nor did she expect others to think her so. Such matters were her playthings, her billiard table, her hounds and hunters, her waltzes and polkas, her picnics and summer-day excursions. She had little else to amuse her, and therefore played at love-making in all its forms. She was now playing at it with Mr. Arabin and did not at all expect the earnestness and truth of his answer.

"All in your power would be nothing," said he; "for Mrs. Bold is, I imagine, already engaged to another."

"Then you own the impeachment yourself."

"You cross-question me rather unfairly," he replied, "and I do not know why I answer you at all. Mrs. Bold is a very beautiful woman, and as intelligent as beautiful. It is impossible to know her without admiring her."

"So you think the widow a very beautiful woman?"

"Indeed I do."

"And one that would grace the parsonage of St. Ewold's."

"One that would well grace any man's house."

"And you really have the effrontery to tell me this," said she;

"to tell me, who, as you very well know, set up to be a beauty myself, and who am at this very moment taking such an interest in your affairs, you really have the effrontery to tell me that Mrs. Bold is the most beautiful woman you know."

"I did not say so," said Mr. Arabin; "you are more beautiful——"

"Ah, come now, that is something like. I thought you could not be so unfeeling."

"You are more beautiful, perhaps more clever."

"Thank you, thank you, Mr. Arabin. I knew that you and I should be friends."

"But——"

"Not a word further. I will not hear a word further. If you talk till midnight, you cannot improve what you have said."

"But Madame Neroni, Mrs. Bold——"

"I will not hear a word about Mrs. Bold. Dread thoughts of strychnine did pass across my brain, but she is welcome to the second place."

"Her place——"

"I won't hear anything about her or her place. I am satisfied, and that is enough. But, Mr. Arabin, I am dying with hunger; beautiful and clever as I am, you know I cannot go to my food, and yet you do not bring it to me."

This at any rate was so true as to make it necessary that Mr. Arabin should act upon it, and he accordingly went into the dining-room and supplied the signora's wants.

"And yourself?" said she.

"Oh," said he, "I am not hungry; I never eat at this hour."

"Come, come, Mr. Arabin, don't let love interfere with your appetite. It never does with mine. Give me half a glass more champagne, and then go to the table. Mrs. Bold will do me an injury if you stay talking to me any longer."

Mr. Arabin did as he was bid. He took her plate and glass from her, and going into the dining-room, helped himself to a sandwich from the crowded table and began munching it in a corner.

As he was doing so, Miss Thorne, who had hardly sat down for a moment, came into the room, and seeing him standing, was greatly distressed.

"Oh, my dear Mr. Arabin," said she, "have you never sat down yet? I am so distressed. You of all men too."

Mr. Arabin assured her that he had only just come into the room.

"That is the very reason why you should lose no more time. Come, I'll make room for you. Thank'ee, my dear," she said, seeing that Mrs. Bold was making an attempt to move from her chair, "but I would not for worlds see you stir, for all the ladies would think it necessary to follow. But, perhaps, if Mr. Stanhope has done—just for a minute, Mr. Stanhope—till I can get another chair."

And so Bertie had to rise to make way for his rival. This he did, as he did everything, with an air of good-humoured pleasantry which made it impossible for Mr. Arabin to refuse the proffered seat.

"His bishopric let another take," said Bertie; the quotation being certainly not very appropriate, either for the occasion or the person spoken to. "I have eaten and am satisfied; Mr. Arabin, pray take my chair. I wish for your sake that it really was a bishop's seat."

Mr. Arabin did sit down, and as he did so, Mrs. Bold got up as though to follow her neighbour.

"Pray, pray don't move," said Miss Thorne, almost forcing Eleanor back into her chair. "Mr. Stanhope is not going to leave us. He will stand behind you like a true knight as he is. And now I think of it, Mr. Arabin, let me introduce you to Mr. Slope. Mr. Slope, Mr. Arabin." And the two gentlemen bowed stiffly to each other across the lady whom they both intended to marry, while the other gentleman who also intended to marry her stood behind, watching them.

The two had never met each other before, and the present was certainly not a good opportunity for much cordial conversation, even if cordial conversation between them had been possible. As it was, the whole four who formed the party seemed as though their tongues were tied. Mr. Slope, who was wide awake to what he hoped was his coming opportunity, was not much concerned in the interest of the moment. His wish was to see Eleanor move, that he might pursue her. Bertie was not exactly in the same frame of mind; the evil day was near enough; there was no reason why he should precipitate it. He had made up his mind to marry Eleanor Bold if he could, and was resolved to-day to take the first preliminary step towards doing so. But there was time enough before him. He was not going to make an offer of marriage over the table-cloth. Having thus good-naturedly made way for Mr. Arabin, he was willing also to let him talk to the future Mrs. Stanhope as long as they remained in their present position.

Mr. Arabin having bowed to Mr. Slope, began eating his food without saying a word further. He was full of thought, and though he ate he did so unconsciously.

But poor Eleanor was the most to be pitied. The only friend on whom she thought she could rely, was Bertie Stanhope, and he, it seemed, was determined to desert her. Mr. Arabin did not attempt to address her. She said a few words in reply to some remarks from Mr. Slope, and then feeling the situation too much for her, started from her chair in spite of Miss Thorne, and hurried from the room. Mr. Slope followed her, and young Stanhope lost the occasion.

Madeline Neroni, when she was left alone, could not help

pondering much on the singular interview she had had with this singular man. Not a word that she had spoken to him had been intended by her to be received as true, and yet he had answered her in the very spirit of truth. He had done so, and she had been aware that he had so done. She had wormed from him his secret; and he, debarred as it would seem from man's usual privilege of lying, had innocently laid bare his whole soul to her. He loved Eleanor Bold, but Eleanor was not in his eye so beautiful as herself. He would fain have Eleanor for his wife, but yet he had acknowledged that she was the less gifted of the two. The man had literally been unable to falsify his thoughts when questioned, and had been compelled to be true *malgrè lui*, even when truth must have been so disagreeable to him.

This teacher of men, this Oxford pundit, this double-distilled quintessence of university perfection, this writer of religious treatises, this speaker of ecclesiastical speeches, had been like a little child in her hands; she had turned him inside out, and read his very heart as she might have done that of a young girl. She could not but despise him for his facile openness, and yet she liked him for it too. It was a novelty to her, a new trait in a man's character. She felt also that she could never so completely make a fool of him as she did of the Slopes and Thornes. She felt that she never could induce Mr. Arabin to make protestations to her that were not true, or to listen to nonsense that was mere nonsense.

It was quite clear that Mr. Arabin was heartily in love with Mrs. Bold, and the signora, with very unwonted good nature, began to turn it over in her mind whether she could not do him a good turn. Of course Bertie was to have the first chance. It was an understood family arrangement that her brother was, if possible, to marry the widow Bold. Madeline knew too well his necessities and what was due to her sister to interfere with so excellent a plan, as long as it might be feasible. But she had strong suspicion that it was not feasible. She did not think it likely that Mrs. Bold would accept a man in her brother's position, and she had frequently said so to Charlotte. She was inclined to believe that Mr. Slope had more chance of success; and with her it would be a labour of love to rob Mr. Slope of his wife.

And so the signora resolved, should Bertie fail, to do a good-natured act for once in her life, and give up Mr. Arabin to the woman whom he loved.

CHAPTER XXXIII

ULLATHORNE SPORTS—ACT II

"THAT which has made them drunk, has made me bold." 'Twas thus that Mr. Slope encouraged himself, as he left the dining-room in pursuit of Eleanor. He had not indeed seen in that room any person really intoxicated; but there had been a good deal of wine drunk, and Mr. Slope had not hesitated to take his share, in order to screw himself up to the undertaking which he had in hand. He is not the first man who has thought it expedient to call in the assistance of Bacchus on such an occasion.

Eleanor was out through the window, and on the grass before she perceived that she was followed. Just at that moment the guests were nearly all occupied at the tables. Here and there were to be seen a constant couple or two, who preferred their own sweet discourse to the jingle of glasses, or the charms of rhetoric which fell from the mouths of the Honourable George and the bishop of Barchester; but the grounds were as nearly vacant as Mr. Slope could wish them to be.

Eleanor saw that she was pursued, and as a deer, when escape is no longer possible, will turn to bay and attack the hounds, so did she turn upon Mr. Slope.

"Pray don't let me take you from the room," said she, speaking with all the stiffness which she knew how to use. "I have come out to look for a friend. I must beg of you, Mr. Slope, to go back."

But Mr. Slope would not be thus entreated. He had observed all day that Mrs. Bold was not cordial to him, and this had to a certain extent oppressed him. But he did not deduce from this any assurance that his aspirations were in vain. He saw that she was angry with him. Might she not be so because he had so long tampered with her feelings,—might it not arise from his having, as he knew was the case, caused her name to be bruited about in conjunction with his own, without having given her the opportunity of confessing to the world that henceforth their names were to be one and the same? Poor lady! He had within him a certain Christian conscience-stricken feeling of remorse on this head. It might be that he had wronged her by his tardiness. He had, however, at the present moment inbibed too much of Mr. Thorne's champagne to have any inward misgivings. He was right in repeating the boast of Lady Macbeth: he was not drunk; but he was bold enough for anything. It was a pity that in such a state he could not have encountered Mrs. Proudie.

"You must permit me to attend you," said he; "I could not think of allowing you to go alone."

"Indeed you must, Mr. Slope," said Eleanor still very stiffly; "for it is my special wish to be alone."

The time for letting the great secret escape him had already come. Mr. Slope saw that it must be now or never, and he was determined that it should be now. This was not the first attempt at winning a fair lady. He had been on his knees, looked unutterable things with his eyes, and whispered honeyed words before this. Indeed he was somewhat an adept at these things, and had only to adapt to the perhaps different taste of Mrs. Bold the well-remembered rhapsodies which had once so much gratified Olivia Proudie.

"Do not ask me to leave you, Mrs. Bold," said he with an impassioned look, impassioned and sanctified as well, with that sort of look which is not uncommon with gentlemen of Mr. Slope's school, and which may perhaps be called the tender-pious. "Do not ask me to leave you, till I have spoken a few words with which my heart is full; which I have come hither purposely to say."

Eleanor saw how it was now. She knew directly what it was she was about to go through, and very miserable the knowledge made her. Of course she could refuse Mr. Slope, and there would be an end of that, one might say. But there would not be an end of it as far as Eleanor was concerned. The very fact of Mr. Slope's making an offer to her would be a triumph to the archdeacon, and in a great measure a vindication of Mr. Arabin's conduct. The widow could not bring herself to endure with patience the idea that she had been in the wrong. She had defended Mr. Slope, she had declared herself quite justified in admitting him among her acquaintance, had ridiculed the idea of his considering himself as more than an acquaintance, and had resented the archdeacon's caution in her behalf: now it was about to be proved to her in a manner sufficiently disagreeable that the archdeacon had been right, and she herself had been entirely wrong.

"I don't know what you can have to say to me, Mr. Slope, that you could not have said when we were sitting at table just now;" and she closed her lips, and steadied her eyeballs, and looked at him in a manner that ought to have frozen him.

But gentlemen are not easily frozen when they are full of champagne, and it would not at any time have been easy to freeze Mr. Slope.

"There are things, Mrs. Bold, which a man cannot well say before a crowd; which perhaps he cannot well say at any time; which indeed he may most frevently desire to get spoken, and which he may yet find it almost impossible to utter. It is such things as these, that I now wish to say to you;" and then the tender-pious look was repeated, with a little more emphasis even than before.

Eleanor had not found it practicable to stand stock still before the dining-room window, and there receive his offer in full view of Miss Thorne's guests. She had therefore in self defence walked on, and thus Mr. Slope had gained his object of walking with her. He now offered her his arm.

"Thank you, Mr. Slope, I am much obliged to you; but for the very short time that I shall remain with you I shall prefer walking alone."

"And must it be so short?" said he; "must it be——"

"Yes," said Eleanor, interrupting him; "as short as possible, if you please, sir."

"I had hoped, Mrs. Bold—I had hoped——"

"Pray hope nothing, Mr. Slope, as far as I am concerned; pray do not; I do not know, and need not know what hope you mean. Our acquaintance is very slight, and will probably remain so. Pray, pray let that be enough; there is at any rate no necessity for us to quarrel."

Mrs. Bold was certainly treating Mr. Slope rather cavalierly, and he felt it so. She was rejecting him before he had offered himself, and informed him at the same time that he was taking a great deal too much on himself to be so familiar. She did not even make an attempt

> From such a sharp and waspish word as "no"
> To pluck the sting.

He was still determined to be very tender and very pious, seeing that in spite of all Mrs. Bold had said to him, he not yet abandoned hope; but he was inclined also to be somewhat angry. The widow was bearing herself, as he thought, with too high a hand, was speaking of herself in much too imperious a tone. She had clearly no idea that an honour was being conferred on her. Mr. Slope would be tender as long as he could, but he began to think, if that failed, it would not be amiss if he also mounted himself for a while on his high horse. Mr. Slope could undoubtedly be very tender, but he could be very savage also, and he knew his own abilities.

"That is cruel," said he, "and unchristian too. The worst of us are all still bidden to hope. What have I done that you should pass on me so severe a sentence?" and then he paused a moment, during which the widow walked steadily on with measured step, saying nothing further.

"Beautiful woman," at last he burst forth; "beautiful woman, you cannot pretend to be ignorant that I adore you. Yes, Eleanor, yes, I love you. I love you with the truest affection which man can bear to woman. Next to my hopes of heaven are my hopes of possessing you." (Mr. Slope's memory here played him false, or he would not have omitted the deanery.) "How sweet to walk to heaven with you by my side, with you for my guide, mutual guides. Say, Eleanor, dearest Eleanor, shall we walk that sweet path together?"

Eleanor had no intention of ever walking together with Mr. Slope on any other path than that special one of Miss Thorne's which they now occupied; but as she had been unable to prevent the expression of Mr. Slope's wishes and aspirations, she resolved to hear him out to the end, before she answered him.

"Ah! Eleanor," he continued, and it seemed to be his idea that as he had once found courage to pronounce her Christian name, he could not utter it often enough. "Ah! Eleanor, will it not be sweet, with the Lord's assistance, to travel hand in hand through this mortal valley which his mercies will make pleasant to us, till hereafter we shall dwell together at the foot of his throne?" And then a more tenderly pious glance than ever beamed from the lover's eyes. "Ah! Eleanor——"

"My name, Mr. Slope, is Mrs. Bold," said Eleanor, who, though determined to hear out the tale of his love, was too much disgusted by his blasphemy to be able to bear much more of it.

"Sweetest angel, be not so cold," said he, and as he said it the champagne broke forth, and he contrived to pass his arm round her waist. He did this with considerable cleverness, for up to this point Eleanor had contrived with tolerable success to keep her distance from him. They had got into a walk nearly enveloped by shrubs, and Mr. Slope therefore no doubt considered that as they were now alone it was fitting that he should give her some outward demonstration of that affection of which he talked so much. It may perhaps be presumed that the same stamp of measures had been found to succeed with Olivia Proudie. Be this as it may, it was not successful with Eleanor Bold.

She sprang from him as she would have jumped from an adder, but she did not spring far; not, indeed, beyond arm's length; and then, quick as thought, she raised her little hand and dealt him a box on the ear with such right good will, that it sounded among the trees like a miniature thunder-clap.

"I never, never will speak another word to you," she said, gasping with emotion and the loss of breath which her exertion and violent feelings occasioned her, and so saying she put foot to the ground and ran quickly back along the path to the house.

But how shall I sing the divine wrath of Mr. Slope, or how invoke the tragic muse to describe the rage which swelled the celestial bosom of the bishop's chaplain? Such an undertaking by no means befits the low-heeled buskin of modern fiction. The painter put a veil over Agamemnon's face when called on to depict the father's grief at the early doom of his devoted daughter. The god, when he resolved to punish the rebellious winds, abstained from mouthing empty threats. We will not attempt to tell with what mighty surgings of the inner heart Mr. Slope swore to revenge himself on the woman who had disgraced him, nor will we vainly strive to depict his deep agony of soul.

There he is, however, alone in the garden walk, and we must contrive to bring him out of it. He was not willing to come forth quite at once. His cheek was stinging with the weight of Eleanor's fingers, and he fancied that every one who looked at him would be able to see on his face the traces of what he had endured. He stood awhile, becoming redder and redder with rage. He stood motionless, undecided, glaring with his eyes, thinking of the pains and penalties of Hades, and meditating how he might best devote his enemy to the infernal gods with all the passion of his accustomed eloquence. He longed in his heart to be preaching at her. 'Twas thus that he was ordinarily avenged of sinning mortal men and women. Could he at once have ascended his Sunday rostrum and fulminated at her such denunciations as his spirit delighted in, his bosom would have been greatly eased.

But how preach to Mr. Thorne's laurels, or how preach indeed at all in such a vanity fair as this now going on at Ullathorne? And then he began to feel a righteous disgust at the wickedness of the doings around him. He had been justly chastised for lending, by his presence, a sanction to such worldly lures. The gaiety of society, the mirth of banquets, the laughter of the young, and the eating and drinking of the elders were, for awhile, without excuse in his sight. What had he now brought down upon himself by sojourning thus in the tents of the heathen? He had consorted with idolaters round the altars of Baal; and therefore a sore punishment had come upon him. He then thought of the Signora Neroni, and his soul within him was full of sorrow. He had an inkling—a true inkling— that he was a wicked, sinful man; but it led him in no right direction; he could admit no charity in his heart. He felt debasement coming on him, and he longed to shake it off, to rise up in his stirrup, to mount to high places and great power, that he might get up into a mighty pulpit and preach to the world a loud sermon against Mrs. Bold.

There he stood fixed to the gravel for about ten minutes. Fortune favoured him so far that no prying eyes came to look upon him in his misery. Then a shudder passed over his whole frame; he collected himself, and slowly wound his way round to the lawn, advancing along the path and not returning in the direction which Eleanor had taken. When he reached the tent he found the bishop standing there in conversation with the master of Lazarus. His lordship had come out to air himself after the exertion of his speech.

"This is very pleasant—very pleasant, my lord, is it not?" said Mr. Slope with his most gracious smile, and pointing to the tent; "very pleasant. It is delightful to see so many persons enjoying themselves so thoroughly."

Mr. Slope thought he might force the bishop to introduce him to Dr. Gwynne. A very great example had declared and practised the wisdom of being everything to everybody, and Mr. Slope was desirous of following it. His maxim was never to lose a chance. The bishop, however, at the present moment was not very anxious to increase Mr. Slope's circle of acquaintance among his clerical brethren. He had his own reasons for dropping any marked allusion to his domestic chaplain, and he therefore made his shoulder rather cold for the occasion.

"Very, very," said he without turning round, or even deigning to look at Mr. Slope. "And therefore, Dr. Gwynne, I really think that you will find that the hebdomadal board will exercise as wide and as general an authority as at the present moment. I, for one, Dr. Gwynne——"

"Dr. Gwynne," said Mr. Slope, raising his hat, and resolving not to be outwitted by such an insignificant little goose as the bishop of Barchester.

The master of Lazarus also raised his hat and bowed very politely to Mr. Slope. There is not a more courteous gentleman in the queen's dominions than the master of Lazarus.

"My lord," said Mr. Slope; "pray do me the honour of introducing me to Dr. Gwynne. The opportunity is too much in my favour to be lost."

The bishop had no help for it. "My chaplain, Dr. Gwynne," said he; "my present chaplain, Mr. Slope." He certainly made the introduction as unsatisfactory to the chaplain as possible, and by the use of the word present, seemed to indicate that Mr. Slope might probably not long enjoy the honour which he now held. But Mr. Slope cared nothing for this. He understood the innuendo, and disregarded it. It might probably come to pass that he would be in a situation to resign his chaplaincy before the bishop was in a situation to dismiss him from it. What need the future dean of Barchester care for the bishop, or for the bishop's wife? Had not Mr. Slope, just as he was entering Dr. Stanhope's carriage, received an all important note from Tom Towers of the Jupiter? had he not that note this moment in his pocket?

So disregarding the bishop, he began to open out a conversation with the master of Lazarus.

But suddenly an interruption came, not altogether unwelcome to Mr. Slope. One of the bishop's servants came up to his master's shoulder with a long, grave face, and whispered into the bishop's ear.

"What is it, John?" said the bishop.

"The dean, my lord; he is dead."

Mr. Slope had no further desire to converse with the master of Lazarus, and was very soon on his road back to Barchester.

Eleanor, as we have said, having declared her intention of never holding further communication with Mr. Slope, ran hurriedly

back towards the house. The thought, however, of what she had
done grieved her greatly, and she could not abstain from bursting
into tears. 'Twas thus she played the second act in that day's
melodrame.

CHAPTER XXXIV

MRS. BOLD CONFIDES HER SORROW TO HER FRIEND MISS STANHOPE

WHEN Mrs. Bold came to the end of the walk and faced the
lawn, she began to bethink herself what she should do. Was
she to wait there till Mr. Slope caught her, or was she to go
in among the crowd with tears in her eyes and passion in her face?
She might in truth have stood there long enough without any
reasonable fear of further immediate persecution from Mr. Slope;
but we are all inclined to magnify the bugbears which frighten us.
In her present state of dread she did not know of what atrocity
he might venture to be guilty. Had any one told her a week ago
that he would have put his arm round her waist at this party of
Miss Thorne's, she would have been utterly incredulous. Had she
been informed that he would be seen on the following Sunday
walking down the High-street in a scarlet coat and top-boots, she
would not have thought such a phenomenon more improbable.

But this improbable iniquity he had committed; and now there
was nothing she could not believe of him. In the first place it
was quite manifest that he was tipsy; in the next place, it was to
be taken as proved that all his religion was sheer hypocrisy; and
finally the man was utterly shameless. She therefore stood watching
for the sound of his footfall, not without some fear that he might
creep out at her suddenly from among the bushes.

As she thus stood, she saw Charlotte Stanhope at a little distance
from her walking quickly across the grass. Eleanor's handkerchief
was in her hand, and putting it to her face so as to conceal her
tears, she ran across the lawn and joined her friend.

"Oh, Charlotte," she said, almost too much out of breath to
speak very plainly; "I am so glad I have found you."

"Glad you have found me!" said Charlotte, laughing: "that's
a good joke. Why Bertie and I have been looking for you everywhere. He swears that you have gone off with Mr. Slope, and is
now on the point of hanging himself."

"Oh, Charlotte, don't," said Mrs. Bold.

"Why, my child, what on earth is the matter with you!" said
Miss Stanhope, perceiving that Eleanor's hand trembled on her
own arm, and finding also that her companion was still half choked

by tears. "Goodness heaven! something has distressed you. What is it? What can I do for you?"

Eleanor answered her only by a sort of spasmodic gurgle in her throat. She was a good deal upset, as people say, and could not at the moment collect herself.

"Come here, this way, Mrs. Bold; come this way, and we shall not be seen. What has happened to vex you so? What can I do for you? Can Bertie do anything?"

"Oh, no, no, no, no," said Eleanor. "There is nothing to be done. Only that horrid man——"

"What horrid man?" asked Charlotte.

There are some moments in life in which both men and women feel themselves imperatively called on to make a confidence; in which not to do so requires a disagreeable resolution and also a disagreeable suspicion. There are people of both sexes who never make confidences; who are never tempted by momentary circumstances to disclose their secret; but such are generally dull, close, unimpassioned spirits, "gloomy gnomes, who live in cold dark mines." There was nothing of the gnome about Eleanor; and she therefore resolved to tell Charlotte Stanhope the whole story about Mr. Slope.

"That horrid man; that Mr. Slope," said she: "did you not see that he followed me out of the dining-room?"

"Of course I did, and was sorry enough; but I could not help it. I knew you would be annoyed. But you and Bertie managed it badly between you."

"It was not his fault nor mine either. You know how I disliked the idea of coming in the carriage with that man."

"I am sure I am very sorry if that has led to it."

"I don't know what has led to it," said Eleanor, almost crying again. "But it has not been my fault."

"But what has he done, my dear?"

"He's an abominable, horrid, hypocritical man, and it would serve him right to tell the bishop all about it."

"Believe me, if you want to do him an injury, you had far better tell Mrs. Proudie. But what did he do, Mrs. Bold?"

"Ugh!" exclaimed Eleanor.

"Well, I must confess he's not very nice," said Charlotte Stanhope.

"Nice!" said Eleanor. "He is the most fulsome, fawning, abominable man I ever saw. What business had he to come to me? —I that never gave him the slightest tittle of encouragement—I that always hated him, though I did take his part when others ran him down."

"That's just where it is, my dear. He has heard that, and therefore fancied that of course you were in love with him."

This was wormwood to Eleanor. It was in fact the very thing

which all her friends had been saying for the last month past
and which experience now proved to be true. Eleanor resolved
within herself that she would never again take any man's part.
The world with all its villainy, and all its ill-nature, might wag
as it liked; she would not again attempt to set crooked things
straight.

"But what did he do, my dear?" said Charlotte, who was really
rather interested in the subject.

"He—he—he——"

"Well—come, it can't have been anything so very horrid, for
the man was not tipsy."

"Oh, I am sure he was," said Eleanor. "I am sure he must have
been tipsy."

"Well, I declare I didn't observe it. But what was it, my love?"

"Why, I believe I can hardly tell you. He talked such horrid
stuff that you never heard the like; about religion, and heaven, and
love.—Oh, dear,—he is such a nasty man."

"I can easily imagine the sort of stuff he would talk. Well,—and
then——?"

"And then—he took hold of me."

"Took hold of you?"

"Yes,—he somehow got close to me, and took hold of me——"

"By the waist?"

"Yes," said Eleanor shuddering.

"And then——"

"Then I jumped away from him, and gave him a slap on the
face; and ran away along the path, till I saw you."

"Ha, ha, ha!" Charlotte Stanhope laughed heartily at the
finale to the tragedy. It was delightful to her to think that Mr.
Slope had had his ears boxed.

Charlotte Stanhope was very anxious that her brother should at
once on that very day settle matters with his future wife. Things
had now come to that point between him and his father, and between
him and his creditors, that he must either do so, or leave Barchester;
either do that, or go back to his unwashed associates, dirty lodgings,
and poor living at Carrara. Unless he could provide himself
with an income, he must go to Carrara, or to ——. His father the
prebendary had not said this in so many words, but had he done
so, he could not have signified it more plainly.

This being so, could not this affair of Mr. Slope's be turned to
advantage? Could it not be made the excuse for bringing Bertie
and Mrs. Bold into still closer connection; into such close connection
that they could not fail to throw themselves into each other's arms?
Such was the game which Miss Stanhope now at a moment's
notice resolved to play.

And very well she played it. In the first place, it was arranged
that Mr. Slope should not return in the Stanhope's carriage to

Barchester. It so happened that Mr. Slope was already gone, but of that of course they knew nothing. The signora should be induced to go first, with only the servants and her sister, and Bertie should take Mr. Slope's place in the second journey. Bertie was to be told in confidence of the whole affair, and when the carriage was gone off with its first load, Eleanor was to be left under Bertie's special protection, so as to insure her from any further aggression from Mr. Slope. While the carriage was getting ready, Bertie was to seek out that gentleman and make him understand that he must provide himself with another conveyance back to Barchester. Their immediate object should be to walk about together in search of Bertie. Bertie, in short, was to be the Pegasus on whose wings they were to ride out of their present dilemma.

They first went into the dining-room, looking for their champion, and from thence to the drawing-room. Here they found Mr. Arabin, still hanging over the signora's sofa; or, rather, they found him sitting near her head, as a physician might have sat, had the lady been his patient. There was no other person in the room. The guests were some in the tent, some few still in the dining-room, some at the bows and arrows, but most of them walking with Miss Thorne through the park, and looking at the games that were going on.

All that had passed, and was passing between Mr. Arabin and the lady, it is unnecessary to give in detail. She was doing with him as she did with all others. It was her mission to make fools of men, and she was pursuing her mission with Mr. Arabin. She had almost got him to own his love for Mrs. Bold, and had subsequently almost induced him to acknowledge a passion for herself. He, poor man, was hardly aware what he was doing or saying, hardly conscious whether he was in heaven or hell. So little had he known of female attractions of that peculiar class which the signora owned, that he became affected with a kind of temporary delirium, when first subjected to its power. He lost his head rather than his heart, and toppled about mentally, reeling in his ideas as a drunken man does on his legs.

As soon as Mr. Arabin saw Mrs. Bold enter the room, he blushed and rose from his chair; then he sat down again, and then again got up. The signora saw the blush at once, and smiled at the poor victim, but Eleanor was too much confused to see anything.

"Oh, Madeline," said Charlotte, "I want to speak to you particularly; we must arrange about the carriage, you know," and she stooped down to whisper to her sister. Mr. Arabin immediately withdrew to a little distance, and as Charlotte had in fact much to explain before she could make the new carriage arrangement intelligible, he had nothing to do but to talk to Mrs. Bold.

"Are you returning to Plumstead, Mrs. Bold?" Mr. Arabin

merely asked this by way of making conversation, but he immediately perceived that he was approaching dangerous ground.

"No," said Mrs. Bold, very quietly; "I am going home to Barchester."

"Oh, ah, yes. I had forgotten that you had returned." And then Mr. Arabin, finding it impossible to say anything further, stood silent till Charlotte had completed her plans, and Mrs. Bold stood equally silent, intently occupied as it appeared in the arrangement of her rings.

And yet these two people were thoroughly in love with each other; and though one was a middle-aged clergyman, and the other a lady at any rate past the wishy-washy bread-and-butter period of life, they were as unable to tell their own minds to each other as any Damon and Phillis, whose united ages would not make up that to which Mr. Arabin had already attained.

Madeline Neroni consented to her sister's proposal, and then the two ladies again went off in quest of Bertie Stanhope.

CHAPTER XXXV

ULLATHORNE SPORTS—ACT III

AND now Miss Thorne's guests were beginning to take their departure, and the amusement of those who remained was becoming slack. It was getting dark, and ladies in morning costumes were thinking that if they were to appear by candle-light they ought to readjust themselves. Some young gentlemen had been heard to talk so loud that prudent mammas determined to retire judiciously, and the more discreet of the male sex, whose libations had been moderate, felt that there was not much more left for them to do.

The countess and her noble brood were among the first to leave, and as regarded the Hon. George, it was certainly time that he did so. Her ladyship was in a great fret and fume. Those horrid roads would, she was sure, be the death of her if unhappily she were caught in them by the dark night. The lamps she was assured were good, but no lamp could withstand the jolting of the roads of East Barsetshire. The De Courcy property lay in the western division of the county.

Mrs. Proudie could not stay when the countess was gone. So the bishop was searched for by the Revs. Messrs. Grey and Green, and found in one corner of the tent enjoying himself thoroughly in a disquisition on the hebdomadal board. He obeyed, however, the behests of his lady without finishing the sentence in which he was promising to Dr. Gwynne that his authority at Oxford should remain unimpaired; and the episcopal horses turned their noses towards the palatial stables. Then the Grantlys went. Before they did so, Mr. Harding managed to whisper a word into his daughter's ear. Of course, he said he would undeceive the Grantlys as to that foolish rumour about Mr. Slope.

"No, no, no," said Eleanor; "pray do not—pray wait till I see you. You will be home in a day or two, and then I will explain to you everything."

"I shall be home to-morrow," said he.

"I am so glad," said Eleanor. "You will come and dine with me, and then we shall be so comfortable."

Mr. Harding promised. He did not exactly know what there was to be explained, or why Dr. Grantly's mind should not be disabused of the mistake into which he had fallen; but nevertheless he promised. He owed some reparation to his daughter, and he thought that he might best make it by obedience.

And thus the people were thinning off by degrees, as Charlotte and Eleanor walked about in quest of Bertie. Their search might have been long, had they not happened to hear his voice. He was comfortably ensconced in the ha-ha, with his back to the sloping side, smoking a cigar, and eagerly engaged in conversation with some youngster from the further side of the county, whom he had never met before, who was also smoking under Bertie's pupilage, and listening with open ears to an account given by his companion of some of the pastimes of Eastern clime.

"Bertie, I am seeking you everywhere," said Charlotte. "Come up here at once."

Bertie looked up out of the ha-ha, and saw the two ladies before him. As there was nothing for him but to obey, he got up and threw away his cigar. From the first moment of his acquaintance with her he had liked Eleanor Bold. Had he been left to his own devices, had she been penniless, and had it then been quite out of the question that he should marry her, he would most probably have fallen violently in love with her. But now he could not help regarding her somewhat as he did the marble workshops at Carrara, as he had done his easel and palette, as he had done the lawyer's chambers in London; in fact, as he had invariably regarded everything by which it had been proposed to him to obtain the means of living. Eleanor Bold appeared before him, no longer as a beautiful woman, but as a new profession called matrimony. It was a profession indeed requiring but little labour, and one in which an income was insured to him. But nevertheless he had been as it were goaded on to it; his sister had talked to him of Eleanor, just as she had talked of busts and portraits. Bertie did not dislike money, but he hated the very thought of earning it. He was now called away from his pleasant cigar to earn it, by offering himself as a husband to Mrs. Bold. The work indeed was made easy enough;

for in lieu of his having to seek the widow, the widow had apparently come to seek him.

He made some sudden absurd excuse to his auditor, and then throwing away his cigar, climbed up the wall of the ha-ha and joined the ladies on the lawn.

"Come and give Mrs. Bold an arm," said Charlotte, "while I set you on a piece of duty which, as a preux chevalier, you must immediately perform. Your personal danger will, I fear, be insignificant, as your antagonist is a clergyman."

Bertie immediately gave his arm to Eleanor, walking between her and his sister. He had lived too long abroad to fall into the Englishman's habit of offering each an arm to two ladies at the same time; a habit, by the bye, which foreigners regard as an approach to bigamy, or a sort of incipient Mormonism.

The little history of Mr. Slope's misconduct was then told to Bertie by his sister, Eleanor's ears tingling the while. And well they might tingle. If it were necessary to speak of the outrage at all, why should it be spoken of to such a person as Mr. Stanhope, and why in her own hearing? She knew she was wrong, and was unhappy and dispirited, and yet she could think of no way to extricate herself, no way to set herself right. Charlotte spared her as much as she possibly could, spoke of the whole thing as though Mr. Slope had taken a glass of wine too much, said that of course there would be nothing more about it, but that steps must be taken to exclude Mr. Slope from the carriage.

"Mrs. Bold need be under no alarm about that," said Bertie, "for Mr. Slope has gone this hour past. He told me that business made it necessary that he should start at once for Barchester."

"He is not so tipsy, at any rate, but what he knows his fault," said Charlotte. "Well, my dear, that is one difficulty over. Now I'll leave you with your true knight, and get Madeline off as quickly as I can. The carriage is here, I suppose, Bertie?"

"It has been here for the last hour."

"That's well. Good bye, my dear. Of course you'll come in to tea. I shall trust to you to bring her, Bertie; even by force if necessary." And so saying, Charlotte ran off across the lawn, leaving her brother alone with the widow.

As Miss Stanhope went off, Eleanor bethought herself that, as Mr. Slope had taken his departure, there no longer existed any necessity for separating Mr. Stanhope from his sister Madeline, who so much needed his aid. It had been arranged that he should remain so as to preoccupy Mr. Slope's place in the carriage, and act as a social policeman to effect the exclusion of that disagreeable gentleman. But Mr. Slope had effected his own exclusion, and there was no possible reason now why Bertie should not go with his sister. At least Eleanor saw none, and she said as much.

"Oh, let Charlotte have her own way," said he. "She has

arranged it, and there will be no end of confusion, if we make another change. Charlotte always arranges everything in our house; and rules us like a despot."

"But the signora?" said Eleanor.

"Oh, the signora can do very well without me. Indeed, she will have to do without me," he added, thinking rather of his studies in Carrara, than of his Barchester hymeneals.

"Why, you are not going to leave us?" asked Eleanor.

It has been said that Bertie Stanhope was a man without principle. He certainly was so. He had no power of using active mental exertion to keep himself from doing evil. Evil had no ugliness in his eyes; virtue no beauty. He was void of any of those feelings which actuate men to do good. But he was perhaps equally void of those which actuate men to do evil. He got into debt with utter recklessness, thinking nothing as to whether the tradesmen would ever be paid or not. But he did not invent active schemes of deceit for the sake of extracting the goods of others. If a man gave him credit, that was the man's look-out; Bertie Stanhope troubled himself nothing further. In borrowing money he did the same; he gave people references to "his governor;" told them that the "old chap" had a good income; and agreed to pay sixty per cent. for the accommodation. All this he did without a scruple of conscience; but then he never contrived active villainy.

In this affair of his marriage, it had been represented to him as a matter of duty that he ought to put himself in possession of Mrs. Bold's hand and fortune; and at first he had so regarded it. About her he had thought but little. It was the customary thing for men situated as he was to marry for money, and there was no reason why he should not do what others around him did. And so he consented. But now he began to see the matter in another light. He was setting himself down to catch this woman, as a cat sits to catch a mouse. He was to catch her, and swallow her up, her and her child, and her houses and land, in order that he might live on her instead of on his father. There was a cold, calculating, cautious cunning about this quite at variance with Bertie's character. The prudence of the measure was quite as antagonistic to his feelings as the iniquity.

And then, should he be successful, what would be the reward? Having satisfied his creditors with half of the widow's fortune, he would be allowed to sit down quietly at Barchester, keeping economical house with the remainder. His duty would be to rock the cradle of the late Mr. Bold's child, and his highest excitement a demure party at Plumstead rectory, should it ultimately turn out that the archdeacon would be sufficiently reconciled to receive him.

There was very little in the programme to allure such a man as Bertie Stanhope. Would not the Carrara workshop, or whatever worldly career fortune might have in store for him, would not almost anything be better than this? The lady herself was undoubtedly all that was desirable; but the most desirable lady becomes nauseous when she has to be taken as a pill. He was pledged to his sister, however, and let him quarrel with whom he would, it behoved him not to quarrel with her. If she were lost to him all would be lost that he could ever hope to derive henceforward from the paternal roof-tree. His mother was apparently indifferent to his weal or woe, to his wants or his welfare. His father's brow got blacker and blacker from day to day, as the old man looked at his hopeless son. And as for Madeline—poor Madeline, whom of all of them he liked the best,—she had enough to do to shift for herself. No; come what might, he must cling to his sister and obey her behests, let them be ever so stern; or at the very least seem to obey them. Could not some happy deceit bring him through in this matter, so that he might save appearances with his sister, and yet not betray the widow to her ruin? What if he made a confederate of Eleanor? 'Twas in this spirit that Bertie Stanhope set about his wooing.

"But you are not going to leave Barchester?" asked Eleanor.

"I do not know," he replied; "I hardly know yet what I am going to do. But it is at any rate certain that I must do something."

"You mean about your profession?" said she.

"Yes, about my profession, if you can call it one."

"And is it not one?" said Eleanor. "Were I a man, I know none I should prefer it to, except painting. And I believe the one is as much in your power as the other."

"Yes, just about equally so," said Bertie, with a little touch of inward satire directed at himself. He knew in his heart that he would never make a penny by either.

"I have often wondered, Mr. Stanhope, why you do not exert yourself more," said Eleanor, who felt a friendly fondness for the man with whom she was walking. "But I know it is very impertinent in me to say so."

"Impertinent!" said he. "Not so, but much too kind. It is much too kind in you to take any interest in so idle a scamp."

"But you are not a scamp, though you are perhaps idle; and I do take an interest in you; a very great interest," she added, in a voice which almost made him resolve to change his mind. "And when I call you idle, I know you are only so for the present moment. Why can't you settle steadily to work here in Barchester?"

"And make busts of the bishop, dean and chapter? or perhaps, if I achieve a great success, obtain a commission to put up an elaborate tombstone over a prebendary's widow, a dead lady with a Grecian nose, a bandeau, and an intricate lace veil; lying of course on a marble sofa, from among the legs of which Death will be creeping out and poking at his victim with a small toasting-fork."

Eleanor laughed; but yet she thought that if the surviving

prebendary paid the bill, the object of the artist as a professional man would, in a great measure, be obtained.

"I don't know about the dean and chapter and the prebendary's widow," said Eleanor. "Of course you must take them as they come. But the fact of your having a great cathedral in which such ornaments are required, could not but be in your favour."

"No real artist could descend to the ornamentation of a cathedral," said Bertie, who had his ideas of the high ecstatic ambition of art, as indeed all artists have, who are not in receipt of a good income. "Buildings should be fitted to grace the sculpture, not the sculpture to grace the building."

"Yes, when the work of art is good enough to merit it. Do you, Mr. Stanhope, do something sufficiently excellent, and we ladies of Barchester will erect for it a fitting receptacle. Come, what shall the subject be?"

"I'll put you in your pony chair, Mrs. Bold, as Dannecker put Ariadne on her lion. Only you must promise to sit for me."

"My ponies are too tame, I fear, and my broad-rimmed straw hat will not look so well in marble as the lace veil of the prebendary's wife."

"If you will not consent to that, Mrs. Bold, I will consent to try no other subject in Barchester."

"You are determined then, to push your fortune in other lands?"

"I am determined," said Bertie, slowly and significantly, as he tried to bring up his mind to a great resolve; "I am determined in this matter to be guided wholly by you."

"Wholly by me!" said Eleanor, astonished at, and not quite liking, his altered manner.

"Wholly by you," said Bertie, dropping his companion's arm, and standing before her on the path. In their walk they had come exactly to the spot in which Eleanor had been provoked into slapping Mr. Slope's face. Could it be possible that this place was peculiarly unpropitious to her comfort? could it be possible that she should here have to encounter yet another amorous swain?

"If you will be guided by me, Mr. Stanhope, you will set yourself down to steady and persevering work, and you will be ruled by your father as to the place in which it will be most advisable for you to do so."

"Nothing could be more prudent, if only it were practicable. But now, if you will let me, I will tell you how it is that I will be guided by you, and why. Will you let me tell you?"

"I really do not know what you can have to tell."

"No,—you cannot know. It is impossible that you should. But we have been very good friends, Mrs. Bold, have we not?"

"Yes, I think we have," said she, observing in his demeanour an earnestness very unusual with him.

"You were kind enough to say just now that you took an interest in me, and I was perhaps vain enough to believe you."

"There is no vanity in that; I do so as your sister's brother,—and as my own friend also."

"Well, I don't deserve that you should feel so kindly towards me," said Bertie; "but upon my word I am very grateful for it," and he paused awhile, hardly knowing how to introduce the subject that he had in hand.

And it was no wonder that he found it difficult. He had to make known to his companion the scheme that had been prepared to rob her of her wealth; he had to tell her that he intended to marry her without loving her, or else that he loved her without intending to marry her; and he had also to bespeak from her not only his own pardon, but also that of his sister, and induce Mrs. Bold to protest in her future communion with Charlotte that an offer had been duly made and duly rejected.

Bertie Stanhope was not prone to be very diffident of his own conversational powers, but it did seem to him that he was about to tax them almost too far. He hardly knew where to begin, and he hardly knew where he should end.

By this time Eleanor was again walking on slowly by his side, not taking his arm as she had heretofore done, but listening very intently for whatever Bertie might have to say to her.

"I wish to be guided by you," said he; "and, indeed, in this matter, there is no one else who can set me right."

"Oh, that must be nonsense," said she.

"Well, listen to me now, Mrs. Bold; and if you can help it, pray don't be angry with me."

"Angry!" said she.

"Oh, indeed you will have cause to be so. You know how very much attached to you my sister Charlotte is."

Eleanor acknowledged that she did.

"Indeed she is; I never knew her to love any one so warmly on so short an acquaintance. You know also how well she loves me?"

Eleanor now made no answer, but she felt the blood tingle in her cheek as she gathered from what he said the probable result of this double-barrelled love on the part of Miss Stanhope.

"I am her only brother, Mrs. Bold, and it is not to be wondered at that she should love me. But you do not yet know Charlotte,—you do not know how entirely the well-being of our family hangs on her. Without her to manage for us, I do not know how we should get on from day to day. You cannot yet have observed all this."

Eleanor had indeed observed a good deal of this; she did not however now say so, but allowed him to proceed with his story.

"You cannot therefore be surprised that Charlotte should be most anxious to do the best for us all."

Eleanor said that she was not at all surprised.

"And she has had a very difficult game to play, Mrs. Bold—a very difficult game. Poor Madeline's unfortunate marriage and terrible accident, my mother's ill health, my father's absence from England, and last, and worst perhaps, my own roving, idle spirit have almost been too much for her. You cannot wonder if among all her cares one of the foremost is to see me settled in the world."

Eleanor on this occasion expressed no acquiescence. She certainly supposed that a formal offer was to be made, and could not but think that so singular an exordium was never before made by a gentleman in a similar position. Mr. Slope had annoyed her by the excess of his ardour. It was quite clear that no such danger was to be feared from Mr. Stanhope. Prudential motives alone actuated him. Not only was he about to make love because his sister told him, but he also took the precaution of explaining all this before he began. 'Twas thus, we may presume, that the matter presented itself to Mrs. Bold.

When he had got so far, Bertie began poking the gravel with a little cane which he carried. He still kept moving on, but very slowly, and his companion moved slowly by his side, not inclined to assist him in the task the performance of which appeared to be difficult to him.

"Knowing how fond she is of yourself, Mrs. Bold, cannot you imagine what scheme should have occurred to her?"

"I can imagine no better scheme, Mr. Stanhope, than the one I proposed to you just now."

"No," said he, somewhat lack-a-daisically; "I suppose that would be the best; but Charlotte thinks another plan might be joined with it.—She wants me to marry you."

A thousand remembrances flashed across Eleanor's mind all in a moment,—how Charlotte had talked about and praised her brother, how she had continually contrived to throw the two of them together, how she had encouraged all manner of little intimacies, how she had with singular cordiality persisted in treating Eleanor as one of the family. All this had been done to secure her comfortable income for the benefit of one of the family!

Such a feeling as this is very bitter when it first impresses itself on a young mind. To the old such plots and plans, such matured schemes for obtaining the goods of this world without the trouble of earning them, such long-headed attempts to convert "tuum" into "meum", are the ways of life to which they are accustomed. 'Tis thus that many live, and it therefore behoves all those who are well to do in the world to be on their guard against those who are not. With them it is the success that disgusts, not the attempt. But Eleanor had not yet learnt to look on her money as a source of danger; she had not begun to regard herself as fair game to be hunted down by hungry gentlemen. She had enjoyed the society of the Stanhopes, she had greatly liked the cordiality of Charlotte, and had been happy in her new friends. Now she saw the cause of all this kindness and her mind was opened to a new phase of human life.

"Miss Stanhope," said she, haughtily, "has been contriving for me a great deal of honour, but she might have saved herself the trouble. I am not sufficiently ambitious."

"Pray don't be angry with her, Mrs. Bold," said he, "or with me either."

"Certainly not with you, Mr. Stanhope," said she, with considerable sarcasm in her tone. "Certainly not with you."

"No—nor with her," said he, imploringly.

"And why, may I ask you, Mr. Stanhope, have you told me this singular story? For I may presume I may judge by your manner of telling it, that—that—that you and your sister are not exactly of one mind on the subject."

"No we are not."

"And if so," said Mrs. Bold, who was now really angry with the unnecessary insult which she thought had been offered to her, "and if so, why has it been worth your while to tell me all this?"

"I did once think, Mrs. Bold,—that you—that you——"

The widow now again became entirely impassive, and would not lend the slightest assistance to her companion.

"I did once think that you perhaps might,—might have been taught to regard me as more than a friend."

"Never!" said Mrs. Bold, "never. If I have ever allowed myself to do anything to encourage such an idea, I have been very much to blame,—very much to blame indeed."

"You never have," said Bertie, who really had a good-natured anxiety to make what he said as little unpleasant as possible. "You never have, and I have seen for some time that I had no chance; but my sister's hopes ran higher. I have not mistaken you, Mrs. Bold, though perhaps she has."

"Then why have you said all this to me?"

"Because I must not anger her."

"And will not this anger her? Upon my word, Mr. Stanhope, I do not understand the policy of your family. Oh, how I wish I was at home!" And as she expressed the wish, she could restrain herself no longer, but burst out into a flood of tears.

Poor Bertie was greatly moved. "You shall have the carriage to yourself going home," said he; "at least you and my father. As for me I can walk, or for the matter of that it does not much signify what I do." He perfectly understood that part of Eleanor's grief arose from the apparent necessity of going back to Barchester in the carriage with her second suitor.

This somewhat mollified her. "Oh, Mr. Stanhope," said she, "why should you have made me so miserable? What will you have gained by telling me all this?"

He had not even yet explained to her the most difficult part of his proposition; he had not told her that she was to be a party to the little deception which he intended to play off upon his sister.

This suggestion had still to be made, and as it was absolutely necessary, he proceeded to make it.

We need not follow him through the whole of his statement. At last, and not without considerable difficulty, he made Eleanor understand why he had let her into his confidence, seeing that he no longer intended her the honour of a formal offer. At last he made her comprehend the part which she was destined to play in this little family comedy.

But when she did understand it, she was only more angry with him than ever: more angry, not only with him, but with Charlotte also. Her fair name was to be bandied about between them in different senses, and each sense false. She was to be played off by the sister against the father; and then by the brother against the sister. Her dear friend Charlotte, with all her agreeable sympathy and affection, was striving to sacrifice her for the Stanhope family welfare; and Bertie, who, as he now proclaimed himself, was over head and ears in debt, completed the compliment of owning that he did not care to have his debts paid at so great a sacrifice of himself. Then she was asked to conspire together with this unwilling suitor, for the sake of making the family believe that he had in obedience to their commands done his best to throw himself thus away!

She lifted up her face when he had finished, and looking at him with much dignity, even through her tears, she said—

"I regret to say it, Mr. Stanhope; but after what has passed, I believe that all intercourse between your family and myself had better cease."

"Well, perhaps it had," said Bertie naïvely; "perhaps that will be better, at any rate for a time; and then Charlotte will think you are offended at what I have done."

"And now I will go back to the house, if you please," said Eleanor. "I can find my way by myself, Mr. Stanhope; after what has passed," she added, "I would rather go alone."

"But I must find the carriage for you, Mrs. Bold, and I must tell my father that you will return with him alone, and I must make some excuse to him for not going with you; and I must bid the servant put you down at your own house, for I suppose you will not now choose to see them again in the close."

There was a truth about this, and a perspicuity in making arrangements for lessening her immediate embarrassment, which had some effect in softening Eleanor's anger. So she suffered herself to walk by his side over the now deserted lawn, till they came to the drawing-room window. There was something about Bertie Stanhope which gave him, in the estimation of everyone, a different standing from that which any other man would occupy under similar circumstances. Angry as Eleanor was, and great as was her cause for anger, she was not half as angry with him as she would have been with any one else. He was apparently so simple, so good-natured, so unaffected and easy to talk to, that she had already half-forgiven him before he was at the drawing-room window. When they arrived there, Dr. Stanhope was sitting nearly alone with Mr. and Miss Thorne; one or two other unfortunates were there, who from one cause or another were still delayed in getting away; but they were every moment getting fewer in number.

As soon as he had handed Eleanor over to his father, Bertie started off to the front gate, in search of the carriage, and there waited leaning patiently against the front wall, and comfortably smoking a cigar, till it came up. When he returned to the room Dr. Stanhope and Eleanor were alone with their hosts.

"At last, Miss Thorne," said he cheerily, "I have come to relieve you. Mrs. Bold and my father are the last roses of the very delightful summer you have given us, and desirable as Mrs. Bold's society always is, now at least you must be glad to see the last flowers plucked from the tree."

Miss Thorne declared that she was delighted to have Mrs. Bold and Dr. Stanhope still with her; and Mr. Thorne would have said the same, had he not been checked by a yawn, which he could not suppress.

"Father, will you give your arm to Mrs. Bold?" said Bertie: and so the last adieux were made, and the prebendary led out Mrs. Bold, followed by his son.

"I shall be home soon after you," said he, as the two got into the carriage.

"Are you not coming in the carriage?" said the father.

"No, no; I have some one to see on the road, and shall walk. John, mind you drive to Mrs. Bold's house first."

Eleanor looking out of the window, saw him with his hat in his hand, bowing to her with his usual gay smile, as though nothing had happened to mar the tranquillity of the day. It was many a long year before she saw him again. Dr. Stanhope hardly spoke to her on her way home; and she was safely deposited by John at her own hall-door, before the carriage drove into the close.

And thus our heroine played the last act of that day's melodrame.

CHAPTER XXXVI

MR. AND MRS. QUIVERFUL ARE MADE HAPPY.
MR. SLOPE IS ENCOURAGED BY THE PRESS

BEFORE she started for Ullathorne, Mrs. Proudie, careful soul, caused two letters to be written, one by herself and one by her lord, to the inhabitants of Puddingdale vicarage, which made happy the hearth of those within it.

As soon as the departure of the horses left the bishop's stable-groom free for other services, that humble denizen of the diocese started on the bishop's own pony with the two despatches. We have had so many letters lately that we will spare ourselves these. That from the bishop was simply a request that Mr. Quiverful would wait upon his lordship the next morning at 11 A.M.; and that from the lady was as simply a request that Mrs. Quiverful would do the same by her, though it was couched in somewhat longer and more grandiloquent phraseology.

It had become a point of conscience with Mrs. Proudie to urge the settlement of this great hospital question. She was resolved that Mr. Quiverful should have it. She was resolved that there should be no more doubt or delay, no more refusals and resignations, no more secret negotiations carried on by Mr. Slope on his own account in opposition to her behests.

"Bishop," she said, immediately after breakfast, on the morning of that eventful day, "have you signed the appointment yet?"

"No, my dear, not yet; it is not exactly signed as yet."

"Then do it," said the lady.

The bishop did it; and a very pleasant day indeed he spent at Ullathorne. And when he got home he had a glass of hot negus in his wife's sitting-room, and read the last number of the "Little Dorrit" of the day with great inward satisfaction. Oh, husbands, oh, my marital friends, what great comfort is there to be derived from a wife well obeyed!

Much perturbation and flutter, high expectation and renewed hopes, were occasioned at Puddingdale, by the receipt of these episcopal despatches. Mrs. Quiverful, whose careful ear caught the sound of the pony's feet as he trotted up to the vicarage kitchen door, brought them in hurriedly to her husband. She was at the moment concocting the Irish stew destined to satisfy the noonday wants of fourteen young birds, let alone the parent couple. She had taken the letters from the man's hands between the folds of her capacious apron, so as to save them from the contamination of the stew, and in this guise she brought them to her husband's desk.

They at once divided the spoil, each taking that addressed to the other. "Quiverful," said she with impressive voice, "you are to be at the palace at eleven tomorrow."

"And so you are, my dear," said he, almost gasping with the importance of the tidings: and then they exchanged letters.

"She'd never have sent for me again," said the lady, "if it wasn't all right."

"Oh! my dear, don't be too certain," said the gentleman. "Only think if it should be wrong."

"She'd never have sent for me, Q., if it wasn't all right," again argued the lady. "She's stiff and hard and proud as pie-crust, but I think she's right at bottom." Such was Mrs. Quiverful's verdict about Mrs. Proudie, to which in after times she always adhered. People when they get their income doubled usually think that those through whose instrumentality this little ceremony is performed are right at bottom.

"Oh Letty!" said Mr. Quiverful, rising from his well-worn seat.

"Oh Q.!" said Mrs. Quiverful: and then the two, unmindful of the kitchen apron, the greasy fingers, and the adherent Irish stew, threw themselves warmly into each other's arms.

"For heaven's sake don't let any one cajole you out of it again," said the wife.

"Let me alone for that," said the husband, with a look of almost fierce determination, pressing his fist as he spoke rigidly on his desk, as though he had Mr. Slope's head below his knuckles, and meant to keep it there.

"I wonder how soon it will be," said she.

"I wonder whether it will be at all," said he, still doubtful.

"Well, I won't say too much," said the lady. "The cup has slipped twice before, and it may fall altogether this time; but I'll not believe it. He'll give you the appointment to-morrow. You'll find he will."

"Heaven send he may," said Mr. Quiverful, solemnly. And who that considers the weight of the burden on this man's back, will say that the prayer was an improper one? There were fourteen of them —fourteen of them living—as Mrs. Quiverful had so powerfully urged in the presence of the bishop's wife. As long as promotion cometh from any human source, whether north or south, east or west, will not such a claim as this hold good, in spite of all our examination tests, *detur digniori's* and optimist tendencies? It is fervently to be hoped that it may. Till we can become divine we must be content to be human, lest in our hurry for a change we sink to something lower.

And then the pair sitting down lovingly together, talked over all their difficulties, as they so often did, and all their hopes, as they so seldom were enabled to do.

"You had better call on that man, Q., as you come away from the palace," said Mrs. Quiverful, pointing to an angry call for money from the Barchester draper, which the postman had left at the vicarage that morning. Cormorant that he was, unjust, hungry cormorant! When rumour first got abroad that the Quiverfuls were to go to the hospital, this fellow with fawning eagerness had pressed his goods upon the wants of the poor clergyman. He had done so, feeling that he should be paid from the hospital funds, and flattering himself that a man with fourteen children, and money wherewithal to clothe them, could not but be an excellent customer. As soon as the second rumour reached him, he applied for his money angrily.

And "the fourteen"—or such of them as were old enough to hope and discuss their hopes, talked over their golden future. The tall-grown girls whispered to each other of possible Barchester parties, of possible allowances for dress, of a possible piano—the one they had in the vicarage was so weather-beaten with the storms of years and children as to be no longer worthy of the name—of the pretty garden, and the pretty house. 'Twas of such things it most behoved them to whisper.

And the younger fry, they did not content themselves with whispers, but shouted to each other of their new play-ground beneath our dear ex-warden's well-loved elms, of their future own gardens, of marbles to be procured in the wished-forcity, and of the rumour which had reached them of a Barchester school.

'Twas in vain that their cautious mother tried to instil into their breasts the very feeling she had striven to banish from that of their father; 'twas in vain that she repeated to the girls that "there's many a slip 'twixt the cup and the lip;" 'twas in vain she attempted to make the children believe that they were to live at Puddingdale all their lives. Hopes mounted high and would not have themselves quelled. The neighbouring farmers heard the news, and came in to congratulate them. 'Twas Mrs. Quiverful herself who had kindled the fire, and in the first outbreak of her renewed expectations she did it so thoroughly, that it was quite past her power to put it out again.

Poor matron! good honest matron! doing thy duty in the state to which thou hast been called, heartily if not contentedly; let the fire burn on;—on this occasion the flames will not scorch; they shall warm thee and thine. 'Tis ordained that that husband of thine, that Q. of thy bosom, shall reign supreme for years to come over the bedesmen of Hiram's hospital.

And the last in all Barchester to mar their hopes, had he heard and seen all that passed at Puddingdale that day, would have been Mr. Harding. What wants had he to set in opposition to those of such a regiment of young ravens? There are fourteen of them living! with him at any rate, let us say, that that argument would have been sufficient for the appointment of Mr. Quiverful.

In the morning, Q. and his wife kept their appointments with that punctuality which bespeaks an expectant mind. The friendly farmer's gig was borrowed, and in that they went, discussing many things by the way. They had instructed the household to expect them back by one, and injunctions were given to the eldest pledge to have ready by that accustomed hour the remainder of the huge stew which the provident mother had prepared on the previous day. The hands of the kitchen clock came round to two, three, four, before the farmer's gig-wheels were again heard at the vicarage gate. With what palpitating hearts were the returning wanderers greeted!

"I suppose, children, you all thought we were never coming back any more?" said the mother, as she slowly let down her solid foot till it rested on the step of the gig. "Well, such a day as we've had!"

and then leaning heavily on a big boy's shoulder, she stepped once more on terra firma.

There was no need for more than the tone of her voice to tell them that all was right. The Irish stew might burn itself to cinders now.

Then there was such kissing and hugging, such crying and laughing. Mr. Quiverful could not sit still at all, but kept walking from room to room, then out into the garden, then down the avenue into the road, and then back again to his wife. She, however, lost no time so idly.

"We must go to work at once, girls; and that in earnest. Mrs. Proudie expects us to be in the hospital house on the 15th of October."

Had Mrs. Proudie expressed a wish that they should all be there on the next morning, the girls would have had nothing to say against it.

"And when will the pay begin?" asked the eldest boy.

"To-day, my dear," said the gratified mother.

"Oh,—that is jolly," said the boy.

"Mrs. Proudie insisted on our going down to the house," continued the mother; "and when there I thought I might save a journey by measuring some of the rooms and windows; so I got a knot of tape from Bobbins. Bobbins is as civil as you please, now."

"I wouldn't thank him," said Letty the younger.

"Oh, it's the way of the world, my dear. They all do just the same. You might just as well be angry with the turkey cock for gobbling at you. It's the bird's nature." And as she enunciated to her bairns the upshot of her practical experience, she pulled from her pocket the portions of tape which showed the length and breadth of the various rooms at the hospital house.

And so we will leave her happy in her toils.

The Quiverfuls had hardly left the palace, and Mrs. Proudie was still holding forth on the matter to her husband, when another visitor was announced in the person of Dr. Gwynne. The master of Lazarus had asked for the bishop, and not for Mrs. Proudie, and therefore, when he was shown in to the study, he was surprised rather than rejoiced to find the lady there.

But we must go back a little, and it shall be but a little, for a difficulty begins to make itself manifest in the necessity of disposing of all our friends in the small remainder of this one volume. Oh, that Mr. Longman would allow me a fourth! It should transcend the other three as the seventh heaven transcends all the lower stages of celestial bliss.

Going home in the carriage that evening from Ullathorne, Dr. Gwynne had not without difficulty brought round his friend the archdeacon to a line of tactics much less bellicose than that which his own taste would have preferred. "It will be unseemly in us to show ourselves in a bad humour: and moreover we have no power in this matter, and it will therefore be bad policy to act as though we had." 'Twas thus the master of Lazarus argued. "If," he continued, "the bishop be determined to appoint another to the hospital, threats will not prevent him, and threats should not be lightly used by an archdeacon to his bishop. If he will place a stranger in the hospital, we can only leave him to the indignation of others. It is probable that such a step may not eventually injure your father-in-law. I will see the bishop, if you will allow me,—alone." At this the archdeacon winced visibly; "yes, alone; for so I shall be calmer: and then I shall at any rate learn what he does mean to do in the matter."

The archdeacon puffed and blew, put up the carriage window and then put it down again, argued the matter up to his own gate, and at last gave way. Everybody was against him, his own wife, Mr. Harding, and Dr. Gwynne.

"Pray keep him out of hot water, Dr. Gwynne," Mrs. Grantly had said to her guest. "My dearest madam, I'll do my best," the courteous master had replied. 'Twas thus he did it; and earned for himself the gratitude of Mrs. Grantly.

And now we may return to the bishop's study.

Dr. Gwynne had certainly not foreseen the difficulty which here presented itself. He,—together with all the clerical world of England,—had heard it rumoured about that Mrs. Proudie did not confine herself to her wardrobes, still-rooms, and laundries; but yet it had never occurred to him that if he called on a bishop at one o'clock in the day, he could by any possibility find him closeted with his wife; or that if he did so, the wife would remain longer than necessary to make her curtsey. It appeared, however, as though in the present case Mrs. Proudie had no idea of retreating.

The bishop had been very much pleased with Dr. Gwynne on the preceding day, and of course thought that Dr. Gwynne had been as much pleased with him. He attributed the visit solely to compliment, and thought it an extremely gracious and proper thing for the master of Lazarus to drive over from Plumstead specially to call at the palace so soon after his arrival in the country. The fact that they were not on the same side either in politics or doctrines made the compliment the greater. The bishop, therefore, was all smiles. And Mrs. Proudie, who liked people with good handles to their names, was also very well disposed to welcome the master of Lazarus.

"We had a charming party at Ullathorne, Master, had we not?" said she. "I hope Mrs. Grantly got home without fatigue."

Dr. Gwynne said that they had all been a little tired, but were none the worse this morning.

"An excellent person, Miss Thorne," suggested the bishop.

"And an exemplary Christian, I am told," said Mrs. Proudie.

Dr. Gwynne declared that he was very glad to hear it.

"I have not seen her Sabbath-day schools yet," continued the lady, "but I shall make a point of doing so before long."

Dr. Gwynne merely bowed at this intimation. He had heard something of Mrs. Proudie and her Sunday schools, both from Dr. Grantly and Mr. Harding.

"By the bye, Master," continued the lady, "I wonder whether Mrs. Grantly would like me to drive over and inspect her Sabbath-day school. I hear that it is most excellently kept."

Dr. Gwynne really could not say. He had no doubt Mrs. Grantly would be most happy to see Mrs. Proudie any day Mrs. Proudie would do her the honour of calling: that was, of course, if Mrs. Grantly should happen to be at home.

A slight cloud darkened the lady's brow. She saw that her offer was not taken in good part. This generation of unregenerated vipers was still perverse, stiffnecked, and hardened in their iniquity. "The archdeacon, I know," said she, "sets his face against these institutions."

At this Dr. Gwynne laughed slightly. It was but a smile. Had he given his cap for it he could not have helped it.

Mrs. Proudie frowned again. "'Suffer little children, and forbid them not,'" said she. "Are we not to remember that, Dr. Gwynne? 'Take heed that ye despise not one of these little ones.' Are we not to remember that, Dr. Gwynne?" And at each of these questions she raised at him her menacing forefinger.

"Certainly, madam, certainly," said the master, "and so does the archdeacon, I am sure, on week days as well as on Sundays."

"On week days you can't take heed not to despise them," said Mrs. Proudie, "because then they are out in the fields. On week days they belong to their parents, but on Sundays they ought to belong to the clergyman." And the finger was again raised.

The master began to understand and to share the intense disgust which the archdeacon always expressed when Mrs. Proudie's name was mentioned. What was he to do with such a woman as this? To take his hat and go would have been his natural resource; but then he did not wish to be foiled in his object.

"My lord," said he, "I wanted to ask you a question on business, if you could spare me one moment's leisure. I know I must apologise for so disturbing you; but in truth I will not detain you five minutes."

"Certainly, Master, certainly," said the bishop; "my time is quite yours,—pray make no apology, pray make no apology."

"You have a great deal to do just at the present moment, bishop. Do not forget how extremely busy you are at present," said Mrs. Proudie, whose spirit was now up; for she was angry with her visitor.

"I will not delay his lordship much above a minute," said the master of Lazarus, rising from his chair, and expecting that Mrs. Proudie would now go, or else that the bishop would lead the way into another room.

But neither event seemed likely to occur, and Dr. Gwynne stood for a moment silent in the middle of the room.

"Perhaps it's about Hiram's hospital?" suggested Mrs. Proudie. Dr. Gwynne, lost in astonishment, and not knowing what else on earth to do, confessed that his business with the bishop was connected with Hiram's hospital.

"His lordship has finally conferred the appointment on Mr. Quiverful this morning," said the lady.

Dr. Gwynne made a simple reference to the bishop, and finding that the lady's statement was formally confirmed, he took his leave. "That comes of the reform bill," he said to himself as he walked down the bishop's avenue. "Well, at any rate the Greek play bishops were not so bad as that."

It has been said that Mr. Slope, as he started for Ullathorne, received a despatch from his friend, Mr. Towers, which had the effect of putting him in that high good-humour which subsequent events somewhat untowardly damped. It ran as follows. Its shortness will be its sufficient apology.

"My dear Sir,—I wish you every success. I don't know that I can help you, but if I can, I will.

"Yours ever,
"T.T.
"30/9/185—"

There was more in this than in all Sir Nicholas Fitzwhiggin's flummery; more than in all the bishop's promises, even had they been ever so sincere; more than in any archbishop's good word, even had it been possible to obtain it. Tom Towers would do for him what he could.

Mr. Slope had from his youth upwards been a firm believer in the public press. He had dabbled in it himself ever since he had taken his degree, and regarded it as the great arranger and distributor of all future British terrestrial affairs whatever. He had not yet arrived at the age, an age which sooner or later comes to most of us, which dissipates the golden dreams of youth. He delighted in the idea of wresting power from the hands of his country's magnates, and placing it in a custody which was at any rate nearer to his own reach. Sixty thousand broad sheets dispersing themselves daily among his reading fellow-citizens, formed in his eyes a better depôt for supremacy than a throne at Windsor, a cabinet in Downing Street, or even an assembly at Westminster. And on this subject we must not quarrel with Mr. Slope, for the feeling is too general to be met with disrespect.

Tom Towers was as good, if not better than his promise. On the following morning the Jupiter, spouting forth public opinion with sixty thousand loud clarions, did proclaim to the world that Mr. Slope was the fitting man for the vacant post.

It had been well for Mr. Slope that Dr. Trefoil had died in the autumn. Those caterers for our morning repast, the staff of the

G

Jupiter, had been sorely put to it for the last month to find a suffi-
ciency of proper pabulum. Just then there was no talk of a new
American president. No wonderful tragedies had occurred on
railway trains in Georgia, or elsewhere. There was a dearth of
broken banks, and a dead dean with the necessity for a live one was
a godsend. Had Dr. Trefoil died in June, Mr. Towers would probably
not have known so much about the piety of Mr. Slope.

And here we will leave Mr. Slope for a while in his triumph;
explaining, however, that his feelings were not altogether of a
triumphant nature. His rejection by the widow, or rather the
method of his rejection, galled him terribly. For days to come he
positively felt the sting upon his cheek, whenever he thought of what
had been done to him. He could not refrain from calling her by
harsh names, speaking to himself as he walked through the streets
of Barchester. When he said his prayers, he could not bring himself
to forgive her. When he strove to do so, his mind recoiled from the
attempt, and in lieu of forgiving ran off in a double spirit of vindic-
tiveness, dwelling on the extent of the injury he had received.
And so his prayers dropped senseless from his lips.

And then the signora; what would he not have given to be able to
hate her also? As it was, he worshipped the very sofa on which she
was ever lying. And thus it was not all rose colour with Mr. Slope,
although his hopes ran high.

CHAPTER XXXVII

MRS. BOLD AT HOME

Poor Mrs. Bold, when she got home from Ullathorne on the evening
of Miss Thorne's party, was very unhappy, and moreover, very
tired. Nothing fatigues the body so much as weariness of spirit, and
Eleanor's spirit was indeed weary.

Dr. Stanhope had civilly but not very cordially asked her into tea,
and her manner of refusal convinced the worthy doctor that he need
not repeat the invitation. He had not exactly made himself a party
to the intrigue which was to convert the late Mr. Bold's patrimony
into an income for his hopeful son, but he had been well aware what
was going on. And he was well aware also, when he perceived that
Bertie declined accompanying them home in the carriage, that the
affair had gone off.

Eleanor was very much afraid that Charlotte would have darted
out upon her, as the prebendary got out at his own door, but Bertie
had thoughtfully saved her from this, by causing the carriage to go
round by her own house. This also Dr. Stanhope understood, and
allowed to pass by without remark.

When she got home, she found Mary Bold in the drawing-room with the child in her lap. She rushed forward, and, throwing herself on her knees, kissed the little fellow till she almost frightened him.

"Oh, Mary, I am so glad you did not go. It was an odious party."

Now the question of Mary's going had been one greatly mooted between them. Mrs. Bold, when invited, had been the guest of the Grantlys, and Miss Thorne, who had chiefly known Eleanor at the hospital or at Plumstead rectory, had forgotten all about Mary Bold. Her sister-in-law had implored her to go under her wing, and had offered to write to Miss Thorne, or to call on her. But Miss Bold had declined. In fact, Mr. Bold had not been very popular with such people as the Thornes, and his sister would not go among them unless she were specially asked to do so.

"Well then," said Mary, cheerfully, "I have the less to regret."

"You have nothing to regret; but oh! Mary, I have—so much—so much;"—and then she began kissing her boy, whom her caresses had aroused from his slumbers. When she raised her head, Mary saw that the tears were running down her cheeks.

"Good heavens, Eleanor, what is the matter? what has happened to you?—Eleanor—dearest Eleanor—what is the matter?" and Mary got up with the boy still in her arms.

"Give him to me—give him to me," said the young mother. "Give him to me, Mary," and she almost tore the child out of her sister's arms. The poor little fellow murmured somewhat at the disturbance, but nevertheless nestled himself close into his mother's bosom.

"Here, Mary, take the cloak from me. My own, own darling, darling, darling jewel. You are not false to me. Everybody else is false; everybody else is cruel. Mamma will care for nobody, nobody, nobody, but her own, own, own little man;" and she again kissed and pressed the baby, and cried till the tears ran down over the child's face.

"Who has been cruel to you, Eleanor?" said Mary. "I hope I have not."

Now, in this matter, Eleanor had great cause for mental uneasiness. She could not certainly accuse her loving sister-in-law of cruelty; but she had to do that which was more galling; she had to accuse herself of imprudence against which her sister-in-law had warned her. Miss Bold had never encouraged Eleanor's acquaintance with Mr. Slope, and she had positively discouraged the friendship of the Stanhopes as far as her usual gentle mode of speaking had permitted. Eleanor had only laughed at her, however, when she said that she disapproved of married women who lived apart from their husbands, and suggested that Charlotte Stanhope never went to church. Now however, Eleanor must either hold her tongue, which was quite impossible, or confess herself to have been utterly wrong, which was nearly equally so. So she staved off the evil day by more tears, and consoled herself by inducing little Johnny to rouse himself sufficiently to return her caresses.

"He is a darling—as true as gold. What would mamma do without him? Mamma would lie down and die if she had not her own Johnny Bold to give her comfort." This and much more she said of the same kind, and for a time made no other answer to Mary's inquiries.

This kind of consolation from the world's deceit is very common. Mothers obtain it from their children, and men from their dogs. Some men even do so from their walking-sticks, which is just as rational. How is it that we can take joy to ourselves in that we are not deceived by those who have not attained the art to deceive us? In a true man, if such can be found, or a true woman, much consolation may indeed be taken.

In the caresses of her child, however, Eleanor did receive consolation; and may ill befall the man who would begrudge it to her. The evil day, however, was only postponed. She had to tell her disagreeable tale to Mary, and she had also to tell it to her father. Must it not, indeed, be told to the whole circle of her acquaintance before she could be made to stand all right with them? At the present moment there was no one to whom she could turn for comfort. She hated Mr. Slope; that was a matter of course, in that feeling she revelled. She hated and despised the Stanhopes; but that feeling distressed her greatly. She had, as it were, separated herself from her old friends to throw herself into the arms of this family; and then how had they intended to use her? She could hardly reconcile herself to her own father, who had believed ill of her. Mary Bold had turned Mentor. That she could have forgiven had the Mentor turned out to be in the wrong; but Mentors in the right are not to be pardoned. She could not but hate the archdeacon; and now she hated him worse than ever, for she must in some sort humble herself before him. She hated her sister, for she was part and parcel of the archdeacon. And she would have hated Mr. Arabin if she could. He had pretended to regard her, and yet before her face he had hung over that Italian woman as though there had been no beauty in the world but hers—no other woman worth a moment's attention. And Mr. Arabin would have to learn all this about Mr. Slope! She told herself that she hated him, and she knew that she was lying to herself as she did so. She had no consolation but her baby, and of that she made the most. Mary, though she could not surmise what it was that had so violently affected her sister-in-law, saw at once that her grief was too great to be kept under control, and waited patiently till the child should be in his cradle.

"You'll have some tea, Eleanor," she said.

"Oh, I don't care," said she; though in fact she must have been very hungry, for she had eaten nothing at Ullathorne.

Mary quietly made the tea, and buttered the bread, laid aside the cloak, and made things look comfortable.

"He's fast asleep," said she, "you're very tired; let me take him up to bed."

But Eleanor would not let her sister touch him. She looked wistfully at her baby's eyes, saw that they were lost in the deepest slumber, and then made a sort of couch for him on the sofa. She was determined that nothing should prevail upon her to let him out of her sight that night.

"Come, Nelly," said Mary, "don't be cross with me. I at least have done nothing to offend you."

"I an't cross," said Eleanor.

"Are you angry then? Surely you can't be angry with me."

"No, I an't angry; at least not with you."

"If you are not, drink the tea I have made for you. I am sure you must want it."

Eleanor did drink it, and allowed herself to be persuaded. She ate and drank, and as the inner woman was recruited she felt a little more charitable towards the world at large. At last she found words to begin her story, and before she went to bed, she had made a clean breast of it, and told everything—everything that is, as to the lovers she had rejected; of Mr. Arabin she said not a word.

"I know I was wrong," said she, speaking of the blow she had given to Mr. Slope; "but I didn't know what he might do, and I had to protect myself."

"He richly deserved it," said Mary.

"Deserved it!" said Eleanor, whose mind as regarded Mr. Slope was almost bloodthirsty. "Had I stabbed him with a dagger, he would have deserved it. But what will they say about it at Plumstead?"

"I don't think I should tell them," said Mary. Eleanor began to think that she would not.

There could have been no kinder comforter than Mary Bold. There was not the slightest dash of triumph about her when she heard of the Stanhope scheme, nor did she allude to her former opinion when Eleanor called her late friend Charlotte a base, designing woman. She re-echoed all the abuse that was heaped on Mr. Slope's head, and never hinted that she had said as much before. "I told you so, I told you so!" is the croak of a true Job's comforter. But Mary, when she found her friend lying in her sorrow and scraping herself with potsherds, forbore to argue and to exult. Eleanor acknowledged the merit of the forbearance, and at length allowed herself to be tranquillised.

On the next day she did not go out of the house. Barchester she thought would be crowded with Stanhopes and Slopes; perhaps also with Arabins and Grantlys. Indeed there was hardly any one among her friends whom she could have met, without some cause of uneasiness.

In the course of the afternoon she heard that the dean was dead;
and she also heard that Mr. Quiverful had been finally appointed to
the hospital.

In the evening her father came to her, and then the story, or as
much of it as she could bring herself to tell him, had to be repeated.
He was not in truth much surprised at Mr. Slope's effrontery; but he
was obliged to act as though he had been, to save his daughter's
feelings. He was, however, anything but skilful in his deceit, and she
saw through it.

"I see," said she, "that you think it only in the common course of
things that Mr. Slope should have treated me in this way." She had
said nothing to him about the embrace, nor yet of the way in which
it had been met.

"I do not think it at all strange," said he, "that any one should
admire my Eleanor."

"It is strange to me," said she, "that any man should have so much
audacity, without ever having received the slightest encouragement."

To this Mr. Harding answered nothing. With the archdeacon it
would have been the text for a rejoinder, which would not have
disgraced Bildad the Shuhite.

"But you'll tell the archdeacon?" asked Mr. Harding.

"Tell him what?" said she sharply.

"Or Susan?" continued Mr. Harding. "You'll tell Susan; you'll
let them know that they wronged you in supposing that this man's
addresses would be agreeable to you."

"They may find that out their own way," said she; "I shall not
ever willingly mention Mr. Slope's name to either of them."

"But I may."

"I have no right to hinder you from doing anything that may be
necessary to your own comfort, but pray do not do it for my sake.
Dr. Grantly never thought well of me, and never will. I don't
know now that I am even anxious that he should do so."

And then they went to the affair of the hospital. "But is it true,
papa?"

"What, my dear?" said he. "About the dean? Yes, I fear quite
true. Indeed I know there is no doubt about it."

"Poor Miss Trefoil. I am so sorry for her. But I did not mean
that," said Eleanor. "But about the hospital, papa?"

"Yes, my dear. I believe it is true that Mr. Quiverful is to have
it."

"Oh, what a shame!"

"No, my dear, not at all, not at all a shame; I am sure I hope it
will suit him."

"But, papa, you know it is a shame. After all your hopes, all your
expectations to get back to your old house, to see it given away in
this way to a perfect stranger!"

"My dear, the bishop had a right to give it to whom he pleased."

"I deny that, papa. He had no such right. It is not as though you were a candidate for a new piece of preferment. If the bishop has a grain of justice——"

"The bishop offered it to me on his terms, and as I did not like the terms, I refused it. After that, I cannot complain."

"Terms! he had no right to make terms."

"I don't know about that; but it seems he had the power. But to tell you the truth, Nelly, I am as well satisfied as it is. When the affair became the subject of angry discussion, I thoroughly wished to be rid of it altogether."

"But you did want to go back to the old house, papa. You told me so yourself."

"Yes, my dear, I did. For a short time I did wish it. And I was foolish in doing so. I am getting old now; and my chief worldly wish is for peace and rest. Had I gone back to the hospital, I should have had endless contentions with the bishop, contentions with his chaplain, and contentions with the archdeacon. I am not up to this now, I am not able to meet such troubles; and therefore I am not ill-pleased to find myself left to the little church of St. Cuthbert's. I shall never starve," added he, laughing, "as long as you are here."

"But will you come and live with me, papa?" she said earnestly, taking him by both his hands. "If you will do that, if you will promise that, I will own that you are right."

"I will dine with you to-day at any rate."

"No, but live here altogether. Give up that close, odious little room in High Street."

"My dear, it's a very nice little room; and you are really quite uncivil."

"Oh, papa, don't joke. It's not a nice place for you. You say you are growing old, though I am sure you are not."

"Am not I, my dear?"

"No, papa, not old—not to say old. But you are quite old enough to feel the want of a decent room to sit in. You know how lonely Mary and I are here. You know nobody ever sleeps in the big front bed-room. It is really unkind of you to remain up there alone, when you are so much wanted here."

"Thank you, Nelly—thank you. But, my dear——"

"If you had been living here, papa, with us, as I really think you ought to have done, considering how lonely we are, there would have been none of all this dreadful affair about Mr. Slope."

Mr. Harding, however, did not allow himself to be talked over into giving up his own and only little *pied à terre* in the High Street. He promised to come and dine with his daughter, and stay with her, and visit her, and do everything but absolutely live with her. It did not suit the peculiar feelings of the man to tell his daughter that though she had rejected Mr. Slope, and been ready to reject Mr. Stanhope, some other more favoured suitor would probably soon appear; and that on the appearance of such a suitor the big front bed-room might perhaps be more frequently in requisition than at present. But doubtless such an idea crossed his mind, and added its weight to the other reasons which made him decide on still keeping the close, odious little room in High Street.

The evening passed over quietly and in comfort. Eleanor was always happier with her father than with any one else. He had not, perhaps, any natural taste for baby-worship, but he was always ready to sacrifice himself, and therefore made an excellent third in a trio with his daughter and Mary Bold in singing the praises of the wonderful child. They were standing together over their music in the evening, the baby having again been put to bed upon the sofa, when the servant brought in a very small note in a beautiful pink envelope. It quite filled the room with perfume as it lay upon the small salver. Mary Bold and Mrs. Bold were both at the piano, and Mr. Harding was sitting close to them, with the violoncello between his legs; so that the elegancy of the epistle was visible to them all.

"Please, ma'am, Dr. Stanhope's coachman says he is to wait for an answer," said the servant.

Eleanor got very red in the face as she took the note in her hand. She had never seen the writing before. Charlotte's epistles, to which she was well accustomed, were of a very different style and kind. She generally wrote on large note-paper; she twisted up her letters into the shape and sometimes into the size of cocked hats; she addressed them in a sprawling manly hand, and not unusually added a blot or a smudge, as though such were her own peculiar sign-manual. The address of this note was written in a beautiful female hand, and the gummed wafer bore on it an impress of a gilt coronet. Though Eleanor had never seen such a one before, she guessed that it came from the signora. Such epistles were very numerously sent out from any house in which the signora might happen to be dwelling, but they were rarely addressed to ladies. When the coachman was told by the lady's maid to take the letter to Mrs. Bold, he openly expressed his opinion that there was some mistake about it. Whereupon the lady's maid boxed the coachman's ears. Had Mr. Slope seen in how meek a spirit the coachman took the rebuke, he might have learnt a useful lesson, both in philosophy and religion.

The note was as follows. It may be taken as a faithful promise that no further letter whatever shall be transcribed at length in these pages.

"My dear Mrs. Bold,—May I ask you, as a great favour, to call on me to-morrow? You can say what hour will best suit you; but quite early, if you can. I need hardly say that if I could call upon you I should not take this liberty with you.

"I partly know what occurred the other day, and I promise you that you shall meet with no annoyance if you will come to me. My brother leaves us for London to-day; from thence he goes to Italy.

"It will probably occur to you that I should not thus intrude on you, unless I had that to say to you which may be of considerable moment. Pray therefore excuse me, even if you do not grant my request, and believe me,

"Very sincerely yours,
"M. VESEY NERONI.

"Thursday Evening."

The three of them sat in consultation on this epistle for some ten or fifteen minutes, and then decided that Eleanor should write a line saying that she would see the signora the next morning, at twelve o'clock.

CHAPTER XXXVIII

THE STANHOPES AT HOME

WE must now return to the Stanhopes, and see how they behaved themselves on their return from Ullathorne.

Charlotte, who came back in the first homeward journey with her sister, waited in palpitating expectation till the carriage drove up to the door a second time. She did not run down or stand at the window, or show in any outward manner that she looked for anything wonderful to occur; but, when she heard the carriage-wheels, she stood up with erect ears, listening for Eleanor's footfall on the pavement or the cheery sound of Bertie's voice welcoming her in. Had she heard either, she would have felt that all was right; but neither sound was there for her to hear. She heard only her father's slow step, as he ponderously let himself down from the carriage, and slowly walked along the hall, till he got into his own private room on the ground floor. "Send Miss Stanhope to me," he said to the servant.

"There's something wrong now," said Madeline, who was lying on her sofa in the back drawing-room.

"It's all up with Bertie," replied Charlotte. "I know, I know," she said to the servant, as he brought up the message. "Tell my father I will be with him immediately."

"Bertie's wooing has gone astray," said Madeline; "I knew it would."

"It has been his own fault then. She was ready enough, I am quite sure," said Charlotte, with that sort of ill-nature which is not uncommon when one woman speaks of another.

"What will you say to him now?" By "him," the signora meant their father.

"That will be as I find him. He was ready to pay two hundred pounds for Bertie, to stave off the worst of his creditors, if this marriage had gone on. Bertie must now have the money instead, and go and take his chance."

"Where is he now?"

"Heaven knows! smoking in the bottom of Mr. Thorne's ha-ha, or philandering with some of those Miss Chadwicks. Nothing will ever make an impression on him. But he'll be furious if I don't go down."

"No; nothing ever will. But don't be long, Charlotte, for I want my tea."

And so Charlotte went down to her father. There was a very black cloud on the old man's brow; blacker than his daughter could ever yet remember to have seen there. He was sitting in his own arm-chair, not comfortably over the fire, but in the middle of the room, waiting till she should come and listen to him.

"What has become of your brother?" he said, as soon as the door was shut.

"I should rather ask you," said Charlotte. "I left you both at Ullathorne, when I came away. What have you done with Mrs. Bold?"

"Mrs. Bold! nonsense. The woman has gone home as she ought to do. And heartily glad I am that she should not be sacrificed to so heartless a reprobate."

"Oh, papa!"

"A heartless reprobate! Tell me now where he is, and what he is going to do. I have allowed myself to be fooled between you. Marriage, indeed! Who on earth that has money, or credit, or respect in the world to lose, would marry him?"

"It is no use your scolding me, papa. I have done the best I could for him and you."

"And Madeline is nearly as bad," said the prebendary, who was in truth very, very angry.

"Oh, I suppose we are all bad," replied Charlotte.

The old man emitted a huge leonine sigh. If they were all bad, who had made them so? If they were unprincipled, selfish, and disreputable, who was to be blamed for the education which had had so injurious an effect?

"I know you'll ruin me among you," said he.

"Why, papa, what nonsense that is. You are living within your income this minute, and if there are any new debts, I don't know of them. I am sure there ought to be none, for we are dull enough here."

"Are those bills of Madeline's paid?"

"No, they are not. Who was to pay them?"

"Her husband may pay them."

"Her husband! would you wish me to tell her you say so? Do you wish to turn her out of your house?"

"I wish she would know how to behave herself."

"Why, what on earth has she done now? Poor Madeline! To-day is only the second time she has gone out since we came to this vile town."

He then sat silent for a time, thinking in what shape he would declare his resolve. "Well, papa," said Charlotte, "shall I stay here, or may I go up-stairs and give mamma her tea?"

"You are in your brother's confidence. Tell me what he is going to do?"

"Nothing, that I am aware of."

"Nothing—nothing! nothing but eat and drink, and spend every shilling of my money he can lay his hands upon. I have made up my mind, Charlotte. He shall eat and drink no more in this house."

"Very well. Then I suppose he must go back to Italy."

"He may go where he pleases."

"That's easily said, papa; but what does it mean? You can't let him——"

"It means this," said the doctor, speaking more loudly than was his wont, and with wrath flashing from his eyes; "that as sure as God rules in heaven, I will not maintain him any longer in idleness."

"Oh, ruling in heaven!" said Charlotte. "It is no use talking about that. You must rule him here on earth; and the question is, how you can do it. You can't turn him out of the house penniless, to beg about the street."

"He may beg where he likes."

"He must go back to Carrara. That is the cheapest place he can live at, and nobody there will give him credit for above two or three hundred pauls. But you must let him have the means of going."

"As sure as——"

"Oh, papa, don't swear. You know you must do it. You were ready to pay two hundred pounds for him if this marriage came off. Half that will start him to Carrara."

"What? give him a hundred pounds!"

"You know we are all in the dark, papa," said she, thinking it expedient to change the conversation. "For anything we know, he may be at this moment engaged to Mrs. Bold."

"Fiddlestick," said the father, who had seen the way in which Mrs. Bold had got into the carriage, while his son stood apart without even offering her his hand.

"Well, then, he must go to Carrara," said Charlotte.

Just at this moment the lock of the front door was heard, and Charlotte's quick ears detected her brother's cat-like step in the hall. She said nothing, feeling that for the present Bertie had better keep out of her father's way. But Dr. Stanhope also heard the sound of the lock.

"Who's that?" he demanded. Charlotte made no reply, and he asked again. "Who is that that has just come in? Open the door. Who is it?"

"I suppose it is Bertie."

"Bid him come here," said the father. But Bertie, who was close to the door and heard the call, required no further bidding, but walked in with a perfectly unconcerned and cheerful air. It was this peculiar *insouciance* which angered Dr. Stanhope, even more than his son's extravagance.

"Well, sir?" said the doctor.

"And how did you get home, sir, with your fair companion?" said Bertie. "I suppose she is not up-stairs, Charlotte?"

"Bertie," said Charlotte, "papa is in no humour for joking. He is very angry with you."

"Angry!" said Bertie, raising his eyebrows, as though he had never yet given his parent cause for a single moment's uneasiness.

"Sit down, if you please, sir," said Dr. Stanhope very sternly, but not now very loudly. "And I'll trouble you to sit down too, Charlotte. Your mother can wait for her tea a few minutes."

Charlotte sat down on the chair nearest to the door, in somewhat of a perverse sort of manner; as much as though she would say— Well, here I am; you shan't say I don't do what I am bid; but I'll be whipped if I give way to you. And she was determined not to give way. She too was angry with Bertie; but she was not the less ready on that account to defend him from his father. Bertie also sat down. He drew his chair close to the library-table, upon which he put his elbow, and then resting his face comfortably on one hand, he began drawing little pictures on a sheet of paper with the other. Before the scene was over he had completed admirable figures of Miss Thorne, Mrs. Proudie, and Lady De Courcy, and begun a family piece to comprise the whole set of the Lookalofts.

"Would it suit you, sir," said the father, "to give me some idea as to what your present intentions are?—what way of living you propose to yourself?"

"I'll do anything you can suggest, sir," replied Bertie.

"No, I shall suggest nothing further. My time for suggesting has gone by. I have only one order to give, and that is, that you leave my house."

"To-night?" said Bertie; and the simple tone of the question left the doctor without any adequately dignified method of reply.

"Papa does not quite mean to-night," said Charlotte, "at least I suppose not."

"To-morrow, perhaps," suggested Bertie.

"Yes, sir, to-morrow," said the doctor. "You shall leave this to-morrow."

"Very well, sir. Will the 4.30 P.M. train be soon enough?" and Bertie, as he asked, put the finishing touch to Miss Thorne's high-heeled boots.

"You may go how and when and where you please, so that you leave my house to-morrow. You have disgraced me, sir; you have disgraced yourself, and me, and your sisters."

"I am glad at least, sir, that I have not disgraced my mother," said Bertie.

Charlotte could hardly keep her countenance; but the doctor's brow grew still blacker than ever. Bertie was executing his *chef d'œuvre* in the delineation of Mrs. Proudie's nose and mouth.

"You are a heartless reprobate, sir; a heartless, thankless, good-for-nothing reprobate. I have done with you. You are my son—that I cannot help; but you shall have no more part or parcel in me as my child, nor I in you as your father."

"Oh, papa, papa! you must not, shall not say so," said Charlotte.

"I will say so, and do say so," said the father, rising from his chair. "And now leave the room, sir."

"Stop, stop," said Charlotte; "why don't you speak, Bertie? why don't you look up and speak? It is your manner that makes papa so angry."

"He is perfectly indifferent to all decency, to all propriety," said the doctor; and then he shouted out, "Leave the room, sir! Do you hear what I say?"

"Papa, papa, I will not let you part so. I know you will be sorry for it." And then she added, getting up and whispering into his ear, "Is he only to blame? Think of that. We have made our own bed, and, such as it is, we must lie on it. It is no use for us to quarrel among ourselves," and as she finished her whisper Bertie finished off the countess's bustle, which was so well done that it absolutely seemed to be swaying to and fro on the paper with its usual lateral motion.

"My father is angry at the present time," said Bertie, looking up for a moment from his sketches, "because I am not going to marry Mrs. Bold. What can I say on the matter? It is true that I am not going to marry her. In the first place——"

"That is not true, sir," said Dr. Stanhope; "but I will not argue with you."

"You were angry just this moment because I would not speak," said Bertie, going on with a young Lookaloft.

"Give over drawing," said Charlotte, going up to him and taking the paper from under his hand. The caricatures, however, she preserved, and showed them afterwards to the friends of the Thornes, the Proudies, and De Courcys. Bertie, deprived of his occupation, threw himself back in his chair and waited further orders.

"I think it will certainly be for the best that Bertie should leave this at once, perhaps to-morrow," said Charlotte; "but pray, papa, let us arrange some scheme together."

"If he will leave this to-morrow, I will give him 10*l.*, and he shall be paid 5*l.* a month by the banker at Carrara as long as he stays permanently in that place."

"Well, sir! it won't be long," said Bertie; "for I shall be starved to death in about three months."

"He must have marble to work with," said Charlotte.

"I have plenty there in the studio to last me three months," said Bertie. "It will be no use attempting anything large in so limited a time; unless I do my own tombstone."

Terms, however, were ultimately come to, somewhat more liberal than those proposed, and the doctor was induced to shake hands with his son, and bid him good night. Dr. Stanhope would not go up to tea, but had it brought to him in his study by his daughter.

But Bertie went up-stairs and spent a pleasant evening. He finished the Lookalofts, greatly to the delight of his sisters, though the manner of portraying their *décolleté* dresses was not the most refined. Finding how matters were going, he by degree allowed it to escape from him that he had not pressed his suit upon the widow in a very urgent way.

"I suppose, in point of fact, you never proposed at all?" said Charlotte.

"Oh, she understood that she might have me if she wished," said he.

"And she didn't wish," said the signora.

"You have thrown me over in the most shameful manner," said Charlotte. "I suppose you told her all about my little plan?"

"Well, it came out somehow; at least the most of it."

"There's an end of that alliance," said Charlotte; "but it doesn't matter much. I suppose we shall all be back at Como soon."

"I am sure I hope so," said the signora; "I'm sick of the sight of black coats. If that Mr. Slope comes here any more, he'll be the death of me."

"You've been the ruin of him, I think," said Charlotte.

"And as for a second black-coated lover of mine, I am going to make a present of him to another lady with most singular disinterestedness."

The next day, true to his promise, Bertie packed up and went off by the 4.30 P.M. train, with 20*l.* in his pocket, bound for the marble quarries of Carrara. And so he disappears from our scene.

At twelve o'clock on the day following that on which Bertie went, Mrs. Bold, true also to her word, knocked at Dr. Stanhope's door with a timid hand and palpitating heart. She was at once shown up to the back drawing-room, the folding doors of which were closed, so that in visiting the signora Eleanor was not necessarily thrown into any communion with those in the front room. As she went up the stairs, she saw none of the family, and was so far saved much of the annoyance which she had dreaded.

"This is very kind of you, Mrs. Bold; very kind, after what has happened," said the lady on the sofa with her sweetest smile.

"You wrote in such a strain that I could not but come to you."

"I did, I did; I wanted to force you to see me."

"Well, signora; I am here."

"How cold you are to me. But I suppose I must put up with that. I know you think you have reason to be displeased with us all. Poor Bertie! if you knew all, you would not be angry with him."

"I am not angry with your brother—not in the least. But I hope you did not send for me here to talk about him."

"If you are angry with Charlotte, that is worse; for you have no warmer friend in all Barchester. But I did *not* send for you to talk about this,—pray bring your chair nearer, Mrs. Bold, so that I may look at you. It is so unnatural to see you keeping so far off from me."

Eleanor did as she was bid, and brought her chair close to the sofa.

"And now, Mrs. Bold, I am going to tell you something which you may perhaps think indelicate; but yet I know that I am right in doing so."

Hereupon Mrs. Bold said nothing, but felt inclined to shake in her chair. The signora, she knew, was not very particular, and that which to her appeared to be indelicate might to Mrs. Bold appear to be extremely indecent.

"I believe you know Mr. Arabin?"

Mrs. Bold would have given the world not to blush, but her blood was not at her own command. She did blush up to her forehead, and the signora, who had made her sit in a special light in order that she might watch her, saw that she did so.

"Yes,—I am acquainted with him. That is, slightly. He is an intimate friend of Dr. Grantly, and Dr. Grantly is my brother-in-law."

"Well; if you know Mr. Arabin, I am sure you must like him. I know and like him much. Everybody that knows him must like him."

Mrs. Bold felt it quite impossible to say anything in reply to this. Her blood was rushing about her body she knew not how or why. She felt as though she were swinging in her chair; and she knew that she was not only red in the face, but also almost suffocated with heat. However, she sat still and said nothing.

"How stiff you are with me, Mrs. Bold," said the signora; "and I the while am doing for you all that one woman can do to serve another."

A kind of thought came over the widow's mind that perhaps the signora's friendship was real, and that at any rate it could not hurt her; and another kind of thought, a glimmering of a thought, came to her also,—that Mr. Arabin was too precious to be lost. She despised the signora; but might she not stoop to conquer? It should be but the smallest fraction of a stoop!

"I don't want to be stiff," she said, "but your questions are so very singular."

"Well, then, I will ask you one more singular still," said Madeline Neroni, raising herself on her elbow and turning her own face full upon her companion's. "Do you love him, love him with all your

heart and soul, with all the love your bosom can feel? For I can tell
you that he loves you, adores you, worships you, thinks of you and
nothing else, is now thinking of you as he attempts to write his
sermon for next Sunday's preaching. What would I not give to be
loved in such a way by such a man, that is, if I were an object fit for
any man to love!"

Mrs. Bold got up from her seat and stood speechless before the
woman who was now addressing her in this impassioned way. When
the signora thus alluded to herself, the widow's heart was softened,
and she put her own hand, as though caressingly, on that of her
companion which was resting on the table. The signora grasped it
and went on speaking.

"What I tell you is God's own truth; and it is for you to use it as
may be best for your own happiness. But you must not betray me.
He knows nothing of this. He knows nothing of my knowing his
inmost heart. He is simple as a child in these matters. He told me
his secret in a thousand ways because he could not dissemble; but
he does not dream that he has told it. You know it now, and I
advise you to use it."

Eleanor returned the pressure of the other's hand with an in-
finitesimal *soupçon* of a squeeze.

"And remember," continued the signora, "he is not like other
men. You must not expect him to come to you with vows and oaths
and pretty presents, to kneel at your feet, and kiss your shoe-strings.
If you want that, there are plenty to do it; but he won't be one of
them." Eleanor's bosom nearly burst with a sigh; but Madeline,
not heeding her, went on. "With him, yea will stand for yea, and
nay for nay. Though his heart should break for it, the woman who
shall reject him once, will have rejected him once and for all.
Remember that. And now, Mrs. Bold, I will not keep you, for you
are fluttered. I partly guess what use you will make of what I have
said to you. If ever you are a happy wife in that man's house,
we shall be far away; but I shall expect you to write me one line to
say that you have forgiven the sins of the family."

Eleanor half whispered that she would, and then, without uttering
another word, crept out of the room, and down the stairs, opened
the front door for herself without hearing or seeing any one, and
found herself in the close.

It would be difficult to analyse Eleanor's feelings as she walked
home. She was nearly stupefied by the things that had been said to
her. She felt sore that her heart should have been so searched and
riddled by a comparative stranger, by a woman whom she had
never liked and never could like. She was mortified that the man
whom she owned to herself that she loved should have concealed
his love from her and shown it to another. There was much to vex
her proud spirit. But there was, nevertheless, an under-stratum of
joy in all this which buoyed her up wondrously. She tried if she

could disbelieve what Madame Neroni had said to her; but she found that she could not. It was true; it must be true. She could not, would not, did not doubt it.

On one point she fully resolved to follow the advice given her. If it should ever please Mr. Arabin to put such a question to her as that suggested, her "yea" should be "yea". Would not all her miseries be at an end, if she could talk of them to him openly, with her head resting on his shoulder?

CHAPTER XXXIX

MR. SLOPE'S PARTING INTERVIEW WITH THE SIGNORA

On the following day the signora was in her pride. She was dressed in her brightest of morning dresses, and had quite a *levée* round her couch. It was a beautifully bright October afternoon; all the gentlemen of the neighbourhood were in Barchester, and those who had the entry of Dr. Stanhope's house were in the signora's back drawing-room. Charlotte and Mrs. Stanhope were in the front room, and such of the lady's squires as could not for the moment get near the centre of attraction had to waste their fragrance on the mother and sister.

The first who came and the last to leave was Mr. Arabin. This was the second visit he had paid to Madame Neroni since he had met her at Ullathorne. He came he knew not why, to talk about he knew not what. But, in truth, the feelings which now troubled him were new to him, and he could not analyse them. It may seem strange that he should thus come dangling about Madame Neroni because he was in love with Mrs. Bold; but it was nevertheless the fact; and though he could not understand why he did so, Madame Neroni understood it well enough.

She had been gentle and kind to him, and had encouraged his staying. Therefore he stayed on. She pressed his hand when he first greeted her; she made him remain near her; and whispered to him little nothings. And then her eye, brilliant and bright, now mirthful, now melancholy, and invincible in either way! What man with warm feelings, blood unchilled, and a heart not guarded by a triple steel of experience could have withstood those eyes! The lady, it is true, intended to do him no mortal injury; she merely chose to inhale a slight breath of incense before she handed the casket over to another. Whether Mrs. Bold would willingly have spared even so much is another question.

And then came Mr. Slope. All the world now knew that Mr. Slope was a candidate for the deanery, and that he was generally considered to be the favourite. Mr. Slope, therefore, walked rather largely upon the earth. He gave to himself a portly air, such as might become a dean, spoke but little to other clergymen, and shunned the bishop as much as possible. How the meagre little prebendary, and the burly chancellor, and all the minor canons and vicars choral, ay, and all the choristers too, cowered and shook and walked about with long faces when they read or heard of that article in the Jupiter. Now were coming the days when nothing would avail to keep the impure spirit from the cathedral pulpit. That pulpit would indeed be his own. Precentors, vicars, and choristers might hang up their harps on the willows. Ichabod! Ichabod! the glory of their house was departing from them.

Mr. Slope, great as he was with embryo grandeur, still came to see the signora. Indeed, he could not keep himself away. He dreamed of that soft hand which he had kissed so often, and of that imperial brow which his lips had once pressed, and he then dreamed also of further favours.

And Mr. Thorne was there also. It was the first visit he had ever paid to the signora, and he made it not without due preparation. Mr. Thorne was a gentleman usually precise in his dress, and prone to make the most of himself in an unpretending way. The grey hairs in his whiskers were eliminated perhaps once a month; those on his head were softened by a mixture which we will not call a dye; it was only a wash. His tailor lived in St. James Street, and his bootmaker at the corner of that street and Piccadilly. He was particular in the article of gloves, and the getting up of his shirts was a matter not lightly thought of in the Ullathorne laundry. On the occasion of the present visit he had rather overdone his usual efforts, and caused some little uneasiness to his sister, who had not hitherto received very cordially the proposition for a lengthened visit from the signora at Ullathorne.

There were others also there—young men about the city who had not much to do, and who were induced by the lady's charms to neglect that little; but all gave way to Mr. Thorne, who was somewhat of a grand signior, as a country gentleman always is in a provincial city.

"Oh, Mr. Thorne, this is so kind of you!" said the signora. "You promised to come; but I really did not expect it. I thought you country gentlemen never kept your pledges."

"Oh, yes, sometimes," said Mr. Thorne, looking rather sheepish. and making his salutations a little too much in the style of the last century.

"You deceive none but your consti—stit—stit; what do you call the people that carry you about in chairs and pelt you with eggs and apples when they make you a member of Parliament?"

"One another also, sometimes, signora," said Mr. Slope, with a deanish sort of smirk on his face. "Country gentlemen do deceive one another sometimes, don't they, Mr. Thorne?"

Mr. Thorne gave him a look which undeaned him completely for the moment; but he soon remembered his high hopes, and recovering himself quickly, sustained his probable coming dignity by a laugh at Mr. Thorne's expense.

"I never deceive a lady, at any rate," said Mr. Thorne; "especially when the gratification of my own wishes is so strong an inducement to keep me true, as it now is."

Mr. Thorne went on thus awhile with antediluvian grimaces and compliments which he had picked up from Sir Charles Grandison, and the signora at every grimace and at every bow smiled a little smile and bowed a little bow. Mr. Thorne, however, was kept standing at the foot of the couch, for the new dean sat in the seat of honour near the table. Mr. Arabin the while was standing with his back to the fire, his coat tails under his arms, gazing at her with all his eyes—not quite in vain, for every now and again a glance came up at him, bright as a meteor out of heaven.

"Oh, Mr. Thorne, you promised to let me introduce my little girl to you. Can you spare a moment?—will you see her now?"

Mr. Thorne assured her that he could, and would see the young lady with the greatest pleasure in life. "Mr. Slope, might I trouble you to ring the bell?" said she; and when Mr. Slope got up she looked at Mr. Thorne and pointed to the chair. Mr. Thorne, however, was much too slow to understand her, and Mr. Slope would have recovered his seat had not the signora, who never chose to be unsuccessful, somewhat summarily ordered him out of it.

"Oh, Mr. Slope, I must ask you to let Mr. Thorne sit here just for a moment or two. I am sure you will pardon me. We can take a liberty with you this week. Next week, you know, when you move into the dean's house, we shall all be afraid of you."

Mr. Slope, with an air of much indifference, rose from his seat, and, walking into the next room, became greatly interested in Mrs. Stanhope's worsted work.

And then the child was brought in. She was a little girl, about eight years of age, like her mother, only that her enormous eyes were black, and her hair quite jet. Her complexion, too, was very dark, and bespoke her foreign blood. She was dressed in the most outlandish and extravagant way in which clothes could be put on a child's back. She had great bracelets on her naked little arms, a crimson fillet braided with gold round her head, and scarlet shoes with high heels. Her dress was all flounces, and stuck out from her as though the object were to make it lie off horizontally from her little hips. It did not nearly cover her knees; but this was atoned for by a loose pair of drawers, which seemed made throughout of lace; then she had on pink silk stockings. It was thus that the last of the Neros was habitually dressed at the hour when visitors were wont to call.

"Julia, my love," said the mother,—Julia was ever a favourite name with the ladies of that family. "Julia, my love, come here. I was telling you about the beautiful party poor mamma went to. This is Mr. Thorne; will you give him a kiss, dearest?''

Julia put up her face to be kissed, as she did to all her mother's visitors; and then Mr. Thorne found that he had got her, and, which was much more terrific to him, all her finery, into his arms. The lace and starch crumpled against the waistcoat and trowsers, the greasy black curls hung upon his cheek, and one of the bracelet clasps scratched his ear. He did not at all know how to hold so magnificent a lady, nor holding her what to do with her. However, he had on other occasions been compelled to fondle little nieces and nephews, and now set about the task in the mode he always had used.

"Diddle, diddle, diddle, diddle," said he, putting the child on one knee, and working away with it as though he were turning a knife-grinder's wheel with his foot.

"Mamma, mamma," said Julia, crossly, "I don't want to be diddle diddled. Let me go, you naughty old man, you."

Poor Mr. Thorne put the child down quietly on the ground, and drew back his chair; Mr. Slope, who had returned to the pole star that attracted him, laughed aloud; Mr. Arabin winced and shut his eyes; and the signora pretended not to hear her daughter.

"Go to Aunt Charlotte, lovey," said the mamma, "and ask her if it is not time for you to go out."

But little Miss Julia, though she had not exactly liked the nature of Mr. Thorne's attention, was accustomed to be played with by gentlemen, and did not relish the idea of being sent so soon to her aunt.

"Julia, go when I tell you, my dear." But Julia still went pouting about the room. "Charlotte, do come and take her," said the signora. "She must go out; and the days get so short now." And thus ended the much-talked-of interview between Mr. Thorne and the last of the Neros.

Mr. Thorne recovered from the child's crossness sooner than from Mr. Slope's laughter. He could put up with being called an old man by an infant, but he did not like to be laughed at by the bishop's chaplain, even though that chaplain was about to become a dean. He said nothing, but he showed plainly enough that he was angry.

The signora was ready enough to avenge him. "Mr. Slope," said she, "I hear that you are triumphing on all sides."

"How so?" said he, smiling. He did not dislike being talked to about the deanery, though, of course, he strongly denied the imputation.

"You carry the day both in love and war." Mr. Slope hereupon did not look quite satisfied as he had done.

"Mr. Arabin," continued the signora, "don't you think Mr. Slope is a very lucky man?"

"Not more so than he deserves, I am sure," said Mr. Arabin.

"Only think, Mr. Thorne, he is to be our new dean; of course we all know that."

"Indeed, signora," said Mr. Slope, "we all know nothing about it. I can assure you I myself——"

"He *is* to be the new dean—there is no manner of doubt of it, Mr. Thorne."

"Hum!" said Mr. Thorne.

"Passing over the heads of old men like my father and Arch-deacon Grantly——"

"Oh—oh!" said Mr. Slope.

"The archdeacon would not accept it," said Mr. Arabin; where-upon Mr. Slope smiled abominably, and said, as plainly as a look could speak, that the grapes were sour.

"Going over all our heads," continued the signora; "for, of course, I consider myself one of the chapter."

"If I am ever dean," said Mr. Slope—"that is, were I ever to become so, I should glory in such a canoness."

"Oh, Mr. Slope, stop; I haven't half done. There is another canoness for you to glory in. Mr. Slope is not only to have the deanery, but a wife to put in it."

Mr. Slope again looked disconcerted.

"A wife with a large fortune too. It never rains but it pours, does it, Mr. Thorne?"

"No, never," said Mr. Thorne, who did not quite relish talking about Mr. Slope and his affairs.

"When will it be, Mr. Slope?"

"When will what be?" said he.

"Oh! we know when the affair of the dean will be: a week will settle that. The new hat, I have no doubt, has been already ordered. But when will the marriage come off?"

"Do you mean mine or Mr. Arabin's?" said he, striving to be facetious.

"Well, just then I meant yours, though, perhaps, after all, Mr. Arabin's may be first. But we know nothing of him. He is too close for any of us. Now all is open and above board with you; which, by the bye, Mr. Arabin, I beg to tell you I much like the best. He who runs can read that Mr. Slope is a favoured lover. Come, Mr. Slope, when is the widow to be made Mrs. Dean?"

To Mr. Arabin this badinage was peculiarly painful; and yet he could not tear himself away and leave it. He believed, still believed with that sort of belief which the fear of a thing engenders, that Mrs. Bold would probably become the wife of Mr. Slope. Of Mr. Slope's little adventure in the garden he knew nothing. For aught he knew Mr. Slope might have had an adventure of quite a different character. He might have thrown himself at the widow's feet, been accepted, and then returned to town a jolly, thriving wooer. The signora's jokes were bitter enough to Mr. Slope, but they were quite as bitter to Mr. Arabin. He still stood leaning against the fire-place, fumbling with his hands in his trowsers pockets.

"Come, come, Mr. Slope, don't be so bashful," continued the signora. "We all know that you proposed to the lady the other day at Ullathorne. Tell us with what words she accepted you. Was it with a simple 'yes,' or with two 'no no's,' which make an affirmative? or did silence give consent? or did she speak out with that spirit which so well becomes a widow, and say openly, 'By my troth, sir, you shall make me Mrs. Slope as soon as it is your pleasure to do so'?"

Mr. Slope had seldom in his life felt himself less at his ease. There sat Mr. Thorne, laughing silently. There stood his old antagonist, Mr. Arabin, gazing at him with all his eyes. There round the door between the two rooms were clustered a little group of people, including Miss Stanhope and the Rev. Messrs. Gray and Green, all listening to his discomfiture. He knew that it depended solely on his own wit whether or no he could throw the joke upon the lady. He knew that it stood him to do so if he possibly could; but he had not a word. "'Tis conscience that makes cowards of us all." He felt on his cheek the sharp points of Eleanor's fingers, and did not know who might have seen the blow, who might have told the tale to this pestilent woman who took such delight in jeering him. He stood there, therefore, red as a carbuncle and mute as a fish; grinning just sufficiently to show his teeth; an object of pity.

But the signora had no pity; she knew nothing of mercy. Her present object was to put Mr. Slope down, and she was determined to do it thoroughly, now that she had him in her power.

"What, Mr. Slope, no answer? Why it can't possibly be that the woman has been fool enough to refuse you? She can't surely be looking out after a bishop. But I see how it is, Mr. Slope. Widows are proverbially cautious. You should have let her alone till the new hat was on your head; till you could show her the key of the deanery."

"Signora," said he at last, trying to speak in a tone of dignified reproach, "you really permit yourself to talk on solemn subjects in a very improper way."

"Solemn subjects—what solemn subjects? Surely a dean's hat is not such a solemn subject."

"I have no aspirations such as those you impute to me. Perhaps you will drop the subject."

"Oh certainly, Mr. Slope; but one word first. Go to her again with the prime minister's letter in your pocket. I'll wager my shawl to your shovel she does not refuse you then."

"I must say, signora, that I think you are speaking of the lady in a very unjustifiable manner."

"And one other piece of advice, Mr. Slope; I'll only offer you one other;" and then she commenced singing—

"It's gude to be merry and wise, Mr. Slope;
    It's gude to be honest and true;
  It's gude to be off with the old love—Mr. Slope,
    Before you are on with the new.—

"Ha, ha, ha!"

And the signora, throwing herself back on her sofa, laughed merrily. She little recked how those who heard her would, in their own imaginations, fill up the little history of Mr. Slope's first love. She little cared that some among them might attribute to her the honour of his earlier admiration. She was tired of Mr. Slope and wanted to get rid of him; she had ground for anger with him; and she chose to be revenged.

How Mr. Slope got out of that room he never himself knew. He did succeed ultimately, and probably with some assistance, in getting his hat and escaping into the air. At last his love for the signora was cured. Whenever he again thought of her in his dreans, it was not as of an angel with azure wings. He connected her rather with fire and brimstone, and though he could still believe her to be a spirit, he banished her entirely out of heaven, and found a place for her among the infernal gods. When he weighed in the balance, as he not seldom did, the two women to whom he had attached himself in Barchester, the pre-eminent place in his soul's hatred was usually allotted to the signora.

CHAPTER XL

THE DEAN ELECT

DURING the entire next week Barchester was ignorant who was to be its new dean on Sunday morning. Mr. Slope was decidedly the favourite; but he did not show himself in the cathedral, and then he sank a point or two in the betting. On Monday, he got a scolding from the bishop in the hearing of the servants, and down he went till nobody would have him at any price; but on Tuesday he received a letter, in an official cover, marked private, by which he fully recovered his place in the public favour. On Wednesday, he was said to be ill, and that did not look well; but on Thursday morning he went down to the railway station, with a very jaunty air; and when it was ascertained that he had taken a first-class ticket for London, there was no longer any room for doubt on the matter.

While matters were in this state of ferment at Barchester, there was not much mental comfort at Plumstead. Our friend the archdeacon had many grounds for inward grief. He was much displeased at the result of Dr. Gwynne's diplomatic mission to the palace, and did not even scruple to say to his wife that had he gone himself, he would have managed the affair much better. His wife did not agree with him, but that did not mend the matter.

Mr. Quiverful's appointment to the hospital was, however, a *fait accompli*, and Mr. Harding's acquiescence in that appointment was not less so. Nothing would induce Mr. Harding to make a public appeal against the bishop; and the Master of Lazarus quite approved of his not doing so.

"I don't know what has come to the Master," said the archdeacon over and over again. "He used to be ready enough to stand up for his order."

"My dear archdeacon," Mrs. Grantly would say in reply, "what is the use of always fighting? I really think the Master is right." The Master, however, had taken steps of his own, of which neither the archdeacon nor his wife knew anything.

Then Mr. Slope's successes were henbane to Dr. Grantly; and Mrs. Bold's improprieties were as bad. What would be all the world to Archdeacon Grantly if Mr. Slope should become Dean of Barchester and marry his wife's sister! He talked of it, and talked of it till he was nearly ill. Mrs. Grantly almost wished that the marriage were done and over, so that she might no more hear about it.

And there was yet another ground of misery which cut him to the quick, nearly as closely as either of the others. That paragon of a clergyman, whom he had bestowed upon St. Ewold's, that college friend of whom he had boasted so loudly, that ecclesiastical knight before whose lance Mr. Slope was to fall and bite the dust, that worthy bulwark of the church as it should be, that honoured representative of Oxford's best spirit, was—so at least his wife had told him half a dozen times—misconducting himself!

Nothing had been seen of Mr. Arabin at Plumstead for the last week, but a good deal had, unfortunately, been heard of him. As soon as Mrs. Grantly had found herself alone with the archdeacon, on the evening of the Ullathorne party, she had expressed herself very forcibly as to Mr. Arabin's conduct on that occasion. He had, she declared, looked and acted and talked very unlike a decent parish clergyman. At first the archdeacon had laughed at this, and assured her that she need not trouble herself; that Mr. Arabin would be found to be quite safe. But by degrees he began to find that his wife's eyes had been sharper than his own. Other people coupled the signora's name with that of Mr. Arabin. The meagre little prebendary who lived in the close, told him to a nicety how often Mr. Arabin had visited at Dr. Stanhope's, and how long he had remained on the occasion of each visit. He had asked after Mr. Arabin at the cathedral library, and an officious little vicar choral had offered to go and see whether he could be found at Dr. Stanhope's. Rumour, when she has contrived to sound the first note on her trumpet, soon makes a loud peal audible enough. It was too clear that Mr. Arabin had succumbed to the Italian woman, and that the archdeacon's credit would suffer fearfully if something were not done to rescue the brand from the burning. Besides, to give the archdeacon his due, he was really attached to Mr. Arabin, and grieved greatly at his backsliding.

They were sitting, talking over their sorrows, in the drawing-room before dinner on the day after Mr. Slope's departure for London; and on this occasion Mrs. Grantly spoke out her mind freely. She had opinions of her own about parish clergymen, and now thought it right to give vent to them.

"If you would have been led by me, archdeacon, you would never have put a bachelor into St. Ewold's."

"But, my dear, you don't mean to say that all bachelor clergymen misbehave themselves."

"I don't know that clergymen are so much better than other men," said Mrs. Grantly. "It's all very well with a curate whom you have under your own eye, and whom you can get rid of if he persists in improprieties."

"But Mr. Arabin was a fellow, and couldn't have had a wife."

"Then I would have found some one who could."

"But, my dear, are fellows never to get livings?"

"Yes, to be sure they are, when they get engaged. I never would put a young man into a living unless he were married, or engaged to be married. Now here is Mr. Arabin. The whole responsibility lies upon you."

"There is not at this moment a clergyman in all Oxford more respected for morals and conduct than Arabin."

"Oh, Oxford!" said the lady, with a sneer. "What men choose to do at Oxford, nobody ever hears of. A man may do very well at Oxford who would bring disgrace on a parish; and, to tell you the truth, it seems to me that Mr. Arabin is just such a man."

The archdeacon groaned deeply, but he had no further answer to make.

"You really must speak to him, archdeacon. Only think what the Thornes will say if they hear that their parish clergyman spends his whole time philandering with this woman."

The archdeacon groaned again. He was a courageous man, and knew well enough how to rebuke the younger clergymen of the diocese, when necessary. But there was that about Mr. Arabin which made the doctor feel that it would be very difficult to rebuke him with good effect.

"You can advise him to find a wife for himself, and he will understand well enough what that means," said Mrs. Grantly.

The archdeacon had nothing for it but groaning. There was Mr. Slope; he was going to be made dean; he was going to take a wife; he was about to achieve respectability and wealth; an excellent family mansion, and a family carriage; he would soon be among the

comfortable *élite* of the ecclesiastical world of Barchester; whereas
his own *protégé*, the true scion of the true church, by whom he had
sworn, would be still but a poor vicar, and that with a very indifferent character for moral conduct! It might be all very well
recommending Mr. Arabin to marry, but how would Mr. Arabin
when married support a wife!

Things were ordering themselves thus in Plumstead drawing-
room when Dr. and Mrs. Grantly were disturbed in their sweet
discourse by the quick rattle of a carriage and pair of horses on the
gravel sweep. The sound was not that of visitors, whose private
carriages are generally brought up to country-house doors with
demure propriety, but betokened rather the advent of some person
or persons who were in a hurry to reach the house, and had no
intention of immediately leaving it. Guests invited to stay a week,
and who were conscious of arriving after the first dinner bell, would
probably approach in such a manner. So might arrive an attorney
with the news of a granduncle's death, or a son from college with all
the fresh honours of a double first. No one would have had himself
driven up to the door of a country house in such a manner who had
the slightest doubt of his own right to force an entry.

"Who is it?" said Mrs. Grantly, looking at her husband.

"Who on earth can it be?" said the archdeacon to his wife. He
then quietly got up and stood with the drawing-room door open in
his hand. "Why, it's your father!"

It was indeed Mr. Harding, and Mr. Harding alone. He had
come by himself in a post-chaise with a couple of horses from Barchester, arriving almost after dark, and evidently full of news. His
visits had usually been made in the quietest manner; he had rarely
presumed to come without notice, and had always been driven up
in a modest old green fly, with one horse, that hardly made itself
heard as it crawled up to the hall door.

"Good gracious, Warden, is it you?" said the archdeacon, forgetting in his surprise the events of the last few years. "But come in;
nothing the matter, I hope."

"We are very glad you are come, papa," said his daughter. "I'll
go and get your room ready at once."

"I an't warden, archdeacon," said Mr. Harding. "Mr. Quiverful
is warden."

"Oh, I know, I know," said the archdeacon, petulantly. "I forgot
all about it at the moment. Is anything the matter?"

"Don't go this moment, Susan," said Mr. Harding; "I have
something to tell you."

"The dinner bell will ring in five minutes," said she.

"Will it?" said Mr. Harding. "Then, perhaps, I had better
wait." He was big with news which he had come to tell, but which
he knew could not be told without much discussion. He had hurried
away to Plumstead as fast as two horses could bring him; and now,

finding himself there, he was willing to accept the reprieve which dinner would give him.

"If you have anything of moment to tell us," said the archdeacon, "pray let us hear it at once. Has Eleanor gone off?"

"No, she has not," said Mr. Harding, with a look of great displeasure.

"Has Slope been made dean?"

"No, he has not; but——"

"But what?" said the archdeacon, who was becoming very impatient.

"They have——"

"They have what?" said the archdeacon.

"They have offered it to me," said Mr. Harding, with a modesty which almost prevented his speaking.

"Good heavens!" said the archdeacon, and sank back exhausted in an easy-chair.

"My dear, dear father," said Mrs. Grantly, and threw her arms round her father's neck.

"So I thought I had better come out and consult with you at once," said Mr. Harding.

"Consult!" shouted the archdeacon. "But, my dear Harding, I congratulate you with my whole heart—with my whole heart; I do indeed. I never heard anything in my life that gave me so much pleasure;" and he got hold of both his father-in-law's hands, and shook them as though he were going to shake them off, and walked round and round the room, twirling a copy of the Jupiter over his head, to show his extreme exultation.

"But——" began Mr. Harding.

"But me no buts," said the archdeacon. "I never was so happy in my life. It was just the proper thing to do. Upon my honour, I'll never say another word against Lord —— the longest day I have to live."

"That's Dr. Gwynne's doing, you may be sure," said Mrs. Grantly, who greatly liked the Master of Lazarus, he being an orderly married man with a large family.

"I suppose it is," said the archdeacon.

"Oh, papa, I am so truly delighted!" said Mrs. Grantly, getting up and kissing her father.

"But, my dear," said Mr. Harding.— It was all in vain that he strove to speak; nobody would listen to him.

"Well, Mr. Dean," said the archdeacon, triumphing; "the deanery gardens will be some consolation for the hospital elms. Well, poor Quiverful! I won't begrudge him his good fortune any longer."

"No, indeed," said Mrs. Grantly. "Poor woman, she has fourteen children. I am sure I am very glad they have got it."

"So am I," said Mr. Harding.

"I would give twenty pounds," said the archdeacon, "to see

how Mr. Slope will look when he hears it." The idea of Mr. Slope's discomfiture formed no small part of the archdeacon's pleasure.

At last Mr. Harding was allowed to go up-stairs and wash his hands, having, in fact, said very little of all that he had come out to Plumstead on purpose to say. Nor could anything more be said till the servants were gone after dinner. The joy of Dr. Grantly was so uncontrollable that he could not refrain from calling his father-in-law Mr. Dean before the men; and therefore it was soon matter of discussion in the lower regions how Mr. Harding, instead of his daughter's future husband, was to be the new dean, and various were the opinions on the matter. The cook and butler, who were advanced in years, thought that it was just as it should be; but the footman and lady's maid, who were younger, thought it was a great shame that Mr. Slope should lose his chance.

"He's a mean chap all the same," said the footman; "and it an't along of him that I says so. But I always did admire the missus's sister; and she'd well become the situation."

While these were the ideas down-stairs, a very great difference of opinion existed above. As soon as the cloth was drawn and the wine on the table, Mr. Harding made for himself an opportunity of speaking. It was, however, with much inward troubling that he said:—

"It's very kind of Lord —— very kind, and I feel it deeply, most deeply. I am, I must confess, gratified by the offer——"

"I should think so," said the archdeacon.

"But, all the same, I am afraid that I can't accept it."

The decanter almost fell from the archdeacon's hand upon the table; and the start he made was so great as to make his wife jump up from her chair. Not accept the deanship! If it really ended in this, there would be no longer any doubt that his father-in-law was demented. The question now was whether a clergyman with low rank, and preferment amounting to less than 200*l.* a year, should accept high rank, 1200*l.* a year, and one of the most desirable positions which his profession had to afford!

"What!" said the archdeacon, gasping for breath, and staring at his guest as though the violence of his emotion had almost thrown him into a fit.

"What!"

"I do not find myself fit for new duties," urged Mr. Harding.

"New duties! What duties," said the archdeacon, with unintended sarcasm.

"Oh, papa," said Mrs. Grantly, "nothing can be easier than what a dean has to do. Surely you are more active than Dr. Trefoil."

"He won't have half as much to do as he has at present," said Dr. Grantly.

"Did you see what the Jupiter said the other day about young men?"

"Yes; and I saw that the Jupiter said all that it could to induce the appointment of Mr. Slope. Perhaps you would wish to see Mr. Slope made dean."

Mr. Harding made no reply to this rebuke, though he felt it strongly. He had not come over to Plumstead to have further contention with his son-in-law about Mr. Slope, so he allowed it to pass by.

"I know I cannot make you understand my feeling," he said, "for we have been cast in different moulds. I may wish that I had your spirit and energy and power of combating; but I have not. Every day that is added to my life increases my wish for peace and rest."

"And where on earth can a man have peace and rest if not in a deanery?" said the archdeacon.

"People will say that I am too old for it."

"Good heavens! people! what people? What need you care for any people?"

"But I think myself I am too old for any new place."

"Dear papa," said Mrs. Grantly, "men ten years older than you are appointed to new situations day after day."

"My dear," said he, "it is impossible that I should make you understand my feelings, nor do I pretend to any great virtue in the matter. The truth is, I want the force of character which might enable me to stand against the spirit of the times. The call on all sides now is for young men, and I have not the nerve to put myself in opposition to the demand. Were the *Jupiter*, when it hears of my appointment, to write article after article, setting forth my incompetency, I am sure it would cost me my reason. I ought to be able to bear with such things, you will say. Well, my dear, I own that I ought. But I feel my weakness, and I know that I can't. And, to tell you the truth, I know no more than a child what the dean has to do."

"Pshaw!" exclaimed the archdeacon.

"Don't be angry with me, archdeacon: don't let us quarrel about it, Susan. If you knew how keenly I feel the necessity of having to disoblige you in this matter, you would not be angry with me."

This was a dreadful blow to Dr. Grantly. Nothing could possibly have suited him better than having Mr. Harding in the deanery. Though he had never looked down on Mr. Harding on account of his recent poverty, he did fully recognise the satisfaction of having those belonging to him in comfortable positions. It would be much more suitable that Mr. Harding should be dean of Barchester than vicar of St. Cuthbert's and precentor to boot. And then the great discomfiture of that arch enemy of all that was respectable in Barchester, of that new low-church clerical *parvenu* that had fallen amongst them, that alone would be worth more, almost, than the situation itself. It was frightful to think that such unhoped-for good fortune should be marred by the absurd crotchets and unwholesome hallucinations by which Mr. Harding allowed himself to be led astray. To have the cup so near his lips and then to lose the drinking of it, was more than Dr. Grantly could endure.

And yet it appeared as though he would have to endure it. In vain he threatened and in vain he coaxed. Mr. Harding did not indeed speak with perfect decision of refusing the proffered glory, but he would not speak with anything like decision of accepting it. When pressed again and again, he would again and again allege that he was wholly unfitted to new duties. It was in vain that the archdeacon tried to insinuate, though he could not plainly declare, that there were no new duties to perform. It was in vain he hinted that in all cases of difficulty he, the archdeacon, was willing and able to guide a weak-minded dean. Mr. Harding seemed to have a foolish idea, not only that there were new duties to do, but that no one should accept the place who was not himself prepared to do them.

The conference ended in an understanding that Mr. Harding should at once acknowledge the letter he had received from the minister's private secretary, and should beg that he might be allowed two days to make up his mind; and that during those two days the matter should be considered.

On the following morning the archdeacon was to drive Mr. Harding back to Barchester.

CHAPTER XLI

MISS THORNE SHOWS HER TALENT AT MATCH-MAKING

On Mr. Harding's return to Barchester from Plumstead, which was effected by him in due course in company with the arch-deacon, more tidings of a surprising nature met him. He was, during the journey, subjected to such a weight of unanswerable argument, all of which went to prove that it was his bounden duty not to interfere with the paternal government that was so anxious to make him a dean, that when he arrived at the chemist's door in High Street, he hardly knew which way to turn himself in the matter. But, perplexed as he was, he was doomed to further perplexity. He found a note there from his daughter begging him most urgently to come to her immediately. But we must again go back a little in our story.

Miss Thorne had not been slow to hear the rumours respecting Mr. Arabin, which had so much disturbed the happiness of Mrs. Grantly. And she, also, was unhappy to think that her parish clergyman should be accused of worshipping a strange goddess. She, also, was of opinion, that rectors and vicars should all be married, and with that good-natured energy which was characteristic of her, she put her wits to work to find a fitting match for Mr. Arabin. Mrs. Grantly, in this difficulty, could think of no better remedy than a lecture from the archdeacon. Miss Thorne thought that a young lady, marriageable, and with a dowry, might be of more efficacy. In looking through the catalogue of her unmarried friends, who might possibly be in want of a husband, and might also be fit for such promotion as a country parsonage affords, she could think of no one more eligible than Mrs. Bold; and, consequently, losing no time, she went into Barchester on the day of Mr. Slope's discomfiture, the same day that her brother had had his interesting interview with the last of the Neros, and invited Mrs. Bold to bring her nurse and baby to Ullathorne and make them a protracted visit.

Miss Thorne suggested a month or two, intending to use her influence afterwards in prolonging it so as to last out the winter, in order that Mr. Arabin might have an opportunity of becoming fairly intimate with his intended bride. "We'll have Mr. Arabin too," said Miss Thorne to herself; "and before the spring they'll know each other; and in twelve or eighteen months' time, if all goes well, Mrs. Bold will be domiciled at St. Ewold's;" and then the kind-hearted lady gave herself some not undeserved praise for her match-making genius.

Eleanor was taken a little by surprise, but the matter ended in her promising to go to Ullathorne for at any rate a week or two; and on the day previous to that on which her father drove out to Plumstead, she had had herself driven out to Ullathorne.

Miss Thorne would not perplex her with her embryo lord on that same evening, thinking that she would allow her a few hours to make herself at home; but on the following morning Mr. Arabin arrived. "And now," said Miss Thorne to herself, "I must contrive to throw them in each other's way." That same day, after dinner, Eleanor, with an assumed air of dignity which she could not maintain, with tears that she could not suppress, with a flutter which she could not conquer, and a joy which she could not hide, told Miss Thorne that she was engaged to marry Mr. Arabin, and that it behoved her to get back home to Barchester as quick as she could.

To say simply that Miss Thorne was rejoiced at the success of the scheme, would give a very faint idea of her feelings on the occasion. My readers may probably have dreamt before now that they have had before them some terribly long walk to accomplish, some journey of twenty or thirty miles, an amount of labour frightful to anticipate, and that immediately on starting they have ingeniously found some accommodating short cut which has brought them without fatigue to their work's end in five minutes. Miss Thorne's waking feelings were somewhat of the same nature. My readers may perhaps have had to do with children, and may on some occasion have promised to their young charges some great gratification intended to come off, perhaps at the end of the winter, or at the beginning of summer. The impatient juveniles, however, will not wait, and clamorously demand their treat before they go to bed. Miss Thorne had a sort of feeling that her children were equally unreasonable. She was like an inexperienced gunner, who has ill calculated the length of the train that he has laid. The gunpowder exploded much too soon, and poor Miss Thorne felt that she was blown up by the strength of her own petard.

Miss Thorne had had lovers of her own, but they had been gentlemen of old-fashioned and deliberate habits. Miss Thorne's heart also had not always been hard, though she was still a virgin spinster; but it had never yielded in this way at the first assault. She had intended to bring together a middle-aged studious clergyman, and a discreet matron who might possibly be induced to marry again; and in doing so she had thrown fire among tinder. Well, it was all as it should be, but she did feel perhaps a little put out by the precipitancy of her own success; and perhaps a little vexed at the readiness of Mrs. Bold to be wooed.

She said, however, nothing about it to any one, and ascribed it all to the altered manners of the new age. Their mothers and grandmothers were perhaps a little more deliberate; but it was admitted on all sides that things were conducted very differently now than in former times. For aught Miss Thorne knew of the matter, a couple of hours might be quite sufficient under the new regime to complete that for which she in her ignorance had allotted twelve months.

But we must not pass over the wooing so cavalierly. It has been told, with perhaps tedious accuracy, how Eleanor disposed of two of her lovers at Ullathorne; and it must also be told with equal accuracy, and if possible with less tedium, how she encountered Mr. Arabin.

It cannot be denied that when Eleanor accepted Miss Thorne's invitation, she remembered that Ullathorne was in the parish of St. Ewold's. Since her interview with the signora she had done little else than think about Mr. Arabin, and the appeal that had been made to her. She could not bring herself to believe or try to bring herself to believe, that what she had been told was untrue. Think of it how she would, she could not but accept it as a fact that Mr. Arabin was fond of her; and then when she went further, and asked herself the question, she could not but accept it as a fact also that she was fond of him. If it were destined for her to be the partner of his hopes and sorrows, to whom could she look for friendship so properly as to Miss Thorne? This invitation was like an ordained step towards the fulfilment of her destiny, and when she also heard that Mr. Arabin was expected to be at Ullathorne on the following day, it seemed as though all the world were conspiring in her favour. Well, did she not deserve it? In that affair of Mr. Slope, had not all the world conspired against her?

She could not, however, make herself easy and at home. When in the evening after dinner Miss Thorne expatiated on the excellence of Mr. Arabin's qualities, and hinted that any little rumour which might be ill-naturedly spread abroad concerning him really meant nothing, Mrs. Bold found herself unable to answer. When Miss Thorne went a little further and declared that she did not know a prettier vicarage-house in the county than St. Ewold's, Mrs. Bold remembering the projected bow-window and the projected priestess still held her tongue; though her ears tingled with the conviction that all the world knew that she was in love with Mr. Arabin. Well; what would that matter if they could only meet and tell each other what each now longed to tell?

And they did meet. Mr. Arabin came early in the day, and found the two ladies together at work in the drawing-room. Miss Thorne, who had she known all the truth would have vanished into air at once, had no conception that her immediate absence would be a blessing, and remained chatting with them till luncheon-time. Mr. Arabin could talk about nothing but the Signora Neroni's beauty, would discuss no people but the Stanhopes. This was very distressing to Eleanor, and not very satisfactory to Miss Thorne. But yet there was evidence of innocence in his open avowal of admiration.

And then they had lunch, and then Mr. Arabin went out on parish duty, and Eleanor and Miss Thorne were left to take a walk together.

"Do you think the Signora Neroni is so lovely as people say?" Eleanor asked as they were coming home.

"She is very beautiful certainly, very beautiful," Miss Thorne answered; "but I do not know that any one considers her lovely. She is a woman all men would like to look at; but few I imagine would be glad to take her to their hearths, even were she unmarried and not afflicted as she is."

There was some little comfort in this. Eleanor made the most of it till she got back to the house. She was then left alone in the drawing-room, and just as it was getting dark Mr. Arabin came in.

It was a beautiful afternoon in the beginning of October, and Eleanor was sitting in the window to get the advantage of the last daylight for her novel. There was a fire in the comfortable room, but the weather was not cold enough to make it attractive; and as she could see the sun set from where she sat, she was not very attentive to her book.

Mr. Arabin when he entered stood awhile with his back to the fire in his usual way, merely uttering a few commonplace remarks about the beauty of the weather, while he plucked up courage for more interesting converse.

"It is a lovely sunset," said Eleanor.

"Very lovely," said he.

H

Eleanor found that it was quite impossible for herself to commence a conversation. In the first place she could find nothing to say; words, which were generally plenty enough with her, would not come to her relief. And, moreover, do what she would, she could hardly prevent herself from crying.

"Do you like Ullathorne?" said Mr. Arabin.

"Yes, indeed, very much!"

"I don't mean Mr. and Miss Thorne. I know you like them; but the style of the house."

"I like everything old-fashioned," said Eleanor; "old-fashioned things are so much the honestest."

"I don't know about that," said Mr. Arabin, gently laughing. "That is an opinion on which very much may be said on either side."

"And you, Mr. Arabin, what do you think?" said Eleanor.

"What do I think, Mrs. Bold?" and then he rumbled his money with his hands in his trowsers pockets, and looked and spoke very little like a thriving lover. "It is the bane of my life that on important subjects I acquire no fixed opinion."

"I think the world grows more worldly every day," said Eleanor.

"That is because you see more of it as you grow up."

Eleanor made no answer to this. She felt thoroughly dissatisfied with herself. She was most anxious not to show to him any special emotion, and yet she felt that if he looked at her he would at once see that she was not at ease.

But he did not look at her. Instead of doing so, he left the fire-place and began walking up and down the room. She was afraid that her tears would get the better of her, and was preparing for an escape from the room, when Mr. Arabin in his walk stood opposite to her.

"Mrs. Bold," said he, "I owe you retribution for a great offence of which I have been guilty towards you. I have thought much of it since, and I am now aware that I was wholly unwarranted in putting to you a question which I once asked you. It was indelicate on my part, and perhaps unmanly. No intimacy which may exist between myself and your connection, Dr. Grantly, could justify it. Nor could the acquaintance which existed between ourselves." This word acquaintance struck cold on Eleanor's heart. Was this to be her doom after all? "I therefore think it right to beg your pardon in a humble spirit, and I now do so."

What was Eleanor to say to him? She could not say much, because she was crying, and yet she must say something. She was most anxious to say that something graciously, kindly, and yet not in such a manner as to betray herself. She had never felt herself so much at a loss for words.

"Indeed I took no offence, Mr. Arabin."

"Oh, but you did! And had you not done so, you would not have been yourself. You were as right to be offended, as I was wrong so to offend you. I have not forgiven myself, but I hope to hear that you forgive me."

She was now past speaking calmly, though she still continued to hide her tears, and Mr. Arabin, after pausing a moment in vain for her reply, was walking off towards the door. She felt that she could not allow him to go unanswered without grievously sinning against all charity; so, rising from her seat, she gently touched his arm and said: "Oh, Mr. Arabin, do not go till I speak to you! I do forgive you. You know that I forgive you."

He took the hand that had so gently touched his arm, and then gazed into her face as if he would peruse there, as though written in a book, the whole future destiny of his life; and as he did so, there was a sober sad seriousness in his own countenace, which Eleanor found herself unable to sustain. She could only look down upon the carpet, let her tears trickle as they would, and leave her hand within his.

It was but for a minute that they stood so, but the duration of that minute was sufficient to make it ever memorable to them both. Eleanor was sure now that she was loved. No words, be their eloquence what it might, could be more impressive than that eager, melancholy gaze.

Why did he look so into her eyes? Why did he not speak to her? Could it be that he looked for her to make the first sign?

And he, though he knew but little of women, even he knew that he was loved. He had only to ask and it would be all his own, that inexpressible loveliness, those ever speaking but yet now mute eyes, that feminine brightness and eager loving spirit which had so attracted him since first he had encountered it at St. Ewold's. It might, must all be his own now. On no other supposition was it possible that she should allow her hand to remain thus clasped within his own. He had only to ask. Ah! but that was the difficulty. Did a minute suffice for all this? Nay, perhaps it might be more than a minute.

"Mrs. Bold——" at last he said, and then stopped himself. "Eleanor!" he then said, in his softest tone, as though the courage of a lover were as yet but half assumed, as though he were still afraid of giving offence by the freedom which he took.

"Eleanor!" he again exclaimed; and in a moment he had her clasped to his bosom. There was now that sympathy between them which hardly admitted of individual motion. They were one and the same,—one flesh,—one spirit,—one life.

"Eleanor, my own Eleanor, my own, my wife!" She ventured to look up at him through her tears, and he, bowing his face down over hers, pressed his lips upon her brow; his virgin lips, which since a beard first grew upon his chin, had never yet tasted the luxury of a woman's cheek.

She had been told that her yea must be yea, or her nay, nay;

but she was called on for neither the one nor the other. She told
Miss Thorne that she was engaged to Mr. Arabin, but no such
words had passed between them, no promises had been asked or
given.

"Oh, let me go," said she; "let me go now. I am too happy to
remain,—let me go, that I may be alone." He did not try to hinder
her; he did not repeat the kiss; he did not press another on her lips.
He might have done so had he been so minded. She was now all his
own. He took his arm from round her waist, his arm that was
trembling with a new delight, and let her go. She fled like a roe to
her own chamber, and then, having turned the bolt, she enjoyed the
full luxury of her love. She idolised, almost worshipped this man
who had so meekly begged her pardon. And he was now her own.
Oh, how she wept and cried and laughed, as the hopes and fears
and miseries of the last few weeks passed in remembrance through
her mind.

She got up and rang for her maid that she might tell her little
boy of his new father; and in her own way she did tell him. She
desired her maid to leave her, in order that she might be alone with
her child; and then, while he lay sprawling on the bed, she poured
forth the praises, all unmeaning to him, of the man she had selected
to guard his infancy.

She could not be happy, however, till she had made Mr. Arabin
take the child to himself, and thus, as it were, adopt him as his own.
The moment the idea struck her she took the baby up in her arms,
and, opening her door, ran quickly down to the drawing-room. She
at once found, by his step still pacing on the floor, that he was there;
and a glance within the room told her that he was alone. She
hesitated a moment, and then hurried in with her precious
charge.

Mr. Arabin met her in the middle of the room. "There," said
she, breathless with her haste; "there, take him—take him and love
him."

Mr. Arabin took the little fellow from her, and kissing him again
and again, prayed God to bless him. "He shall be all as my own—
all as my own," said he. Eleanor, as she stooped to take back her
child, kissed the hand that held him, and then rushed back with her
treasure to her chamber.

It was thus that Mr. Harding's younger daughter was won for
the second time. At dinner neither she nor Mr. Arabin were very
bright, but their silence occasioned no remark. In the drawing-
room, as we have before said, she told Miss Thorne what had
occurred. The next morning she returned to Barchester, and Mr.
Arabin went over with his budget of news to the archdeacon. As
Doctor Grantly was not there, he could only satisfy himself by telling
Mrs. Grantly how that he intended himself the honour of becoming
her brother-in-law. In the ecstasy of her joy at hearing such tidings,

Mrs. Grantly vouchsafed him a warmer welcome than any he had
yet received from Eleanor.

"Good heavens!" she exclaimed—it was the general exclamation
of the rectory. "Poor Eleanor! Dear Eleanor! What a monstrous
injustice has been done her!—Well, it shall all be made up now."
And then she thought of the signora. "What lies people tell," she
said to herself.

But people in this matter had told no lies at all.

CHAPTER XLII

THE ENGAGEMENT

ELEANOR had no opportunity of speaking another word to Mr.
Arabin that evening, except such words as all the world might
hear; and these, as may be supposed, were few enough. Miss Thorne
did her best to leave them in privacy; but Mr. Thorne, who knew
nothing of what had occurred, and another guest, a friend of his,
entirely interfered with her good intentions. So poor Eleanor had
to go to bed without one sign of affection. Her state, nevertheless,
was not be to pitied.

The next morning she was up early. It was probable, she thought,
that by going down a little before the usual hour of breakfast, she
might find Mr. Arabin alone in the dining-room. Might it not be
that he also would calculate that an interview would thus be possible?
Thus thinking, Eleanor was dressed a full hour before the time
fixed in the Ullathorne household for morning prayers.

When she found herself in the dining-room, facing him, she
hardly yet knew how to address him.

He, however, soon relieved her from her embarrassment. He
came up to her, and taking both her hands in his, he said: "So,
Eleanor, you and I are to be man and wife. Is it so?"

She looked up into his face, and her lips formed themselves into a
single syllable. She uttered no sound, but he could read the affirmative plainly in her face.

"It is a great trust," said he; "a very great trust."

"It is—it is," said Eleanor, not exactly taking what he had said
in the sense that he had meant. "It is a very, very great trust, and I
will do my utmost to deserve it."

"And I also will do my utmost to deserve it," said Mr. Arabin,
very solemnly. And then, winding his arm round her waist, he
stood there gazing at the fire, and she with her head leaning on his
shoulder, stood by him, well satisfied with her position. They
neither of them spoke, or found any want of speaking. All that was
needful for them to say had been said. The yea, yea, had been

spoken by Eleanor in her own way—and that way had been perfectly satisfactory to Mr. Arabin.

It had been Mr. Harding's intention to hurry over to Ullathorne as soon as possible after his return to Barchester, in order to secure the support of his daughter in his meditated revolt against the archdeacon as touching the deanery; but he was spared the additional journey by hearing that Mrs. Bold had returned unexpectedly home. As soon as he had read her note he started off, and found her waiting for him in her own house.

How much each of them had to tell the other, and how certain each was that the story which he or she had to tell would astonish the other!

"My dear, I am so anxious to see you," said Mr. Harding, kissing his daughter.

"Oh, papa, I have so much to tell you!" said the daughter, returning the embrace.

"My dear, they have offered me the deanery!" said Mr. Harding, anticipating by the suddenness of the revelation the tidings which Eleanor had to give him.

"Oh, papa," said she, forgetting her own love and happiness in her joy at the surprising news; "oh, papa, can it be possible? Dear papa, how thoroughly, thoroughly happy that makes me!"

"But, my dear, I think it best to refuse it."

"Oh, papa!"

"I am sure you will agree with me, Eleanor, when I explain it to you. You know, my dear, how old I am. If I live, I——"

"But, papa, I must tell you about myself."

"Well, my dear."

"I do so wonder how you'll take it."

"Take what?"

"If you don't rejoice at it, if it doesn't make you happy, if you don't encourage me, I shall break my heart."

"If that be the case, Nelly, I certainly will encourage you."

"But I fear you won't. I do so fear you won't. And yet you can't but think I am the most fortunate woman living on God's earth."

"Are you, dearest? Then I certainly will rejoice with you. Come, Nelly, come to me, and tell me what it is."

"I am going——"

He led her to the sofa, and seating himself beside her, took both her hands in his. "You are going to be married, Nelly. Is not that it?"

"Yes," she said, faintly. "That is if you will approve;" and then she blushed as she remembered the promise which she had so lately volunteered to him, and which she had so utterly forgotten in making her engagement with Mr. Arabin.

Mr. Harding thought for a moment who the man could be whom he was to be called upon to welcome as his son-in-law. A week since he would have had no doubt whom to name. In that case he would have been prepared to give his sanction, although he would have done so with a heavy heart. Now he knew that at any rate it would not be Mr. Slope, though he was perfectly at a loss to guess who could possibly have filled the place. For a moment he thought that the man might be Bertie Stanhope, and his very soul sank within him.

"Well, Nelly?"

"Oh, papa, promise to me that, for my sake, you will love him."

"Come, Nelly, come; tell me who it is."

"But will you love him, papa?"

"Dearest, I must love any one that you love." Then she turned her face to his, and whispered into his ear the name of Mr. Arabin.

No man that she could have named could have more surprised or more delighted him. Had he looked round the world for a son-in-law to his taste, he could have selected no one whom he would have preferred to Mr. Arabin. He was a clergyman; he held a living in the neighbourhood; he was of a set to which all Mr. Harding's own partialities most closely adhered; he was the great friend of Dr. Grantly; and he was, moreover, a man of whom Mr. Harding knew nothing but what he approved. Nevertheless, his surprise was so great as to prevent the immediate expression of his joy. He had never thought of Mr. Arabin in connection with his daughter; he had never imagined that they had any feeling in common. He had feared that his daughter had been made hostile to clergymen of Mr. Arabin's stamp by her intolerance of the archdeacon's pretensions. Had he been put to wish, he might have wished for Mr. Arabin for a son-in-law; but had he been put to guess, the name would never have occurred to him.

"Mr. Arabin!" he exclaimed; "impossible!"

"Oh, papa, for heaven's sake don't say anything against him! If you love me, don't say anything against him. Oh, papa, it's done, and mustn't be undone—oh, papa!"

Fickle Eleanor! where was the promise that she would make no choice for herself without her father's approval? She had chosen, and now demanded his acquiescence. "Oh, papa, isn't he good? isn't he noble? isn't he religious, highminded, everything that a good man possibly can be?" and she clung to her father, beseeching him for his consent.

"My Nelly, my child, my own daughter! He is; he is noble and good and highminded; he is all that a woman can love and a man admire. He shall be my son, my own son. He shall be as close to my heart as you are. My Nelly, my child, my happy, happy child!"

We need not pursue the interview any further. By degrees they returned to the subject of the new promotion. Eleanor tried to prove to him, as the Grantlys had done, that his age could be no bar

to his being a very excellent dean; but those arguments had now
even less weight on him than before. He said little or nothing, but sat
meditative. Every now and then he would kiss his daughter, and
say "yes," or "no," or "very true," or "well, my dear, I can't quite
agree with you there," but he could not be got to enter sharply into
the question of "to be, or not to be" dean of Barchester. Of her and
her happiness, of Mr. Arabin and his virtues, he would talk as much
as Eleanor desired; and, to tell the truth, that was not a little; but
about the deanery he would now say nothing further. He had got a
new idea into his head—Why should not Mr. Arabin be the new
dean?

CHAPTER XLIII

THE ARCHDEACON IS SATISFIED WITH THE STATE OF AFFAIRS

THE archdeacon, in his journey into Barchester, had been assured
by Mr. Harding that all their prognostications about Mr. Slope
and Eleanor were groundless. Mr. Harding, however, had found it
very difficult to shake his son-in-law's faith in his own acuteness.
The matter had, to Dr. Grantly, been so plainly corroborated by
such patent evidence, borne out by such endless circumstances, that
he at first refused to take as true the positive statement which Mr.
Harding made to him of Eleanor's own disavowal of the impeachment. But at last he yielded in a qualified way. He brought himself
to admit that he would at the present regard his past convictions as a
mistake; but in doing this he so guarded himself, that if, at any
future time, Eleanor should come forth to the world as Mrs. Slope,
he might still be able to say: "There, I told you so. Remember what
you said and what I said; and remember also for coming years, that I
was right in this matter,—as in all others."

He carried, however, his concession so far as to bring himself to
undertake to call at Eleanor's house, and he did call accordingly,
while the father and daughter were yet in the middle of their
conference. Mr. Harding had had so much to hear and to say that
he had forgotten to advertise Eleanor of the honour that awaited her,
and she heard her brother-in-law's voice in the hall, while she was
quite unprepared to see him.

"There's the archdeacon," she said, springing up.

"Yes, my dear. He told me to tell you that he would come and
see you; but, to tell the truth, I had forgotten all about it."

Eleanor fled away, regardless of all her father's entreaties. She
could not now, in the first hours of her joy, bring herself to bear all
the archdeacon's retractions, apologies, and congratulations. He
would have so much to say, and would be so tedious in saying it;

consequently, the archdeacon, when he was shown into the drawing-room, found no one there but Mr. Harding.

"You must excuse Eleanor," said Mr. Harding.

"Is anything the matter?" asked the doctor, who at once anticipated that the whole truth about Mr. Slope had at last come out.

"Well, something is the matter. I wonder now whether you will be much surprised?"

The archdeacon saw by his father-in-law's manner that after all, he had nothing to tell him about Mr. Slope. "No," said he, "certainly not—nothing will ever surprise me again." Very many men now-a-days, besides the archdeacon, adopt or affect to adopt the *nil admirari* doctrine; but nevertheless, to judge from their appearrance, they are just as subject to sudden emotions as their grandfathers and grandmothers were before them.

"What do you think Mr. Arabin has done?"

"Mr. Arabin! It's nothing about that daughter of Stanhope's, I hope?"

"No, not that woman," said Mr. Harding, enjoying his joke in his sleeve.

"Not that woman! Is he going to do anything about any woman? Why can't you speak out if you have anything to say? There is nothing I hate so much as these sort of mysteries."

"There shall be no mystery with you, archdeacon; though of course, it must go no further at present."

"Well."

"Except Susan. You must promise me you'll tell no one else."

"Nonsense!" exclaimed the archdeacon, who was becoming angry in his suspense. "You can't have any secret about Mr. Arabin."

"Only this—that he and Eleanor are engaged."

It was quite clear to see, by the archdeacon's face, that he did not believe a word of it. "Mr. Arabin! It's impossible!"

"Eleanor, at any rate, has just now told me so."

"It's impossible," repeated the archdeacon.

"Well, I can't say I think it impossible. It certainly took me by surprise; but that does not make it impossible."

"She must be mistaken."

Mr. Harding assured him that there was no mistake; that he would find, on returning home, that Mr. Arabin had been at Plumstead with the express object of making the same declaration, that even Miss Thorne knew all about it; and that, in fact, the thing was as clearly settled as any such arrangement between a lady and a gentleman could well be.

"Good heavens!" said the archdeacon, walking up and down Eleanor's drawing-room. "Good heavens! Good heavens!"

Now, these exclamations certainly betokened faith. Mr. Harding properly gathered from it that, at last, Dr. Grantly did believe the fact. The first utterance clearly evinced a certain amount of distaste at the information he had received; the second, simply indicated surprise; in the tone of the third, Mr. Harding fancied that he could catch a certain gleam of satisfaction.

The archdeacon had truly expressed the workings of his mind. He could not but be disgusted to find how utterly astray he had been in all his anticipations. Had he only been lucky enough to have suggested this marriage himself when he first brought Mr. Arabin into the country, his character for judgment and wisdom would have received an addition which would have classed him at any rate next to Solomon. And why had he not done so? Might he not have foreseen that Mr. Arabin would want a wife in his parsonage? He had foreseen that Eleanor would want a husband; but should he not also have perceived that Mr. Arabin was a man much more likely to attract her than Mr. Slope? The archdeacon found that he had been at fault, and of course could not immediately get over his discomfiture.

Then his surprise was intense. How sly this pair of young turtle doves had been with him. How egregiously they had hoaxed him. He had preached to Eleanor against her fancied attachment to Mr. Slope, at the very time that she was in love with his own protégé, Mr. Arabin; and had absolutely taken that same Mr. Arabin into his confidence with reference to his dread of Mr. Slope's alliance. It was very natural that the archdeacon should feel surprise.

But there was also great ground for satisfaction. Looking at the match by itself, it was the very thing to help the doctor out of his difficulties. In the first place, the assurance that he should never have Mr. Slope for his brother-in-law, was in itself a great comfort. Then Mr. Arabin was, of all men, the one with whom it would best suit him to be so intimately connected. But the crowning comfort was the blow which this marriage would give to Mr. Slope. He had now certainly lost his wife; rumour was beginning to whisper that he might possibly lose his position in the palace; and if Mr. Harding would only be true, the great danger of all would be surmounted. In such case it might be expected that Mr. Slope would own himself vanquished, and take himself altogether away from Barchester. And so the archdeacon would again be able to breathe pure air.

"Well, well," said he. "Good heavens! good heavens!" and the tone of the fifth exclamation made Mr. Harding fully aware that content was reigning in the archdeacon's bosom.

And then slowly, gradually, and craftily Mr. Harding propounded his own new scheme. Why should not Mr. Arabin be the new dean?

Slowly, gradually, and thoughtfully Dr. Grantly fell into his father-in-law's views. Much as he liked Mr. Arabin, sincere as was his admiration for that gentleman's ecclesiastical abilities, he would not have sanctioned a measure which would rob his father-in-law of his fairly-earned promotion, were it at all practicable to induce his father-in-law to accept the promotion which he had earned. But the archdeacon had, on a former occasion, received proof of the obstinacy with which Mr. Harding could adhere to his own views in opposition to the advice of all his friends. He knew tolerably well that nothing would induce the meek, mild man before him to take the high place offered to him, if he thought it wrong to do so. Knowing this, he also said to himself more than once: "Why should not Mr. Arabin be Dean of Barchester?" It was at last arranged between them that they would together start to London by the earliest train on the following morning, making a little *détour* to Oxford on their journey. Dr. Gwynne's counsels, they imagined, might perhaps be of assistance to them.

These matters settled, the archdeacon hurried off, that he might return to Plumstead and prepare for his journey. The day was extremely fine, and he came into the city in an open gig. As he was driving up the High Street he encountered Mr. Slope at a crossing. Had he not pulled up rather sharply, he would have run over him. The two had never spoken to each other since they had met on a memorable occasion in the bishop's study. They did not speak now; but they looked each other full in the face, and Mr. Slope's countenance was as impudent, as triumphant, as defiant as ever. Had Dr. Grantly not known to the contrary, he would have imagined that his enemy had won the deanship, the wife, and all the rich honours, for which he had been striving. As it was, he had lost everything that he had in the world, and had just received his *congé* from the bishop.

In leaving the town the archdeacon drove by the well-remembered entrance of Hiram's hospital. There, at the gate, was a large, untidy, farmer's wagon, laden with untidy-looking furniture; and there, inspecting the arrival, was good Mrs. Quiverful—not dressed in her Sunday best—not very clean in her apparel—not graceful as to her bonnet and shawl; or, indeed, with many feminine charms as to her whole appearance. She was busy at domestic work in her new house, and had just ventured out, expecting to see no one on the arrival of the family chattels. The archdeacon was down upon her before she knew where she was.

Her acquaintance with Dr. Grantly or his family was very slight indeed. The archdeacon, as a matter of course, knew every clergyman in the archdeaconry, it may almost be said in the diocese, and had some acquaintance, more or less intimate, with their wives and families. With Mr. Quiverful he had been concerned on various matters of business; but of Mrs. Q. he had seen very little. Now, however, he was in too gracious a mood to pass her by unnoticed. The Quiverfuls, one and all, had looked for the bitterest hostility from Dr. Grantly; they knew his anxiety that Mr. Harding should return to his old home at the hospital, and they did not know that a new home had been offered to him at the deanery. Mrs. Quiverful was therefore not a little surprised and not a little rejoiced also, at the tone in which she was addressed.

"How do you do, Mrs. Quiverful?—how do you do?" said he, stretching his left hand out of the gig, as he spoke to her. "I am very glad to see you employed in so pleasant and useful a manner; very glad indeed."

Mrs. Quiverful thanked him, and shook hands with him, and looked into his face suspiciously. She was not sure whether the congratulations and kindness were or were not ironical.

"Pray tell Mr. Quiverful from me," he continued, "that I am rejoiced at his appointment. It's a comfortable place, Mrs. Quiverful, and a comfortable house, and I am very glad to see you in it. Good-bye—good-bye." And he drove on, leaving the lady well pleased and astonished at his good-nature. On the whole things were going well with the archdeacon, and he could afford to be charitable to Mrs. Quiverful. He looked forth from his gig smilingly on all the world, and forgave every one in Barchester their sins, excepting only Mrs. Proudie and Mr. Slope. Had he seen the bishop, he would have felt inclined to pat even him kindly on the head.

He determined to go home by St. Ewold's. This would take him some three miles out of his way; but he felt that he could not leave Plumstead comfortably without saying one word of good fellowship to Mr. Arabin. When he reached the parsonage the vicar was still out; but, from what he had heard, he did not doubt but that he would meet him on the road between their two houses. He was right in this, for about halfway home, at a narrow turn, he came upon Mr. Arabin, who was on horseback.

"Well, well, well, well;" said the archdeacon, loudly, joyously, and with supreme good humour; "well, well, well, well; so, after all, we have no further cause to fear Mr. Slope."

"I heard from Mrs. Grantly that they have offered the deanery to Mr. Harding," said the other.

"Mr. Slope has lost more than the deanery, I find, and then the archdeacon laughed jocosely. "Come, come, Arabin, you have kept your secret well enough. I know all about it now."

"I have had no secret, archdeacon," said the other with a quiet smile. "None at all—not for a day. It was only yesterday that I knew my own good fortune, and to-day I went over to Plumstead to ask your approval. From what Mrs. Grantly has said to me, I am led to hope that I shall have it."

"With all my heart, with all my heart," said the archdeacon cordially, holding his friend fast by the hand. "It's just as I would have it. She is an excellent young woman; she will not come to you empty-handed; and I think she will make you a good wife. If she does her duty by you as her sister does by me, you'll be a happy man;

that's all I can say." And as he finished speaking, a tear might have been observed in each of the doctor's eyes.

Mr. Arabin warmly returned the archdeacon's grasp, but he said little. His heart was too full for speaking, and he could not express the gratitude which he felt. Dr. Grantly understood him as well as though he had spoken for an hour.

"And mind, Arabin," said he, "no one but myself shall tie the knot. We'll get Eleanor out to Plumstead, and it shall come off there. I'll make Susan stir herself, and we'll do it in style. I must be off to London to-morrow on special business. Harding goes with me. But I'll be back before your bride has got her wedding dress ready." And so they parted.

On his journey home the archdeacon occupied his mind with preparations for the marriage festivities. He made a great resolve that he would atone to Eleanor for all the injury he had done her by the munificence of his future treatment. He would show her what was the difference in his eyes between a Slope and an Arabin. On one other thing also he decided with a firm mind: if the affair of the dean should not be settled in Mr. Arabin's favour, nothing should prevent him putting a new front and bow-window to the dining-room at St. Ewold's parsonage.

"So we're sold after all, Sue," said he to his wife, accosting her with a kiss as soon as he entered his house. He did not call his wife Sue above twice or thrice a year, and these occasions were great high days.

"Eleanor has had more sense than we gave her credit for," said Mrs. Grantly.

And there was great content in Plumstead rectory that evening; and Mrs. Grantly promised her husband that she would now open her heart, and take Mr. Arabin into it. Hitherto she had declined to do so.

CHAPTER XLIV

MR. SLOPE BIDS FAREWELL TO THE PALACE AND ITS INHABITANTS

WE must now take leave of Mr. Slope, and of the bishop also, and of Mrs. Proudie. These leave-takings in novels are as disagreeable as they are in real life; not so sad, indeed, for they want the reality of sadness; but quite as perplexing, and generally less satisfactory. What novelist, what Fielding, what Scott, what George Sand, or Sue, or Dumas, can impart an interest to the last chapter of his fictitious history? Promises of two children and superhuman happiness are of no avail, nor assurance of extreme

respectability carried to an age far exceeding that usually allotted
to mortals. The sorrows of our heroes and heroines, they are your
delight, oh public! their sorrows, or their sins, or their absurdities;
not their virtues, good sense, and consequent rewards. When we
begin to tint our final pages with *couleur de rose*, as in accordance with
fixed rule we must do, we altogether extinguish our own powers of
pleasing. When we become dull we offend your intellect; and we
must become dull or we should offend your taste. A late writer,
wishing to sustain his interest to the last page, hung his hero at
the end of the third volume. The consequence was, that no one
would read his novel. And who can apportion out and dovetail
his incidents, dialogues, characters, and descriptive morsels, so as
to fit them all exactly into 439 pages, without either compressing
them unnaturally, or extending them artificially at the end of his
labour? Do I not myself know that I am at this moment in want of a
dozen pages, and that I am sick with cudgelling my brains to find
them? And then when everything is done, the kindest-hearted
critic of them all invariably twits us with the incompetency and
lameness of our conclusion. We have either become idle and
neglected it, or tedious and over-laboured it. It is insipid or unnatural, overstrained or imbecile. It means nothing, or attempts
too much. The last scene of all, as all last scenes we fear must be,

> Is second childishness, and mere oblivion,
> Sans teeth, san eyes, sans taste, sans everything.

I can only say that if some critic, who thoroughly knows his work,
and has laboured on it till experience has made him perfect, will
write the last fifty pages of a novel in the way they should be
written, I, for one, will in future do my best to copy the example.
Guided by my own light only, I confess that I despair of success.

For the last week or ten days, Mr. Slope had seen nothing of Mrs.
Proudie, and very little of the bishop. He still lived in the palace,
and still went through his usual routine work; but the confidential
doings of the diocese had passed into other hands. He had seen this
clearly, and marked it well; but it had not much disturbed him. He
had indulged in other hopes till the bishop's affairs had become dull
to him, and he was moreover aware that, as regarded the diocese,
Mrs. Proudie had checkmated him. It has been explained, in the
beginning of these pages, how three or four were contending
together as to who, in fact, should be bishop of Barchester. Each of
these had now admitted to himself (or boasted to herself) that Mrs.
Proudie was victorious in the struggle. They had gone through a
competitive examination of considerable severity, and she had come
forth the winner, *facile princeps*. Mr. Slope had, for a moment, run her
hard, but it was only for a moment. It had become, as it were,
acknowledged that Hiram's hospital should be the testing point

between them, and now Mr. Quiverful was already in the hospital, the proof of Mrs. Proudie's skill and courage.

All this did not break down Mr. Slope's spirit, because he had other hopes. But, alas, at last there came to him a note from his friend Sir Nicholas, informing him that the deanship was disposed of. Let us give Mr. Slope his due. He did not lie prostrate under this blow, or give himself up to vain lamentations; he did not henceforward despair of life, and call upon gods above and gods below to carry him off. He sat himself down in his chair, counted out what monies he had in hand for present purposes, and what others were coming in to him, bethought himself as to the best sphere for his future exertions, and at once wrote off a letter to a rich sugar-refiner's wife in Baker Street, who, as he well knew, was much given to the entertainment and encouragement of serious young evangelical clergymen. He was again, he said, "upon the world, having found the air of a cathedral town, and the very nature of cathedral services, uncongenial to his spirit;" and then he sat awhile, making firm resolves as to his manner of parting from the bishop, and also as to his future conduct.

> At last he rose, and twitched his mantle blue (black),
> To-morrow to fresh woods and pastures new.

Having received a formal command to wait upon the bishop, he rose and proceeded to obey it. He rang the bell and desired the servant to inform his master that if it suited his lordship, he, Mr. Slope, was ready to wait upon him. The servant, who well understood that Mr. Slope was no longer in the ascendent, brought back a message, saying that "his lordship desired that Mr. Slope would attend him immediately in his study." Mr. Slope waited about ten minutes more to prove his independence, and then he went into the bishop's room. There, as he had expected, he found Mrs. Proudie, together with her husband.

"Hum, ha,—Mr. Slope, pray take a chair," said the gentleman bishop.

"Pray be seated, Mr. Slope," said the lady bishop.

"Thank ye, thank ye," said Mr. Slope, and walking round to the fire, he threw himself into one of the arm-chairs that graced the hearth-rug.

"Mr. Slope," said the bishop, "it has become necessary that I should speak to you definitively on a matter that has for some time been pressing itself on my attention."

"May I ask whether the subject is in any way connected with myself?" said Mr. Slope.

"It is so,—certainly,—yes, it certainly is connected with yourself, Mr. Slope."

"Then, my lord, if I may be allowed to express a wish, I would prefer that no discussion on the subject should take place between us in the presence of a third person."

"Don't alarm yourself, Mr. Slope," said Mrs. Proudie, "no discussion is at all necessary. The bishop merely intends to express his own wishes."

"I merely intend, Mr. Slope, to express my own wishes,—no discussion will be at all necessary," said the bishop, reiterating his wife's words.

"That is more, my lord, than we any of us can be sure of," said Mr. Slope; "I cannot, however, force Mrs. Proudie to leave the room; nor can I refuse to remain here if it be your lordship's wish that I should do so."

"It is his lordship's wish, certainly," said Mrs. Proudie.

"Mr. Slope," began the bishop, in a solemn, serious voice, "it grieves me to have to find fault. It grieves me much to have to find fault with a clergyman; but especially so with a clergyman in your position."

"Why, what have I done amiss, my lord?" demanded Mr. Slope, boldly.

"What have you done amiss, Mr. Slope?" said Mrs. Proudie, standing erect before the culprit, and raising that terrible forefinger. "Do you dare to ask the bishop what you have done amiss? does not your conscience——"

"Mrs. Proudie, pray let it be understood, once for all, that I will have no words with you."

"Ah, sir, but you will have words," said she; "you must have words. Why have you had so many words with that Signora Neroni? Why have you disgraced yourself, you a clergyman too, by constantly consorting with such a woman as that,—with a married woman—with one altogether unfit for a clergyman's society?"

"At any rate, I was introduced to her in your drawing-room," retorted Mr. Slope.

"And shamefully you behaved there," said Mrs. Proudie, "most shamefully. I was wrong to allow you to remain in the house a day after what I then saw. I should have insisted on your instant dismissal."

"I have yet to learn, Mrs. Proudie, that you have the power to insist either on my going from hence or on my staying here."

"What!" said the lady; "I am not to have the privilege of saying who shall and who shall not frequent my own drawing-room! I am not to save my servants and dependents from having their morals corrupted by improper conduct! I am not to save my own daughters from impurity! I will let you see, Mr. Slope, whether I have the power or whether I have not. You will have the goodness to understand that you no longer fill any situation about the bishop; and as your room will be immediately wanted in the palace for another chaplain, I must ask you to provide yourself with apartments as soon as may be convenient to you."

"My lord," said Mr. Slope, appealing to the bishop, and so turning his back completely on the lady, "will you permit me to ask that I may have from your own lips any decision that you may have come to on this matter?"

"Certainly, Mr. Slope, certainly," said the bishop; "that is but reasonable. Well, my decision is that you had better look for some other preferment. For the situation which you have lately held I do not think that you are well suited."

"And what, my lord, has been my fault?"

"That Signora Neroni is one fault," said Mrs. Proudie; "and a very abominable fault she is; very abominable and very disgraceful. Fie, Mr. Slope, fie! You an evangelical clergyman indeed!"

"My lord, I desire to know for what fault I am turned out of your lordship's house."

"You hear what Mrs. Proudie says," said the bishop.

"When I publish the history of this transaction, my lord, as I decidedly shall do in my own vindication, I presume you will not wish me to state that you have discarded me at your wife's bidding— because she has objected to my being acquainted with another lady, the daughter of one of the prebendaries of the chapter?"

"You may publish what you please, sir," said Mrs. Proudie. "But you will not be insane enough to publish any of your doings in Barchester. Do you think I have not heard of your kneelings at that creature's feet—that is if she has any feet—and of your constant slobbering over her hand? I advise you to beware, Mr. Slope, of what you do and say. Clergymen have been unfrocked for less than what you have been guilty of."

"My lord, if this goes on I shall be obliged to indict this woman— Mrs. Proudie I mean—for defamation of character."

"I think, Mr. Slope, you had better now retire," said the bishop. "I will enclose to you a cheque for any balance that may be due to you; and, under the present circumstances, it will of course be better for all parties that you should leave the palace at the earliest possible moment. I will allow you for your journey back to London, and for your maintenance in Barchester for a week from this date."

"If, however, you wish to remain in this neighbourhood," said Mrs. Proudie, "and will solemnly pledge yourself never again to see that woman, and will promise also to be more circumspect in your conduct, the bishop will mention your name to Mr. Quiverful, who now wants a curate at Puddingdale. The house is, I imagine, quite sufficient for your requirements: and there will moreover be a stipend of fifty pounds a year."

"May God forgive you, madam, for the manner in which you have treated me," said Mr. Slope, looking at her with a very heavenly look; "and remember this, madam, that you yourself may still have a fall;" and he looked at her with a very worldly look. "As to the bishop, I pity him!" And so saying, Mr. Slope left the room. Thus ended the intimacy of the Bishop of Barchester with his first confidential chaplain.

Mrs. Proudie was right in this; namely, that Mr. Slope was not insane enough to publish to the world any of his doings in Barchester. He did not trouble his friend Mr. Towers with any written statement of the iniquity of Mrs. Proudie, or the imbecility of her husband. He was aware that it would be wise in him to drop for the future all allusions to his doings in the cathedral city. Soon after the interview just recorded, he left Barchester, shaking the dust off his feet as he entered the railway carriage; and he gave no longing lingering look after the cathedral towers, as the train hurried him quickly out of their sight.

It is well known that the family of the Slopes never starve: they always fall on their feet like cats, and let them fall where they will, they live on the fat of the land. Our Mr. Slope did so. On his return to town he found that the sugar-refiner had died, and that his widow was inconsolable: or, in other words, in want of consolation. Mr. Slope consoled her, and soon found himself settled with much comfort in the house in Baker Street. He possessed himself, also, before long, of a church in the vicinity of the New Road, and became known to fame as one of the most eloquent preachers and pious clergymen in that part of the metropolis. There let us leave him.

Of the bishop and his wife very little further need be said. From that time forth nothing material occurred to interrupt the even course of their domestic harmony. Very speedily, a further vacancy on the bench of bishops gave to Dr. Proudie the seat in the House of Lords, which he at first so anxiously longed for. But by this time he had become a wiser man. He did certainly take his seat, and occasionally registered a vote in favour of Government views on ecclesiastical matters. But he had thoroughly learnt that his proper sphere of action lay in close contiguity with Mrs. Proudie's wardrobe. He never again aspired to disobey, or seemed even to wish for autocratic diocesan authority. If ever he thought of freedom, he did so, as men think of the millennium, as of a good time which may be coming, but which nobody expects to come in their day. Mrs. Proudie might be said still to bloom, and was, at any rate, strong; and the bishop had no reason to apprehend that he would be speedily visited with the sorrows of a widower's life.

He is still Bishop of Barchester. He has so graced that throne, that the Government has been averse to translate him, even to higher dignities. There may he remain, under safe pupilage, till the new-fangled manners of the age have discovered him to be super-annuated, and bestowed on him a pension. As for Mrs. Proudie, our prayers for her are that she may live for ever.

CHAPTER XLV

THE NEW DEAN TAKES POSSESSION OF THE DEANERY, AND THE NEW WARDEN OF THE HOSPITAL

MR. HARDING and the archdeacon together made their way to Oxford, and there, by dint of cunning argument, they induced the Master of Lazarus also to ask himself this momentous question: "Why should not Mr. Arabin be Dean of Barchester?" He of course for a while tried his hand at persuading Mr. Harding that he was foolish, overscrupulous, self-willed, and weak-minded; but he tried in vain. If Mr. Harding would not give way to Dr. Grantly, it was not likely he would give way to Dr. Gwynne; more especially now that so admirable a scheme as that of inducting Mr. Arabin into the deanery had been set on foot. When the master found that his eloquence was vain, and heard also that Mr. Arabin was about to become Mr. Harding's son-in-law, he confessed that he also would, under such circumstances, be glad to see his old friend and protégé, the fellow of his college, placed in the comfortable position that was going a-begging.

"It might be the means, you know, Master, of keeping Mr. Slope out," said the archdeacon with grave caution.

"He has no more chance of it," said the master, "than our college chaplain. I know more about it than that."

Mrs. Grantly had been right in her surmise. It was the Master of Lazarus who had been instrumental in representing in high places the claims which Mr. Harding had upon the Government, and he now consented to use his best endeavours towards getting the offer transferred to Mr. Arabin. The three of them went on to London together, and there they remained a week, to the great disgust of Mrs. Grantly, and most probably also of Mrs. Gwynne. The minister was out of town in one direction, and his private secretary in another. The clerks who remained could do nothing in such a matter as this, and all was difficulty and confusion. The two doctors seemed to have plenty to do; they bustled here and they bustled there, and complained at their club in the evenings that they had been driven off their legs; but Mr. Harding had no occupation. Once or twice he suggested that he might perhaps return to Barchester. His request, however, was peremptorily refused, and he had nothing for it but to while away his time in Westminster Abbey.

At length an answer from the great man came. The Master of Lazarus had made his proposition through the Bishop of Belgravia. Now this bishop, though but newly gifted with his diocesan honours, was a man of much weight in the clerico-political world. He was, if

not as pious, at any rate as wise as St. Paul, and had been with so
much effect all things to all men, that though he was great among
the dons of Oxford, he had been selected for the most favourite seat
on the bench by a Whig Prime Minister. To him Dr. Gwynne had
made known his wishes and his arguments, and the bishop had made
them known to the Marquis of Kensington Gore. The marquis, who
was Lord High Steward of the Pantry Board, and who by most men
was supposed to hold the highest office out of the cabinet, trafficked
much in affairs of this kind. He not only suggested the arrangement
to the minister over a cup of coffee, standing on a drawing-room
rug in Windsor Castle, but he also favourably mentioned Mr.
Arabin's name in the ear of a distinguished person.

And so the matter was arranged. The answer of the great man
came, and Mr. Arabin was made Dean of Barchester. The three
clergymen who had come up to town on this important mission dined
together with great glee on the day on which the news reached them.
In a silent, decent, clerical manner, they toasted Mr. Arabin with
full bumpers of claret. The satisfaction of all of them was supreme.
The Master of Lazarus had been successful in his attempt, and
success is dear to us all. The archdeacon had trampled upon Mr.
Slope, and had lifted to high honours the young clergyman whom
he had induced to quit the retirement and comfort of the university.
So at least the archdeacon thought; though, to speak sooth, not he,
but circumstances, had trampled on Mr. Slope. But the satisfaction
of Mr. Harding was, of all, perhaps, the most complete. He laid
aside his usual melancholy manner, and brought forth little quiet
jokes from the inmost mirth of his heart; he poked his fun at the archdeacon about Mr. Slope's marriage, and quizzed him for his improper love for Mrs. Proudie. On the following day they all returned
to Barchester.

It was arranged that Mr. Arabin should know nothing of what
had been done till he received the minister's letter from the hands
of his embryo father-in-law. In order that no time might be lost,
a message had been sent to him by the preceding night's post,
begging him to be at the deanery at the hour that the train from
London arrived. There was nothing in this which surprised Mr.
Arabin. It had somehow got about through all Barchester that Mr.
Harding was the new dean, and all Barchester was prepared to
welcome him with pealing bells and full hearts. Mr. Slope had
certainly had a party; there had certainly been those in Barchester
who were prepared to congratulate him on his promotion with
assumed sincerity, but even his own party was not broken-hearted
by his failure. The inhabitants of the city, even the high-souled
ecstatic young ladies of thirty-five, had begun to comprehend that
their welfare, and the welfare of the place, was connected in some
mysterious manner with daily chants and bi-weekly anthems. The
expenditure of the palace had not added much to the popularity

of the bishop's side of the question; and, on the whole, there was a strong reaction. When it became known to all the world that Mr. Harding was to be the new dean, all the world rejoiced heartily.

Mr. Arabin, we have said, was not surprised at the summons which called him to the deanery. He had not as yet seen Mr. Harding since Eleanor had accepted him, nor had he seen him since he had learnt his future father-in-law's preferment. There was nothing more natural, more necessary, than that they should meet each other at the earliest possible moment. Mr. Arabin was waiting in the deanery parlour when Mr. Harding and Dr. Grantly were driven up from the station.

There was some excitement in the bosoms of them all, as they met and shook hands; by far too much to enable either of them to begin his story and tell it in a proper equable style of narrative. Mr. Harding was some minutes quite dumbfounded, and Mr. Arabin could only talk in short, spasmodic sentences about his love and good fortune. He slipped in, as best he could, some sort of congratulation about the deanship, and then went on with his hopes and fears,—hopes that he might be received as a son, and fears that he hardly deserved such good fortune. Then he went back to the dean; it was the most thoroughly satisfactory appointment, he said, of which he had ever heard.

"But! but! but——" said Mr. Harding; and then failing to get any further, he looked imploringly at the archdeacon.

"The truth is, Arabin," said the doctor, "that, after all, you are not destined to be son-in-law to a dean. Nor am I either: more's the pity."

Mr. Arabin looked at him for explanation. "Is not Mr. Harding to be the new dean?"

"It appears not," said the archdeacon. Mr. Arabin's face fell a little, and he looked from one to the other. It was plainly to be seen from them both that there was no cause of unhappiness in the matter, at least not of unhappiness to them; but there was as yet no elucidation of the mystery.

"Think how old I am," said Mr. Harding, imploringly.

"Fiddlestick!" said the archdeacon.

"That's all very well, but it won't make a young man of me," said Mr. Harding.

"And who is to be dean?" asked Mr. Arabin.

"Yes, that's the question," said the archdeacon. "Come, Mr. Precentor, since you obstinately refuse to be anything else, let us know who is to be the man. He has got the nomination in his pocket."

With eyes brim full of tears, Mr. Harding pulled out the letter and handed it to his future son-in-law. He tried to make a little speech, but failed altogether. Having given up the document, he turned round to the wall, feigning to blow his nose, and then sat himself down on the old dean's dingy horse-hair sofa. And here we find it necessary to bring our account of the interview to an end.

Nor can we pretend to describe the rapture with which Mr. Harding was received by his daughter. She wept with grief and wept with joy; with grief that her father should, in his old age, still be without that rank and worldly position which, according to her ideas, he had so well earned; and with joy in that he, her darling father, should have bestowed on that dear one the other good things of which he himself would not open his hand to take possession. And here Mr. Harding again showed his weakness. In the *mêlée* of this exposal of their loves and reciprocal affection, he found himself unable to resist the entreaties of all parties that the lodgings in the High Street should be given up. Eleanor would not live in the deanery, she said, unless her father lived there also. Mr. Arabin would not be dean, unless Mr. Harding would be co-dean with him. The archdeacon declared that his father-in-law should not have his own way in everything, and Mrs. Grantly carried him off to Plumstead, that he might remain there till Mr. and Mrs. Arabin were in a state to receive him in their own mansion.

Pressed by such arguments as these, what could a weak old man do but yield?

But there was yet another task which it behoved Mr. Harding to do before he could allow himself to be at rest. Little has been said in these pages of the state of those remaining old men who had lived under his sway at the hospital. But not on this account must it be presumed that he had forgotten them, or that in their state of anarchy and in their want of due government he had omitted to visit them. He visited them constantly, and had latterly given them to understand that they would soon be required to subscribe their adherence to a new master. There were now but five of them, one of them having been but quite lately carried to his rest,—but five of the full number, which had hitherto been twelve, and which was now to be raised to twenty-four, including women. Of these old Bunce, who for many years had been the favourite of the late warden, was one; and Abel Handy, who had been the humble means of driving that warden from his home, was another.

Mr. Harding now resolved that he himself would introduce the new warden to the hospital. He felt that many circumstances might conspire to make the men receive Mr. Quiverful with aversion and disrespect; he felt also that Mr. Quiverful might himself feel some qualms of conscience if he entered the hospital with an idea that he did so in hostility to his predecessor. Mr. Harding therefore determined to walk in, arm in arm with Mr. Quiverful, and to ask from these men their respectful obedience to their new master.

On returning to Barchester, he found that Mr. Quiverful had not yet slept in the hospital house or entered on his new duties.

He accordingly made known to that gentleman his wishes, and his proposition was not rejected.

It was a bright clear morning, though in November, that Mr. Harding and Mr. Quiverful, arm in arm, walked through the hospital gate. It was one trait in our old friend's character that he did nothing with parade. He omitted, even in the more important doings of his life, that sort of parade by which most of us deem it necessary to grace our important doings. We have housewarmings, christenings, and gala days; we keep, if not our own birthdays, those of our children; we are apt to fuss ourselves if called upon to change our residences, and have, almost all of us, our little state occasions. Mr. Harding had no state occasions. When he left his old house, he went forth from it with the same quiet composure as though he were merely taking his daily walk; and now that he re-entered it with another warden under his wing, he did so with the same quiet step and calm demeanour. He was a little less upright than he had been five years, nay, it was now nearly six years ago; he walked perhaps a little slower; his footfall was perhaps a thought less firm; otherwise one might have said that he was merely returning with a friend under his arm.

This friendliness was everything to Mr. Quiverful. To him, even in his poverty, the thought that he was supplanting a brother clergyman so kind and courteous as Mr. Harding, had been very bitter. Under his circumstances it had been impossible for him to refuse the proffered boon; he could not reject the bread that was offered to his children, or refuse to ease the heavy burden that had so long oppressed that poor wife of his; nevertheless, it had been very grievous to him to think that in going to the hospital he might encounter the ill will of his brethren in the diocese. All this Mr. Harding had fully comprehended. It was for such feelings as these, for the nice comprehension of such motives, that his heart and intellect were peculiarly fitted. In most matters of worldly import the archdeacon set down his father-in-law as little better than a fool. And perhaps he was right. But in some other matters, equally important if they be rightly judged, Mr. Harding, had he been so minded, might with as much propriety have set down his son-in-law for a fool. Few men, however, are constituted as was Mr. Harding. He had that nice appreciation of the feelings of others which belongs of right exclusively to women.

Arm in arm they walked into the inner quadrangle of the building, and there the five old men met them. Mr. Harding shook hands with them all, and then Mr. Quiverful did the same. With Bunce Mr. Harding shook hands twice, and Mr. Quiverful was about to repeat the same ceremony, but the old man gave him no encouragement.

"I am very glad to know that at last you have a new warden," said Mr. Harding in a very cheery voice.

"We be very old for any change," said one of them; "but we do suppose it be all for the best."

"Certainly—certainly it is for the best," said Mr. Harding. "You will again have a clergyman of your own church under the same roof with you, and a very excellent clergyman you will have. It is a great satisfaction to me to know that so good a man is coming to take care of you, and that it is no stranger, but a friend of my own, who will allow me from time to time to come in and see you."

"We be very thankful to your reverence," said another of them.

"I need not tell you, my good friends," said Mr. Quiverful, "how extremely grateful I am to Mr. Harding for his kindness to me,—I must say his uncalled for, unexpected kindness."

"He be always very kind," said a third.

"What I can do to fill the void which he left here, I will do. For your sake and my own I will do so, and especially for his sake. But to you who have known him, I can never be the same well-loved friend and father that he has been."

"No, sir, no," said old Bunce, who hitherto had held his peace; "no one can be that. Not if the new bishop sent a hangel to us out of heaven. We doesn't doubt you'll do your best, sir, but you'll not be like the old master; not to us old ones."

"Fie, Bunce, fie! how dare you talk in that way?" said Mr. Harding; but as he scolded the old man he still held him by his arm, and pressed it with warm affection.

There was no getting up any enthusiasm in the matter. How could five old men tottering away to their final resting-place be enthusiastic on the reception of a stranger? What could Mr. Quiverful be to them, or they to Mr. Quiverful? Had Mr. Harding indeed come back to them, some last flicker of joyous light might have shone forth on their aged cheeks; but it was in vain to bid them rejoice because Mr. Quiverful was about to move his fourteen children from Puddingdale into the hospital house. In reality they did no doubt receive advantage, spiritual as well as corporal; but this they could neither anticipate nor acknowledge.

It was a dull affair enough, this introduction of Mr. Quiverful; but still it had its effect. The good which Mr. Harding intended did not fall to the ground. All the Barchester world, including the five old bedesmen, treated Mr. Quiverful with the more respect, because Mr. Harding had thus walked in arm in arm with him, on his first entrance to his duties.

And here in their new abode we will leave Mr. and Mrs. Quiverful and their fourteen children. May they enjoy the good things which Providence has at length given to them!

CHAPTER XLVI

CONCLUSION

THE end of a novel, like the end of a children's dinner-party, must be made up of sweetmeats and sugar-plums. There is now nothing else to be told but the gala doings of Mr. Arabin's marriage, nothing more to be described than the wedding dresses, no further dialogue to be recorded than that which took place between the arch-deacon who married them, and Mr. Arabin and Eleanor who were married. "Wilt thou have this woman to thy wedded wife," and "Wilt thou have this man to thy wedded husband, to live together according to God's ordinance?" Mr. Arabin and Eleanor each answered, "I will." We have no doubt that they will keep their promises; the more especially as the Signora Neroni had left Barchester before the ceremony was performed.

Mrs. Bold had been somewhat more than two years a widow before she was married to her second husband, and little Johnnie was then able with due assistance to walk on his own legs into the drawing-room to receive the salutations of the assembled guests. Mr. Harding gave away the bride, the archdeacon performed the service, and the two Miss Grantlys, who were joined in their labours by other young ladies of the neighbourhood, performed the duties of bridesmaids with equal diligence and grace. Mrs. Grantly super-intended the breakfast and bouquets, and Mary Bold distributed the cards and cake. The archdeacon's three sons had also come home for the occasion. The eldest was great with learning, being regarded by all who knew him as a certain future double first. The second, however, bore the palm on this occasion, being resplendent in a new uniform. The third was just entering the university, and was probably the proudest of the three.

But the most remarkable feature in the whole occasion was the excessive liberality of the archdeacon. He literally made presents to everybody. As Mr. Arabin had already moved out of the parsonage of St. Ewold's, that scheme of elongating the dining-room was of course abandoned; but he would have refurnished the whole deanery had he been allowed. He sent down a magnificent piano by Erard, gave Mr. Arabin a cob which any dean in the land might have been proud to bestride, and made a special present to Eleanor of a new pony chair that had gained a prize in the Exhibition. Nor did he even stay his hand here; he bought a set of cameos for his wife, and a sapphire bracelet for Miss Bold; showered pearls and workboxes on his daughters, and to each of his sons he presented a cheque for 20*l*. On Mr. Harding he bestowed a magnificent violoncello with all the new-fashioned arrangements and expensive additions, which,

on account of these novelties, that gentleman could never use with
satisfaction to his audience or pleasure to himself.

Those who knew the archdeacon well, perfectly understood the
cause of his extravagance. 'Twas thus that he sang his song of
triumph over Mr. Slope. This was his pæan, his hymn of thanks-
giving, his loud oration. He had girded himself with his sword, and
gone forth to the war; now he was returning from the field laden
with the spoils of the foe. The cob and the cameos, the violoncello
and the pianoforte, were all as it were trophies reft from the tent of his
now conquered enemy.

The Arabins after their marriage went abroad for a couple of
months, according to the custom in such matters now duly established,
and then commenced their deanery life under good auspices. And
nothing can be more pleasant than the present arrangement of
ecclesiastical affairs in Barchester. The titular bishop never interfered, and Mrs. Proudie not often. Her sphere is more extended,
more noble, and more suited to her ambition than that of a cathedral
city. As long as she can do what she pleases with the diocese, she is
willing to leave the dean and chapter to themselves. Mr. Slope tried
his hand at subverting the old-established customs of the close, and
from his failure she has learnt experience. The burly chancellor
and the meagre little prebendary are not teased by any application
respecting Sabbath-day schools, the dean is left to his own dominions,
and the intercourse between Mrs. Proudie and Mrs. Arabin is
confined to a yearly dinner given by each to the other. At these
dinners Dr. Grantly will not take a part; but he never fails to ask
for and receive a full account of all that Mrs. Proudie either does
or says.

His ecclesiastical authority has been greatly shorn since the
palmy days in which he reigned supreme as mayor of the palace to
his father, but nevertheless such authority as is now left to him he
can enjoy without interference. He can walk down the High Street
of Barchester without feeling that those who see him are comparing
his claims with those of Mr. Slope. The intercourse between Plumstead and the deanery is of the most constant and familiar description. Since Eleanor has been married to a clergyman, and especially
to a dignitary of the church, Mrs. Grantly has found many more
points of sympathy with her sister; and on a coming occasion, which
is much looked forward to by all parties, she intends to spend a
month or two at the deanery. She never thought of spending a
month in Barchester when little Johnny Bold was born!

The two sisters do not quite agree on matters of church doctrine,
though their differences are of the most amicable description. Mr.
Arabin's church is two degrees higher than that of Mrs. Grantly.
This may seem strange to those who will remember that Eleanor
was once accused of partiality to Mr. Slope; but it is no less the fact.
She likes her husband's silken vest, she likes his adherence to the

rubric, she specially likes the eloquent philosophy of his sermons, and she likes the red letters in her own prayer-book. It must not be presumed that she has a taste for candles, or that she is at all astray about the real presence; but she has an inkling that way. She sent a handsome subscription towards certain very heavy ecclesiastical legal expenses which have lately been incurred in Bath, her name of course not appearing; she assumes a smile of gentle ridicule when the Archbishop of Canterbury is named, and she has put up a memorial window in the cathedral.

Mrs. Grantly, who belongs to the high and dry church, the high church as it was some fifty years since, before tracts were written and young clergymen took upon themselves the highly meritorious duty of cleaning churches, rather laughs at her sister. She shrugs her shoulders, and tells Miss Thorne that she supposes Eleanor will have an oratory in the deanery before she has done. But she is not on that account a whit displeased. A few high church vagaries do not, she thinks, sit amiss on the shoulders of a young dean's wife. It shows at any rate that her heart is in the subject; and it shows moreover that she is removed, wide as the poles asunder, from that cesspool of abomination in which it was once suspected that she would wallow and grovel. Anathema maranatha! Let anything else be held as blessed, so that that be well cursed. Welcome kneelings and bowings, welcome matins and complines, welcome bell, book, and candle, so that Mr. Slope's dirty surplices and ceremonial Sabbaths be held in due execration!

If it be essentially and absolutely necessary to choose between the two, we are inclined to agree with Mrs. Grantly that the bell, book, and candle are the lesser evil of the two. Let it however be understood that no such necessity is admitted in these pages.

Dr. Arabin (we suppose he must have become a doctor when he became a dean) is more moderate and less outspoken on doctrinal points than his wife, as indeed in his station it behoves him to be. He is a studious, thoughtful, hard-working man. He lives constantly at the deanery and preaches nearly every Sunday. His time is spent in sifting and editing old ecclesiastical literature, and in producing the same articles new. At Oxford he is generally regarded as the most promising clerical ornament of the age. He and his wife live together in perfect mutual confidence. There is but one secret in her bosom which he has not shared. He has never yet learned how Mr. Slope had his ears boxed.

The Stanhopes soon found that Mr. Slope's power need no longer operate to keep them from the delight of their Italian villa. Before Eleanor's marriage they had all migrated back to the shores of Como. They had not been resettled long before the signora received from Mrs. Arabin a very pretty though very short epistle, in which she was informed of the fate of the writer. This letter was answered by another, bright, charming, and witty, as the signora's letters always were; and so ended the friendship between Eleanor and the Stanhopes.

One word of Mr. Harding, and we have done.

He is still Precentor of Barchester, and still pastor of the little church of St. Cuthbert's. In spite of what he has so often said himself, he is not even yet an old man. He does such duties as fall to his lot well and conscientiously, and is thankful that he has never been tempted to assume others for which he might be less fitted.

The Author now leaves him in the hands of his readers; not as a hero, not as a man to be admired and talked of, not as a man who should be toasted at public dinners and spoken of with conventional absurdity as a perfect divine, but as a good man without guile, believing humbly in the religion which he has striven to teach, and guided by the precepts which he has striven to learn.